Smoke Wade

Look for these other **Age of Aces Books**

Captain Babyface:
The Complete Adventures
BY STEVE FISHER

The Red Falcon:
The Dare-Devil Aces Years (Vol. 1-4)
BY ROBERT J. HOGAN

The Adventures of
The Three Mosquitoes:
The Wizard Ace
The Magic Inferno
BY RALPH OPPENHEIM

Chinese Brady:
The Complete Adventures
BY C.M. MILLER

Sky Devil: Hell's Skipper
BY HAROLD F. CRUICKSHANK

Murder of The Admiral/
Murder of The Pigboat Skipper
AN AGE OF ACES DOUBLE
BY STEVE FISHER

The Black Sheep of Belogue
THE BEST OF O.B. MYERS

Satan's Playmates:
The Adventures of
Molloy & McNamara
BY WILLIAM HARTLEY

COMING SOON!

From the tattered pages of

POPULAR PUBLICATIONS

THE ADVENTURES OF SMOKE WADE

VOLUME 1

by **ROBERT J. HOGAN**

ILLUSTRATED BY

FREDERICK BLAKESLEE

and **JOHN FLEMING GOULD**

AGE OF ACES BOOKS

ORCHARD PARK • NY

SMOKE WADE stories were first published in the following issues
of BATTLE ACES magazine:
"Six Gun Eagle," August 1932
of DARE-DEVIL ACES magazine:
"Dead Man's Staffel," December 1932
and BATTLE BIRDS magazine:
"Ghost Drome," December 1932
"Buzzard's Trap," January 1933
"The Death Fokker," February 1933
"The Flaming Patrol," March 1933
"The Cowboy Flight," July 1933
"The Death Circus," August 1933
"Steel Coffin Ace," September 1933
"The Gotha Ghost," October 1933
"The Secret Squadron," November 1933
"Sixgun Circus," December 1933
"Injun Buzzards," January 1934

All illustrations by Frederick Blakeslee except "Six Gun Eagle" frontspiece by John Fleming Gould.
The original illustrations in this volume have been digitally edited to better fit the layout.

Edited by Bill Mann
Designed by David Kalb • Art Direction by Chris Kalb
Printed on demand by BookSurge Publishing beginning in March 2009

The Editor gratefully wishes to acknowledge the contributions of
Joel Frieman, Don Hutchison and Colonel McGill.

ISBN: 978-0-9820950-1-0

TABLE OF CONTENTS

Six Gun Eagle

There are more ways than one of trapping ornery coyotes like von Stolz, and Smoke Wade, six-gun rider of the devil's sky range, knew all of 'em!

Six Gun Eagle

YEARS of hard riding under scorching Arizona sun had baked the bronze color of Captain "Smoke" Wade's thin, square-jawed face deep into his leathery skin—a color that months in the blood-red skies of the Front, behind the snarling Hisso motor and jabbering Vickers of his Pinto Spad, had only made still more indelible.

The lanky C.O. of the 66th pursuit squadron at Dombley shifted his weight, towered to his full six feet two of hard brawn, hooked his thumbs in his gun belt, that hung slantwise from the left hip and supported his old six-gun hung well down on his right leg, and scrutinized a slim youngster in the dim light of early day. Then he drawled, with characteristic leisure and calm—

"New replacement, eh? What's your handle, pardner?"

"Havens, sir."

Smoke nodded and grinned slightly.

"Good name. Knew a cowpoke named Havens back in Arizona. What's the other handle? What did they call yuh—back where you come from?"

Another flood of a whiter shade crossed the thin, young face of the replacement, but changed to a faint, sensitive pinkish hue as he spoke, with plain embarrassment.

"Jitters," he answered. Then, with a struggle, "They called me that because—I went haywire after a crash in early training." He straightened his shoulders in a defiant gesture. "But—but that's all gone now. I'm all right and ready for duty, sir."

A soft light came into the sometimes hard, but now half-shut gray eyes of the big, Western-bred squadron commander.

"Sure you are, sonny. But from now on, we'll forget that Jitter handle, eh? We'll be shovin' off directly, I reckon, just as soon as we can get the crates hot."

His words sounded assuring. There was no trace of the sudden worry that had come over Smoke Wade. The 66th had been catching hell of late, what with von Stolz and his devil's brood that outnumbered the 66th three to one, and the sector suddenly teeming with the thunderous undertone of a great push getting in motion.

To him, his men were of great importance—like his own flesh and blood. Every pilot of the 66th was a pal to Smoke Wade, a buddy to be protected and made the most of. A big job, with half-scared kids being hurled at him at a moment when, the best the air could offer were needed in the sector.

He glanced quickly down the tarmac, and his head moved in a sidewise jerk in the direction of two others of the brood. First Lieutenants Brant and Quinn moved more swiftly toward him.

"This here's Havens," he told them. "We're going on a little initiation party right now, the four of us, in the usual way."

Smoke turned to Havens once more with his slow grin of confidence.

"We're going for a little hop over the lines, just to let you see what the Front looks like, son," he told him. "Brant and Quinn, they're leaders of A and B Flights. You're to be attached to Brant's flight. We sort of like to take you new men out to make sure you'll get along. Savvy?"

Havens nodded rather automatically.

"I'll fly point, Brant takes left tip and Quinn right and you close in between. Stick with us. If things get hot, take a crack at a Heinie if you get a good chance, and then beat it for home, ridin' like hell."

"Yes, sir." Haven's voice was steady for those two words, but the hand that came up in salute trembled a little.

"And another thing, Havens," Smoke admonished. "This is war up here. You were supposed to learn salutin' and sech back behind. We don't go on that much here at the Front. Ain't got the time, mostly, I reckon, for sech foolishness. When I can't make my men respect me, without forcin' 'em to salute and say 'sir' just because I'm the C.O. in a monkey suit, then I'll quit this outfit and go herdin' sheep."

"Yes, sir—certainly."

But ten minutes later, when four Spads droned toward the Front as the morning sun split over the horizon in a half huge coin of blazing gold, the grin of assurance was gone from the bronze face of Smoke Wade. He sat hunched a little over his stick in the cockpit of the Pinto Spad. His lips moved slightly with words drowned by the thunder of the great Hisso.

"Reckon you know, Jake," he mumbled, caressing the padding about the cockpit as though it were flesh and blood. "Reckon, you old critter, we got to make the best of it, hey, fella?"

Smoke hadn't forgotten his horse back in Arizona, his old pinto pony, Jake. And the Spad, painted in a pinto design to match his pony, thousands of miles away, had in part taken the place of the four-legged animal of flesh and blood.

Once, Smoke turned half round in his seat and grinned back at Havens. He waved to reassure him, but when he turned back and faced the front the grin was gone from his face.

"Damn you, von Stolz," he muttered. "I hope you and your coyotes ain't out this mornin'." He shook his head sadly. "Ain't no use scarin' the life out of this kid first time over. Lord knows, he's scared enough now, without seein' a Jerry crate. Reckon it'll take a damn good handlin' to make somethin' of this poor kid, but—"

SMOKE suddenly sat bolt upright in his seat and whirled his broad shoulders toward the east. He couldn't be sure yet, because of the blinding rays of the sun, but something had told him. A sound—like warming Spandaus guns, far off. His lips moved in an angry curse as he knew. The ships were still in the sun, far to the east, but coming like the mill tails of Hades. He knew that much before he could tell how many.

He glanced swiftly below to orient himself, and a puzzled look came over his leathery features. Below was the most deserted part of that sector. Almost directly under him stood a long building. An old French farm house, half shot away by gun fire. Even from the five thousand feet altitude he held, he could see it plainly. About the house, trucks moved. Something brown—or black—in them. Trucks moving toward the house and away again. Funny, that. The roads from the house seemed to run in all directions and spread a brown look over the surrounding country.

He could not see much in that one fleeting glance below, before the Jerries snarled in close. But he saw enough to arouse his curiosity to fever heat.

Smoke's hand went up in signal for battle. He shot another glance at Havens to reassure him with a grin that he didn't feel. The flight of four spun and, heading for the Fokker flight, began to climb frantically. Up came the Fokkers, too. Smoke made them out plainly, for they were out of the blinding sun now.

Ten of them. He cursed again. At point he could see the leader and he cursed him more than the rest. Von Stolz was there. Arrogant, cocky, little von Stolz was leading his buzzards to attack a smaller flight. His attacks were always like that. That was why Smoke hated him to begin with. Twice since he'd moved opposite in the same sector, von Stolz had been caught in a small flight when Spads outnumbered his brood two to one—and had he fought gallantly? Not von Stolz. He'd high-tailed it for home.

"Ornery coyote," Smoke had drawled then, "Yuh cain't shoot somethin' unless you can get close enough to it."

Smoke led his flight in a desperate climb, but it was not enough. Like plummeting king-fishers from lofty pines, the ten Fokkers devils snarled down, with rattling Spandaus guns shooting tongues of blue flames in orange and yellow tracer ribbons.

Then came the answering movement from the flight of Smoke Wade. There came an instant flash to the left. The tightly bunched flight flashed into their vertical and out so rapidly and with such skill that the hellions of von Stolz were taken entirely off their guard.

Vickers guns belched flame and steel. White tracers fluffed out in a hell of telltale ribbons that were evidence of dead aims and true shooting.

Havens was closed in by the formation—almost trapped there. But he was firing, too. Smoke shot a glance at him as he whirled and signaled to break formation. Down below, two Fokker D-7s twisted and spun like crazy, dancing things at the end of long, ever increasing strings of black smoke and flame. Two up and eight against four. Still more than two to one. Havens wasn't so hot yet.

As the Boche flight swung into a tight vertical and came slamming back, the leader pulled one of his tricks. Smoke growled with all the savagery of a hungry timber wolf as he saw it coming. Then he whirled and darted after him.

Von Stolz had deliberately looped from the point of his flight and had come in behind the others now. From this protected position he could pounce out in surprise and fall with all the fury of hell on any hapless one who chanced to try to dive out of the fight. He wanted to get all the kills if possible. To be a hero for the glory of the *Vaterland* and—himself.

Smoke had thundered halfway toward him in a crazy, zigzag course, shooting as he came. Suddenly he cursed wildly, and his right hand flashed far down on his right leg as he kicked the rudder. Von Stolz had plunged like a meteor at something. Swinging to follow, Smoke found a snarling Fokker barring his way. There wasn't time or room to maneuver the Spad. But his six-gun was out and blasting away with deadly aim now over the cockpit edge. The Fokker nosed down with a grunt as a six-gun slug found its way into the Mercedes. Smoke glanced after it.

And in that one glimpse, he saw the horror he had feared. Havens had been too eager. He'd held down on his triggers and let his Vickers snarl their way to overheating and the ultimate double jam of both guns. Frantically, the kid was diving for home, working wildly with his jammed guns which, mounted as they were half in the Vee of a Hisso, made it next to impossible to fix.

On his tail rode von Stolz. True to his reputation he was taking his toll of cold meat that was helpless.

Smoke Wade's face was an ugly thing to see as he screamed down from the upper fight, almost plumb in the middle of the snarling Fokkers. Crouched over his sights, he headed hell-bent for the crimson Fokker.

EVEN before he could kick the Spad straight for von Stolz's cockpit, Smoke saw the yellow tracers fluffing from the raving Spandaus straight towards Havens' Spad. He saw the agonized face of Havens turn and stare back. He had been working wildly with his jammed guns. It seemed hopeless now. He was flying a crazy, zigzag course, struggling desperately to keep out of the line of those stabbing fingers of death. Then, in an instant of mortal terror, Havens flung his hands high in the air and held them there in surrender.

As though von Stolz had not seen, he snarled on; his firing increased. Yellow tracers cut their way through the tail group of the new Spad and crept toward the cockpit.

Then Smoke Wade's eye caught the cockpit of von Stolz in the ring-back-sights before him. He pressed with the skill of an expert, which he was. But Smoke Wade, for once in his life, was an instant too long. Von Stolz had sensed his danger and had moved upward. Smoke cursed as he saw his tracers fluff into the rear of the cockpit and spray the tail of the crimson ship.

Frantically, he kicked out and pulled to follow the Boche in his wild Immelman—but it wasn't an Immelman after all. At the top von Stolz didn't turn after the roll. Instead, he whirled toward the north, gave a signal to the rest of his brood and hurtled for home.

Smoke pulled closer to Havens now. The kid's face was white and drawn, but he could smile. Smoke grinned back at him with thin tight lips that were hard to turn upward at the corners in a mirthful expression.

He glanced over his shoulder. The Jerry crates were headed north. Von Stolz was at their head again, but now, where ten had been before, only six remained.

"Huh," grunted Smoke as he spun his Spad and took after them. "Let that be a lesson to yuh. Reckon you wouldn't a' come out if you'd known what was comin' to your flight, you yellow skulkin' coyote."

He waved to Brant and Quinn as they thundered at him looking for orders. Then he pointed back toward Havens, who was making for home, dropping lower and lower in altitude as he flew. Smoke gave them the order to turn back and see that Havens landed safely, while he did a little maneuvering on his own hook.

Steadily, flying in a great circle, he veered to the east, into the sun, and climbed steadily. A pair of powerful binoculars came out of their case at his side and he studied the country to the north, in the direction the Fokkers had taken. He was up in the sun himself now, where they couldn't spot him and where he could see well enough through the glasses.

A slow grin spread across his face as he watched. The Fokkers were circling. They were going down to land. Instantly, Smoke moved closer to the spot where they were coming down. He could make it out easily through the glasses. A puzzled look came over his face.

"Huh. Reckon they'll crack up if they try to land there," he ventured. "They'll crack up sure there, or else I'm a jack rabbit."

Another minute. Three planes came slithering down in long, graceful glides, to the place, landed with seeming ease and rolled to a stop at one edge where they were partly hidden by the foliage of trees.

"Huh," Smoke grunted, more puzzled than ever, "Reckon I am a jack rabbit then."

The other planes were landing there too without trouble, in spite of the fact that the whole field looked from the air like a thin, wooded section where no ship could possibly get down whole. Smoke flew in one great circle, fifteen thousand feet above the place. Then he turned, still puzzled, toward the lone farmhouse he had noticed before.

"Reckon somethin's goin' on they didn't want no one to see," he chuckled. "Then the old coyote, von Stolz, lost his nerve and ran for home, anyway."

The wrecked building, perhaps a full kilometer behind the German front, seemed suddenly abandoned now as he stared down. Where fifteen minutes before, at the beginning of the dogfight, tractors had been running here and there like busy ants, now not a thing moved below. There was the baked, brown look of the earth for some distance about the remains of the building, as though a great scourge had come there and had blighted everything in sight, but that was all.

His brow furrowed with perplexity as he droned toward Dombley and home. He couldn't figure the thing out. That lone shack. Then the sudden ceasing of movement about it. It all tallied up with the transfer of von Stolz and his brood of devils to a new and secret field close to the farm house. Smoke had had plenty of premonitions about that move when von Stolz had come up. Heinie was planning something big. But what?

COLONEL MCGILL, the post commander, wrinkled his gray old brow, too, as Smoke told him what he had seen, twenty minutes later in his private office. His eyes grew worried and puzzled.

"Smoke," he said with unusual seriousness, "this is getting bad. Those Heinies have got something big up their sleeves, and we've got to find out what—"

His words were interrupted by a knock on the door of his office. "Come in," he boomed.

Smoke turned as the door opened, and saw two infantrymen enter half carrying someone between them; his eyes popped out of his head. That jibbering, palsied figure between them was none other than Havens, the new replacement. Behind came Brant and Quinn.

Havens' face was the color of dirty linen as he tried to stammer out words that were unintelligible at first. Smoke pushed a chair toward him and tried to ease him into it.

"There. You're all right now, I reckon, Havens," he said softly. "What in hell's hit yuh? You look like you'd seen a ghost."

"I—I have," gasped Havens, trembling as he sat there. "I—I did see one, I tell yuh."

"Huh?" Smoke stared. "Take it easy, son," he advised. "Then tell us what's gone haywire."

"He's telling the truth maybe," ventured one of the infantrymen. "We seen him crash comin' in. His engine cut out on him, and he just made the lines. We was in the back line trench, about half a kilometer from that old chateau up near the front."

Smoke nodded shortly.

"Yeah. Reckon I know the place. Half blasted away with gun fire, but most of it stands yet. "Go on."

"Well, me buddy here and me, we seen this guy come in to land, and we knew he didn't have a chance in that spot, so we starts after him across the field before he'd crashed. We seen him pile out of his wrecked plane and go runnin' and scream-in' toward the chateau, like he was scared silly."

"I was," stammered Havens, almost in a scream. "I—the crash got me haywire, and I—I guess I didn't know what I was doing. I wanted to get away from it. It seemed that every plane on the Front was after me. I was crazy I guess."

He was shaking violently as he tried to go on.

"I tried to hide in the chateau to get away from it all—to shut it out. Then something else happened there. There were weird, unearthly noises. Some crazy, whispering voice telling me to get out if I valued my life. I—I didn't go. I was too scared to move. It was dark in there and then something came floating across the room at me. A ghost. I'm not lying or crazy. I saw it. It was a terrible white thing with clanking chains, and it came right out of the wall and right at me. Then—then—these two came." He motioned toward the infantrymen. "They saw it just before it disappeared."

Smoke's eyes were blazing with a new light now. He whirled to the two infantrymen.

"You saw this?" he demanded. "Both of yuh saw this here ghost Havens is talkin' about?"

They nodded. "For only an instant," the spokesman told him. "Then it was gone. Seemed to fade right back into the wall on the other side of the room."

Colonel McGill was on his feet.

"Damn it, men," he roared, "you know damn well you didn't see any ghost. There isn't any such thing. Damn it, the morale of our men is low enough, without stories like this coming in."

It was as though Smoke Wade wasn't listening to him at all. He had moved swiftly to the big map of the Front that hung on the wall. He pulled one of the infantrymen with him as he went and pointed to a spot at the map.

"That's the point where the chateau is located, ain't it?" he drawled.

The corporal nodded.

"I ain't sure," Smoke went on, "but I'll gamble that chateau had a reputation for bein' haunted, didn't it?"

The corporal nodded again. "Yes, sir. It did. That might be one of the reasons why we didn't use it. Another was that it was so conspicuous to the enemy fire, the officers preferred to have their headquarters at the Front in dugouts."

Smoke spun and faced Colonel McGill.

"Colonel, I think you're wrong, sir," he said. "I reckon these here men are tellin' the truth about what they saw."

Colonel McGill's face darkened.

"Wade," he barked, "I'd given you more credit than to think you'd believe in such trash as ghosts. We've got enough trouble with—"

"I know, colonel," Smoke cut him off quickly. "But just the same I'll bet you a thousand francs right now that I can clear up this whole business in twenty-four hours and prove to you that this chateau is haunted.

Colonel McGill hadn't forgotten the last time Smoke Wade had taken him for a bet. His sporting blood boiled.

"I'll take that bet, Wade," he boomed.

"And, by George, I'll take that thousand francs away from you so fast that—"

Smoke's confident chuckle cut him off before he had finished.

"It's a go then, colonel," he grinned, "on one condition. You give me a free hand here at this field for the next twenty-four hours and use your rank in giving any orders I suggest. Is that fair?"

Colonel McGill nodded, still smiling. "A go," he said.

FIVE hours later, with meals forgotten and only one thing uppermost in the whirling brain of Smoke Wade, he sat crouched over the table of his office, pouring over a map of the sector.

He looked up quickly and boomed a "come in" as a knock sounded on the door. Havens was framed there, less shaken now, but still a sad picture of shattered nerves. He came in a little uncertainly and stood beside his new commanding officer; as he began to speak, his eyes wandered about and down at the map before Wade, where lines were drawn and places marked.

"Captain," he began. "I—I came to ask you for another chance. I know I went haywire this morning and all that, but it was because of the crash, I think. I—I've got to make good, that's all. I will, if—"

Smoke grinned at him reassuringly, and his big hand rose to his shoulder.

"You've done plenty for one day, Havens," he chuckled. "Reckon somethin' big's goin' to come ridin' out of that haunted chateau story of yours. You'll do all right. But for the next day or so, you better take it easy and stay out of the air."

Havens' face brightened.

"Thanks, captain," he said, earnestly. "I was afraid you'd hold it against me, and I—well, I want to make good here at the 66th."

"Sure. Reckon you will, too, Havens. Now, run along and don't worry about it anymore. I got a lot of figurin' to do yet awhile before I'm set to go into action."

Havens' appearance had put a sudden thought in Smoke's brain. He reached for the phone and called Colonel McGill.

"Colonel, would you use your influence with the infantry and artillery men about the chateau? From what I can find on the map, there aren't any outfits very close, but if possible, have them stay away from and out of that chateau. Have them leave it alone, if you can, colonel, will you?"

He heard the colonel chuckle. "Haven't got any salt on the tail of that ghost yet, have you, Smoke?"

"Not yet, colonel. But if you'll do your part perhaps I'll—"

"I will," McGill assured him. It was late afternoon when Smoke Wade began scribbling words on sheets of paper. They were all alike—read the same—and said:

> *"To Hauptmann von Stolz. You're a yellow, skulking coward of a fighter. We've had reinforcements come up to our field. I'm betting a thousand francs you're afraid to meet us in a dogfight in the dark, by the light of dropped flares. The loser to drop the thousand francs or the equivalent over the field of the winner at dawn tomorrow morning. We'll be there. But I'm betting you won't have the guts. Over St. Miheil then, at midnight, if you're as brave as you try to make us believe.*
>
> *Captain Smoke Wade, 66th squadron pursuit"*

His smile broadened wider and wider as he wrote each message. There were a dozen in all. Calmly, Smoke placed them in as many message cans, tucked them under his arm and went out to the tarmac.

Jake, the pinto Spad, was warming on the line at his phoned order. He climbed to the cockpit, shouted "clear" and kicked round into the wind.

Through machine-gun fire, zigzagging crazily, he roared over the trenches of the enemy. Now and then, his hand reached over the edge of the cockpit and let go one of the cans. These were not alone for von Stolz. Perhaps von Stolz would need some urging.

Half a dozen cans left, he swung toward the spot he had seen that morning, with its mysterious brown surroundings, and climbed as he skirted it. The glasses came into play now as he stared from a distance, and he grinned broadly at what he saw. Below, part of the ground, within several hundred feet of the house in every direction, was gray with troops—enemy troops.

He roared on toward the camouflaged field he had spotted. Down, down he whirled like a mad man now. Fokkers were warming, ticking over on the line. Three spun on the tarmac and roared down the runway.

Smoke grinned. His hand dove into the cockpit time after time, and each time it flung a message can at a mechanic or pilot who was racing for cover. The Fokkers were staggering off now. Smoke waited, hung for a moment, and then yanked over in a shuddering vertical and raced at them as they climbed. Hunched over the stick, his gray eyes narrowed as he stared across the sights of his Vickers guns.

Tac-tac-tac! The Pinto Spad shuddered with the recoil of the Vickers. Tiny tongues of flame, blue and orange, darting like the split tongue of a rattler, showed the spot from whence came those white tracer ribbons of death.

One Fokker folded up and flopped to deathlike stillness, like a headless hen. Another, forced down by the pilot in his sudden fear, crashed as the landing gear gave way and partly disappeared in a cloud of dust among the masses of low shrubbery the enemy had used to make the field look from the air like a heavily wooded section. The third suddenly dove like a plummet and lay still in a twisted mass of wreckage.

His eyes narrowed as he roared above the lone farm house on his way back. There had been many Germans there. Perhaps ten thousand or more. Now there was hardly half that number. They had disappeared like magic with only the house to hide them.

It was nearly dark when he reached his own field again. He called Brant and Quinn to his office.

"Reckon you birds never went on purpose for a dogfight at midnight," he drawled. "Well, you're goin' tonight."

They stared at him in bewilderment.

"I ain't crazy," Smoke insisted, "I got a plan worked out. You, Brant, and Quinn are going to lead every ship out of here a half hour before midnight, see? Every pilot, that is, except Havens. You won't need him. The kid needs a couple of days' rest before he's fit for the slaughter again. Brant, you take my pinto Spad, and I'll take one of the replacement Spads. You're going to meet von Stolz, and I want him to think I'm there with my whole outfit, savvy?"

They both nodded blankly.

"Now, take plenty of flares along. The meeting is at midnight over St. Miheil, and I reckon von Stolz'll be there sure enough. Don't take any chance with the men. Just keep him busy for a while. That's the game. I'll be over in Germany myself, and I don't want him around crampin' my style none."

Brant and Quinn were hardly out of the door, before Smoke was at the phone, calling a friend, Captain Fields of the artillery, now at the Front.

"This you, Fields?" drawled Smoke. "This is Smoke Wade... Yeah... Listen. I got a little job tonight, if you can help... Yep. That's right... You're right close to that there chateau what's supposed to be haunted, ain't yuh?... Thought so. All right. Now get this straight, and we'll pull a fast one on Heinie. First, can you deliver to me about a hundred and fifty pounds of light bombs, maybe fifty pounders, that I can set off without droppin' 'em?... That's right. Like settin' off dynamite... Sure. Now, the next thing—and this is damn important, I reckon—at exactly midnight, blow hell out of that chateau. Enough bombs to blow the whole thing off the map. But you'll have to sneak up on it and not let anybody see you doin' it, see? Enough to blow down deep in the ground, too... That's right, I reckon... Huh? I'll tell you later. I'm countin' on yuh, Fields. Yep."

IT WAS half past eleven when Smoke Wade, with two hundred pounds of high explosive bombs packed gingerly on the floor of his cockpit, roared into the darkness in a strange Spad. The night was dark, but clear.

As he droned north, his eyes gradually became accustomed to the darkness, and he began to make out objects on the ground dimly. Every nerve was tense as an E string as he crossed the lines, flying high. Then, without an instant's hesitation, his hand reached for the throttle and pulled it back. The nose dropped sharply as he pushed the Spad into a glide.

Then he did a thing that took nerves of steel. He reached for the ignition switch and cut that. The engine turned over and over with the race of the wind against it, then slowly died.

No sound came now except the wind playing a chant through the wires of the Spad. Smoke leaned far over the edge of his cockpit and stared down. At first he couldn't make out what he sought, then he found it. A small field that looked merely like a smooth gray blot in the blackness of the surrounding trees.

His hand was firm on the stick as he held the nose as high as possible to cut down the sighing of the wind through the rigging. Turn after turn he made above that field to make sure. A dead engine. Enough bombs to blow a building to kingdom come—and not a tremble.

Skillfully, he slipped in at the spot. A short distance away he made out a small building in the darkness and recognized it. It was the one which stood alone in that peculiarly brown, open space behind the German lines.

His muscles tightened as he heard the *carump-carump* of the wheels as they touched the ground and the plane began to roll. The stick was well back in his lap now as he waited for the roll to cease. Then it came with a slight groan.

Smoke mumbled something under his breath. He thought he'd heard the crack of something giving way in the only thing that would get him back to his own side of the lines. Well, no time for that now.

Cautiously, he unwound his lanky body from the cockpit and controls, and listened. The night was still, except for the booming and rumble of distant guns. He glanced at the luminous dial of his wrist watch.

His hand dropped to his six-gun to make sure. It was there in its holster. Carefully, he lifted each of the four fifty-pound bombs from the cockpit, and with one tucked under each arm, he made his way stealthily toward the place where the half-ruined house stood in the darkness.

Suddenly, he froze in his tracks. Someone had spoken close to what had been the front of the house. He couldn't make anything out against the blackness of the ruined place. It came again. A muffled tread and then a stop. He moved closer.

"*Wer da?*"

A sentry. Of course. He was being challenged. He couldn't make him out at all in the blackness. His hand instinctively felt toward the old six-gun, but that wouldn't do the trick.

Suddenly, the roaring sound of a plane motor sounded from overhead. Smoke had heard it a minute before and had cursed. It was whining angrily, high up, and seemed to be circling. Then the earth was bathed in a radiant light about him.

In that instant, Smoke saw the sentry before him and the sentry saw him. Smoke was half-crouched when the light came. His hands laid the bombs tenderly on the ground, and from that position he leaped like a wild animal. His great fist smacked with a dull thud against the jaw of the German, before the Boche realized what had happened, and he slumped to the ground on legs suddenly turned to rubber.

Smoke crouched low again and waited, cursing the flare and whoever had dropped it. There didn't seem to be anyone else in sight.

The flare was short-lived and burned out rapidly. Smoke moved on under cover of the darkness. He heard angry voices coming from the direction of the building. Cautiously, he skirted it. The voices seemed to be condemning some fool airman who had dropped a flare. He wasn't suspected.

He stopped short now for an instant and oriented himself. Very dimly, he could see something that loomed high and ominous some distance south. That would be the chateau. In another moment now that would be gone—if Fields kept his word.

A blank wall faced the chateau. Smoke stole softly toward it. Then, at the wall and a few feet away from it, he laid the two bombs and darted swiftly toward the place where his plane stood. Halfway there he stopped short for an instant and stared south. High above where St. Miheil should be, flares burst in the sky. He could see their lights plainly, and his face wrinkled in a slow grin.

Two more bombs, the last, were under his arms and he moved swiftly toward the house, skirting it carefully this time. The sound of the voices inside the house came to him again. Through the open roof the Boches had seen the flares in the sky to the south and knew that von Stolz, their revered ace, had answered his challenge.

With the softness and stealth of a bobcat, Smoke stole to the place of the other bombs, and laid the two beside them. Four in all now.

SMOKE glanced at his watch. One minute of twelve. He tensed and watched the seconds tick away. It should be timed to a fine hair. Ten seconds left. He reached for one of the bombs and unscrewed the cap—pressed the handle for the timing fuse that would send them off in five seconds.

Instantly—that done—he leaped to his feet and dashed for the plane. His work was over now. He had only to get back. As he ran, the earth sped beneath him. A flare burst in the sky above. That plane had been coming lower all the time. And with his running and the sound of his feet treading hastily, shouts came from the house. Shouts that were cut off by a terrific explosion behind.

Smoke plunged on, his face in the light of the flare as the bombs went off, shaking the earth under him. And at the same instant another explosion came from some two kilometers to the south. The earth rocked as though possessed. Clods of dirt and stone fell plunking all about him in the fury that followed. Angry voices in guttural accents came to him from the north. Another truckload of troops was arriving. Thank the Lord something had held them up until now. Smoke heard angry shouts behind him. The light of the flare illuminated the Spad in the field as he made for it. It wouldn't have mattered anyway. This new outfit in trucks would have caught him before he could get away.

Down behind a boulder, Smoke crouched with his six-gun in his hand. This was the end. He'd shoot it out with those damn Heinies and die with his boots on. Damn that flare, anyway. And yet it helped him to see and watch them come.

Blam! Blam! Two fat Heinies yelped like hurt dogs as six-gun lead plowed their vitals. They had spotted him now. Knew where he was. Orders came, barked in guttural German. Some men raced toward the gaping hole that had been the little house—their objective. Others, yelling and shouting, galloped in a great circle to surround Smoke Wade, hidden behind his rock.

Another flare burst from overhead. Smoke was cursing and shooting and re-loading like a wild man. That damn Heinie in the plane above. Why didn't he do something? Then he remembered the sound that the din about him now made almost unrecognizable. It wasn't the drone of a Mercedes. It was rather the sharply bitten staccato of a Hisso. Someone in a Spad was up there. And a Spad meant someone on his side.

The Jerries had reached his own Spad there on the field. Eight or ten of them were running about, trying to get closer to him in a wide circle as he crouched behind the rock.

Suddenly a new light burst in the darkness. It came from his Spad. The devils had fired it. He was done. Washed up for sure. But Smoke Wade fought on like a mad man. His gun began to glow cherry. German after German yelped in testimony to his marksmanship. A steel-jacketed bullet spat and whistled as it ricocheted off the boulder, sending a shower of stone dust in his eyes.

And now another sound came to him as he shot, with only one eye that wasn't full of the powdered stone and dust it was the death chant of Vickers guns from just above. The diving Spad was snarling like an angry hornet. Men screamed, leaped in the air and plunked headlong in their last twitch of mortal pain.

But it seemed endless, this fighting. Another truck load of Jerries was coming up—Jerries who were yelling and cursing, running with flame-spatting guns.

Flame belched from Smoke's six-gun. But the odds made it seem futile. The rescue Spad had flipped over in a slithering vertical, climbed for a little altitude and now was snarling down on the new arrivals.

Men fought and kicked and screamed with pain and torture as that Spad whirled and dove with crimson-spitting Vickers. Then it zoomed and dropped another flare. The light of the burning plane helped to show the way. The Spad was landing in the field where Smoke had landed.

Half doubled over, Smoke raced to the point where it should slow enough for him to catch hold. It came leaping and bounding over the rough ground, uncertainly. A hole and it would be gone.

It swerved near. Men were running to stop it, too, but farther away. Smoke leaped for the left wing in a desperate lunge. Made it! Then the Hisso blasted wide again, while hot steel sprayed all about them. He clung to the wires against the ripping slipstream of the whirling prop and stared at the figure in the cockpit.

"Havens!" he gasped. "Well, I'll be a horned toad if—"

Havens' grin suddenly changed to a wince of pain. He seemed suddenly to go limp—then struggle to hold himself. The Spad was still leaping and bucking over the uneven ground. Trees, some distance away, came looming at them dangerously.

Smoke leaned half in the cockpit. His hand grasped the stick.

"Good boy. Hold it. We'll make it. Hit bad?"

Havens' face was white as he shook his head.

"In the left leg," he screamed above the roar of the motor.

"Can you handle the rudder with the other?"

"I'll see—yes."

"Good."

Smoke's hand gripped the stick in a sure hold. The trees came tearing at them. The Spad was off now. Flying laboriously at that obstacle of timber and branches. Smoke held his course. No time now.

His hand brought the stick back with a sure pull. Branches crashed and ripped through the landing gear. The Spad lurched dizzily, wavered and droned into level flight again under the skillful hand of Smoke Wade. Then they were climbing into smooth air and heading for home.

EVERY ship of the 66th, except the one in which Smoke Wade had left, was back on the line when he reached the field and landed in the flare of a gasoline torch. Tenderly, Smoke lifted Havens from the cockpit and placed him in an ambulance. Havens was objecting strenuously, saying it was only a flesh wound, but Smoke was firm.

"Reckon it ought to be took care of, sonny," he grinned, "anyhow. I know when I got a good man in my outfit, and I aim to take care of him."

Colonel McGill, Brant, Quinn and others of their flight were there. McGill's wrinkled face was still more canyoned with his happy smile.

"Splendid!" he exploded. "Marvelous, Wade. I've just received word that the tunnel caved in several places across the Front."

Smoke's brows knit.

"Caved in?" he repeated. "Lord, colonel, I didn't expect that. And how the devil did you know it was a tunnel?"

Colonel McGill chuckled.

"You're not half as surprised as some of the doughboys in a Front-line trench were when they suddenly dropped about six feet into the earth. Of course we all got the idea of the tunnel when I heard how and where the cave-in came. Stupid of me not to have seen it yesterday morning when we were talking. That crazy story about the haunted chateau must have gotten me off the track. How did you figure it out?"

"Wasn't so hard," Smoke admitted. "That brown look around that farm house over the lines got me thinking. Looked like dirt, but I couldn't figure where it could come from. Then the yarn about the haunted chateau gave me a hunch and I bet on it. The only answer could be a tunnel, and the Heinies had to have a place for it to come out behind our lines. Must have rigged up some sound and movie contraption to scare our men away from the chateau. Last evenin' they started pourin' Heinies into the tunnel. More than ten thousand of 'em, I reckon, poor devils! Reckon they'd have cleaned house plenty, if it had worked."

McGill nodded gravely.

"They certainly would have," he agreed. "But that bombing—from both ends at once. How did you contrive to work that to cause the cave-in?"

"Reckon that wasn't all my fault, colonel," he confessed. "I figured on blowin' both ends of the tunnel at once, so's to catch the Heinies in their own trap, sort of, but I didn't figure on a complete cave-in. That's a fact. The blast must have weakened supports comin' from both ends at once like that and let her down."

"Probably," said Colonel McGill. He shoved a big roll of franc notes toward Smoke, and the grin returned to Smoke's face as he took them.

"Oh, sure, colonel," he smiled. "I was comin' to that. Yuh see, I need that money to pay off von Stolz."

"Von Stolz?" gasped McGill.

"Reckon you heard right, colonel," Smoke chuckled. "Von Stolz was apt to be hangin' around tonight, maybe, I thought, so I wanted to be sure I could get rid of him and the whole pack. I knew he wouldn't chance goin' out with a few planes and that he'd take his whole outfit to make sure of his skulkin' hide."

"But, good Lord, man, this is war," McGill objected. "You don't mean to say you're taking my thousand francs to pay von Stolz?"

"Reckon that's what I'm aimin' to do, colonel," he nodded. "Smoke Wade always pays his bets, no matter who they're made with." He broke off in a chuckle. "And besides, major, I got a hunch I'll get it back from von Stolz before long—or take it out of his hide."

The ambulance had not yet left with Havens when Smoke sauntered toward his quarters a minute later. He saw Havens motioning to him from the rear of the ambulance, and his face was worried and earnest.

"I just wanted to make sure, captain, you didn't hold it against me—my coming out tonight and messing into your business. You see, I saw that line on your map when I was in your office talking to you and—well, I had a hunch about where you were going and about the tunnel, and I thought you might need some help. That first flare—" he said apologetically, "I—I guess that was a mistake. I saw as soon as I dropped it that it showed you up and—"

Smoke cut him off with a chuckle.

"Now, don't you be worryin' about that none," he laughed. "That first flare of yours come just right, I reckon—so's I could see that Heinie's chin good and plain."

Dead
Man's
Staffel

Men waited for their midnight raids in terror—this strange Boche staffel, whose ships dove straight into the earth, blowing up pilots and all. What was the secret of this suicide squadron? Could a Yank fight them and live? Grimly Smoke Wade sought the answer, riding his pinto Spad into dead man's skies.

Dead Man's Staffel

A LONE pinto Spad verticaled and zoomed and dove high above the German side of the lines. Three Fokkers hurled about it in a tangle of white-yellow tracer smoke, like a nest of hornets revolting at intrusion.

Under the windshield of that pinto Spad, a lanky, leathery figure hunched over his stick, working frantically with jammed guns. Great bony hands bled from brutal contact with the sharp metal of the twin Vickers, half hidden in the Hisso's Vee.

Angry curses sprayed through clenched white teeth. The pilot slammed back in his seat in disgust. Controls moved with lightning speed. His right hand flashed to his right leg, far down. It came up in a blur and brought with it a big, old-time Western six-gun.

That was Smoke Wade in a tight spot. The Arizona sun-bronzed cow-poke whirled in his seat. His big six-gun spoke.

Blam! Blam!

The cracks came almost as fast as the answering Spandau rattle about him. One of the three remaining Fokkers leaped into the air and plunged for hell.

Two Fokkers snarled in from behind, struggling to get him in their cross-fire. Smoke Wade jerked the controls of his plane and kicked. The pinto Spad leaped into the air, half-rolled and slammed out of the

Immelmann, straight for the crimson ship on his right.

The pinto Spad and the crimson Fokker came very close together in that split second of time. For a reason known only to him Smoke poised his six-gun and waited. His eyes were mere slits as he stared at the red crate. Von Stolz should be in that ship. But something about this Fokker left doubt in his mind.

"Hell," he spat, "you ain't von Stolz!"

The pilot had turned and stared at him, but that hadn't been the deciding factor. More than half hidden under the big helmet and the large goggles, his face might have been that of von Stolz.

Smoke's six-gun flashed out over the cockpit padding. He didn't bother to sight across the top of the barrel, but shot from the cockpit edge.

Blam! Blam! Blam!

Something happened to the Mercedes under that slim, ugly snout of the crimson Fokker. The prop stopped with a jerk. The Jerry pilot shot a scared look around as he stuck the nose for the ground, howling down for a dead stick landing.

"That crate won't be flyin' right soon, not with that engine," Smoke spat as he hurled at the one remaining Fokker.

That Jerry was wise. He kicked over in a tight vertical and howled for home. Smoke grunted in disgust as he watched him go.

"Now, I wonder," he mused as he turned south. "Wonder why that lousy coyote, von Stolz, don't want me to know he ain't in the air opposite me no more."

Ten minutes later, the lanky skipper of the 66th pursuit squadron set his ship down at the field at Dombley and sauntered with a rapid, swinging gait toward headquarters and Colonel McGill's office.

The wise old commander of the field looked up as Smoke entered his office and snapped up a salute.

"It's just like I suspected," Smoke began first. "Reckon von Stolz is up to somethin' and he don't want us to know he's left his *jagdstaffel* number seven across the line. Couldn't be he's injured and in the hospital. That skulkin' coyote ain't never got close enough to a good air lighter to get hurt. I'm sure that he ain't flyin' that red ship what's supposed to be his."

Colonel McGill's wrinkled face grew puzzled.

"You recognized the pilot in the ship, then, Smoke?" he asked.

Smoke shook his head.

"Nope. Told by somethin' else. I cruised around over his drome this mornin' and let 'em come up after me. That damned red ship kept out of reach most of the time. I got two out of the five and sent 'em down before my guns jammed. Got another with the old smoke pole and then I come in close to that red ship."

McGill nodded and waited.

"And it wasn't von Stolz," Smoke affined. "Got a pilot what looks a heap like him with a helmet and big pair of goggles on, but I could tell by the ship. There's a place right back of the cockpit in von Stolz's crimson crate where I put some mighty fancy holes the once I got close enough to him. That ought to have a right big patch on that there spot, but there ain't none on this crate, although the rest seemed mighty like it."

Colonel McGill still looked very much puzzled. The same look was reflected on the leathery face of Smoke Wade.

"Very odd," admitted the colonel. "By the way, General Banks called you from Staff while you were gone. He wants you to come over to his office as soon as you return. He seemed very much agitated about something."

Smoke's face twisted in a slow grin.

"Say what he wanted?" he drawled. "You don't reckon he wants to make another bet like that last one?"

Colonel McGill chuckled at the thought, then sobered.

"I hardly think so this time, Smoke," he said. "Better get right over and see what he wants. It might possibly have something to do with this mysterious act of von Stolz."

Smoke nodded and hurried out of the office.

FOR ten minutes the pinto Spad roared toward the southwest. Then Smoke brought the mottle-colored, heavily-patched crate down lightly to the field outside Staff headquarters and strode to General Banks' office. He found the general in a high state of excitement as he entered. Banks whirled to face him anxiously.

"Thank God you've come, Wade!" he boomed sincerely. "I was afraid you might not get back from the lone patrol the colonel said you were on."

Smoke grinned.

"Reckon Heinie ain't got no mold for the slug what's goin' to snuff out my skinny carcass," he ventured. "What's got yuh all stirred up, general? Young stock been stampedin' out the corral or somethin?"

General Banks was very grave.

"It's something that's just begun over at the 13th bombardment squadron at Rene." He motioned Smoke to a chair and sat down heavily himself. "It's horrible, Wade. No one can fathom it. You're the only man I can think of to put on the job. Your work in stopping the drive at Coucy was damned clever. I'm desperately hoping you can do something about this, although it seems almost hopeless—beyond human power."

Smoke leaned forward in his chair and listened, then, all ears.

"For four nights now the 13th night bombers have been going over to bomb the big supply depot at St. Armand, far behind the German lines. They did fairly well the first two nights. Last night and the night before, the whole lot of them got lost. Only half the ships returned to their field. The rest must have landed somewhere in Germany or crashed. Those who came back reported that somewhere on the way over their compasses went bad on them. Just spun around crazily. It was only by luck that they got back in the dark."

Smoke's eyes narrowed. That was all.

"But that's of minor consequence to the other thing that has happened," General Banks raced on, tensely and anxiously. "On the last two nights, while the 13th has been gone, strange bombers have come from the enemy side of the lines and have raided their drome. They don't drop bombs. The ships themselves come down and blow up—pilots and all. Men of the 13th have found pieces of human bodies and wreckage for miles about the place."

Smoke's eyes almost closed as he stared at General Banks.

"Yuh-yuh mean to tell me, general," he demanded, "thet them Jerry pilots deliberately fly over and crash with their whole load of bombs? Thet's suicide, sir. Don't sound like 'em."

General Banks shrugged with a hopeless gesture.

"What other line of reasoning can we attach to it?" he demanded. "The 13th is about to go crazy. They want their number changed. They think they're hoodooed and I can't say I blame them. But there's a much more deadly possibility behind all this than just the blowing up of part of the field of the 13th. Can you imagine what a squadron of those ships under the hands of those suicidal maniac pilots would do to Paris? They go out knowing they're going to die. They can spot their crashes right in the heart of Paris. Why, good God, man, they could blow up the whole city with a dozen ships!"

Smoke sat very still for a long time and studied the toe of his muddy boot. Then he looked up quickly.

"You want me to go over to the 13th and see what I can do, is that it, sir?" he drawled.

General Banks nodded.

"Yes. As soon as you can, Wade. Staff is desperate. We're hoping you can do something, although it looks—"

Smoke was on his feet.

"I got me a hunch right now," he barked. "Don't be worryin' none for a spell. We'll see what happens tonight."

IT WAS nearly dark when the pinto Spad hurled down on the field of the 13th bombardment squadron and roared to the line. A slim, cocky little captain swaggered up and glared at Smoke as he untangled himself from the cockpit and dropped to the ground.

"You're Wade," he guessed with plain signs of antagonism. "I've received orders from General Banks of Staff that you're coming here to take charge. I'm Captain Turner, the commander of the 13th bombardment."

Smoke nodded and stuck out his hand. Turner ignored it.

"I'm damned if I'm going to have another captain coming around here messing in my squadron," he barked. "These brass hats give me a pain in the neck. How in hell does this general think you're going to solve something that we ourselves can't solve?"

Smoke eyed him narrowly for half a minute without a word.

"If yore thinkin' I come over here to take your squadron of egg layers away from you, Turner, you got a burr under your saddle, I reckon. Got a right good outfit of my own. I'm skipper of the 66th pursuit over Dombley way. And now, if you'll lay off your buckin' and snortin' long enough for me to ask some questions, maybe I can be of some help."

Cocky little Turner didn't answer. He just stood and glared.

"How long was it after you took off on the last two nights to bomb the St. Armand German supply depot that you saw the compasses go haywire?" Smoke drawled. "Sixteen minutes, exactly," snapped Turner.

Smoke unfolded a map from his pocket and checked the approximate point over which they would be at that time.

"How come you couldn't follow the stars and get home theta way after this happened?" he asked calmly.

"Think we're dumb?" Turner flamed. "Both last night and the night before were solid clouds upstairs above five thousand." Smoke nodded.

"Thought maybe yuh had a reason," he said. "Don't recollect myself. Was sleepin' then. Yuh plan to go over tonight again on another bomb raid, I reckon?" Turner shrugged.

"You seem to be running the show from now on, according to some fool brass hats," he snapped. "Do we?"

"Yep," Smoke drawled. "I reckon. Now one more question, if yuh can keep from throwin' a fit before I get through. How many of these mysterious German raids comes off in each of the two nights before?"

"Two," cracked Turner. "One about midnight and the other about four in the morning."

Smoke nodded very calmly.

"We'll take off, the whole crowd, at ten minutes to twelve." He shot a glance at the half dozen blasted hangars far down the field. "Won't be no use to leave what ships yuh got left here anyways. Be safer in the air." He glanced skyward into the lowering darkness. "Be right bright tonight with stars, anyhow."

Then his eyes flashed to the pilots—white, shaken kids, clustered about.

"Any of you birds what don't know how to tell direction by the stars," he said. "I'll show yuh soon's the big dipper comes up full."

He uttered those orders as calmly as though he had been announcing a Sunday school picnic; then he strode toward the mess.

Ships began to warm on the line at eleven-thirty that night. Smoke stood beside his pinto Spad and watched the luminous dials over the cockpit padding. His face wore a troubled look which he was glad the darkness hid from the others. He had a hunch, but that was all. The thing was too baffling. Pilots deliberately committing suicide! It sounded incredible. Still, those Heinies might be inspired to do a lot of things for the *Vaterland.*

His movements were tense and eager as he swung into the cockpit at twelve minutes to twelve. He wanted to get at this and satisfy the curiosity that gnawed his inards.

Liberties in a dozen D.H. night-bombers roared and hauled the lumbering, bomb-laden crates down the field. Smoke sat hunched and crowded in the cockpit of his pinto Spad, packed in close beside a mass of parachute Hares.

Gasoline flares sputtered and flamed in ditches at the side of the field. His hand flashed through the flickering light and signaled for the take-off.

Liberties blasted. Smoke's Hisso snarled. The ground shuddered under the heavy barrage of blasting motors. Smoke grinned twistedly as his pinto Spad leaped into the air and shot north in the lead.

"Poor devils," he mumbled. "If they think they're hoodooed 'cause they're in the 13th Squadron, wonder if any of 'em notices there's thirteen of us takin' off now."

He checked the luminous dial of his compass and glanced at his map, switching on the dash light for a moment. Spurts of flame from below told him they were over the lines. He snapped off the light again when he had made sure they were on the course for St. Armand and droned on.

They were across the enemy lines now. The flashes had diminished behind. Suddenly Smoke blinked and shot the stick ahead with a jerk. Winged things that roared and spurted sparks from exhaust stacks were rushing at him out of the darkness. Instantly his hand dove for a Very pistol and he fired a signal for a dive.

He saw the D.H.'s hurl down beside him, exhaust stacks glowing. Shadowy things swept by just overhead, blotting out the stars here and there, making others twinkle for an instant.

Smoke pulled back on the stick and sent the pinto Spad zooming upward in a screaming climb. His hand clutched flares which he flung overboard. The Very pistol came out again and he fired an order to the D.H.'s to continue toward their objective.

Smoke watched them disappear into the north, then, frantically, he turned back to the south. The flares had burst into day-like brilliance, and in this light he could see five planes, lumbering, wobbly-looking things, hurling toward the field of the 13th. Instantly, while the flares were brilliant, he hurled down after them.

Cautiously he came within range. His thumb poised on the trigger button, then tramped down. Vickers bucked and rattled. They looked like Rumplers, those crates below. By the light of the dying flares, Smoke could see his tracers entering the cockpit of the last Jerry crate. He stared aghast. Nothing happened. Hurling closer, he poured another burst into it. He could make out the pilot's head now, protruding above the cockpit cowling, staring motionlessly ahead.

"Maybe armored," Smoke grunted, speculatively.

He stormed in right beside that last Jerry plane then and stared at it. The flares went out. Screaming ahead and above, he let go with a new batch of flares, then dived down again.

It was almost ghastly. No answering fire came from those lumbering crates. They rumbled on, straight for the field of the 13th, as though drawn there by a great magnet. Pilots took no notice of the flashing pinto Spad. They didn't seem to notice anything except their objective.

SOMETHING like a cold chill ran up Smoke's back as he stared. He swung in close to another plane—but that was the same. It just held formation and hurled on.

His hand dove for his six-gun then. Taking very careful aim at the head of that Jerry pilot, not sixty feet from him, he pulled the trigger.

Blam!

The old smoke-pole spoke. The pilot's head jerked sidewise and flopped against the cockpit cowling—but the heavily-laden crate lumbered on in perfect formation!

Smoke blinked and stared. He roared up and ahead again as the flares went out and hurled more over the side. The Jerry crates had nearly reached the field now. They were going down. Desperately he tried to think what to do—how to turn them. His Vickers flamed until they glowed cherry red, but the ships hurled on.

Blam! Blam! Blam!

They dove with murderous accuracy at the tarmac. The air shuddered as they burst into flame and fell apart, uprooting hangars and field. Two out of the flight missed the drome altogether and blew up a hundred yards on the other side of the road.

Smoke cursed through clenched teeth and checked his time. Then with a vicious kick he banked and headed north, his compass set directly on the course for St. Armand. His hand reached the throttle and he pulled back until the speed of the pinto Spad crept back to the cruising speed of the bomb-laden D. H. ships.

Minutes ticked by.

Thirteen! Fourteen! Fifteen!

His eyes were glued on the compass. The card began to spin slowly. He couldn't go by that now. He took his direction from the stars and hurled on. The compass was spinning like a top.

Sixteen!

Again Smoke hurled flares overboard and stared down. In the brilliant light he made out the ruins of an ancient chateau on the blasted land below. To the north of it was a row of great trees which seemed to shelter something that gleamed through them.

Very slowly, Smoke Wade's face wrinkled into a grin.

"Ain't sure just what's down there yet, but I'm damn well goin' to find out directly," he drawled to himself.

Then, without the slightest hesitation, he whirled and, glancing up at the North Star, thundered south.

Some of the ships of the 13th were back at the field when Smoke landed.

Captain Turner was among them. He was ghastly white. Other pilots were babbling and twitching like half-crazy lunatics.

"Good Lord!" yelled one. "This is the end of the war! The Jerries have got more guts than we. They're deliberately sacrificing themselves to make a clean hit. Paris'll be next."

"Don't you believe it," Smoke bluffed in a booming voice. "Them square-heads ain't got half the guts, mostly, that Yanks have. Don't know how yet, but I got a mighty strong hunch thet these here pilots is some kind of a trick."

Turner cursed in a shaky voice. His hand trembled like a palsied paw as he pointed to a hideous thing lying on the ground a few yards away.

"Bluff your damned head off, you damn string bean of a four-flusher," he almost screamed. "But you can't laugh that off!"

Smoke stared and blinked. Before him on the ground lay the terribly mangled remains of a German. His legs were blown clear off his body. The rest was almost beyond recognition.

"I suppose that guy thought he was starting out on a picnic," shrieked Turner, his nerves going fast. "No, by damn, that guy and all the rest knew they were going to be killed when they started out! They—"

"Shut up!" bellowed Smoke in a voice that echoed through the night. Another minute and he'd have a lunatic asylum about him. "I'll lay a bet with you, Turner, and the rest of your 13th. I'll bet these guys aren't pilots at all. Put in all the franc notes you birds can raise and I'll cover it. And to make it look harder, I'll bet that these birds weren't even killed in the crashes."

Turner stared at him for an instant. Smoke held his calm. He's made the wildest bet of his career for a special reason this time. Men were going mad rapidly. Something had to be done to relieve the tension. That bet was all he could think of.

It worked. It took the minds of the pilots off the horrible circumstances. They rushed forward to lay their money on a sure thing. Franc notes in Captain Turner's hands rose in a great pile that made a heavy crap game look like a ping-pong contest.

"About five thousand francs," he cracked when he had counted.

"Right," said Smoke. He hauled out a roll of franc notes that could choke a hippopotamus. The men of the 13th stared as he counted very slowly. The tension rapidly grew less taut.

"There," he drawled, handing an equal amount of cash to Turner and pocketing the rest. "Reckon that'll start things off."

"It will," Turner exulted. His hand shot forward toward Smoke and held a slip of white paper out to him. "Now, since you've made the craziest bet that was ever laid, maybe you can laugh this off."

Smoke stared at the note and shook his head. It was written in German script. He couldn't make it out.

"It says," Turner grinned, "that this Heinie in whose hand we found the thing clutched is leaving all his worldly possessions to his mother. He hopes that his voluntary death will save the *Vaterland* and win the war for the Kaiser."

Smoke stared blankly for an instant. Turner glared at him.

"We've stood your damn foolishness long enough," he snapped. "I'm getting in touch with General Banks at once and reporting that you've made no progress and that you're just a big four-flusher. I'm going to try to get him over here at once, even at this time of night, if I can. This note will be convincing evidence that you're even crazier than we are."

Smoke stood rigid for an instant. Then he whirled toward his pinto Spad.

"You'll have to make it right pronto," he drawled, " 'cause this here lanky four-flusher, as you says, is takin' off right now—bound for Germany. And I reckon I won't be comin' back until I'm ready to collect that there bet."

He hesitated an instant.

"Maybe if you got a medical officer here I could speak to him."

Turner jerked his head toward the hospital and sent one of his men with orders to bring a medical officer. A few minutes later a portly, irate individual waddled down the tarmac with night shirt hastily thrust into breeches.

"Just like to order an investigation," Smoke cracked. He pointed to the remains of the dead German on the tarmac. "When I come back I'll expect a report from you as to just how long that Jerry's been dead."

Smoke turned without waiting for an answer and trotted toward his warming pinto Spad.

A WANING moon had risen high in the sky when he circled back of the enemy lines. Very dimly he made out the ruined chateau he had sighted in the light of the flares. Beyond he saw tiny lights flickering off and on at the spot where he had seen trees with possible hangars concealed under them. The lights went out as he roared overhead.

He bore on farther into Germany for a few minutes, then turned in a great circle. He had spotted another open space, perhaps a mile or more to the west of the chateau. Now, directly over it, his hand reached for the switch. The Hisso stopped and died. Only the faint swishing of wind through his wires told of his slow glide.

With as little noise as possible, he kicked sidewise at the boundary of the small field and brought the pinto Spad down. Lights again flickered to the east around what he took to be the drome of the mysterious crates.

The Spad slowed its roll at the far end of the field and stopped. Smoke picked the tail cautiously and hauled his ship into the cover of trees, heading into the wind for a hurried take-off.

His right hand crept to his six-gun, poised there ready as he sped, crouching, toward the drome with the lights. A form moved ahead of him. He made it out from his hunched position under cover of a hedge. Slowly, a guard was pacing back and forth along the boundary of the field.

Smoke advanced without a sound. He had difficulty in seeing what his feet tread on. A twig snapped. He cursed under his breath and tensed.

"*Wer da?*" The sentry shot his challenge.

Smoke didn't move. The sentry had stopped.

"*Wer da?*" he repeated, as he moved with bayonet lowered, straight for Smoke's hiding place. Smoke's left hand felt for something heavy near him. It closed over a rock the size of an ostrich egg. Carefully he raised it and tossed it to a point about six feet to the south.

The guard moved swiftly toward that sharp, crashing sound. Smoke's gun hand whirled the six-gun until he clutched the butt in his right hand. He tensed ready to spring. The guard came very close to him.

Like lightning without its noisy thunder, Smoke raised the big six-gun and struck. There was only the sound of a dull thud. All was still again.

Smoke advanced toward the row of hangars he could barely make out under the great trees ahead. He reached the first one and peered around. The vague outlines of five ships flashed before his narrowed eyes. They were Rumplers, too, with peculiar rigging. Lights flashed and flickered about the ship. Men were preparing them for flight.

Smoke's brain spun dizzily. He crept through the side door of one of the hangars and felt about blindly in the darkness. His hand clutched something—a cloth garment, then his heart leaped in wild exultation as he realized what it was—a greaseball's monkey suit. Swiftly he stepped into it and buttoned it up. His own uniform was now hidden, but at the same time, if he happened to be caught, he knew he would be treated as a spy in the garb of a German mechanic.

Chills ran up and down his back as he picked up a wrench and strode toward the first ship, around which mechanics were working. A head was protruding from the pilot's cockpit.

A mechanic flashed a light full on him as he came up—then turned it back again to the engine. Smoke bent down, as though fixing something under the tail. He rose a moment later. A mechanic who had been working in the cockpit, practically in the lap of the motionless pilot, had trotted off toward the nearest hangar.

Smoke stepped forward and bent down in the cockpit. The pilot didn't move. He hadn't expected him to. His hand touched the other's limp fingers—they were stone cold. The German was dead. His body was strapped to the back of the seat and held fast there to look real.

Suddenly, Smoke clutched that limp right hand again. A paper crackled. He tore open the tight fingers, pulled out a sheet and shot it into his own pocket. Then he stared for a moment at the mass of wires and mechanisms in the front of the dead man's cockpit.

"The devils!" he hissed. "Radio controlled. And they put these dead Jerries in the cockpit to make it look real."

Moving away from the ship, he strode confidently toward the next. That was the same. Again he extracted a slip of paper in the hand of a dead Jerry and moved on to the next.

The next ship had only one mechanic working at it. He turned as Smoke came up and shot a stream of German at him that might as well have been Greek for all Smoke's understanding.

"*Jawohl!*" barked Smoke—about all the German he knew.

His fingers worked rapidly with the hand of the dead pilot and got the paper. The mechanic spouted again.

"*Jawohl!*" Smoke repeated, and trotted toward the nearest hangar. Halfway there, the darkness hid him. He had four supposedly last wills and confessions of suicide; grimly he strode on toward the fifth.

Here he had to wait until a mechanic was through fussing in the cockpit with the radio-control apparatus. He advanced then straight for the dead pilot. A mechanic was at the prop whirling it. The engine started with a roar. Smoke dove for the cockpit and for that slip of paper that should be there. It was. He got it and whirled.

A stiff, huge German officer was standing before him, blocking his way. He spouted a guttural command.

Smoke nodded and snapped up his best imitation of a Jerry salute.

"*Jawohl*!" he cracked.

The officer moved toward him menacingly. Smoke dove past and raced for the cover of the hangar. He heard an angry roar from behind. The bellowing stopped presently with a stream of what Smoke took to be curses.

He shot a glance at the luminous dials of his wrist watch. Twenty minutes of four. Those ships would be roaring toward the field of the 13th any minute now!

ACROSS the field and through the darkness, he sped for the ruined chateau. That was where the compasses had been interfered with. It must be the seat of a gigantic radio and electrical control system.

He was puffing like a steam engine when he reached the ruins. Through a crack in the walls he could see a brilliant light burning in what had probably once been the wine vault.

Cautiously, he felt his way about—found a door and tried it. It was open.

Pushing it in a crack, he peered through. His eyes narrowed.

The room was half taken up with a great tangle of wires, tubes and gadgets of all kinds. At a table where levers and switches lay in a mass of regularity, one man worked with his back to the door.

With the grace and silence of a cat, Smoke crept to him. He saw the Boche pull a lever as he came. Instantly he heard the blasting of engines from far away outside and knew that the mystery ships were taking the air, with their dead men for pilots.

The man at the controls glanced up and smiled. Suddenly he whirled, gaping at Smoke. A cry of terror leaped from his throat as his hand flashed to a Luger lying on the table.

Smoke tried to leap and silence him without making the noise of his six-gun bark. But it couldn't be done. The Luger would get him first.

Blam!

The old wine vault echoed with the bark of the smoke-pole. The German pitched over on his face and lay still. Smoke leaped for the control board and stared frantically at it.

The roar of the ships had diminished overhead, roaring south. He must turn them back. An idea flashed into his dizzy brain. St. Armand had to be bombed. Why not—Desperately he examined the objects before him.

There was a chart marked, "15 minutes 54 2-5 seconds—field. Fleugen 180 degrees."

A jeweler's accurate clock stood next to it, with the second hand ticking off the time.

A lever to his right was marked, "*herauf*" and—in the other direction—"*herab*". Smoke guessed it controlled the raising and lowering of the death bombers. Since it now was straight up and down between the two, the planes were evidently flying level.

Another gadget moved in a circle, something like a rheostat. It was marked in degrees and fractions, and was set at the point "180." That controlled the direction.

Desperately, with blood running hot through his veins, Smoke stared at the outfit a second longer, then he took hold of the handle that turned on the round disc marked by degrees and moved it slowly to the point marked "N."

St. Armand was directly over this spot from field 13. If flying due south would reach the field of the 13th, flying due north would hit the huge enemy supply depot.

He tensed and a great thrill raced up his spine as be heard the drone of the five ships once more. They had turned around—and were heading for their own supply station at St. Armand.

Leaping to another table, he studied a great map thereon. He made out the supply depot at St. Armand, gauged the distance, compared the time that it tool to fly south to the field of the 13th and then the time that should bring those ships back.

Swiftly, he computed the time as closely as possible to the split second. By now the ships were hurling back overhead. He checked them with the clock, then tensed at the controls.

He had been so interested in his calculations that he hadn't heard the noiseless approach of an officer down the stone steps.

"So!" barked someone. "Hands up!"

He whirled and snatched for his six-gun, but his hand froze at the butt as he stared.

"Von Stolz!" Smoke hissed. "I had a mighty strong hunch you was in this somehow and—"

"Stand where you are!" von Stolz croaked. His eyes were narrowed to slits. The hair seemed to bristle from his round, close-cropped head. A monocle glinted in his right eye as he swaggered up, Luger trained steadily on the Yank.

Smoke tensed for a spring or a draw. He was cornered like a rat in a trap, but he wasn't through—not yet.

Von Stolz's pig eyes gleamed hideously as he swaggered across the stone floor of the vault.

"I believe I have the honor to kill *Herr* Smoke Wade," he hissed. "You have lived too long already. But you shall defy the Baron von Stolz no longer."

He had moved toward the switchboard. The Luger swerved and he hesitated an instant before prodding it in the middle of Smoke's back.

"First I will take that famous gun for a souvenir, *Herr* Pig," he rasped.

SMOKE didn't move. His arms were half raised above his head. Von Stolz's slim, slinking hand shot to Smoke's holster and yanked the six-gun out.

"Now!" he grinned in fiendish delight.

Smoke moved then with the speed of light; his long legs carried him in an instant leap to the right.

Blam! The Luger spat flame and steel. Smoke felt a hot, burning sensation in his left arm, but his right was moving like a battering ram.

Smack! It clipped von Stolz in a vicious hook to the jaw that sent the arrogant little German staggering back. The Yank leaped like a great cat to follow up. His hands seized both wrists of von Stolz and sent the guns hurling from his grasp.

Thud! Everything Smoke had went behind that crashing right to the point of von Stolz's chin. The Boche's knees buckled. He went down in a limp heap upon the floor.

Smoke leaped for his six-gun and clutched it as his eyes darted to the clock. One minute more, if his figures were correct, and that flight of death-dealers would be over St. Armand.

He heard the sound of many running feet on the stone steps. The next second men were crowding the entrance.

Blam! Blam! Blam!

The big six-gun barked in a demon chatter. Men fell kicking. Others pushed on. Smoke crouched behind a heavy table he'd thrown up and let go again.

Two more Boches screamed and pitched into the vault. He shot a quick glance at the time, while his fingers reloaded with lightning speed. Thirty seconds more! Other Jerries were swarming in through the opening. Splinters flew from the heavy oak table behind which Smoke crouched.

Still his six-gun boomed out in grim defiance. His hand felt along the floor for the lost Luger of von Stolz. Then he had it and was spattering Jerry lead into the Germans while he reloaded his own smoke-pole.

The firing from the doorway ceased for a moment. Smoke struggled with the momentous problem of the lever that con-trolled the diving and climbing movement of those five ships. *Herauf* and *herab*. Which was up and which down? *Auf* meant open, he thought. *Herauf*, therefore, might mean up.

The clock indicated that the time was right to the second. He let go with another blast from his own gun, then dove for the control board and pulled the lever toward Herab.

Blam! Blam! Jerries sprawled about the stone steps, almost filling the opening. Smoke leaped straight toward them, a flaming gun in each hand.

One shot from his six-gun shattered the single electric light. In the sudden darkness, he grabbed the oak table and hurled it into the tangle of wires and gadgets that was the great radio control unit, smashing the affair to bits.

There was a wild scramble at the stairs. Smoke turned, moved backward through the blackness and began climbing, shooting as he went. He felt Germans all about him, dead ones and fighting, struggling ones. They couldn't distinguish him from the others in the inky black.

In a few moments he dove outside and was running wildly. He could feel the blood dripping from his left hand that clutched the Luger, but he could still use it. Behind, men were shouting. The first gray of dawn was showing in the east. They had seen him and were coming to stop his flight.

Smoke reached his pinto Spad in the field where he had hidden it. He was gasping from loss of breath. He whirled the prop with a frantic prayer. The Hisso caught and snorted. The engine was still warm. One leap shot him into the cockpit.

Men were racing across the field in front of him. The heel of his hand battered the gun open wide. The Hisso snarled and yanked the pinto Spad ahead. A rattle of shots slithered and screamed through the ship covering. Smoke's six-gun roared in reply. Then the pinto Spad screamed into the air and swung south.

GENERAL BANKS was at the field of the 13th. He was shaking with rage—raving at Captain Turner like a madman. He stared at Smoke almost as though he were a ghost, then smiled proudly.

As rapidly as possible Smoke told him what had happened. He held out the five supposed last wills he had taken from the dead Germans for proof.

"These here," he ventured, "was part of von Stolz's devilish plan to break down our morale and make us think he was goin' straight to Paris after testin' his murder machines out on the field of the 13th. Maybe he had some crazy idea of forcin' the Allies to surrender or somethin'. But the way I figured it was thet if they could have they'd have sent all them bombers—with dead Germans out of some trench or some-place—straight into Paris to begin with. Reckon, though, they couldn't control 'em that far away, so they put up the bluff at the Front. And thet powerful control station was throwin' your compasses off, Turner."

General Banks whirled to glare at Turner.

"And you, you white-livered, jealous young pup!" he stormed. "You got me out of bed at this ungodly time of night to satisfy your idea that

Smoke Wade here didn't know what he was talkin' about. Why, you—"

"Just a minute, general," Smoke interrupted. "Turner and the rest has had a tough time of it. It damn near got me once or twice. Yuh can't blame them so much." He turned to Turner, standing white and shaking, with a hound-dog expression of defeat on his face. "Now, I reckon I better be collectin' that little bet."

Turner didn't answer. He just handed Smoke a huge roll of franc notes.

"This'll be a lesson to you and your brood, Turner," Smoke chuckled. "A lesson thet Germans and French and Yanks and all of us is just human bein's and thet none of us don't go in much for deliberate suicide."

It was broad daylight now. Smoke climbed into his pinto Spad. Then he stood up in the cockpit and separated a goodly quantity of franc notes from the roll in his hand.

"Yer outfit's had a right tough time of it lately," he said, tossing the notes to Turner. "There's a little donation from Smoke Wade. Go get drunk or whatever the hell you like and forget this war for a couple of days; then you'll come back like human bein's again.

"And speakin' of bein' just human," he grinned. "This here cowpoke has had some real appetizin' exercise of late. Reckon I got just time to get back to muh own field in time for mess."

The Hisso blasted wide. Smoke's arm waved a salute.

"Adios!" he called as the pinto Spad rumbled and took the air.

Ghost Drome

Frederick Blakeslee

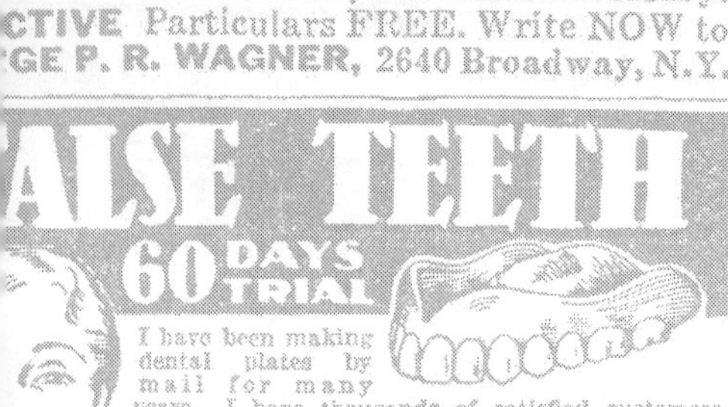

Smoke Wade, six-gun rider of the devil's sky range, scoffed at that Boche message about a dead baron's curse. But when the baron's phantom ship burned his hangars, scared hell out of half his men, he decided it was time to do a little haunting of his own—deep in flaming mystery skies.

Ghost Drome

SMOKE WADE, the leathery-featured, lanky, bronzed, Arizona cowpoke, stopped his nervous pacing of the tarmac abruptly and listened. The faint roar of a Hisso from the north came to him.

He cursed and stared into the gathering darkness of evening toward the sound.

"Hell!" he spat. "Two hours since B Flight left and now one comin' back. Only one."

The shadowy form of a frantic Spad hurled over the boundary, slammed in, cut the gun and prepared to land down wind.

"And that rider ain't takin' no spare time."

With a dull *crrumph*, the speeding plane struck the ground and rolled on. Tires screamed, landing gear groaned, and the Spad ground-looped. The motor blasted wide. It roared straight for Smoke Wade.

The skipper of the 66th pursuit cursed. His eyes shifted once to the north again and for the third time he cursed.

"One back out of seven."

Even before the excited pilot had struggled free of his cockpit, Smoke heard his voice.

"I got him," he cried. "I got von Stolz!"

Smoke's face grew more troubled. He advanced to meet the insanely excited pilot anxiously.

"Howdy, Horton. Couldn't see yuh so good in the dark." Smoke tried to keep his voice calm and soothing.

"I—I tell you I got von Stolz," Horton declared. "I shot him down ten minutes ago north of Camai. He—he went down in flames."

Smoke placed his great hands on the shoulders of the newest replacement to the 66th pursuit and nodded soberly.

"Course yuh did, Horton. Sure. Take it easy, son. This here war's plenty hard even on us old-timers, let alone tenderfoots at the Front. Yuh been dreamin' too much, 'bout this skulkin' coyote von Stolz. I reckon. Yuh'll be all right when yuh get a couple days lay-off and some rest."

Horton's young face colored crimson.

"It's the truth, damn it," he insisted. "You think I'm crazy to say I shot down a great ace like von Stolz. You think because a lot of you birds who've been at the Front a long time haven't been able to knock von Stolz out of the air it can't be done. All right. Ask the rest of B Flight when they get back."

"The others?" demanded Smoke. "They're comin' back—after all. Thank God fer that favor."

The expression on his bronzed features was one of mingled relief and perplexity. His eyes flashed through the dim light from the white face before him to the sounds of roaring Hissos out of the north.

Six Spads romped over the boundary and landed. Smoke shot his uppermost question to Quinn, the skipper of B Flight, when Quinn reached him.

"What's this here stuff Horton's tellin' me about knockin' von Stolz out of the sky?" he demanded.

Horton grinned a little sneeringly—plenty triumph—at his flight commander.

"Go on. Tell him, skipper. You were there and saw it."

Quinn nodded.

"Sure, Smoke. That's straight. Your old enemy, the Baron von Stolz, went down at the end of a column of smoke about ten minutes ago just north of Camai."

Smoke gaped for an instant. He shook his head as though waking from a dream. Slowly, his characteristic grin spread over his face and he stuck out his big hand to Horton.

"I reckon congratulations are plenty in order, son," he beamed, "but I got a good notion to take yuh across my knee and spank hell out of yuh for deprivin' me of the job I al'ays said was mine if I ever got close enough."

Indeed Smoke Wade was not the only man at the field of the 66th who was astonished to hear of the shooting down of the baron by a green replacement. Lucky shot, they all decided. Such things happened in stories and now and then in real life over the lines, but not often.

But the real surprise came next morning. Spads of the 66th were warming on the line. Pilots, rubbing the feathers or straw out of their sleepy eyes, came trotting down the tarmac from quarters. Some were still pulling flying suits hurriedly over their pajamas. Others were dressed. But on every face was less tension than on other mornings. The Baron von Stolz was dead.

Smoke's smile was a little disappointed as he watched them. He hadn't gotten over the shock of the baron's death. The baron was his own meat. He'd sworn it. And then a scatterbrain like Horton had stepped in and finished him with apparent ease. He couldn't fathom the thing, but it was done now and he tried to hide his feelings. He grinned easily as his men gathered about him.

"Reckon for once your goin' to have a easy patrol," he said. "With von Stolz gone that's goin' to be a heap like puttin' a burr under the saddle of every Fokker for a spell. But don't take no chances. Be on the watch to—"

Suddenly he stopped short and listened. Pilots about him tensed. The low throbbing of a Mercedes came to their ears, roaring out of the north. A curse sprayed from between Smoke's clenched teeth. His hand dove for his big six-gun far down on his right leg and brought it out in a blurred movement.

DOWN over the north boundary of the field, a jet black Fokker romped with a deafening scream. Smoke's gun came up. No fire and no bombs came from the diving Fokker. Smoke held his own lead. The black Fokker plunged low. Something fell, tipping end over end as it came. With a dull plunk a message can dropped at his feet and instantly Smoke had it, was pulling the cover.

He frowned, then his lips formed a snarl as he read:

To the conqueror of the Baron von Stolz.

We salute you.

I, as professor of the supernatural of Heidelberg University, have long been interested in the strange history of the family of von Stolz. The only living male heir to that name was killed last night an hour after sundown. This is only significant when it is considered and realized that his father, and his grandfather of the same name, met violent deaths at the hands of enemies at precisely the same hour of the day many years ago. Since then, their ghosts are supposed to have haunted their enemies and those connected with their deaths. All these enemies and many friends have either gone insane or died by their own hand or by other mysterious causes.

Permit me to say here that the following request is in no way connected with the War, but in the interest of science and research. If the deceased Baron von Stolz succeeds in a threat he made in writing before his death to haunt and destroy his enemies we of the science have no doubt of his ghost appearing at least to some of you. What form his spirit may take we cannot tell. His forefather's ghosts appeared twice a day, one hour before sunrise and one hour after sunset, the latter at the exact moment of their death. We assume the ghost of the baron will appear at the same general time.

We urge you in the interest of science to be on the lookout for what apparition may come and to report by dropped message to us on our side of the lines anything connected with it that might be of even the slightest interest.

Yours for science,

Herr Dr. Hugo von Murnster.

"Well, I'll be a ring-tailed thingamajig-jig," Smoke burst out. He stared down at the letter again, his brain turning hand-springs. He heard a gasp at his elbow and turned. Horton was staring into the north like an insane person.

"The—the ghost of the baron," he half sobbed.

Smoke Wade cut in with a laugh that didn't ring true.

"Don't be a damn fool kid, Horton, There ain't no such thing as a ghost."

Horton whirled on him. His face was ghastly white. His lips trembled when he tried to speak.

"That—that's because you never saw one," he stammered. "I was—I was in a haunted house once when I was a kid, All n-night. I—never got over it."

Smoke glared at him. His eyes swept the faces of the other pilots. Mostly they were white—drawn. His hand reached out and grasped Horton by the shirt front and yanked him to him.

"Listen, you damn fool. That's enough of that. If you're putting on this act for the benefit of the rest, you'd better stop it before I kick hell out of you. If you still think you're back in kindergarten I'll see that you're sent back to the states to cut out paper dolls." He whirled to face the rest. "Flyin's off for this morning, seein's how you're lookin' like a bunch of kids scar't of their own shadows. Go down to town and drink up, or do what the hell you like. There's somethin' phony about this and I'm goin' to try and find out what it is."

The pilots moved away uneasily. Smoke called Quinn, who seemed calm like the few other veterans of the 66th.

"Listen," Smoke demanded. "You said you seen Horton shoot down the baron last evenin'."

Quinn nodded.

"Tell me about it."

Quinn shrugged.

"Isn't much to tell," he admitted. "We struck von Stolz's flight north of Camai and went into a fight. It was plenty hot for a while. I had just sent one jerry down out of control and was about to follow him down when I saw Horton having a hell of a time with the baron at the edge of the fight. I banked to go over and help him, when suddenly, Horton pulled—or tried to pull—an Immelmann. It was plenty sloppy, but when he came out there he was right on the Baron von Stolz's tail. I saw tracers jump out front of his Spad toward von Stolz, and then the baron's Fokker flipped over on one ear and began falling.

"He seemed to be fighting like hell to get control when a hell of a cloud of smoke belched out of the side of his Fokker and then flame.

He began slipping like a fool from then on."

Smoke's eyes were fastened on Quinn, but he seemed to be looking through him as he fought with the problem.

"See him crash and burn?" he demanded.

Quinn shook his head.

"Not quite. It was getting dark, even at the ten thousand feet at which we'd been fighting. Just as von Stolz went down, a lot of his gang jumped me and made it hot for me. Horton, I think, dove out of the fight and ran for home. Probably couldn't wait to tell the story. He's that kind. I was fighting like hell, but I sneaked a couple of chances to glance down at the baron's Fokker. I didn't see him crash, but he was almost down and still burning plenty from the light of the flame I could see when I got my last look at him."

Smoke nodded absently.

"Thanks, Quinn," he said. "That's some help. I'm goin' up to see McGill. You better see that the crazy ghost-fearin' buzzards get to town and do a little fancy drinkin' and forget this damned foolishness."

COLONEL MCGILL was very grave when he had finished reading the message. His eyes blazed as he looked up at Smoke.

"This," he said, anxiously, "is damned serious. It's apt to make a mad house of the field. I'll call G.H.Q. at once and notify them so they can be on guard and take whatever steps they see fit."

He talked long and earnestly on the phone. Then he hung up and stared at Smoke.

"You've told me what's happened, Smoke," he said. "Now tell me what you think."

Smoke rubbed his chin meditatively.

"Ain't sure just what I think," he confessed. "It sort of looks to me like if the baron's dead, Heinie is goin' on usin' him—or the idea of his ghost—to scare hell out of our birds. And they sure done it mostly so fer. If we can let 'em lay off fer a couple of days and give 'em time to forget and see there ain't nothin' to it, I reckon it'll come out O. K."

Colonel McGill breathed deeply.

"I hope you're right, Smoke," he said.

But their hopes were destined for a shock when evening came—and the hour of the Baron von Stolz's death. Smoke's pinto Spad was on the line. Pilots stood in tense groups. The very air seemed electrified with suspense.

Even Smoke felt it in his own nervous system. It seemed that, if anything out of the ordinary should happen now, things would blow up. Men would go mad. He tensed, grew rigid and cursed without realizing. A thin, wailing, eerie moan sounded from somewhere in the heavens to the north.

Others heard it at the same instant. Groups broke up and faces shone whiter in the gathering darkness. Smoke could only see dimly about him now. The sound was approaching nearer. It seemed to come from high up in the sky.

Suddenly, the wailing noise increased in tone. It rose to a higher pitch. The heavens from which it came were clear of clouds. Still Smoke strained his eyes in vain to see the thing that hurtled at them with that ghastly sound.

With startling abruptness, the thing appeared in the sky at that instant. It seemed shapeless. It was huge and white and ghastly. It came at a great speed, but without apparent means of motion or shape of rigid structure.

It was white. It seemed made of some form of unearthly substance that appeared and vanished as it came. The thing was gigantic. Perhaps a hundred and fifty feet across. It bulged forward in the middle and diminished in a thin, fluttering tail of the white stuff that disappeared in thin air behind.

Smoke Wade's eyes fairly popped out of his head. He leaped for his Spad and kicked into the wind. His Hisso blasted open wide. Quinn was running for his ship too. The other pilots, mostly green replacements, stood jibbering and gaping and trembling.

Smoke hunched over his stick, let go with a warming burst from his Vickers and hurled at the thing. An angry curse sprayed through his lips. His eyes bulged as he searched the apparition for something tangible. Something that would connect it with earthly things. He could find nothing.

Insanely desperate, he raced down and pressed his gun triggers. Vickers snarled. White tracers fluffed into the mass of ghastly white.

That was all.

Nothing happened. The great, white, shapeless form bore down upon the hangars. Again and again Smoke cursed and raced down at the thing. His guns glowed white hot from constant firing. They jammed from excess heat. But still the monstrous apparition drifted down at the field—over the hangars.

Quinn was hurling in now. His guns rattled and bucked and vibrated. It was like firing into a stone wall, or into thin air itself. There seemed nothing mortal. Nothing vital about the thing. It moved on, stopping at nothing.

It drifted low over the hangars. Even above the roar of his own motor, Smoke could hear that eerie wail it gave off. It was almost dark; then it seemed to be suddenly light again. No! That was a fire below. One of the hangars over which the great, white, shapeless thing had passed was flaming brightly.

Another and another hangar burst into flames as the gigantic thing wailed its drifting way over their tops. The whole row blazed now and Smoke dove and circled and snarled in, with his Vickers stopped and his big six-gun out, blazing away in a vain frantic effort to stop the seemingly supernatural monster of destruction.

Suddenly, it seemed to leap above him beyond the light of the burning hangars. Smoke whirled and glared at the field. He looked up again. The sky was dark now. He could hear the wailing noise still, but the thing seemed suddenly gone, as though the sky had swallowed it up completely.

Vainly, Smoke combed the sky. The wail ceased a moment later and left him cursing and baffled.

SMOKE circled the field slowly while his brain struggled with the situation. Pilots would be crazy when he landed. He must have something definite to tell them. Still, he wasn't good at making up fake yarns.

Suddenly, he hit upon a desperate plan, the next best thing. If it wouldn't work completely, it might help. Otherwise he'd have a bunch of lunatics to command. He wasn't so sure that he wasn't going a little nuts himself.

He landed. Pilots jibbered about him. Horton was worse than the others—seemed about to go mad.

Smoke surveyed them with a calm, wise grin.

"You're gettin' worked up over nothin'," he boomed, trying to keep his own voice calm. "You're actin' like a bunch of kids. I'm damned ashamed of yuh, knowin' what I know."

Questions darted at him from trembling lips.

"I ain't tellin' all I know," Smoke grinned with the same wise look he had managed to hold since landing. "But I'm ready to make a couple of little bets just to show yuh I know what I'm talkin' 'bout."

Horton was before him. He was shaking. His face was like soiled linen, gray on white.

"You—you still mean to tell me there aren't such things as ghosts?" he demanded in a choked voice.

Smoke nodded.

"Reckon that's right, son," he beamed down. "I'm ready to make a bet of a thousand francs, if you ain't too scar't and yella to count and yuh got that much money, thet this here ain't no ghost."

He paused. Inwardly he was as tense as an E string. His keen eyes searched the white faces about him. His heart sank. It hadn't helped to relieve the tension.

"And," he went on, "just to make it look harder I'll add to that bet that the baron von Stolz you shot down last night ain't no more dead than I am—and I reckon that's plenty 'live."

"You can't prove that," Horton flamed. "I saw him go—go down in flames. He couldn't live with his Fokker burning."

Smoke scanned the other faces. "I mentioned a bet. Any takers, or are yuh willin' to agree with me?"

The other pilots hesitated and milled about. Smoke grinned with more genuine pleasure now. Some of the tension and fear had left their faces before his assurance and calm.

"I'll take that bet," Horton gulped. "I—I maybe won't live to collect, but if I do it's—sure money."

"Check!" boomed Smoke. "It's a bet and—"

An orderly snapped up a salute before him.

"Colonel McGill wants to see you, sir," he stammered "At—at once, sir. In his office."

Smoke's big fists were clenched so tightly that the nails bit into his palms as he strode down the tarmac. Mechanics shuddered and trembled as they rolled ships from the burning hangars or tried to fight the flames with a half-hearted, licked air of defeat.

Colonel McGill was in his office in a high state of anxiety. Worry creased his hard old face. Another man was with him there.

"This is terrible, Smoke," McGill gasped in a hushed voice. "I saw that damn thing. I saw you trying to knock it down without luck. The thing isn't human. Something's got to be done."

Smoke nodded wearily now.

"Reckon it has. How?"

"Our only hope is Intelligence, Smoke," boomed McGill. "This—" he jerked his head toward the alert man beside him—"is F-17 of our Secret Service. You're to take him and drop him behind our lines at once. It's dark enough to start. Take the D.H. we use for this purpose. You'll find it on the line at the end of the field, warming. Thank God that wasn't in the hangars when they burned. You'll land him at a small field north of Camai."

He pointed out the spot on the map. Smoke stared at it and his eyes suddenly lighted as he turned to F-17.

"Reckon you ain't so dumb," he grinned with sudden relief. "That there spot ain't but a few miles from the field where the baron von Stolz and his *jagdstaffel* is located. I ain't got no solution fer this, but I'm bettin' that the baron's field ain't a miss by no mile to start lookin' fer the trouble."

F-17 nodded. "I'm glad you agree with me," he said. "The colonel and I hit upon that point after what Colonel McGill has been telling me of this baron. He may be dead, but in that case someone else is carrying on for him."

"Reckon so," nodded Smoke. "And I'm bettin' that the baron ain't dead, but whatever this thing is that's supposed to be his ghost has got me 'bout locoed. There ain't no sound to it but that damned wail and it don't shoot nor drop bombs and every hangar it goes over busts into flames. Let's go. There's a solution fer it someplace and I reckon it's up to us to find it."

McGill shook his head.

"That's F-17's job." he said. "You're simply to take him over, drop him off and fly back. You see, in the rear cockpit, he'll change into the uniform, of a German officer."

THE D.H. lumbered down the field into the wind. It was almost as light as day as the flames played about the ruined hangars of the 66th. Long rows of ships that the mechanics had been successful in saving stood on the line.

The plane took the air and turned north. The light of the fire sank from sight and became a dull glow behind. Higher and higher they climbed as they crossed the lines. Smoke clutched the stick and glared down at enemy territory. The moon was rising slowly on their right. That would help Smoke in landing.

He felt a light tap on the back and turned. He blinked and stared again. A swanky, cocky-looking German officer was smiling and pointing down. Smoke nodded and cut the gun. The Liberty died.

In great spirals he came down toward the dim blotch of a small field below. Lower he settled. The big Liberty idled almost silently.

Smoke peered ahead. The stick moved back as he skillfully brought the D.H. down for its landing. He leveled off. It was darker than he had expected. He must fly by feel.

Crrrrrumph!

Crash!

The D.H. heaved to one side a moment after the wheels touched. It creaked and groaned and jolted. Slowly, the tail came into the air. The prop had stopped with the cutting of the switch by Smoke at the first warning of a crash. The hub dug deep into the uneven ground.

Smoke was getting out of the front cockpit. F-17 scrambled after him. Together they walked around to the nose of the ship where Smoke bent down to inspect the damage.

"Must of struck a hole," he observed rather casually. "Landin' gear's plumb washed out, I reckon."

He straightened and grinned at the Secret Service agent clothed in the uniform of a German office of high rank.

"Well, here we are, F-17. Yuh can't say I don't make deliveries."

F-17 stared at him in the darkness.

"But how the devil are you going to get back to our side of the lines?" he demanded.

Smoke shrugged.

"Ain't thought thet fer yet. I reckon now I'm Here I might's well go along and help out maybe, if I can."

F-17 shook his head.

"That's impossible," he said firmly. "You forget I'm a German officer now, and you—you're still clothed in Yank togs."

Smoke nodded reluctantly.

"Reckon maybe you're right," he admitted. "Reckon you better go your way alone and me—well, I been hankerin' to have a squint at von Stolz's drome for quite a spell. Guess I'll be goin'."

Smoke Wade took a step toward the road he had noticed skirted the one side of the field. He stopped short and froze motionless. F-17 took in a quick breath and tensed beside him.

The sound of running feet from the direction of the road had come to them. They came nearer; then excited voices gutturaled in German.

"Quick," whispered F-17. "This way. They've heard the plane coming down. They suspect a spy is being landed."

The two whirled and dove for the other side of the field. Pursuers were shouting now. A powerful light leaped up at the other side of the field and flooded the place with brilliance. Smoke and F-17 found themselves running in its brightness, with their bodies throwing long, gruesome shadows as they sprang for cover.

Blam! Blam! Blam!

Rapid firing from behind spurred them on. They were running for the small wood at the far side of the field, for dear life. The shouting and firing increased from behind. Smoke cursed and glanced behind him. He could see nothing for the blinding effect of the light. He cursed and raced on.

They gained the wood and plunged through inky darkness. Men shouted behind them. Swarmed into the wood. Then, with startling abruptness, shouts came from ahead in answer.

In desperation, they plunged to the right. Lights flashed through the trees from behind—and again from all sides. They were hemmed in. Caught like rats in a trap. Smoke cursed and drew his gun. He felt F-17's hand on his arm restraining him.

"No," he whispered. "We'll make a bluff. You're my prisoner, see? It may work, but I doubt it."

F-17 snatched Smoke's six-gun before he could answer. Then he felt the cold end of F-17's Luger at his back and relaxed. Germans came running up, shouting, brandishing guns. F-17 spoke to them in perfect German.

"This is my prisoner," he explained. "I was taking a walk down the road in the moonlight when I heard this plane crash. I ran over, but your coming frightened this Yankee dog and I had a hard time catching him."

A towering Prussian officer confronted him and rumbled questions in German that Smoke couldn't get.

Suddenly, he felt himself seized from behind and held.

The German officer knocked the guns from F-17's hands in a powerful surprise movement and bellowed an order. Men leaped forward to seize F-17.

SMOKE got one glance from F-17 as they were being led across the field; then they were being pushed into a big car. The car moved rapidly down the road.

And that look that Smoke got said, "Take it easy."

He did. Even until they were brought before a great, pointed mustached officer whom soldiers and officers alike addressed as *Herr Excellenz.*

He glared at them from under shaggy eyebrows for some time. Then he spoke in good English.

"You," he said, addressing F-17, "are, we believe, the spy we have been expecting. Your papers lead me to believe so. *Ja.* You shall be shot as a spy. And you—" he turned to Smoke—"a prisoner of war, and I am sorry we cannot give you the same treatment." He nodded to the guards. "Take them behind the lines."

The guards moved them from the office before pointed bayonets. An officer followed with the guns and the German officer's orders and dropped to the front seat of the waiting, open car. One of the guards climbed in the back seat between them. Guns bristled. Smoke cursed as he saw his own six-gun holding him at bay in the back seat over the top of the front seat. The car moved off.

For several minutes they traveled a smooth road. Then the car began to lurch. The flashlight that the officer in the front seat held partly blinded him.

The car struck a hole in the road and they bounced. Smoke tensed and thought fast.

The guard beside him had two guns, one in either hand. His arms were crossed so that the muzzle of each gun stuck in both Smoke's and F-17's ribs. Stealthily, Smoke's long leg moved about the floor to the other side of the car. He felt something like a foot with the toe of his boot and pressed back.

A plan flashed through Smoke's brain. He began pressing out a message in the wireless code he knew so well.

N-e-x-t b-u-m-p g-r-a-b g-u-n.

The foot of F-17 pressed back in answer.

Bam!

The car struck a bump. They were shot off the seat together, with the guard between them. At the same instant that Smoke's iron clutches snatched at the gun in his ribs, his foot crashed against the light held by the officer leaning over the back of the front seat.

There was a snarled curse, a flash of light and the bellow of a Luger. The light shot sidewise to the road. The form of the officer in the front seat slumped limp. The Luger that Smoke held in his hand was smoking.

Instantly he raised it and the butt crashed to the head of the guard beside him. Another crack and F-17's Luger spoke—and in turn. The driver slipped under the wheel.

F-17 leaped forward, leaned far over the front seat and snatched the wheel and brake lever. The car jolted to a stop amid squealing of tires.

F-17 worked like lightning now. He pitched the driver out to the side of the road and began stripping the clothes from the big officer's body slumped in front. Smoke carried the body of the guard to the side of the road and watched F-17.

"Here. Put them on quickly," F-17 snapped. "We may have a chance to get out of this alive. I know this country like a book. We're going to von Stolz's field at once by a back road."

Then they were off, with Smoke making fast the last buttons of his newly acquired uniform. His big six-gun was once more in its holster.

When they turned in at the field of von Stolz's drome ten minutes later with darkness to aid them, they looked much the part of two high German officers coming on business. Indeed, they were.

"We may never get out alive," hissed F-17 at the wheel, "but we'll at least have the satisfaction of having a look at where we believe the trouble to be. I can't go on with what I had planned now."

"*Wer da?*" challenged one of the guards at the gate.

The car stopped. The guard flashed his light inside and F-17 gave him his answer in German.

"We're Captain Mueler and Lieutenant Freitag," he said, "on special mission. We demand to see the officer of the guard at once. Bring him."

The guard presented arms and hurried away.

"Quick," hissed F-17.

He pulled Smoke out of the car and away into the darkness. They walked swiftly for a moment, and then, as the sounds of shouting and cries of alarm came to them, they broke into a run toward the dim shadows of great hangars.

More shouts came from behind, accompanied by the sounds of running feet. One by one they passed close to the backs of hangars. Suddenly Smoke clutched F-17's arm and pointed ahead. A great hangar, larger than the rest, loomed before them.

"I'd bet plenty there might be some-thin' in there we'd mighty like to see," he whispered. "That there's a new hangar on this field. It's more'n twice as big as the rest and I reckon I'm makin' a guess as to why."

THEY dove inside, through a small back door. The place was dark as pitch. Not a sound came to them within. Slowly their eyes became accustomed to the darkness.

They could see forms in the hangar now. Smoke kicked his shin against an elevator and cursed. His hand went over the side of that ship—a Fokker D-7. It moved up the turtle back and over the cockpit covering. Then the windshield.

An exclamation, low and vicious, escaped him.

"Von Stolz's," he hissed. "This here's von Stolz's ship or I'm a hungry timber wolf. I'd know this special windshield he's got on his Fokker any place, I reckon."

Swiftly he moved about it, seeing very little and feeling for the rest. At the right side of the plane, he found a long stack protruding from under the engine hood.

"Huh?" he grunted. "I reckon that settles thet much."

Instantly, he whirled. His eyes probed the darkness of the rest of the hangar. Again he cursed and pointed to a great form that loomed in the darkness. F-17 stared beside him; then they moved noiselessly toward it.

"God!" breathed F-17. "A Gotha."

"Reckon so," whispered Smoke. "And ain't no need askin' why thet there ship is here at this field. Look." He pointed into the dim light where long tubes protruded from wings and nose and fuselage. "No wonder they had to build a hell of a hangar like this to house it, with all thet plumbin' stickin' out."

He climbed up the narrow ladder to the rear gunner's cockpit to have a closer look. Suddenly the sound of shouts and running feet came to them from outside the great hangar.

Smoke plunged headlong into the gunner's cockpit. Strange, there were no guns mounted on the turrets, he thought, as he shot under. Then he remembered that the phantom thing hadn't returned any fire.

His brain struggled with the problem as he slithered along the structural work behind the rear gunner's cockpit. F-17 slipped in behind him. Together they crouched, bracing themselves against the frame work behind the partition back of the gunner's cockpit.

The babble of guttural voices. They became aware of lights going on in the hangar. Of men running about searching. The great Gotha trembled a little as several Germans climbed over her and stuck their flash lights here and there.

The sounds were moving back toward the tail. Smoke grasped wires above his head and pulled himself up. F-17 followed his example. Their feet were the only parts of them that would show below that partition ahead. The light flashed back—illuminated the tail of the ship. They heard a grunt of disappointment the sound of someone dropping to the floor—and dared to breathe once more.

The lights went out. The two remained motionless. Hours went by.

"We're goin' to take a ride in this here contraption," Smoke ventured.

He heard F-17 laugh softly.

"A ride in a ghost. That's a new one."

They fell silent once more and tensed. Men were entering the hangar. They saw a dim light coming in under the plywood partition ahead of them. That would probably be the first gray of dawn filtering through the long, narrow hangar windows.

Then the plane was moving, slowly, but unmistakably, toward the doors as they rumbled open with a heavy sound. Engines warmed. Men clambered aboard. Minutes, and then they were moving, rumbling across the field, taking the air.

Smoke drew his big pocket knife and cut a slit in the side of the ship, big enough to peer through. He could see the country below. To the west were gray streaks of light. An hour before dawn, eh? He laughed angrily and peered out again. This time he cursed. A blanket of gray covered the hole, almost smothered him.

"We're goin' to take this crate now," he hissed to F-17.

F-17 held him back. Guttural voices of command sounded even above the wail.

"Whoever is in command is sending someone back to see what's weighing down the tail," F-17 said.

Smoke grew rigid. His six-gun came out, and crouching below the bottom of the partition he looked through. A German soldier was coming down the cat walk. Smoke leveled his six-gun and pulled.

There was a bellow of rage and another Boche leaped down the narrow flooring from up front as his comrade fell.

Blam! Blam!

The German sprawled. Smoke dove from under the plywood partition and leaped down the catwalk toward the pilot's cockpit. He saw the pilot, who seemed to be the one remaining officer on the great bomber, whirl and sieze his Luger. But he was hours too slow. The big smoke pole spoke again and the pilot slumped. And with his death, the great plane dove.

Instantly, Smoke raced ahead. With one hand he yanked the dead pilot from his seat and slammed in behind the controls. The big wheel came back and the Gotha groaned in a climb.

"Get hold of these levers to shut off that smoke or gas or whatever the hell it is," Smoke yelled to F-17. "I can't see nothin' much through this fog."

F-17 was working like mad. Then, suddenly, the blanket of white vapor shopped short and Smoke stared out over Yank ground.

WHEN Smoke Wade brought the trick Gotha down on the field of the 66th, pilots, mechanics and officers gaped and blinked, to gape again. Questions came at him and F-17 in a torrent.

Smoke looked wise, walked around the great ship once and grinned.

"Reckon there ain't much to explain," he said. "Von Stolz ain't no more dead than I am. His ship's in good shape in the big hangar this crate was housed in. Must of got the effect of burnin' from the special pipe he had rigged out the side of the motor. Some hook-up with smoke and fire what wouldn't catch his ship on fire so long as he kept slippin' away from it.

"Then he pulls this here Gotha stunt to scare hell out of everybody—and I reckon he come mighty near doin' it. All them pipes stuck out there dumped out smoke or some kind of gas that disappeared after it covered the ship in flight." He pointed to the pipes that ran much farther out to the side of one wing than the other. "That there is what made 'em hard to hit. Mostly I was shooting at the middle of the damned thing, but this here offset in pipes puts the fuselage to one side of the smoke screen they was flyin' in. They must a got that invisible effect from usin' maybe a gray gas that blended with the light of the sky. And the fire they spread out, I figure now that wasn't nothing but some sort of gasoline bomb, sort of."

He grinned down at Horton's puzzled face.

"So yuh see, sonny, there's your ghost story, all shot to hell."

"But you couldn't know about this when you made that bet, and yet you seemed so sure you were going to win," he challenged. "You must have known something or guessed right."

Smoke shook his head.

"Just a chance, son," he admitted. "I had to be one to act sure it wasn't a ghost with a lot of the rest of you birds scar't green." He let his hand fall on Horton's shoulder. "And that bet," he reminded him. "We'll call thet square if yuh take the boys down to town and buy the drinks. Reckon we all got plenty cause to celebrate," he grinned—"even if von Stolz ain't dead. Tuh me there's considerable satisfaction in thet."

It was then that F-17 put a question to him.

"You know," he said, "I've had a hunch ever since it happened that the crash of the D.H. wasn't entirely unavoidable. If I'm right you've got a lot of guts, Wade. That's bravery indeed."

"Bravery?" chuckled Smoke. "I'd brand it maybe more like curiosity. Yes, sir. Just plain curiosity, I reckon."

Buzzard's Trap
Frederick Blakeslee

Smoke Wade arrived too late to save that green peelot from a coyote sky trap. But that didn't keep him from setting a six gun trap of his own high in the devil's cloud range—with his own pinto Spad as bait.

Buzzard's Trap

SMOKE WADE was coldly calm as he faced his commanding officer at headquarters. With a careless air, he hooked his thumbs in the slantwise belt of his six-gun, and waited for the C.O. to begin. His even grin of anticipation was in striking contrast to the expression of tense anxiety on the wrinkled face of Colonel McGill.

"I've tried my best to avoid this, Smoke," McGill began sadly. "It means that I'm practically sending you on a suicide mission." His voice trembled. "But it's the only choice I have left."

Smoke chuckled.

"Don't need to take it that hard, colonel," he assured him. "I ain't dead yet and I reckon I ain't figurin' on it none."

McGill paused and drew a deep breath as he pronounced what seemed a death sentence.

"G.H.Q. must have information about the coming attack of the enemy. We know through Intelligence that there is going to be one at either La Tore or Camai. It's up to you to find out which sector has the most activity. As commander of the 66th pursuit squadron you've done wonders, Smoke. But as a lone pilot in a pinch; there's no better at the Front. That's why I'm forced to send you. Ten good men have gone out on this job. None of them came back."

Smoke's face suddenly darkened.

"Von Stolz!" he hissed. "They didn't know that louse like I do." His steel, gray eyes closed to slits. "Maybe you could tell me somethin', colonel," he ventured after a moment's deliberation. "About how long was it after most of these ten got over the lines before von Stolz shot 'em down?"

"I haven't any record of most of the poor devils," Colonel McGill answered frankly. "A few were seen from other planes going to their aid. The others just didn't come back and we got confirmation through the Red Cross. But those who were seen were up, I believe, a matter of perhaps fifteen minutes. Most were shot down over Camai."

Smoke gave a quick nod of satisfaction.

"Reckon that'll do the trick," he grinned. "I got an idea, colonel. I'm goin' to set a trap for that louse, von Stolz, and I wouldn't be bettin' far wrong that it'll be good enough so the world might make that beaten path to my door, like the sayin' goes—if I had one."

McGill couldn't help smiling, but the anxiety was still in his old eyes as he rose and held out his hand to Smoke.

"I hope you're right, Smoke," he said gravely. "The lives of thousands of Yanks are in your hands. Good luck!"

Smoke trotted down the tarmac toward his warmed pinto Spad. A graceful leap shot him into the cockpit. His hand pushed on the gun. The Hisso snorted and roared. Smoke kicked the tail round with an expert movement of his foot on the rudder bar and the pinto Spad leaped into the wind and rose.

Smoke cocked his pinto Spad on one ear as he zoomed into the air and turned north. He hunched a little over the stick and stared ahead. And his leathery face was wrinkled in a mysterious grin of confidence. His brain seemed to be doing a cartwheel and a couple of hand springs as he planned swiftly.

"Fifteen minutes," he mused, with the front lines coming into view. "Allow von Stolz ten minutes to get from Camai to La Tore. That's just a guess. Hope it's a good one."

His keen eyes searched the sky above La Tore as he hedge-hopped toward that sector. German gun crews leaped to their death-dealers as they heard him come. They gaped and cursed as he thundered over their heads, flying in a crazy, zigzag course that made him an impossible target. Smoke grinned.

His eyes shifted rapidly back and forth between the watch on his bony wrist and the sights of his Vickers. He tramped down on his trigger button and made the guns spit flame. Lead hurled down at startled Germans.

Smoke Wade flew like a crazy idiot. Every gun crew in sight got a spattering of lead. He was making a hellish nuisance of himself. War on the La Tore sector was momentarily stopped. Men cursed and scattered before his vicious attacks.

"Five minutes," he drawled, checking the time. "Reckon I'll be leavin' now. Von Stolz'll be on his way from Camai and there won't be no way of them stop-pin' him once he's started."

The lone pinto Spad kicked over in a tight vertical and turned south. Smoke shot a last glance behind him at the La Tore sector.

"No more action there than at a quiltin' party," he observed. "Come on, Jake. You and me'll have a look at Camai, now that von Stolz ought to be out of the way."

He hurled back across the lines. Once behind his own trenches, he whirled and headed east, and five minutes later he swerved north again.

SMOKE grinned with satisfaction as he climbed for Camai. He could make out the ruins of the town far ahead. The air was clear of ships.

"Reckon von Stolz walked into that trap," he observed.

Archie burst into gory salute as he came. Smoke kept climbing. Powerful glasses came from their case at the side of the cockpit and he held the stick with his knees while he stared through them.

"Huh!" he grunted, leaning over the side. "This here looks different. No wonder von Stolz didn't want to let nobody come back from Camai after seein' this. Those Heinies are like a bunch of swarmin' bees."

Great lines of trucks were moving troops to the front. The railroad yards to the north were rushing munitions to the heavily guarded, half-hidden munition dump. To the south great tanks moved sluggishly, forming in a line for battle advance.

The air below him became whipped into a muddy yellow froth from bursting archie shells. They were falling short of their mark. He was flying at a very high altitude where they couldn't reach him. The thin air made his movements labored, but he chanced an upraised hand with fingers extended, thumb to the tip of his slightly hooked nose.

He flew in painstaking, deliberate circles above the sector. Nothing escaped his keen eyes. He checked the time every minute. Fifteen minutes should be the limit, for safety.

As he turned south at the end of that time, he swept the country once more with his narrowed eyes. No doubt of where the attack would take place. His observations proved that.

Something moved to the southwest. He jerked bolt upright in his seat and swung the glasses full in that direction. Five tiny winged things hurled up at him. A curse sprayed through clenched teeth.

"You're a foxy bird, von Stolz," he drawled, "but I reckon this here's one time a guy gets back after seein' Camai."

Instantly he kicked over and sent the pinto Spad howling for the lines. The Fokker flight was coming nearer with startling speed. Von Stolz and his brood swerved in their course and headed toward the Front.

"Goin' to try and cut me off," Smoke cracked. "All right, tenderfoot. Look out below."

The stick of the pinto Spad slammed the instrument board. The ship shuddered. The Hisso screamed for mercy. Wings turned up at the tips as though they were rubber—but held.

Down, down like a striking falcon, he plunged for that flight of Fokkers between himself and his own lines. His thumb tramped down on the trigger button for a warming burst. Vickers guns bucked madly and fell silent.

The Fokkers spread out in a wide V to intercept his mad plunge. They were coming at each other with lightning speed. Smoke heard Spandaus rattle to warm. He was hunched far over the stick, his eyes glued across his sights. The big brown thumb hung poised above the trigger button.

Tac-tac-tac!

Spandaus steel fluffed about him at long range. Smoke held his fire. He cursed as he saw von Stolz leap out of the flight and dart to the rear of his wide-spread V.

"You sculkin' coyote!" Smoke rasped. "Stand up and take—"

His thumb tramped on the trigger. Vickers raved. It was only a short burst, but a Fokker leaped like a startled hare and dove.

Instantly Smoke's hand yanked the stick back hard. The pinto Spad shuddered from the shock. It leaped into the air, hovered on its back and shot down in a perfect loop.

Von Stolz's flight shot beneath—surprised by the lightning move. As Smoke plunged and leveled, his Vickers rattled wildly. Von Stolz was there before them for an instant. He moved swiftly in a tight vertical to the side and shot to the west out of range.

"Yella louse," spat Smoke as he dove.

He pushed the stick still farther ahead and raced for the lines. Once he glanced over his shoulder and shouted something that the roar of his Hisso killed at his lips.

"Like to stay for your party, von," he cackled, "but the colonel's expectin' me back to tell him a bedtime story."

Then he hurled down over the front amid a hell of archie fire and slithered into the field of the 66th.

THE pinto Spad skimmed the ground, touching wheels and skid as gently as a proud mother laying her baby in a crib. Its roll stopped directly in front of headquarters' office. Very deliberately, Smoke unwound his lank body from around the stick and climbed out.

A wild exclamation of joy came from the door of the office. Colonel McGill strode to meet him.

"Thank God, you're back, son," he beamed. He hesitated an instant—fearful. The thing seemed too easy. "Did you see both sectors?"

"Reckon you'd make good in a guessin' contest," Smoke smiled. "I guess I seen everything there was to see, includin' von Stolz. You can tell the brass hats that the big push is coming off at Camai. Ain't a bit of doubt of that."

Colonel McGill was ushering him into his office.

"Splendid," he said.

He reached for the phone and called G.H.Q. in an excited voice. When he had finished his hasty report he turned to Smoke again.

"What under the sun did you do to von Stolz and his hellions?" he asked. "Hypnotize them?"

Smoke chuckled.

"Mighty near, I reckon. When you said most of the men shot down had fallen over Camai I made the guess Camai was the place they didn't want 'em to see. So I went over La Tore first and raised particular hell until I was pretty sure they'd call von Stolz over to drive me out. Then I headed back across the lines like I was goin' home, turned east when they couldn't see me and then north to Camai. And von Stolz wasn't there. Had a ring-side seat above archie for considerable time until von Stolz got wise. Then he was too late."

Colonel McGill beamed on him proudly. They both tensed to listen to the distant drone of Hissos, far off.

"That reminds me, Smoke," he said, "I forgot to mention it before, but there's a flight of replacements coming in. That's probably them now."

Smoke listened. The roar came closer. There was a deafening din above the headquarters' office. Motors droned and growled in a slower tempo as ships leaped and lunged in acrobatics.

"Huh!" grunted Smoke, making for the door. "Sounds like a bunch of drunken sailors instead of pilots."

Outside, he and McGill stared at the antics of a flight of five shiny new Spads. They dove and looped and stalled like crazy tumbler pigeons. When it seemed that they were about to spin from some of their ill-flown maneuvers, they slammed down to bumpy landings,

"Poor young fools showin' off," Smoke observed, half to himself. "They could learn a heap about flyin', I reckon."

A slim, nattily dressed youth climbed from the lead plane and swaggered toward them.

"I'm Lieutenant Snell," he announced with a salute. "I'm in charge of this flight of replacements."

His eyes traveled from the colonel's eagles on McGill's shoulders to the oil-smeared leather coat that hid Smoke Wade's captain's bars.

"I suppose you're C.O. here, colonel," Snell snapped, without giving McGill a chance to announce himself.

McGill nodded.

"Yes," he said. "Come into the office with your papers."

Smoke stepped before cocky little Snell with his shiny new first lieutenant's bars and blocked his way.

"Just before that, colonel," he smiled, "I'd like to ask Snell a couple of things."

McGill waited, half smiling.

"I'd like to know," Smoke drawled, "how come a bird what can't fly no better than you can is sent to the Front in charge of a flight?"

Snell's eyes blazed with sudden fire.

"What is this supposed to be, an insult?" he snapped.

"Nope," Smoke drawled. "But I thought you might like to lay a little on my judgment as to just about how many hours you've had. Maybe a couple of hundred francs that you haven't more than fifty hours."

"Fifty hours," Snell snorted. "I'll bet you five hundred francs that I've got much more than that."

Smoke tensed. Another sound had come to his alert ears. It was the very distant drone of a motor. And it wasn't a Hisso. He stood staring up into the clear blue sky for half a minute before he spotted a tiny speck moving slowly in a wide circle over the field. His face was puzzled as he glanced at the colonel. McGill was looking up too, but he couldn't make it out.

"Mercedes!" spat Smoke. "Tell by the sound."

"Huh?" sputtered McGill. "Well, what the devil is he doing over here?"

Smoke shrugged.

"Doesn't think we see him," he ventured. "He's up damned high."

Snell snorted impatiently.

"Well, do you want that bet," he snapped, "or were you just kidding?"

"Oh, that?" Smoke grinned. "Sure. I'll lay you five hundred, like you said, that you haven't more than fifty hours to your credit."

A cocksure, sneering smile crossed Snell's face.

"You must be a philanthropist," he cracked. "Giving money away that easy. That's a bet and I suppose if I can prove that I have three German planes to my credit, you'll be satisfied that you're due to lose your bet."

"Yep," nodded Smoke.

"Come into the office of the colonel, then, and I'll prove it," he announced, moving toward the door with McGill.

Smoke took one more look at the soaring Fokker high above, then followed Snell and the other pilots of the replacement flight into the office.

McGill, seated at his desk, was studying Snell's papers. He looked up with a puzzled frown and nodded to Smoke.

"I guess you lose, Smoke," he announced. "Snell's records say he served for three months at Colombey-Les-Belles and has three enemy planes to his credit."

Smoke stared at Snell for a moment very curiously. Without a word, his big hand dove into his pocket and came out with a bovine-choking roll of franc notes. Very deliberately he counted out five hundred franc notes and handed them to Snell with:

"Reckon this is goin' to end up pretty much like a loan."

Snell glared at him, pocketed the money and refrained from further words. McGill glanced through the papers of the others. He shouted orders through the open doorway to an orderly and turned to the replacements.

"The orderly will show you to your quarters," he announced.

His head jerked sidewise in a sign for Smoke to stay. The pilots filed out. Snell leered triumphantly at Smoke as he passed.

"SMOKE," chuckled Colonel McGill when they were gone and the office door was closed. "You sure got taken in that time. Just what made you do it?" he added seriously.

Smoke grinned at first.

"To begin with, colonel," he admitted, "that bird Snell was too cocky. I thought I'd take it out of him right off the bat, but he had his records to prove what he said, so I reckon there wasn't nothin' to do but pay the money." He shook his head stubbornly. "But just the same, colonel, I know pilots when I see 'em, and if that bird Snell's got more'n fifty hours, from the sloppy exhibition I just saw him pull, I'll kiss his big toe in the Champs Elyses at midnight."

The colonel's chuckle was broken off short by the increasing roar of the same motor they had heard before. Smoke tensed an instant. It was coming closer. That hovering Fokker was diving on the field.

The colonel was close behind as Smoke shot through the door. Smoke reached the tarmac in time to see something round and cylindrical hurl out in the slip stream of the whirling prop and fall to the deadline some distance away, almost directly in front of the astonished replacements.'

"Damn that bird von Stolz," he rasped as he ran. "That's one of his pack droppin' a message. Wonder what hellish trick he's tryin' now?"

As Smoke ran for the can his right hand shot to his big six-gun. It flashed out with a blurred movement and he whirled. The Fokker was just out of range. He cursed and slid the gun back into its holster as he came on the group of replacements.

Snell had been first to retrieve the can. His hands were trembling a little as he held the message before him. Smoke's eyes bulged. He read the note over Snell's shoulder. McGill glared at it beside him.

To Lieutenant Snell:

The Baron von Stolz requests the pleasure of a personal duel in the air at once over La Tore.

Snell leaped forward, but not before Smoke's big hand shot out and grasped him by the collar.

"Hey, what's the idea?" he drawled. "You ain't goin' no place. This is just a trick of—"

Snell moved quickly and spun around to Colonel McGill.

"This is a damned outrage," he stormed. "This big chain store cowboy has insulted me enough. First he cracks wise about my flying. Now he says I can't go to fight an enemy who has challenged me. There's damned sloppy management here, colonel. And believe me, my uncle will hear of this!"

Colonel McGill glared. His face purpled with his rage.

"Silence," he bellowed. "I've had enough of your insolence, damn you! Who is this uncle you're threatening us with?"

"General Banks," snapped Snell. "General Banks of Staff."

Colonel McGill paused, stunned for the moment. He struggled for words, but he was too late.

Down the field a Spad was being warmed for another patrol. Snell broke from Smoke Wade's hold with a wild leap and twisting motion. Smoke lunged for him, but Snell was like lightning on his feet.

He broke ten flat on the way to that warming Spad and Smoke Wade fell farther and farther behind.

Snell was in the cockpit in a mad scramble. Smoke reached the Spad in time to get a face full of dust as the Spad whirled. He stood cursing on the deadline for a moment, spitting out the dirt. The Spad soared into the air and hurled north.

SMOKE was yelling orders to the gaping hangar crews. His own pinto Spad was on the line. It was cold by now. Would take valuable time to warm up.

He cursed as he raced for the cockpit. Mechanics came running.

"Contact!"

The prop whirled. The Hisso sneezed in a fit of hay fever. Again the prop spun over with a grunting, red-faced greaseball on the lower end.

Bam! She caught, snorted and roared.

It seemed an eternity before the instruments before him moved to show an increase in temperature. The air became blue about the big lanky Westerner coiled in the seat, but somehow the hot flow of language from his thin lips had no effect on the temperature gauges. He glared at the needles under their glass fronts. Another minute and he eased the gun full on.

He was off in a cloud of dust and flying rocks. Down over the field he hurled like a madman. His take-off was cross wind. No time for further precautions. A crazy young devil was racing to throw himself into a trap. Von Stolz would win, unless Smoke Wade and his pinto Spad could head him off or pull him through.

Smoke's plans were a bit hazy. He cursed Snell and his ancestry for five generations. He saw him only as a speck to the north, too far ahead to cut him off.

Smoke climbed into the sun as he neared La Tore. He made out a crimson ship racing out of the east. Von Stolz! Smoke's face was puzzled. He was sure of a trick. Still, these two might be old enemies, Snell and von Stolz. But how would von Stolz know that Snell was moving up?

"Hell," spat Smoke Wade at the thought, "the young cub just can't fly, that's all! Somethin' loco in them records."

He poised, undecided as to his next move. Suddenly, he jerked upright and spun in the cockpit. A black flight of Fokker devils snarled out of the clouds behind Snell, directly on his tail. Snell didn't see them.

Angrily, Smoke slammed the stick ahead. The pinto Spad screamed down out of the sun. Massed flights of Fokkers swung beneath him and raved at Snell. Von Stolz had signaled.

Snell half turned in his seat. His face went ghastly white as he saw them. Desperately, he tried to break out and run for home. But he was late for quitting time now. Half a dozen Fokkers shot from behind and hurled down to cut him off.

Smoke was almost within range. His guns bucked insanely to warm. A flock of Fokkers banked and deliberately plunged between him and Snell. His guns chattered a demon chorus. One Fokker went down the twisting way of death in the air. Smoke leveled his sights, with a snarled curse, at another and pressed the trigger button.

Half his instrument board vanished. He ground his teeth and held his course on the tail of the second Jerry. Vickers bucked. The crate wavered and plunged madly, seeming in a hurry to die.

Smoke was fighting to get close to Snell—to protect him. When he looked for him next he was gone! No! He was there, far below, with a mob of Fokkers swirling about him.

Frantically Smoke jammed the stick ahead and sent the pinto Spad howling down. Fokkers stormed up under him in a tangle of plunging ships. He was forced to shift his course to go on living.

Once in the howling dogfight that followed, Smoke stole a glance downward. Far below, Snell was desperately trying to land.

Smoke plunged again. Fokkers swarmed before him. *Blam! Blam!* Spandaus tracers and flaming steel were coming from every angle. One of his own guns was jammed, the other worked badly. The Hisso was coughing and gasping in the last stages of lung trouble.

He saw Snell land near La Tore. Damn von Stolz and his traps! They had forced Snell to land. That much Smoke knew, although he couldn't figure the reason. He cursed and dove. Might pick him up. But even as the nose dropped and the Spad screamed, he realized it was futile. The Hisso sputtered. He brought the ship level. The motor wouldn't hold for a landing and take-off, even if he had the luck to live. Mad with rage he hurled out of the tangle and headed south—for home.

The pinto Spad was vibrating like a shimmy dancer as he staggered it over the boundary and headed for the repair hangar.

"Old Jake's in tough shape," he grinned a little sadly to the mechanics.

He had named his pinto Spad after his pinto cow pony back on the Arizona ranges and had almost the same feeling for this battle-scarred machine as for his horse of flesh and bone.

"Put her in shape pronto. Reckon I'll be needin' her before long again."

Mechanics saluted. Smoke stared at the figure hurrying down the tarmac toward him. It was Colonel McGill. The old colonel seemed to understand before either spoke.

"Snell's gone?" he asked hoarsely.

"Gone down, colonel," Smoke nodded. "Captured, I believe, though. I saw him land. Von Stolz and his brood forced him down. They were thick as flies on a dead steer."

Colonel McGill eyed Smoke speculatively for a moment.

"Strange," he observed, thoughtfully. "Damned strange, Smoke."

Smoke shook his head as they walked toward headquarters.

"Nothin' much strange about von Stolz settin' a trap for Snell like he done," he insisted. "First comes this crazy kid Snell what can't fly, with a record of three Germans to his credit. And when he comes in there's a Fokker high up watchin' for him to arrive. He sees him and his flight dive down and drops that challenge from von Stolz. Von Stolz, the louse, had some damn good reason why he wanted to force Snell down on their side. Don't think they harmed a hair of his head."

Colonel McGill looked very puzzled.

"You believe all that is true?" he asked, a bit hazily.

"Believe it?" declared Smoke. "I'd bet everything I got to my name that it's so. But I'd feel a heap better about it if I could figure out just why von Stolz done all this."

SMOKE was still struggling with the problem an hour later as he watched three mechanics work on the pinto Spad. It was nearly finished. A new prop slipped into place and the key nut spun on the hub end.

The distant drone of a Hisso came to Smoke's keen ears. He tensed for an instant to listen, then dove outside. The Spad was tearing down at full gun. It slammed down on the field cross-wind and rolled straight for McGill's office, bumping into a three-bound landing as it struck the ground.

A slim young figure leaped from the cockpit and dove for the office. Smoke knew him at once—Snell. His leathery face became more puzzled as he broke into a run and followed.

He reached the office in time to see two things. McGill was staring open-mouthed at Snell. And Snell, hardly noticing the colonel, was shouting frantically into the phone.

"Yes. General Banks. At once. Tell him his nephew must speak to him at once. Damned important. . . . Hello, general? This is Jack, Jack Snell. Yes. I've just been in Germany. The drive is coming off at La Tore. I can understand German, you know. And they have a new kind of gas. I saw the horrible stuff. . . . Yes, sir. They were taking me back from my ship after I was forced down. A large quantity of the gas got out of control some distance away. Horrible stuff. Germans fell kicking all around. I got away in the confusion and knocked the mechanic over who was starting my ship."

Snell paused to listen.

"Yes, sir," he snapped. "Just a moment."

He handed the phone to Colonel McGill.

"General Banks wants to speak to you, sir," he panted.

McGill took the phone.

"But general," he boomed, "Lieutenant Wade went over this morning and reports that. . . . Yes sir. . . . But, sir. . . . .Yes, sir."

His hand shook as he held the receiver, then tried frantically to wobble the hook to awaken the dead line.

"Damn!" he cursed. "Wouldn't give me a chance to explain. General Banks orders every plane held ready at the field for cooperation with troops at La Tore for the big defensive. He's advising the movements of all possible troops from Camai sector to the La Tore sector to—"

"Hey, where you going?" cracked Colonel McGill.

"Flying to staff headquarters," Smoke called over his shoulder. "I'll fight this out with General Banks man to—"

His voice died away as he lunged for the pinto Spad.

The crazy-colored crate screamed over the boundary of the little field at staff headquarters. Smoke was out before the roll stopped and racing for the headquarters building.

A sentry barred his way. Banks was very busy. Couldn't be disturbed. Instantly, Smoke side-stepped the out-thrust bayonet. His right fist crashed out and the guard slumped. Smoke dove past.

Banks glared at him. Smoke snapped a salute.

"I'm Captain Wade, skipper of the 66th," he snapped. "You're goin' to listen to me. You don't know what's goin' on at the front."

General Banks glared under his shaggy white eyebrows—speechless.

"I was over both sectors this morning," Smoke raced on. "I seen things that ten others didn't get back to tell. La Tore is quiet. Camai has got the certain signs of a big push. Everything. Troops and munitions moving up. Why, damn it, I'd bet ten thousand francs that the drive comes off at Camai!" General Banks sprang to his feet. "Damn your impudence!" he stormed. "My nephew has eyes and ears. I'll bank on him and I'll take that bet you mentioned."

For the very slightest instant, Smoke wavered.

"Right sir," he snapped. "Ten thousand francs that the drive comes at Camai and not La Tore. I'll prove that this damn nephew of yours simply fell into a trap. Snell's records look phony to me. Von Stolz is behind that too, I think. He planted the whole thing to get your nephew across the lines to see and hear what he wanted him to. He knew he'd come back when they let him escape and tell you. Von Stolz is a clever, sneakin' coyote and that nephew of yours can't fly for sour thorn apples. He never got three Germans and I doubt if he was on the Front before, let alone Colombey-Les-Belles."

Smoke's fists crashed the desk top as he played his trump card.

"But you take his word for it just the same," he roared. "You'll advise troops moved from Camai to La Tore. You, like the rest of the brass hats, sit in a safe office and sends thousands of Yanks to hell, because you haven't got the guts to go over and see for yourselves."

The old war dog seemed about to spring. His jaw shot out defiantly.

"Silence!" he bellowed. "Am I to understand that you insinuate I'm a coward?"

Bam! His own big fist smacked the desk top.

"By Gad, I'll take that challenge! I have one thing more to attend to. I'll be at your field in half an hour."

SMOKE went straight to Colonel McGill on his return to the field. McGill hesitated at first as he laid his plan before him, then he smiled in agreement. Smoke sent for Brant, leader of A flight, and imparted certain things he had in mind; Brant grinned, nodded and shouted orders to the hangar crews, relative to preparing his Spad.

The big staff car, bearing the flag with three stars, brought General Banks to the field as he had promised. The one D.H. of the drome stood warming on the line. Banks strode toward it. Smoke snapped a salute before him. "Ready, sir?" he chirped. "Quite," Banks snapped. Smoke hesitated at the side of the D. H. "Know how to use a Lewis machine gun?" he asked anxiously.

"Certainly, you fool!" roared the general in disgust. "Think I've spent twenty years in this man's army cutting out paper dolls?"

Smoke tried to hide a grin as he helped Banks to the rear cockpit.

Motors blasted all along the line. Every Spad on the field, save Brant's, thundered into the air and fell in behind the lumbering D. H. Bombs nestled in the racks of every crate. The great flight thundered toward the Front.

Far ahead Smoke made out La Tore. A minute later he signaled for a dive. Down, down hurled the D.H., with Spads behind, for the enemy side of the lines. Smoke was pointing below where the war had taken on a slow, inactive appearance.

"There's your drive preparation at La Tore," he drawled.

Banks stared down. Smoke heard his curse come through the tube.

Out of the southwest, riding at them, stormed von Stolz with his entire *jagdstaffel.* Smoke pointed them out to General Banks, who promptly whirled to his twin guns on their turrets.

Smoke led his Spads into a small steeper dive. Directly behind the D.H. rode Snell and his flight in the safest position.

Von Stolz and his buzzards were coming like angry hornets, but they were late for the egg laying.

Smoke's arm went up and cut the air like a saber's slash. Dozens of vained bombs left their racks and hurled downward; the earth below grunted and heaved wildly.

Blam! Blam! Again and again those bombs-hurled down in a gentle arc. They blasted the enemy side of the lines until it seemed that particular part of the world had come to an end.

The air filled with snarling, chattering crates. Desperately, Smoke tried to get within range of von Stolz, but the Boche ace always avoided him.

Tracers slashed through the D.H. wings and tail and fuselage. General Banks was spinning about in the back cockpit, aiming and firing like a madman. Two Fokkers, one from the flaming guns of General Banks and one from Smoke Wade's Vickers, had folded up like bankrupt circus tents and plunged to eternity.

Through the tube Smoke could hear Banks cursing. Often Snell's name tangled with his oaths. He turned in a half roll and glanced back. Snell was fighting for his life with Quinn and the rest of B flight, but had little luck. The kid was game, but lack of experience held him back. Where Quinn's men verticalled and rolled and plunged smoothly, Snell and his green replacements skidded crazily.

Cursing, Smoke raced toward von Stolz again. But the baron saw death written in his flaming guns and veered away at a replacement.

Suddenly von Stolz made a sign. Every Fokker cut out of the fight and hurled west toward Camai. Smoke banked on one ear, to race after them with a signal to his Spads. The pursuits were held back by the lead of the lumbering D.H.

The general uttered a sharp exclamation. He was pointing down excitedly. Action at Camai had already started. The drive was on! The earth rocked from the barrage of heavy guns from the German side of the lines. Even at their altitude, they could make out the retreating Yanks, moving back before murderous fire.

Von Stolz and his brood dove. Viciously they strafed fleeing Yanks. Spandaus bucked and chattered. Smoke leaped on their tails in a flash.

General Banks was firing and cursing like a wild man from Borneo. Another *jagdstaffel* hurled out of the west—it was two Fokkers to one Spad now.

"Gad!" groaned the general. "I should have known."

Smoke gasped. Perhaps he'd been too late at General Banks' office. Maybe he'd already sent through his advice for troop transfer.

His guns bucked like wild horses. One Vickers jammed from excessive firing. A moment later the other stopped with a jerk. The Lewis guns ceased to function behind. Smoke spun in his seat and stared. The general wasn't in sight.

Something slashed through Smoke's helmet. It smacked his skull with sledge-hammer force. Things reeled and went blank. He felt the ship flying herself— fought wildly to get back his fast-waning consciousness. He brought up his big brown palm and slapped himself smartly in the face. Things began to clear, but somehow he couldn't see. Blood, running down into his eyes blinded him. Cursing, sweating and bleeding, he clutched at his face with a grease-smeared paw and wiped it clear.

He blinked and stared, with the D.H. half over in a loop. A perfect bedlam of hell had broken loose about him. Spads were spitting flame and steel from cherry-red guns. A Fokker half rolled to dive.

Smoke's right hand flashed to his six-gun and drew lightning fast. He poured slugs into the belly of the rolling crate, saw it waver, then went blind again.

He clutched at his face, but the blood stuck to his eyeballs and lids. He managed to see out of one eye. A sound came from the rear cockpit. General Banks, his left arm hanging limp, was pouring lead into an unwary Jerry devil who had come in.

A wild exclamation escaped Banks' lips and crashed through the tube. He was pointing with frantic joy toward the ground where the action had suddenly reversed. Over the shattered earth, headed for Berlin, ran thousands of Yank troops. The barrage had ceased.

Smoke became aware of another change. Von Stolz had signaled. Jerry crates fell in behind his lead and hurled north. The enemy had lost, ground and air forces alike. Von Stolz had had enough!

THE Liberty was limping on ten cylinders as Smoke sloshed over the boundary of the home field and cut the gun for a landing. When the roll had stopped and the D.H. stood on the deadline, he turned in his seat and grinned at Banks. The old general was white-lipped, but triumphant, as he smiled back at him.

"Reckon we put on a regular stampede of them coyotes," Smoke drawled.

"Gad, what a fight!" Banks boomed, a little shaky now that it was over. "Wouldn't have missed that for the world."

"You're hurt, general," Smoke warned.

Banks shrugged and eyed Smoke's blood-covered face—dry now.

"No more than you, captain," he blustered. "But before we have first-aid treatment I want to know what's been going on here."

Smoke helped him out of the rear cockpit. He jerked his head toward Brant, coming toward them from his holey Spad.

"It was him—Lieutenant Brant—mostly," Smoke grinned. "You see, I figured if I could get you mad enough, you'd accept my challenge and would postpone advising the whole general staff to move troops from Camai to La Tore sector until you'd seen things yourself. That worked right nice. We all went over and bombed hell out of La Tore and that made the Heinies sure we expected the attack to start there. Reckon they assumed that we'd moved troops already, so they didn't waste time in startin' the drive at Camai as planned."

General Banks nodded.

"Clever," he admitted. "Damn clever. But what stopped the German barrage?"

Smoke chuckled and winked at Brant.

"You see, general," he drawled, "I figured that while we was over La Tore, drawin' von Stolz and his buzzards away from Camai, it'd be a good time to act there. That's where Brant here had his eggs in their basket, you might say. He took off in my Spad just after we'd left and headed for Camai with a load of bombs for the ammunition dump I spotted there. It worked just at the right time. They'd started their drive and they couldn't get stocked up again before our boys made their counter-attack."

Colonel McGill hurried up at that moment with a message which he handed the general. Silence reigned while General Banks read. Then he exploded.

"Where's that damned nephew of mine?" he stormed.

His eyes blazed over the tarmac. They caught Snell in the act of leaving his bullet-riddled Spad. He bellowed a command and Snell answered on rubbery legs.

"What's the meaning of this outrage," Banks demanded. "I started an investigation into your records just before I came. I find that you've only had forty hours in the air. I find that you were chummy with a Lieutenant Feldman of the records department. And Feldman has confessed to fixing your records for you—and more. He shot himself an hour ago, rather than face a firing squad as a German spy."

Snell's face went gray like a dirty towel.

"I—I didn't suspect Feldman of that," he gasped. "I only wanted to make you proud of me, I wanted to amount to something—come to the Front as a flight leader and—"

"Proud?" snorted the indignant general. "Why, damn you, we might have lost this war by this insane trick. I'll break you, by gad. Break you to a—"

Smoke Wade intervened.

"Beggin' pardin', general," he hastened. "But I reckon Snell ain't so bad. He made a right bad mistake, I'll admit, but he's got guts and we need men like him in the air. If you'll let me handle him the way I like, I reckon I'll turn out something that you can be proud of."

General Banks hesitated, then he nodded his consent without a word.

Smoke grinned at Snell and drew him aside.

"That bet, Snell," he reminded him. "Ought to be a thousand francs comin' my way, I reckon."

Snell's eyes shifted.

"I—I got the five hundred you gave me," he said nervously. "But the other five hundred—I haven't got it. That was just a bluff too. You'll have to take it out of my pay."

"I'll make a deal with you on it," Smoke proposed kindly. "Just so long as you behave like a well-broke mustang, we'll forget it." Smoke's face darkened. "But if you slip up, son, so help me, I'll take it out of your hide. Better gallop off to quarters now."

Banks was smiling twistedly as Smoke turned to face him.

"That reminds me of a bet we had, captain," he said. "But I'm afraid perhaps you'll think I'm like my nephew. All bluff. I'll have to send you your winnings."

Smoke winked at Colonel McGill.

"Not all of it comes to me, general," he chuckled. "You see, we're all sort of at fault maybe. When I made that bet with you I didn't know just where all the money was comin' from if I lost. 'Course I was right sure of winning. I been takin' the colonel over the ropes somethin' scandalous now and then, so I let him go in for half with me."

The Death
Fokker

Frederick
Blakeslee

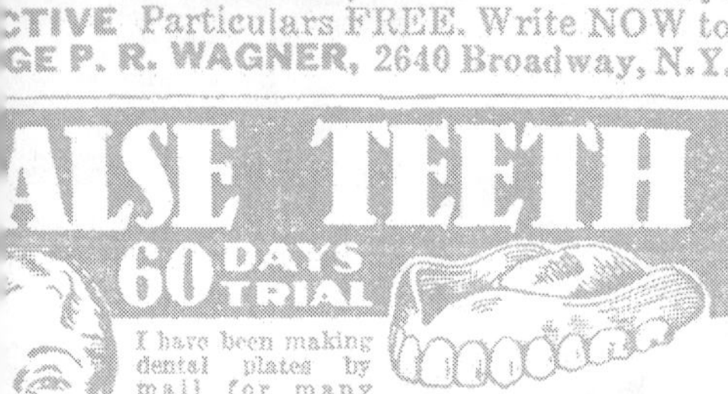

Men said it was haunted—this white Fokker that crossed the lines at dusk, defying Allied bullets like a winged ghost. But it would take more than a ghost to scare Smoke Wade, cowboy eagle—and grimly he set out to lay this one with sky rider's guns!

The Death Fokker

THE leathery face of "Smoke" Wade, lanky, Arizona-bronzed, cowboy skipper of the 66th pursuit squadron, had a worried look. His thumbs were hooked carelessly in the big belt from which hung his old Western six-gun far down on his right leg.

"This is the biggest crisis of the war so far," the kind-faced old C.O., Colonel McGill, was saying. "Our forces are ready for the coming drive at Varette. Our Intelligence in Germany tells us we've kept Heinie fooled. The Boches think the drive is going to start here at Ramou. They must continue to think so or thousands of Yanks will die. No enemy plane must come over on this last day of preparation to see our strategic shift. The Boches must be taken entirely by surprise."

Smoke Wade nodded gravely.

"Reckon you can count on us, colonel," he said. "But I come to—"

The door behind him burst open and cut short his words. A small, swaggering, nervously important officer bustled in. Smoke frowned. He saw the gold star on each shoulder. A general.

Colonel McGill leaped to his feet and saluted.

"Er, Smoke—Captain Wade—this is General Prine from general headquarters," Colonel McGill hurried. "He'll be in charge of this sector for the duration of the drive and—"

A short nod from the general interrupted McGill's words.

"What I want to know," he blustered, "is why in blazes you aren't in the air now?"

"Ain't daylight yet, general," Smoke drawled. "Heinie won't be able to see nothin' fer half an hour yet, I reckon, and—"

The general glared.

"Anyone ask you to do the thinking?" he retorted. "Your orders are to have every plane in the air at once and stay there. Return at intervals for gas and ammunition. Keep enemy planes from crossing the lines at all cost. Understand?"

"Reckon I ain't deaf, general," he nodded. A dangerous light flared in Smoke's gray eyes. "But look here, general. I come to say something and I reckon I'm goin' to say it. I got a new replacement come up this mornin', name of Reed. Ain't never been over the lines before. Ain't no sense in makin' him go this time. Only make trouble and probably be plain murder."

Prine purpled. His small fists clenched.

"Every man of the 66th goes on this flight," he shouted. "Now get out before I have you thrown out."

The corners of Smoke's tight lips curled up. General Prine Whirled to Colonel McGill.

"If I were in command of this outfit I'd make some changes," he snarled with a meaning glance at Smoke. "I'm already making one change. I'm having a new gunnery officer sent up in charge, and if I hear any more of this sort of thing, there'll be a new squadron commander as well."

Smoke chuckled to himself as he trotted down the tarmac.

"One of them sort of coyotes," he grinned. "Well, we'll see. Bringin' up a new gunnery officer, eh? Reckon maybe there'll be more too. Friends of his'n. And if they're all like him I reckon it won't hurt my feelin's none to give up my job. Ain't nothin' much worse'n a flock of chummy kiwis too big fer their hardware, I reckon."

It was still dark. Dim outlines of warming Spads roared or idled along the line. All three flights would go today. The three leaders, Quinn of B Flight, Brant of A Flight and Snell of C came toward Smoke.

"Goin' to be a long drag today, boys, like you already know, I reckon," he drawled. He glanced toward the lighting sky, patched with clouds. "Got that much in our favor anyhow. We'll hide behind them clouds and jump down on any Heinies what try to come across. Always at least one flight stays up there in case others come sneakin' over. Each flight'll take turns goin' back for gas and ammunition. Take it easy and let's give 'em hell."

The three flight leaders shouted orders to their men. Pilots sucked last drags from cigarettes and heeled them.

Smoke strode toward his pinto Spad. He swerved toward a new Spad into which a white-faced, firm-jawed youngster was scrambling.

"Look here, Reed," he advised kindly, "best you hang pretty well out the fightin' today. You just sort of stay around the edge and see how it's done, eh, son?"

Set teeth. Tight lips. A short nod. A choked, "I'll be all right, sir." The kid was in his cockpit, gripping the controls.

TEN minutes later when Smoke led his three flights above a large cloud and gray dawn showed in the east, he was still plenty worried over young Reed. There was something in that look he couldn't fathom. Something akin to fear and yet not fear. A look of grim determination to bash down the enemy, but yet not quite that either.

He forgot the incident for the moment when the first Fokker flight of nine planes came hurling for the lines. Then when flaming steel and yellow and white tracers slashed the clear morning as Smoke led two flights of his hellions down into the fight, it came back to him.

Fokkers and Spads tangled in wild bursts of death and destruction. One Fokker snarled down in flames from the flaming Vickers of Smoke Wade. Another went down before Quinn. All about them were whirling ships and rattling machine guns.

Smoke gasped and jerked upright in his seat as he saw Reed, in the center of the fight, whirling and diving and firing like a madman. His hand shot the controls hard over as Reed darted out of the fight suddenly.

"Come on, Jake," Smoke pleaded to his pinto Spad which he had named for his favorite pinto pony of the Arizona ranges. "Give 'em hell!"

For Reed was streaking away straight into Germany with two Fokkers bearing down on his tail, trapping him in their cross-fire. *Tac-tac-tac!*

Smoke's guns belched flame as his pinto Spad half rolled and snarled down on the two Fokkers. One hurled down out of control. The other burst into flame.

Instantly, Smoke hurled down beside Reed. He saw the white face peer at him. He saw relief there now and gratitude. Two more Fokkers tumbled past, heading earthward. Those which remained whirled and streaked for home.

Smoke motioned Reed home. Then gave orders to Quinn, by sign, to take command of the squadron until he returned. And when he was roaring toward his own lines with Reed close by his side, he saw Quinn leading the two flights once more into the clouds.

Back at the field, as soon as he and Reed had landed, he faced the youngster. There was mingled anger and perplexity on his leathery face.

"What the hell goes on here, son?" he demanded. "I give you orders to stay outside and look on, and first fight comes along you're right plumb in the middle of it. How come? Aimin' to commit suicide, was yuh?"

To his astonishment, Reed nodded a bit sheepishly.

"Yes," he said. "I thought maybe that would be an easy way out."

"Out?" Smoke snapped. "Out of what? You didn't look like no yella dog to me." Smoke's eyes narrowed. Crimson was flowing from Reed's shoulder, smearing his shirt. "Sufferin' rattlesnakes! They did get yuh, too."

Reed glanced at his shoulder and shrugged.

"Not enough to help," he said, almost sadly.

Smoke's face clouded.

"Say, what the devil you drivin' at?"

Reed hesitated for an instant; then he spoke quite calmly.

"I suppose it'll sound sort of foolish to you if I tell you," he admitted. From his pocket, he produced a crumpled letter, "Read that," he said. "I got it just before I was sent up here."

Smoke drew out the letter from the envelope and stared.

> *"Dear Mr. Reed:*
>
> *I regret to inform you that your mother's condition requires the services of the best specialist possible. If it were something I could do, the money would be no item, but unless the finest specialist in New York can operate upon her, she will be doomed to a cripple's chair for the rest of her life.*
>
> *Paul G. Harvey, M. D."*

Smoke looked into the young face with much more understanding.

"So you thought you'd help by goin' out and gettin' yourself killed off, is that it son?"

Reed nodded.

"Yes. I figured she'd get my war risk insurance if I died and that would—"

"Well, I'll be a ring-tailed thingamajig," Smoke exploded. "Thet's guts fer yuh, son, but did yuh stop to think thet your mother'd a heap rather sit in a wheel chair all her life than lose a son like you? Why, jumpin' Judas, money ain't nothin'. I'll lend yuh the money. I got lots of it, made from bets and thet."

Reed shook his head.

"I probably couldn't pay it back," he said firmly. "But what you said about mother not wanting to lose me sort of puts another light on it. I hadn't thought of that."

Smoke grinned and patted him on the shoulder.

"You want to, son," he counseled. "And you're goin' to take the money from me soon's this busy day's over. But right now I'll say I'm a heap glad you got thet Spandau slug in the shoulder, because it's goin' to keep yuh out the air from now on—at least today. It's only a little flesh wound but I'm puttin' you on sick list right now.

"I'll go and get it bound up," Reed agreed. "I'll be back for work, though, captain. And thanks a lot for the offer of the money, but I'm not taking something I can't pay back soon."

Smoke turned and glared at Reed. Glared at where he had been. For Reed was trotting toward the hospital, his arm dripping blood as he went. Slowly the corners of Smoke's thin lips twisted in a grin. He half turned to his pinto Spad. His eyes narrowed. An officer that he had never seen before was beside his plane.

"Morning," the stranger greeted. "I'm Captain Evans, the new gunnery officer here. How's your ammunition?"

Smoke's eyes narrowed. So this was the new kiwi Prine had brought there? Instantly, he took a keen dislike to the man, probably because he had been brought by the swaggering little General Prine. He shot a glance at his gun belts.

"Wouldn't hurt to have full belts of cartridges," Smoke observed. "Tough fight this morning."

Captain Evans barked an order to a gunnery mechanic. Smoke called for the gas truck. The pinto Spad was alive with men working over her. Tanks, filling with gas. New belts of Vickers cartridges being fitted. Oil. Water.

Captain Evans shot a question at Smoke as his foot was in the stirrup of his pinto Spad.

"Haven't seen anything of the Phantom Fokker this morning, have you?" he asked quite matter-of-factly.

Smoke stopped short and stared at him. His eyes narrowed.

"Huh?" he demanded. "Say, what in hell you talkin' about?"

The gunnery officer laughed.

"Can it be you haven't heard of the Phantom Fokker?" he chuckled.

Smoke shook his head and removed his foot from the stirrup.

"Reckon I ain't, stranger," he drawled.

"Not much to tell," Evans explained. "Over at Colombey Les Belles from where I was transferred, they had plenty of trouble with him. A Fokker comes over the line straight for some point where we're planning a drive. Nothing seems to stop him."

Smoke's face darkened.

"Mean to tell me there ain't a Yank on the Front what can knock this bird fer a loop? What's he supposed to be, clever pilot or a ghost?"

Evans shrugged.

"Neither, in a way. He simply flies a straight course for the point he wants to see and flies home again. All I know is what I've heard, but bullets don't seem to have any effect on him. Might just as well be flying in a bullet-proof car from what they say about him."

An angry curse sprayed from Smoke's tight lips. He took one long step. It brought him face to face with Captain Evans.

"Listen, you," Smoke snarled. "We got enough to worry about around here without none of your fairy tales. I'm givin' you warnin'. If you breathe a word of this to any of my pilots I'll break you in two."

Evans' lip curled in a sneer.

"Sure," he said, "if that's the way you feel about it. I guess maybe you're one of these winged wonders who can solve anything without help. A guy that doesn't take tips, eh?"

Smoke's head jerked in a short nod as he leaped for his cockpit.

"Maybe I am," he snapped back, "but I ain't wantin' good pilots scared about somethin' that maybe don't concern 'em."

AS SMOKE zoomed his pinto Spad from the field of the 66th he saw Quinn leading his flight back for gas and ammunition. Snell and Brant would still be back there. He grinned and waved as he hurled north. Later the others would be back in their turn for gas and ammunition to go out again and hold the front against enemy invasion by air.

His mind was torn between two problems as he hurled back to those clouds high above the front. No enemy plane must come over. But what of this damnable Phantom Fokker this new gunnery officer was talking about? Had trouble with it over at Colombey Les Belles, Evans had said. Smoke remembered some of the circumstances. A big shift had been made there for a drive by Yanks. It had failed, he remembered—vaguely, because the enemy had found out about the change. He stiffened. That mustn't happen here. Thousands of Yank lives in his hands.

And he was thinking, too, of the poor gutty kid, Reed. The kid who would willingly die to give his mother his war risk insurance so that she could have a needed operation to keep her from being condemned to a wheel chair.

"Reckon thet's mighty near more guts than I got myself," Smoke mumbled as the pinto Spad hurled up at the cloud. "Kid's proud too. Won't take money no how. Got to figure a way to make him take it somehow."

Smoke raved up in the lead of Snell's and Brant's flight and waved a greeting. Together, with motors throttled back, they circled the edge of the cloud. The sun rose higher behind and above them.

One by one flights went over, filled with gas and ammunition and returned. Quinn had come back. Snell had gone. Then Brant had gone. All returned.

As time wore on and noon approached, Smoke's face grew more and more troubled.

"Don't like this crazy thing one little bit," he drawled, searching the sky below with keen eyes. "Ain't seen hide nor hair nor tail group of a Fokker since dawn this morning. Ain't right somehow. Here on the one day when Jerry'd want to be comin' over to see what's goin' on, they send over one flight and that's the—"

He sat up with a start suddenly and stared toward the north. Nine Fokkers in a tight Vee were hurling toward the front. His steel gray eyes burned toward the tiny Vee far in the distance still. Instantly, his powerful glasses came from their rack beside his seat and snapped to his eyes.

"Hell," he burst out. "Might have knowed. Von Stolz is comin' now. And—" he jerked up straighter and sprayed a curse through his clenched teeth—"I'll bet a flight of Spads against a crashed Fokker thet that baron devil is behind this phony business of clear skies. Somethin's up and I'm a-goin' to find out what it is."

Smoke's big fist shot up and down rapidly in a sign to the other flights. They were all there behind him. All filled with gas and ammunition. Ready to fight. Champing at the bit of inactivity that had chafed them for hours since that first flight at dawn.

He led them back well behind the cloud. They circled there, killing time until the right moment. Smoke swung around the edge of the great cloud. He peered down and saw and cursed with delight. Von Stolz would be caught in a trap.

The signal. Spads turned up their tails. Hissos roared and raced into a screaming mass of diving, plunging death.

Down, down they hurled.

Smoke was first. His thumb was on the trigger button. He held his fire. His eyes glared across his sights. He had von Stolz dead to rights.

Then, too late, von Stolz stared up into the blinding light of the sun and saw the hell raining down from above.

Instantly, he signaled. Fokkers whirled. But Spads snarled down, raving like fiends on their tails.

Smoke followed von Stolz in a tight vertical. He cut in closer. His pinto Spad shuddered from the strain. Von Stolz was in Smoke's sights. Smoke held, roared closer. Across his sights he placed that bullet-shaped head of the baron.

Bam! Down went his thumb on the trigger button.

Tac-tac-tac! Tiny white tracers fluffed out straight for von Stolz. They died out before they reached him, but Smoke hardly noticed. He was sure. He was positive that the baron was on his one-way trip to hell for once.

His heart leaped for an instant as he saw von Stolz's head snap forward on his chest. The crimson Fokker of the baron leaped, hurled over on one wing, and the plane began to fall.

Then it was that something akin to remorse smote Smoke Wade. His enemy was gone. He was plunging for the earth in a twisting spiral. No more would he be in the air with that crimson ship to trick and flaunt Smoke. No more would Smoke be able to make counter traps against the baron to beat him at his own game. From now on, the war for Smoke Wade would lose some of its interest. The baron was gone. Hurling down for hell out of control.

Smoke didn't wait to see von Stolz crash. He was feeling a little sick over the affair. It was as though the baron in being such an arch-enemy of his had almost become a friend. At least a very close acquaintance.

Fokkers and Spads tangled in a froth of wings and tracer ribbons. Smoke clenched his teeth and snarled up under another Fokker. He saw the startled pilot glance over the edge of that cockpit as he pressed his trigger and his Vickers rattled their chant of death.

That Fokker, too, whirled and stormed down in a flopping fall, with the pilot hanging limp in the cockpit.

Then something below caused Smoke to jerk upright in his seat. A lower cloud, three thousand feet below, fascinated him. Something seemed to have moved at its edge. He couldn't be sure. It had only been a sidewise glance. A catch of his eye. But in that split second, he was almost positive he had seen a crimson Fokker plunge into the cloud and disappear.

He yanked over in a tight vertical and stared down, far down to the earth. Von Stolz should have cracked up down there, leaving a crimson smear of plane and von blood against the dull brown of the blasted earth. Smoke rubbed his eyes in a bewildered fashion and stared again. He couldn't make out anything red below him.

Tac-tac-tac! The rattle of Spandaus on his tail yanked him out of his thoughts for the moment. He whirled, kicked and pulled. His pinto Spad rolled, half looped in an outside swirl and raved at the attacking Fokker with flaming guns.

Instantly the Fokker plunged. Down, down, with Smoke hugging his tail and holding down on his trigger button. White ribbons flashed out from in front of his Vickers, straight for the cockpit of that hurling Fokker.

The Fokker leaped high above him, wavered for an instant and then plunged for earth in a screaming dive.

Instantly, Smoke pulled up and scanned the sky. Other Fokkers were plunging down. Two were streaking for home. None had crossed the lines.

The air was clear. Smoke glanced about at his Spads. He counted fearfully. Close to the end, his heart leaped. Every Spad was still in the sky.

A puzzled expression crossed his face as he led his three flights toward another large cloud. Seven Fokkers shot to hell. Seven enemy planes hurled down out of the blue to fly no more, and not one of them went down in flames.

From the edge of their cloud he searched the ground through his glasses. His heart almost stopped a beat. He should have been able to pick out at least two or three of those wrecked Fokkers below. But he couldn't find one of them.

Suddenly, his teeth clenched. His powerful glasses had swerved far to the north, back into Germany. He made out planes flying. Two—no, three of them. They were hedge-hopping, hurling north.

Bafflement was written all over his face. He'd been tricked with the oldest trick of the air. Enemy ships playing possum. His thoughts flashed to that crimson shadow he had thought he'd seen at the edge of the cloud far down.

"Thet's too much to swaller, I reckon," he mouthed angrily to himself. "I didn't learn to shoot yesterday. I know when my bullets is goin' some place, and I'll be a ring-tailed whatyuhmacallit if I didn't have von Stolz' square head straight in my sights."

QUIET settled down over the Front once more. A quiet that was more annoying to Smoke than action and fighting.

"One thing," he drawled later, "I know none of them Fokkers got across the lines. Kept a good watch out in thet direction. Maybe thet's why I didn't see them others pullin' out of their death dives and streakin' fer home, I reckon."

Later Snell and his flight went back for gas and ammunition. He returned. Quinn and Brant took their flights back for the same in turn. Short messes were eaten by each, while the other two flights held the Front.

It was mid-afternoon when Smoke decided it was his turn. Gas was low. Ammunition belts were drawing toward their end. He signaled Brant to take charge in his place and turned for the field.

His wheels had hardly ceased their roll at the dead-line when an orderly saluted and announced that Colonel McGill wished to see him at once.

In his characteristic long stride, Smoke walked to headquarters office. He found Colonel McGill with a worried look on his creased face. He also found little general Prine pacing with his usual swagger up and down before the desk. Prine spoke first.

"I was wondering how long you were going to stay up with that last tank full of gas," he snapped. "What's this I hear about your trouble with Captain Evans?"

Smoke glared.

"Wasn't no trouble, fer as I was concerned," he answered coldly. "I simply told him to keep his mouth shut about that crazy fairy tale of a Phantom Fokker. Ain't no use of scarin' my pilots half to death about somethin' that maybe they don't need to worry about."

General Prine's face was purple with rage.

"I've warned you before, captain, not to take too much under your command," he snapped. "I'll do the thinking and planning here. The fact is that this Phantom Fokker, will, without a doubt, be something for your men to worry about."

Smoke stared.

"What the hell do yuh mean, general?"

"Just this. We've checked up on the fairy tale, as you like to call it. Two weeks ago it happened at Colombey Les Belles. Captain Evans was brought from there for this special mission. He has a record of being the best gunnery officer on the Front. But we didn't take his word for this phantom alone. We've checked with the command at Colombey Les Belles. They were playing the same trick there we're trying here—a quick shift of forces for a surprise drive at another point. An hour before sundown this Phantom Fokker came over. Up to that time, all day, the air forces had been successful in keeping enemy aircraft back of their own lines. But this Phantom Fokker was a different proposition. Bullets had no effect on him or the plane. He simply went straight: over, saw what he wanted to and returned. And I may say that his report resulted in the loss of two thousand Yank lives and our losing ground instead of gaining it."

Smoke stared. His eyes shifted to Colonel McGill. The old colonel nodded gravely.

"It's the truth, Smoke," he said sadly. "We checked up."

General Prine glanced at his watch nervously.

"It's two hours before sundown, captain," he snapped. "You can be on the lookout for that fairy tale of yours to take shape. You seem to be one of these birds who thinks he can take care of anything. Let's see you handle this one. If you fail, there'll be a new squadron commander for the 66th. That's all. Get going."

Smoke didn't take time to eat. He hurried to his pinto Spad. Already it was full of gas, oil and ammunition. He turned as a familiar voice called to him; then he saw young Reed, his shoulder bulging with bandages, running toward his ship across the tarmac.

"How—how's it coming, captain?"

Smoke forced a grin of assurance.

"Just swell, son," he confided. "Won't be long now."

Reed hesitated.

"You—you haven't seen anything of the Phantom Fokker, have you, captain?"

Smoke stared at him. He glared across the tarmac for Captain Evans. The gunnery officer wasn't in evidence.

"Say, how the devil did you hear about that crazy thing?" Smoke demanded.

Reed looked surprised."

"Why, everybody at the field seems to know about it."

The grin that Smoke beamed on him came plenty forced now.

"Don't you be worryin' 'bout thet," he said. "I reckon we'll settle the hash of this supposed Phantom feller if he comes sneakin' around."

Then with a roar and a cloud of dust left behind, Smoke Wade hauled his pinto Spad back into the air.

His brain was a tangle of problems. The young kid needing money for his mother. Gamest kid ever, Reed. A Phantom Fokker, eh? Thousands of Yank lives at stake. He shuddered at the last and pushed the gun full on.

But the air behind the German lines was still calm. He fell in the lead of the three flights and circled above the cloud. Minutes swept by. Ten, fifteen. A half hour. Three-quarters of an hour—

SMOKE straightened in his seat and stared over the rim of the cloud as he skirted above it. A lone Fokker, still tiny, was coming from the north. Something like a chill ran up and down his spine. Instantly Brant was beside him, waving and pointing at the crate.

It came like any ordinary Fokker. It drew nearer. Smoke's face wrinkled in puzzlement. Nothing strange or phantom-like about that crate. It had wings and a tail. It was painted pure white. Just a conventional Fokker.

His arm shot up with clenched fist and jerked up and down rapidly. The sign for attack.

Every plane in the three flights stuck its nose down and howled. The white Fokker came straight on for the Front. It held a straight course.

Closer and closer snarled the three flights of Spads. Then, as they came close enough to see, they stared at the pilot of that Fokker. He was making no pretense of fleeing. He was simply flying straight on toward Yank lines. And he was actually grinning.

Smoke Wade sprayed a curse through clenched teeth. The nonchalance of that lone pilot baffled him. He stared pop-eyed as he hurled down closer. Could this man who grinned in the face of sure death be human? Perhaps he wasn't a man at all. Yet, there was a lifelike expression on the face of the Jerry pilot.

Smoke let go with a warming burst. Spads hurled down behind him. He heard their guns buck as they warmed. But still there was no sign from the Fokker pilot that he would try to get away. Then Smoke Wade lunged in his death dive. His Vickers raved and rattled like mad. White lines fluffed out before his guns, straight for the cockpit of the white Fokker behind.

Other Spads hurled down close behind. Their guns staccatoed with a pulsating sound. White lines of tracer ribbon fluffed out before them as well.

But nothing happened. Nothing except that the head of the Fokker pilot turned and faced them full. And he was laughing at them!

Again and again Smoke lunged down with flaming guns. The air about the slithering Fokker seemed whipped to a froth by Vickers guns and whirling Spads. They dove and cut down and zoomed under to fire into the belly of the seeming Phantom thing, but the white Fokker roared on.

Smoke snarled curse after curse as he tore in and fired burst after burst. The thing had him about crazy. He smacked himself on the cheek almost hard enough to knock an ordinary man out. That was to make sure he wasn't dreaming.

The pilot of the white Fokker screamed on without a pause. Only that fiendish grin of his came back. Now and then he stared maddeningly over the side of his crate down at the sights below that no German must see. His head raised again and the grin seemed broader each time. Then, very deliberately, he thumbed his nose.

He was well over the Yank lines now, and hurling on. Headed for Ramou and Smoke's field behind it.

Guns glowed cherry red from excessive firing. Ahead Smoke could make out his own drome. His throat was sore from cursing and shouting. The whole thing was like a nightmare.

Slowly, as the speed of the diving Spads decreased, the Fokker drew away—it seemed, inch by inch at first. Frantically Smoke pushed on his gun, but the Hisso was doing her best. The Phantom Fokker was gaining. The drive would be a failure. Thousands of Yanks would die.

In a sudden fit of baffled rage, Smoke tore down at his own field. No use fighting a ghost. No need going on driving yourself crazy, trying to fight a thing that bullets didn't harm.

Down Smoke tore. Vaguely he had an idea, but he wasn't sure yet. The Fokker had drawn away from him and his Spads. A souped-up Mercedes perhaps. The cause didn't matter. Later, the Fokker would come back, come hurling back on its way home to give his report that the concentration was at Varette and not Ramou. Might be a chance then, if—

He nosed down, with a curse, at the edge of the field. Over his sights he saw splotches of mud on the edge of the field. Just what he had been looking for.

His thumb pressed the trigger button. Vickers bucked and staccatoed. White lines fluffed out in front of Smoke's guns. His eyes bulged then. No spatters of mud appeared below where his flaming steel should have struck the dirty water. He stared harder and pressed again. The same thing took place. Nothing. Bullets should have whipped that one mud hole to a froth. But the stagnant water remained calm and unruffled.

Smoke cursed himself for his stupidity. He snatched a cartridge out of one of the gun belts and clamped his teeth on the bullet part. A twist of his wrist while his strong white teeth held, and the bullet broke brittlely in two.

He circled the field once and glared at the bullet. It was of a semi-hard cement substance like Plaster of Paris, but with a harder shell. Material that broke up into fine white powder that sprayed from the gun muzzles when the cartridge was fired and gave the effect of tracer smoke for a little way.

"Why, damn my hide," Smoke raved. "If I'd thought of thet a minute sooner, before thet Fokker got away, I'd have pulled the old smoke pole and let him have it. Never occurred to me thet it might be the bullets in the machine guns. Too simple, I reckon."

He hesitated a second before landing. He'd go back up and stop that Fokker on his way back. Stop him with nothing-more than his six-gun. Instantly, he decided against that. Too much of a chance with too much at stake. He couldn't do nearly as well with his six-gun as with his Vickers in an air fight.

RAPIDLY, a plan was taking shape in his quick brain. The whole thing was clear to him now. Captain Evans was the man behind this. Evans wasn't the man's name, of course. He was a German spy. No wonder they'd had such tough luck with the Phantom Fokker at Colombey Les Belles. Evans had been gunnery officer there too. He had taken all the real cartridges and substituted blanks or just as bad. That's what he had done here.

But Smoke knew another trick. Into his mind flashed the recollection of a box of genuine cartridges. He'd saved them almost a year ago.

He snarled down and landed, with a fast roll taking him to the tarmac. No time to argue the thing out with General Prine concerning Evans. That could come later perhaps. Now that Phantom Fokker must be stopped before it returned to Germany.

He saw Colonel McGill and General Prine coming toward him in a high state of excitement as he leaped from the cockpit.

"He's gone," wailed Prine. "You let him go, damn you! Thousands of Yank lives will be lost now, you blundering, cocksure idiot. I'd give anything to stop that damnable white Fokker. I'll break you to a buck private. I'll—"

Smoke drew up before the little general in a flashing salute.

"I'm plumb interested," he drawled, "in that crack about givin' anything to have thet white Fokker shot down. Would it be worth, say, ten thousand francs to yuh, to be paid to the man who brings him down?"

"Why, you traitorous, bragging—" General Prine exploded. He said many uncomplimentary things regarding several past generations of the Arizona Wades. But at the end he managed to gasp an eager "yes."

"I'll see that there money is collected, I reckon," Smoke shouted over his shoulder as he raced for his quarters.

There was a swift rummage for the almost forgotten box of Vickers cartridges and then they came to light. He was racing down the tarmac again. Now he shouted for Reed.

Any minute the Fokker would be back. He kept one eye on the south, the other on his idling pinto Spad and shouted the name Reed, again and again—In fact, until a mechanic came running out and saluted before him.

"Reed, the new replacement, took off in his new Spad just after the Phantom Fokker passed over, sir," he announced.

"Huh? What was thet? Reed gone? Jumpin' Judas!"

Like a flash, Smoke Wade was in his pinto Spad. The ship roared, took the air and almost scraped the ground with one wing as he pulled for the south.

His eyes fairly stuck out of his head as he raced on. Out ahead, coming toward him now, he saw two tiny winged things hurling along. His fingers seemed all thumbs for an instant as he drew out the dummy blanks from his belt and inserted the genuine Vickers, steel-nosed slugs from his hoarded cartridge box.

Nearer and nearer hurled the two crates. Smoke stared and groaned. His voice was hoarse from yelling, but he had more yelling to do.

"Yuh cain't get him with them blank cartridges, Reed," he yelled. "Get out the way and let me finish him."

But Reed couldn't hear him and he didn't seem particularly interested. He was riding the tail of that white phantom Fokker for dear life. White lines fluffed out in front of his guns.

Smoke groaned and cursed. Then he sat bolt upright in his seat. The Fokker had whirled. The first sign that the man was human. He couldn't understand the movement. He was turning to give young Reed the fight of his life.

Up and over and down they raved. Reed whirled with him. Smoke still out of range, hurled closer and yelled until he couldn't yell any more.

Suddenly he saw Reed yank the new Spad straight up. For a minute it looked like the finish. The white Fokker hurled tip, too, but not soon enough. Reed was over, had half rolled and his guns were blazing.

The thing that happened next caused even Smoke Wade to gasp. The white Phantom Fokker shuddered. A lick of fire spurted from the gas tank. Then the whole thing was a mass of flame, falling toward the edge of the drome of the 66th.

REED beat Smoke Wade to a landing by only a split second. Colonel McGill, General Prine and almost the whole field were running madly toward them.

"How in the devil did you do thet?" Smoke gasped hoarsely.

Reed grinned.

"You'll laugh when I tell you, maybe," he admitted. "I—I guess I'm just a kid. You see, back at training field, I wanted to be a great flyer. I heard that knocking down balloons was the toughest job on the front and that they only let veteran pilots try it, so I got hold of a box of incendiary bullets and hid them in my trunk. Makes me feel kind of foolish, now, but—"

Smoke's frown grew more puzzled.

"Yeah. Sure. But how in hell did yuh get the idea thet these here bullets was blanks and—"

Reed laughed again rather sheepishly.

"Just a kid again," he chuckled. "I remember reading some place once about in the Indian wars how some Indians sneaked up and took all the bullets out of the cartridges or something like that, and I was just dumb enough to think maybe it might be tried in modern times. So I took one of the bullets out of the belt that had been replenished in my own ship after I heard about this Phantom Fokker they couldn't hit. You see, honest, captain, I was going sort of nutty here alone while you fellows were out there fighting, and I had to have something to think about and—"

"Huh," Smoke said huskily, "I should think you did. Well, of all the dumb clucks at this field, I'm it this time fer not thinkin' of this trick myself. Why, it was so simple I guess I just took for granted it was out of the question."

By now General Prine and Colonel McGill were letting go with a heavy barrage of questions. And it didn't take Smoke Wade long to tell them the story. He could hardly keep from laughing as he saw the cocky little general's face turning white as he mentioned Captain Evans, by whom Prine had laid such store.

Suddenly a motor blasted wide open down the line. Smoke leaped out and stared. His own pinto Spad, Jake was moving. He saw a familiar head in the cockpit—A head without a helmet or goggles. The new gunnery officer known as Captain Evans was about to escape.

"Stop that man," came the voice of General Prine from behind.

But Smoke Wade's big six-gun was already out. It was a long shot for a six-gun. He took easy aim and pulled three times.

Blam-blam-blam. Almost as fast as the stutter of a machine gun. The head of the man known as Evans danced and jerked and fell limp on the side of the cockpit.

Smoke turned, his six-gun smoking in his hand.

"Reckon thet'll hold thet varment fer a spell," he drawled. He turned to General Prine. "Figure Reed here'll want to be sendin' thet money of his'n home directly. How soon can yuh have it?"

Prine nodded nervously.

"I'll have it for him," he assured, "just as soon as I can write him a check. Ten thousand francs is a lot of money and—"

"Ten thousand francs." Reed blurted. "I don't understand."

So Smoke told him. Later, when it was growing dark and Jerry could no longer come over and learn their secret and McGill and Prine had gone to headquarters, Reed held out his hand to Smoke Wade. His voice was choked with gratitude.

"Gee, Captain Wade," he said, "You're—you're a swell guy, sir."

The big lanky cowboy grinned and took the youngster's hand in his own big one.

"Forget the 'sir', son, and call me Smoke," he said. "And thet sentiment goes double."

The Flaming Patrol

Frederick Blakeslee

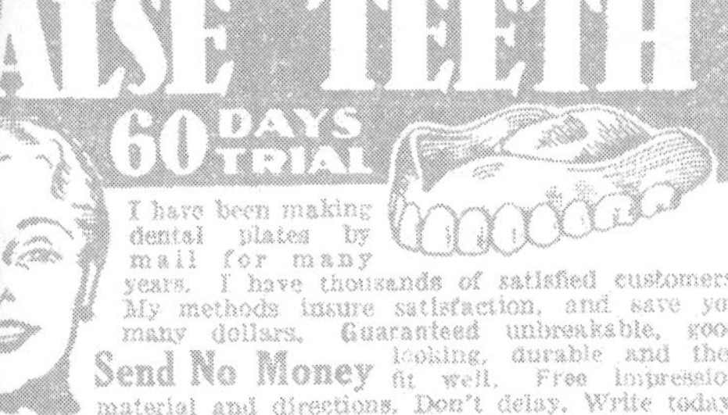

A wall of fire three miles high—this was the terrible barrier that guarded Bocheland's newest ammunition base from Allied raiders. But it takes more than hell flames to trick Smoke Wade when he sets out to beat von Stolz to the draw in a death game.

The Flaming Patrol

DESPERATELY, a lone pinto Spad hurled upward in the lowering afternoon sun. The face of "Smoke" Wade, lanky Arizona-bronzed cowboy skipper of the 66th pursuit squadron, was tense as he stared ahead. Fokkers were storming up at him from far to the north. Nine Fokkers in that one flight, and behind came another flight of seven. One against sixteen. Plenty of odds, but there was a job to be done. Smoke's breath came in short gasps as he hunched over his stick. His whole lithe, muscular body was weak. Every movement was labored. Still, he hurled the pinto Spad higher and higher until the altimeter read well over twenty thousand feet. No man could live in much higher altitude without oxygen.

Smoke's head throbbed. His ears rang with the low air pressure about him and the last words of kindly old Colonel McGill, his C.O. back at Ramou.

"I know it's out of your sector, but every Yank at the Front west of us is counting on you, Smoke," he had said gravely. "Just got wind of a great enemy drive through Intelligence. We know there's a huge drive coming off to the west, but we're not sure just where. You're the sixth master pilot to be sent out. The others didn't come back. Good luck and God bless you, Smoke."

Smoke's teeth clenched as he saw he wasn't going to get over the top of those Fokkers. Fear of a fight was farthest from his mind. But he must avoid combat if possible. Thousands of Yanks were counting on him to bring back the news that meant life or death to them.

Fokkers hurled up to cut him off from the rear lines which he must not see. They were still over Allied soil. They'd come out to meet him as they had the others. One consolation at least came to him as he scanned the sky above and about him.

"Reckon no Jerry coyote's goin' to come skulkin' down on my tail from upstairs. They cain't fly no higher'n I can."

His drawled words, drowned by the road of his Hisso, came with an effort.

Nearer and nearer came the Fokkers. They were almost up to his level. All ships at that altitude were flying sloppily. Engines didn't deliver much more than half their horse power. Propellers churned thin air.

Smoke sat up and searched those Fokkers storming up at him. His face grew puzzled.

"Reckon thet's funny," he drawled to himself. "I'd a swore I'd find a red Fokker in thet pack when I got here. But there just ain't none there. Well, Jake, reckon there's goin' to be a fight in spite of my climbin'. Let's go boy!"

All that very calmly. But instantly the nose of the pinto Spad hurled down. Vickers warmed and bucked. Straight for the lead Fokker of the first flight of nine, Smoke Wade plunged.

The leader wavered and, at the last instant, dove out of his way. White Vickers tracers flashed out and crucified him to his cockpit. Like a snapping rat terrier, Smoke's pinto Spad whirled and struck and struck again.

Another Fokker hurled down for hell. Another veered off and began a fast glide back into Germany with the prop stopped dead.

Then a convulsion seemed to seize the pinto Spad. It whirled in a series of barrel rolls as the second flight of seven Fokkers hurled up to the attack.

The speed of Smoke Wade's dive had been terrific. The snap rolls were almost like lightning. It was as though he were literally boring his way through that second flight.

Bam! The pinto Spad hurled out into the open and screamed like a wild thing gone crazy.

Fokkers tore after the flashing Spad. The Spad had the lead now. It raced like mad for the rear of the German lines.

"Sorry I cain't stay to play with you boys right now," came in a slow drawl over his shoulder. "Got a little sight-seein' of mah own to do."

His great power glasses came out and rose to his eyes. Spandau tracers fluffed after him and died, falling in a slow downward arc as he plunged out of range.

"Let's see now," Smoke drawled in the monotone of the announcer of a rubber neck bus. "On our right we got Reims, ladies and gentlemen. An on our left we got Chauteau Thierry. Don't look like nothin' more goin' on there in the line of war than they is at a Sunday School picnic."

He sat up with a jerk. He was down in lower altitude again. He could breathe and move more freely now. Through his powerful glasses he had spotted something far ahead. There at Fismes, just behind the German lines, was action aplenty. Long trains of trucks moved up from the rear. The ground far below was alive with activity.

Smoke stared harder and grunted with satisfaction. The trucks, most of them, seemed to be heading for a wood to the left of the ruined town.

"And I reckon," Smoke drawled, grinning now, "thet I know right where the supply and ammunition dump is tethered."

Swiftly, he made a mark on his map. He cast a glance over his shoulder. The Fokkers still hurled at him from behind just out of range. He was cut off from his own lines now.

Another flight of Fokkers stormed up from near the Front. Only an instant Smoke hesitated in his decision. Then he took the bull by the horns and yanked the stick.

The pinto Spad hurled up and over in a shudder. Down, down he plunged for the nearest Fokkers. He came in a slithering, twisting lunge, with flame darting from his gun tips.

"Might's well get it over with right soon," he mumbled.

He sure was, one way or the other. One Fokker screamed down before him. In return, his own instrument board vanished from before him and hot oil scalded his face.

It was then, blinded by his hot oil, that he pulled his controls again.

Over and over and over plunged that pinto Spad until it seemed human endurance could no longer stand snap rolls.

He had no time to see tracers fluffing blindly about him. He only knew that as long as he continued to roll he was reasonably safe. His heart yearned to stay and give the Jerries the fight of their lives. But he had business back home.

Down, down. Over and over he hurled. The flight ahead couldn't get within range as he roared above them. Smoke's big bony hand came up before his face, and he grinned as he thumbed his nose while he pulled out of his rolls and roared for the southeast and home,

HE WAS more serious when he stood before Colonel McGill a half hour later. The old colonel's face was beaming. Smoke had already told him of his find, and McGill was hurrying the good news by phone to G.H.Q.

"That's right," he was saying. "Yes, General Banks. Lucky, isn't it? Of course. You can send a bombing squadron over tonight and blow up the dump Captain Wade has spotted . . . No, sir. I don't think we'll see any drive starting at dawn tomorrow. Thank you sir."

The receiver slammed on the hook with a triumphant click.

But still Smoke Wade looked plenty worried.

"Reckon I don't like the look of it no how," he drawled. "Near as I cain figure, there's some trick to it somewhere, colonel."

The shaggy gray eyebrows of the old colonel lowered in perplexity.

"I don't quite understand. Smoke," he said. "You've spotted the place of the drive without question, and you've done better than that. You've found the place where their supplies are stored."

Smoke nodded.

"Reckon so. But the dump ain't blown up yet."

"Of course not," McGill hastened. "But it will be. Even if it isn't we know where the attack's to take place. I'll wager that Yank troops are getting ready to reinforce that point south of Fismes right now."

"Sure," nodded Smoke, "but just the same, when I don't see von Stolz's red Fokker in the sky for more 'n a week and I ain't heard nothin' of his being killed, I reckon to figure somethin's goin' on thet ain't healthy fer Allied troops and pilots. Sort of figured when I didn't see him around this sector fer a week and I heard of this comin' drive, he might have been rushed over around Chateau Thierry sector to help in the drive. But there wasn't a red plane in the sky this evenin'. Not unless I've gone color blind lately, which ain't likely."

Smoke Wade was still worrying about von Stolz's absence from the Front when he turned in a few hours later that night. His troubled sleep was of very short duration.

He sat up with a jerk at the first loud rap on his door. He blinked and stared about him. Through the half open window came a weird light. It mingled with the husky, excited voice of Colonel McGill to make a strange effect upon the half-awake cowpoke.

"Von Stolz!" Smoke barked as in a dream.

"Yes," the colonel cut in hurriedly. "I'm afraid you were right. There's hell up front. General Banks wants you at once over at G.H.Q.

Smoke's hands were working like magic. His big flying suit glided on over his pajamas. He jerked his head toward the strange, flickering light that filtered in through the window.

"What in hell is thet, colonel?"

McGill shook his head.

"I don't know for sure. Looks like a wall of flame, from what I can see from here. It's a long way away to the west and toward the Front. Seems to cover most of the Front we can see from here. That's probably what General Banks wants to—"

But Smoke Wade was gone. Gone in a headlong dive for his pinto Spad that mechanics already were starting on the line.

One wild leap and he was in the cockpit. His hand battered the gun open wide. The pinto Spad shot out across the dark drome and roared into the air.

Almost the very second that his wheels left the ground. Smoke cocked the ship on one wing, slammed over the boundary and stared ahead at the cause of the weird light he had first seen from his room.

It was a gigantic, wholly unbelievable spectacle, that sight before his eyes. To the west, the whole front and for some distance behind the German lines, the sky was crimson with leaping, mounting flame. The whole Front seemed on fire, with flames licking upward thousands of feet in the air.

He lunged nearer to get a closer look at the sight. It was appalling. Hellish. A real hell on earth now. The world seemed surely at an end in that sector a little way behind the German lines.

But as Smoke Wade swerved in his course and tore for G.H.Q. he was sure there was nothing supernatural about it. He couldn't explain the gigantic conflagration. He couldn't even guess in what manner it was caused. But of one thing he was certain. German brains were behind that huge wall of flames that shut the concentration point at Fismes off from the Yanks and their Allies. German brains of a fiendish kind. And but one man could be responsible here under the circumstances. Von Stolz would be that man. So this at last was the reason why Smoke hadn't seen him or his crimson Fokker in the skies for a week.

"Yuh sure pulled a lulu this time, I reckon, Von," Smoke drawled as he hurled toward G.H.Q., "Thet sure is about the biggest bafflin' show of magic or somethin' I ever did see."

FIVE minutes later, when he was hurried into General Banks office at G.H.Q., and he found his friend of high command madly pacing the floor, he ventured a little further in his guess about von Stolz's trick—if it was a trick at all,

"He sure put up somethin' in thet wall of flame thet'll stop bombers from goin' over to rotten egg the concentration supply depot for the drive, general," he drawled.

General Banks turned a haggard, white face toward him.

"Yes," he said bitterly, "that's the hell of it all. Thank God you've come, Smoke. I couldn't think of any other way out than to send for you."

Smoke grinned.

"Take it easy, general," he said. "Reckon I'll do all I can. Now you just put the responsibility on me and tell me the whole works from the beginnin'. My old ears is plumb tinglin' to listen."

"You've seen that wall of flame behind the German lines," General Banks began breathlessly. "We're indeed greatly indebted to you for your valiant services in locating the point of concentration at Fismes and even more than that in locating the supply depot. If we could bomb that and blow it to hell there would be no drive, not until we can rush reinforcements to the Front to meet it."

Smoke's eyes narrowed in a flash.

"Yuh mean to tell me, general thet you ain't got the reinforcements up to the Front yet?" he demanded.

General Banks nodded anxiously.

"That's the very hell of the whole business," he said in a cracked voice. "We started the move at once this evening when we got your report. A few of the men, one company or so, got by just after dark. The rest were coming on. Then about two dozen Gothas came over and blasted the very devil out of every road leading to the Front. We're cut off. All lines are down. All roads are shot to Hades. A motorcycle can't even get by." The great general's hands opened and closed convulsively.

"Our only hope is in bombing that supply depot at Fismes!" His words came almost in a sob. Desperately he pointed out of the window behind him through which came the weird light of the wall of flame behind the German Front.

"I gave orders for every bombing plane on this sector to start over, loaded to the gills with eggs. That means the whole 13th squadron. It's all we have in the line of bombers here. Those D.H.s will do the trick—if they can get through."

Smoke Wade's teeth clenched angrily. He tried to hide the baffled expression he knew must be on his leathery features.

"I'm putting it in your hands, Smoke. I'm powerless. Licked. I'll stand behind you in anything you do. The life of every one of those Yanks out there cut off from us for reinforcements is in your hands. Bombers have got to get through those flames and blast the supplies before the drive starts."

He turned and held out his hand. His words came more in the tone of a prayer than a command. He held out his hand to Smoke.

"God help you, Smoke," he said, "and protect you from harm."

A short grip of the great general's hand and Smoke dove from the office. It was a matter of seconds later that his pinto Spad shot into the air.

Smoke banked close to the ground and hurled toward the gigantic wall of flame. The nose of the pinto Spad was high in the air, climbing as he went. As he roared nearer, he studied the flaming mass. He made a guess as to the height of the highest masses of flame. Three miles high, perhaps. Maybe more. No plane could fly over that and live. The heat from that hellish conflagration would be deadly, even above the topmost tongues high above him.

He sat up straight in his cockpit suddenly and stared at something else that hurled along to the east in the same direction he was taking—straight toward that wall of flame.

He made them out clearly in the light of the fire wall ahead. A whole flight of D.H. night bombers thundering north in tight formation. They too were climbing for the top of those licking flames.

Smoke pushed frantically on his gun, but the Hisso was snarling like a wild thing. They had a lead on him. They would reach the hell ahead of his pinto Spad.

In his brain, reason fought a terrific struggle with fact. He was actually staring at a wall of flame a mile ahead. Still there wasn't reason in it. He'd never heard of flame from the most gigantic fire in the world mounting to three miles in height. It wasn't possible. Yet there it was before him.

And as his brain fought with the fantastic problem, he saw the noses of those bombers dip for a dive. Straight for the licking flames they roared. Down, down, like striking hawks.

They spread out in a wide area as they raced down. On a line now and not in a vee formation, they lunged toward that crimson wall where flames danced and flickered to trap them in seering hellfire.

Then one tore out ahead of the rest and screamed insanely for the barricade. The others seemed to hesitate, awaiting the outcome of that first to dare the hell.

Smoke gasped as he watched that lone plane. Never once did it falter after it had started that deadly plunge.

Down, down it tore. Flames were licking about it. It seemed to stagger, half hidden by the flames. Smoke was shouting like a madman in panic.

"Go on! Go on through. Don't dive any more. Don't—"

His words choked off in the back of his throat. He saw the D.H. turn over on one wing and start down. Flames covered it more and more. Licked at it and darted from its wings, making a funeral pyre as it hurled down.

It lurched suddenly at that instant almost hidden by the flames. Smoke's eyes bulged in his frantic effort to follow the lone D.H.

It seemed to have struck something; half-turned—and then was lost in the dancing flames of the hell.

HE WAS shouting again until he was hoarse. Shouting to the four remaining bombers to turn back before it was too late. They were already acting as though they had heard his warning command. They swirled in tight verticals at the very edge of the flaming wall and plunged down toward the south and their own field.

Smoke hesitated for an instant. His keen eyes swept the sky all about him. Searchlights blinded him as they slashed the heavens from far below and to the south of the wall.

Archie opened up and made a hell of the place about him until his pinto Spad danced and hopped about in the blasts like a monkey on a string.

Suddenly, Smoke's eyes, staring upward for the moment at the top of the wall of flame, caught something in the gleam of one of the searchlights.

It was a sphere shooting upward at a rapid rate of climb. It was round—looked like a basketball a mile above him.

The first faint ray of hope leaped within his heart. Instantly, the pinto Spad stuck its nose high along the flaming wall and Smoke was tearing after the strange thing.

The searchlight that had focused upon the round, drifting object shifted, but Smoke held it with his eyes in the light of the flames. Insanely, he tore up after it. The Hisso groaned in the steep climb, but inch by inch. Smoke was gaining on the thing that had caught his eye.

Seconds swept by. He was getting higher and higher. He was to the south of the wall of flame, but not high enough to see how thick it was.

Then he cursed. His thumb tramped down on his trigger button, and Vickers guns slashed out with tracers and steel and incendiary bullets.

He made out the thing now. A balloon, alone in the sky and rising rapidly. It was a simple affair. Like the old fashioned hot air balloons used once at fairs, but much smaller. This one would not support a man, he guessed. And there was no basket hanging beneath it for the purpose.

He cursed again as the flickering light below fooled him. He was still out of range. He punched on up at the floating gas bag. Once he stared down at the flames, and instantly focused on the balloon again so he wouldn't lose it. The light was getting dimmer at the higher altitude.

But in that glance downward, his heart sank. He had hoped that the wall of flame was not wide. That there might be a chance to get over it. A bare chance. Luck wasn't with him. The flickering fingers of flame extended far beyond the front of the wall.

Again he peered through his sights and pressed. This time he had followed the small balloon for at least a minute. Perhaps two. He hadn't glanced down this time.

Tac-tac-tac! His heart leaped. The balloon burst into a mass of flame before him and began to fall like a great, blazing ball of oil.

Smoke's cry of joy was short-lived. It ended in a hacking, choking cough that shook him from head to toe. He couldn't seem to get his breath. He gasped and heaved frantically. He began to feel weak and exhausted. His head throbbed. His whole body seemed about to burst.

Instinctively, he stuck the nose of his pinto Spad down and stared about him. Something like a chill raced down his spine. And at the same instant he realized something he hadn't thought of before when he noted his position.

The balloon must have drifted back directly over the wall of flame, but a bit higher than the highest licking fingers of flame. He was above the fire. He should be burning to a cinder at that very moment. Instead, there was no sensation of heat.

Down, down screamed his pinto Spad. He felt himself being smothered by some invisible force. Then, slowly, his consciousness was returning. He was out of the wall that seemed to flame.

He was certain from what he saw that flames were there. Hell, he wasn't blind. But flame had heat. There was no heat from that wall. He recalled now that at no time had he felt heat from the gigantic conflagration. But somehow he hadn't thought of that as queer. Hadn't thought of it, in fact, at all with the many other things to think of.

And yet there was the lone D.H. that had so gamely dived into the wall in a frantic effort to get through. He'd seen that burst into flames and mingle with the perfect hell.

His head was clearing. He was out in front of the wall of flame again. Archie was going crazy down below, trying to get him as he hurled back toward the field of the 13th bombardment squadron.

The whole thing was too baffling, too maddening, to figure out. Yet it was up to him. Banks was counting on him. Thousands of Yanks were unknowingly betting their lives on him.

His throat and lungs felt raw as he hurled south toward the field of the 13th bombardment squadron. He began to reason out that phase of it.

Flames there in that wall, to all appearance, but no heat. Flame without heat just wasn't done. Then his coughing and gagging and now the raw feeling in his breathing pipes. Must be gas of some sort.

That was as far as he got in his mental deductions as he stormed down on the field of the 13th. D.H. bombers were pulled up to the line, their engines still idling or dying as the pilots returned from their horrible experience turned off switches.

WITH a roar, Smoke shot his pinto Spad to the line beside the larger D.H.s and leaped to the ground.

Men came running toward him. He made out one pilot, larger than the rest, lunging at him like an angry bull. He, the leader, was fully as large as Smoke Wade and more heavily built. His face as he came nearer in the dying light of a gasoline trench flare was ugly, menacing.

"You, damn you!" he roared as he drew nearer. "You're Smoke Wade and I don't give a damn if you're a general, much less a captain, and I am only a first lieutenant. I'm going to damn well tell you what I think of you, and then when I get through I'm going to lick hell out of you to make up for Turner's death that you're to blame for."

Smoke Wade moved only slightly. His feet came wider apart. He braced himself, and his face with its narrowed eyes and clenched teeth had taken on a sudden, hands-off expression.

The big first lieutenant hesitated, standing eye to eye with the six-gun toting cowpoke.

Smoke's voice came like the crack of a cattle whip.

"Ferget, stranger, thet I outrank yuh," he said. "We'll chew this thing over man to man like we was alone out in the Arizona country. Start talkin'. My ears is plumb burnin' to listen, but yuh better get started pronto, 'cause I ain't got much time fer no kid argumentations. Now, who in hell do yuh think yuh are and why?"

The big first lieutenant hesitated for an instant. Part of the fight had already been taken out of him. His voice was not so ugly as he spoke now.

"I'm First Lieutenant Bolan, senior flight commander of the 13th, In place of Captain Turner who plunged into that flaming wall and was burned."

Smoke gasped.

"Turner?" he exploded. "You mean to tell me thet was Turner what dove into that red wall—" he pointed to the north—"and went out of sight?"

Bolan's fists clenched. His voice rose again.

"Yes, damn you!" he hissed. "Turner went through because of you. Said you taught him a couple of months ago on another deal that there wasn't anything real about some of these strange things that happened at the Front. You proved to him, he said, that everything that looked strange or perhaps supernatural was just another German trick. That's why he went through that wall of flame first—to prove to the rest of us that it wasn't flame at all, but just some trick that he couldn't explain until later.

"He burned!" Bolan's voice screamed now in horror. "We were there and saw his whole plane smothered with flame. I suppose you're going to tell us now that it was all in fun. Just a simple trick of Jerry, eh? Well, I'll show you a simple little trick myself, damn you!"

Big Lieutenant Bolan lunged. His fist, the right one, flashed out for Smoke's face. But somehow, Smoke Wade had moved in a lightning side step and the terrific blow breathed past his face.

Smoke's long, bony arms shot out before Bolan could recover his balance. They came together around the frantically, insanely struggling senior flight commander and held him as though in a vise of steel.

Smoke's brain whirled with planning. It seemed fearfully sluggish though. He'd have to think of something to stop this mad house at the 13th. His eyes swept the other faces in the dim light that reflected from the wall of flame miles away.

There was fear and anger on those faces. The other pilots of the 13th agreed heartily with their senior flight leader. Smoke was in a tight spot. He was thinking fast. As fast as he had ever thought in his life. Thousands of Yank lives depended on these already half crazy bombing pilots accomplishing the blowing up of the supply dump at Fismes. And it was all up to Smoke Wade now.

He had all he could do to hold the fighting Bolan in his clenched arms. His mouth was close to Bolan's ear.

"Listen, you damn yellow kid," Smoke hissed. "You think Turner was burned, but you're wrong. I'll lay you a little bet of, say, ten thousand francs, you and the rest of your scarecrow outfit, that Turner never burned. And it'll be up to me to prove it. If I can't, you win."

He felt the struggling of the big flight leader subside as his words sank in. Gradually. Smoke let go his hold and pushed Bolan a safe distance away from him. Bolan was staring through narrowed eyes.

"Say," he demanded. "How the hell do you know so much?"

Smoke's laugh that answered him was very sure.

"It's my business to know things," he chuckled. "But it's goin' to cost you and the rest of your outfit plenty money to find out. You say you seen Turner and his plane burned. I'm givin' you a chance to clean up ten thousand francs on your eyesight, if you got thet much, and it's up to me to prove it. Is it a bet, or are you birds goin' to keep on actin' like a bunch of scared kids?"

The challenge was out. Bolan hesitated. His eyes shifted among his men. He got ready nods for their answers.

"It's a bet," he snapped. "We'll raise that much money somehow, but God help you if you fail!"

Smoke nodded, still grinning.

"Reckon I'll need his help if I fail," he said. "I'm goin' over now and start work on winnin' thet ten thousand. Maybe you birds'll want to come over in an hour or so with your bombers and lay around out of danger just to see what's goin' on. Course, if yuh should see anything like the fire goin' out, yuh might get nerve enough to go over and bomb the Heinie supply dump, but I wouldn't be so cruel as to ask yuh to do nothin' dangerous if yuh didn't want to."

Bolan and his pilots leaped forward to deny their fear, to still the insults that Smoke had hurled at them calmly. But Smoke was out ahead of them.

One leap shot him into the cockpit of his Spad. The hisso blasted wide open. The pinto Spad whirled on the tarmac and thundered into the air, heading north.

ALMOST the instant that Smoke was out of sight of Bolan and his pilots of the 13th, his face grew troubled. He wasn't sure just exactly what his next move might be. One thing was necessary above all else. He must in some way get over into Germany and cause those three-mile high flames to subside in another hour or so. Yank lives in the balance. The bombers must go through.

His heart leaped as he hurled toward the wall that seemed to be flame. There in one spot, directly before him, there appeared a gap in the flames. He sat up with sudden realization.

"Well, I'll be darned!" he mouthed. "If thet ain't the same place thet Turner tried to dive through, then I'm a—"

His words cut off as though a sharp knife had severed his tongue. The gap was filling up. From below came darting fingers that rose higher and higher from the ground, filling the gap before him.

An angry curse sprayed through his lips. He hunched forward over his stick. His hand smacked the gun and the Hisso screamed like a thing possessed.

Up, up he raced in a slashing climb for the point above that rising flame that was closing the gap. He must get through that gap. That was his only hope now. And the gap was closing before his two mile a minute advance.

Searchlights slashed up from below and focused upon him. Archie grunted insanely as he tore on. The gap was closing. All about him blinding flashes told that archie was getting the range.

But Smoke Wade had no time to swerve and duck and dodge those archie bursts. Every second counted. He must break through that wall of seeming flame before the gap closed.

Blam! Blam! Blam! The pinto Spad was leaping and bounding about like a crazy kite in a storm as he tore through mushroom bursts. On and on and on, with the gap closing.

That other plunge after the balloon above the wall told him there was gas there. Gas, but no heat.

The gap was almost closed before him. Now or never was his chance. He was there. He didn't hesitate. With one great intake of air, he filled his lungs to bursting and hurled the Spad through the almost closed gap.

His lungs were bursting. All about him seemed to swirl tongues of flame, but still there was no heat. Then he was sitting bolt upright in his seat, looking down and through the red haze toward his own lines. Far down below, in front of the wall that seemed to flame, he saw crimson lights that flickered and danced.

That told him more, but was far from solving his problem. The Germans were sending up a gas screen and playing red lights upon it to make it look like a flaming wall. It was probably poison gas. It was choking him now. His lungs were bursting for air. His eyes watered so he couldn't see. Then sudden relief came as his Spad shot out the other side of the wall, and he was behind the wall of gas.

His hand brushed tears from his eyes until he could see plainly. He was coming down in a great enclosure, perhaps five miles square. It was completely surrounded by a wall of reddish gas that he had just plunged over by a scant margin. The concentration point for the German drive at dawn was completely surrounded by the wall. It was very dim inside the great aerial enclosure, with the pinkish tinge making things look weird.

Smoke's keen eyes stared down below. Instinctively, he grasped his stick between his legs and his right hand drew out his old six-gun. Cautiously, he spun the cylinder and inspected the loading. Everything seemed ready if he should need it.

He slipped the gun back in to the holster, far down on his right leg and grasped the stick. His eyes peered over the side for a place to land. His mind had made a mental map of the whole territory about Fismes that afternoon. He had spotted several fields then that would serve to land in. He must get down and do something about this fiendish wall that kept Yank bombers from crossing the lines. After that, he had no plans.

He remembered a field near the gap through which he had just passed. He could see it even now in the dim light within the enclosure. Strange, no searchlights slashed up at him. Doubtless every searchlight on the front was playing red shadows on the wall of gas or piercing the sky to keep Allied aircraft from crossing into the concentration territory. Lucky, that.

His hand reached for the throttle and closed it. Then he ticked off the switch. The prop stopped. There was no going back now. He must land.

Everything seemed still and quiet about the place he had chosen for his landing. His hopes rose as he heard his wheels rumble softly in the landing. His hand flashed to his six-gun as he leaped from the plane. First he'd scout along the line under the wall of gas, lighted red, and try to find the source.

Suddenly, he froze beside his pinto Spad. Shadows moved at one side of the field, not more than a hundred feet from him. He crouched and cursed. They came nearer; then there was a wild yell behind him.

Smoke's six-gun blasted and blasted again. Tongues of flame told of 45 slugs spitting from the muzzle. Screams, shouts. Men falling and writhing on the ground of the pink-lighted field.

More Germans came, closing in upon him from all sides. He was trapped. Half crouched, he dove for the cover of a wood. The rattle of a machine gun behind him put wings to his flying feet.

Blam! All the stars in the heavens came out in one burst. Something had struck him in the head. He was falling. Going down in a heap, with his smoking six-gun still clutched in his hand, and he couldn't seem to get up. Then darkness.

GRIMLY, he felt the jolting motion of men walking. He was being carried between stalwart German guards. He moved slightly. His hands and feet were free. That was something.

Suddenly, his ears picked up a sound. It was the sharp-bitten bark of Liberty motors. Liberties on D.H. bombers. He must have been out for some time. Bolan and the 13th were already scouting on the other side of the red gas wall that kept them from dropping their eggs.

Smoke groaned and relaxed. He wondered where they were taking him. He knew in another minute.

He saw the outline of a frame building before them. There came the sound of guttural voices before a half open door. Then a triumphant laugh came from that door. A laugh he had heard before. No one else could laugh like that. It must be von Stolz.

Smoke lay limp and closed his eyes again as they carried him through the door. He felt a smart slap on the face and again that laugh. He opened his eyes and stared into the evil face of von Stolz grinning down at him. The monode, as usual, was in one eye. There before him was his arch-enemy, the Baron von Stolz, with his close-cropped, bullet-shaped head, his cocky little body in spotless uniform, and the saber scars on the left cheek.

"*Ach, Mein Herr* Smoke Wade," von Stolz was laughing, "at last my time of triumph has come!"

Smoke was being seated in a chair. His eyes flashed about the interior of the one-room building. Then, in spite of his determination to act weak and exhausted, he sat up with a start and brushed the blood away that was flowing from his scalp wound down over one eye. There, across the room from him, was Captain Turner, the skipper of the 13th bombardment. Turner's right arm hung limp at his side. Guards took their places. Four great Germans, they were, with Lugers trained on them,

"Thank God you're O. K., Turner," Smoke cracked.

Von Stolz cut in with a laugh.

"Your friend is all right except for a broken arm, which will be fixed shortly," he said. "The fool tried to dive through my wall of flame and he accidentally collided with the cable that held one of my many balloons. We captured him after his plane crashed, *Herr* Smoke Wade. I tried to send up another balloon to take its place, but you got through before we had finished. It is well the way it has turned out."

The cocky little German laughed triumphantly. Turner cut in then angrily.

"This whole wall of flame is a fake, just as you said everything the Germans did would be, months ago. Captain Wade," he said. "If I hadn't happened to hit that cable I might have gotten through the gas all right, but it had me goofy. That's what the damned stuff is, too. Not flame at all, but a wall of gas going up three miles in the air, with red lights playing on the front of it to make it look hot."

Smoke gave a short nod to Turner.

"I guessed about thet," he drawled calmly, "but I ain't figured yet just how they get it to go up so straight for three miles or more." He turned to the proud baron very meekly now. "Reckon you got us where we cain't get out, baron," he said calmly. "Sort of looks as though the war is over as fer as Turner and me's concerned. You sure done a neat job this trip. Ain't nobody I ever seen as clever as you."

The Baron von Stolz bowed in acknowledgment of the compliment. His narrow set eyes swept over Smoke for an instant and he turned to one of the guards.

"You have searched *Herr* Smoke Wade for weapons?"

"Jofwohl, Excellens!" The guard advanced and laid Smoke's own big six-gun on the table between Smoke and Turner.

Von Stolz eyes gleamed as he saw the famous gun.

"*Ach*, what joy I feel at sight of that gun. The old gun of my famous enemy. Smoke Wade. I shall keep it always for a souvenir of my final victory, *nicht wahr?* But to explain my marvelous trick. You know the flames are not flame. *Ja!* Then I go back and tell you of a gas which our chemical warfare department invented a short time ago. It is a deadly gas, but it was learned after much of it had been made hurriedly, that it's lighter than air and rises, therefore making it impossible to use for ground work, because it will not stay on the ground.

"So I invent this use of it. I can tell you this, for we will use it over and over again in our great drives to come. You will never go back—alive. Not before we win the war, *Mein Herren*, so you will not be able to give away the secret."

Smoke was growing tense by the second. The drones of those D.H. bombers, hovering at the other side of the gas wall, was driving him insane. He thought of making a lunge for his six-gun on the table ten feet away. But the muzzles of those Lugers trained upon him held him back, told him it was crazy.

Von Stolz laughed and went on in fiendish delight.

"So you do not know how it is possible to get the gas up in a such straight wall, *ja?* I do it by balloons like the one *Herr* Turner cut loose. These balloons extend on three mile cables and along the cables run tubes with outlets for the gas every hundred feet or so. The gas comes out of all these openings and rises, hiding the balloons at the top."

He turned proudly to a great control valve in a large pipe line that passed through the building.

"By turning this on or off, I control the flow of the white colored gas. It makes a good screen to play my searchlights upon, and these searchlights, placed in front, are fitted with automatic moving red plates that dance up and down and give the effect of licking flames against the white gas. I control the lights from here as well by this switch," He placed his hand on it proudly. "Is it not wonderful, *Mein Herren*?"

"Reckon it sure is," Smoke drawled. His whole body was tense as an E string. The drone of the D.H. bombers was diminishing in volume. They were going away. Returning home with their eggs that must be laid over the supply dump. He was failing.

Frantically, he eyed his six-gun on the table. He never could reach that gun unless—

"But, baron," he said, trying to sound sincere, "there seems to be something wrong with the outfit. The lights are dimming down. See?" He stared out of the window in the building. "They're dying."

Von Stolz gasped and turned toward the window. Smoke's eyes flashed to the four guards at the other end of the room. A restless move from them and they too turned to stare for the briefest second.

SMOKE moved like lightning. He leaped like a panther. His hand was on the butt of his six-gun and flame darted from the muzzle. *Blam! Blam! Blam! Blam!* The shots came so fast they seemed to merge into one roar. He whirled for von Stolz as the four guards crumpled on the floor.

Crack! Hot steel slammed through Smoke's shoulder and almost knocked him off his feet. The shot had come from behind. He spun just as pitch dark filled the room.

"Out the door," he hear Turner yell. "Von Stolz took a crack at you and turned off the lights. Then—"

"I reckon," hissed Smoke. "Quick. Light a match. There, This valve has got to go shut, I reckon. Pronto."

His shoulders, where the bullet had creased him, burned horribly as he struggled, closing the valve.

"Shut and bolt the door," he shouted to Turner as he worked.

He shot a glance out of the window and his heart leaped. The lights were still playing red on the white wall of gas, but the volume of gas was now truly diminishing.

Smoke's hand flashed to the control switch for the lights and he pulled. Instantly, the red lights went out. And with that two other things happened. The droning of Liberty motors increased to a triumphant roar. The 13th was coming back with their eggs now. And another noise came to them that wasn't so pleasant. That was yelling and shouting from outside the building. They were completely surrounded now. Smoke clutched Turner by the arm in the darkness.

"Stick close," he hissed. "We got a minute to work. They won't dare turn on any lights with those bombers going over."

His shoulder pained him terrifically, but he clenched his teeth and tore at the boards of the floor beneath him. One came loose with a groan that was drowned by the yells outside. Another came up. He guided Turner through the opening in the floor; then, flat on their stomachs they crawled under the floor and to the edge of the building.

There Smoke tensed and stared. Pitch black. Men running about the place, shouting in guttural sounds. He pulled Turner with him until they were out and merging with the other dark forms.

In the darkness they couldn't be distinguished from others about the building. Slowly, they worked their way to the edge of the yelling Germans and then broke into a run toward the spot where Smoke judged his pinto Spad should be.

His six-gun was clutched tightly in his hand as he ran. Turner panted beside him. They slowed at the border of the field and peered through a hedge there. The pinto Spad was still there. So were four Germans guarding it. Their forms were dim ahead.

"I'll pick 'em off with the smoke pole," Smoke hissed. "Then you jump for the cockpit while I spin the prop. I can hang on better outside."

Blam! Blam! Blam! Blam! Flame and slugs hurled from the six-gun and four Heinies sprawled before they sensed what had happened. The two dove from their cover. Turner to the cockpit with Smoke's help. Smoke leaped for the prop and whirled. The Hisso grunted.

Frantically, Smoke whirled that prop. Then the Hisso caught and burst into a roar. In a flash, Smoke lay sprawled on a lower wing, close to the fuselage.

"Give him hell," he shouted to Turner.

Turner sure did. The pinto Spad shot across the field and into the air, amid a storm of screaming slugs from behind. Smoke took just long enough to thumb his nose downward and stared toward the north and the enemy store depot.

Flashes of light darted up here and there as the D.H. bombers of the 13th laid their sanguinary eggs. Then the earth seemed to heave in a convulsion. A huge building rose out of the woods below and broke into a million pieces. The ammunition dump of the enemy was gone.

Smoke grinned.

"Reckon thet finishes Heine's drive at Fismes,"

The pinto Spad, with its lanky passenger on the wing and the pilot with one broken arm, hovered about the Front until the D.H.'s of the 13th turned for home. Then they droned back together. There was first aid for Smoke with his creased shoulder, and Turner's arm went in a sling. Then they were all gathered in the mess over bowls of steaming coffee.

"You certainly won that bet. Captain Wade," Bolan admitted, "and we'll pay it just as soon as we can. Maybe two or three months before you get it all. But it'll be worth it if you'll tell us how you were so sure that Turner didn't burn."

Smoke chuckled.

"Fact is, I didn't know nothin' fer sure 'cept thet there wasn't no heat from the flames I got into. But I had to figure some way to bring you birds over with all your bombs. Figurin' on human nature like I know it, I says if they think I'm sure about somethin' and can prove it, they'll come over like I suggest, and yuh done just thet, thank the Lord!"

Bolan laughed.

"I'll say you got our curiosity hot," he said. "After that bet and your offer to prove it and then beating it before we could get any more out of you, it would have taken the whole German army to make us stay home."

Smoke grinned.

“I reckoned so. And about thet bet, boys, just ferget it, sort of. It was just fer effect. I don’t need the money.”

He yawned with a deep-throated yowl, and turned toward the door.

“Reckon I’ll be goin’ now. ‘Bout three hours ago I was right in the middle of a swell dream, I’m goin’ back and see if I can pick it up where I left off,”

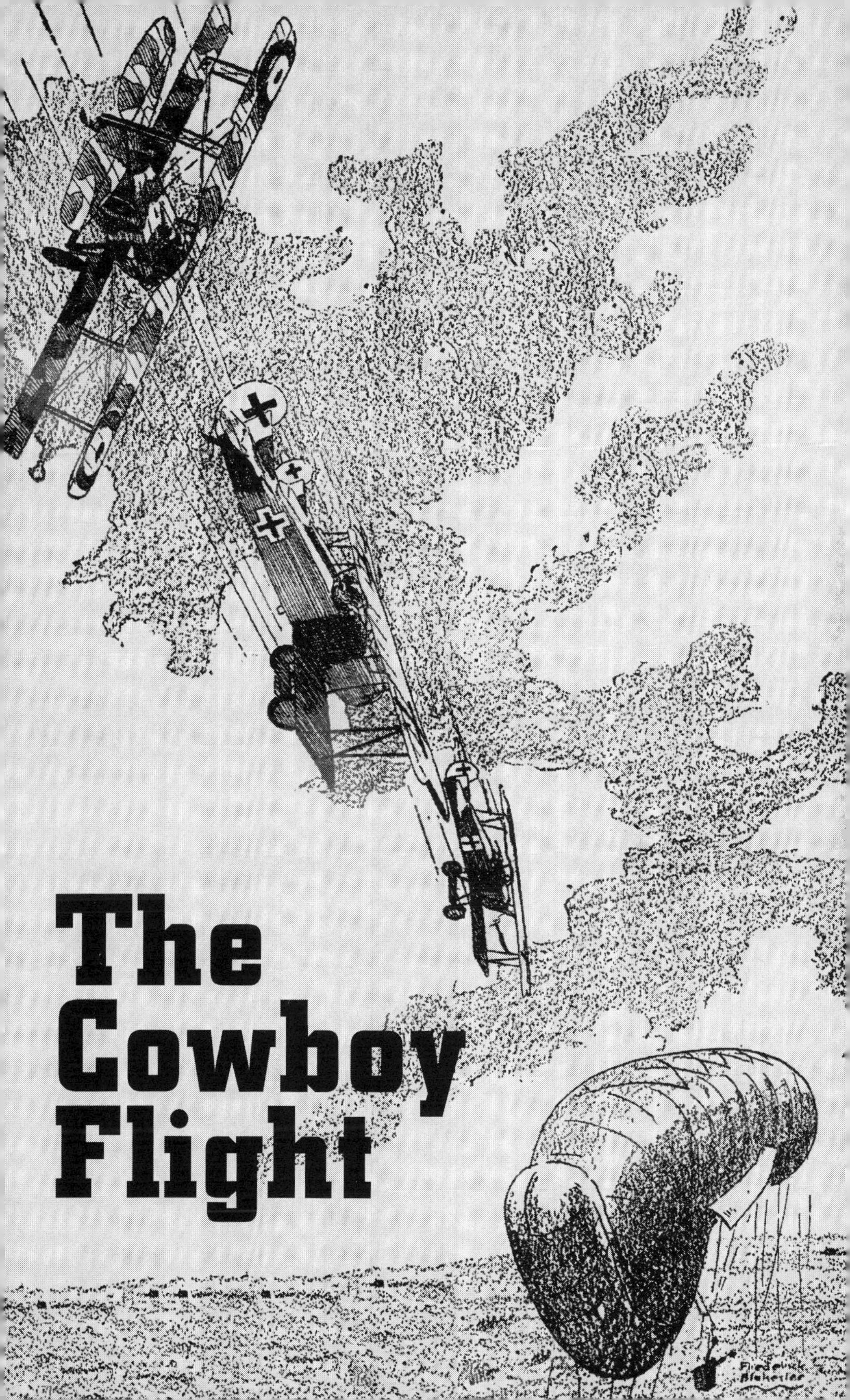
The
Cowboy
Flight

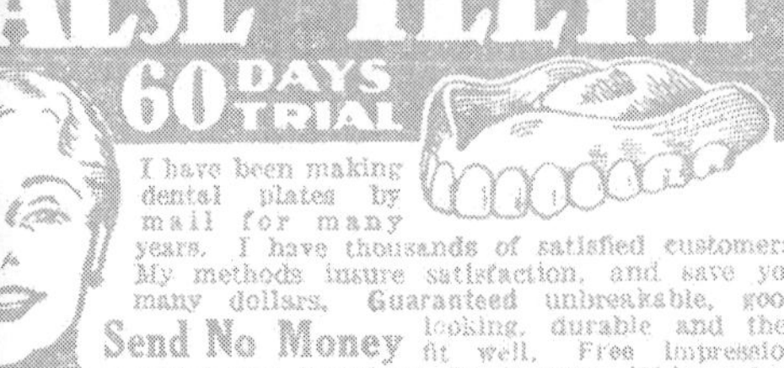

Smoke Wade teams up with a couple of redskin buddies, from out West—and the sky shooting is fast and furious with the Boches on the wrong end of the round-up!

The Cowboy Flight

"PLUMB queer where thet hombre, von Stolz, has slunk to!" Those words, mumbled by Smoke Wade, lanky Arizona skipper of the 66th pursuit, were cut off at his thin lips by the thunder of his Hisso as he swerved his pinto Spad around the edge of a cloud and peered down through slitted eyes. There was a frown of perplexity on his leathery face. He lifted his powerful glasses to his keen gray eyes. "Ain't seen hide nor hair of the von varmint fer maybe ten days or more. Been askin' along the line, and nobody else ain't seen thet red ship of his neither. Somethin's up, I reckon. Von Stolz ain't layin' low, takin' no rest cure. He ain't thet kind no how."

His eyes, peering through the glasses, swerved the focuses on the spot known on the maps of the front as Hill 167. He grunted in disgust as he sighted it, spotted here and there now with German guns, somewhat camouflaged, on the great mound that commanded a view of the surrounding country for miles in every direction.

"This whole war's goin' plumb to hell," he growled. "Why, only day before yesterday, Heinie took thet bump the Frogs call a mountain over here as easy as takin' candy off kids. Cain't figure what's got inter them Yanks of ourn lately. Just folded up their mess kits and started a hike fer Paris right off the nicest gun positions on thet Hill 167 thet I reckon they is along the front."

He banked his Spad, stuck the nose down and shot a quick glance about him. The sky was empty of ships other than that flashing Spad his own expert hand dropped to a lower level. The puzzled expression increased.

"Ain't right, I reckon. 'S why I come out this mornin' to have a look. Ain't a E.A. in sight, and things below is plenty too peaceful. Like the calm before the storm, sort of. Things is goin' to bust wide open directly or I'm a curly-tailed thingamajig."

He left the protection of his cloud and headed south back toward his own drome at Ramou. Constantly, his eyes, through the powerful glasses, roved the enemy lines thousands of feet below. An angry curse sprayed from his lips as he surveyed the ground that had been held by the Yanks, now swarming with Germans. Archie grunted up from the land which should be Allied, grunted up and blasted well below him in mushroom bursts of dirty brownish-yellow smoke that hid the flying death inside.

On toward the Yank lines, the new twisting trenches a mile or more to the south, Smoke's eyes traveled. One lone observation balloon swayed at the end of its cable from behind new Yank lines. Smoke spotted it and glared angrily.

"It don't seem possible thet anything von Stolz could do would have anything to do with our boys losin' so much ground," he drawled. "Why, they walked out and left this before Heinie's advance like a bunch of white-livered kids what was homesick. Von Stolz is clever, but there ain't nothin' of this he might have—"

Smoke's drawl broke off in a short gasp. He came up straight, as though his backbone had suddenly become a crowbar. His narrowed eyes, bulging and straining, were staring through his glasses. And the glasses were focused on the tiny figure in the swaying basket of the balloon.

Instantly the stick of the pinto Spad shot forward. The Hisso screamed in a long dive. Wind whipped at the Spad wings, threatened to tear them away in the headlong plunge.

"What the hell?" he spat. "Never while I've been on the Front have I seen a guy in a balloon basket signalin' with flags to the enemy. Why, the—"

Down, down Smoke streaked in that flashing pinto Spad. He came at the balloon like a hurling meteor from some other planet. Before him in the basket, a figure stood, feet wide apart, braced against his belt. In either hand he held a wigwag signal flag. He was waving them in signal. But strangest of all, the Yank in the basket was facing Hill number 167—now held by the Germans.

Smoke's recollection of the wigwag code was a bit hazy, but now and then he could pick up a letter. Not enough to make sense.

Angrily he whirled his glasses back to the hill and cursed. No one could see those flags from Hill 167 with the naked eye. But if someone were there with powerful glasses like his own they could make out the message very plainly.

"Why, damn a guy with nerve like that," Smoke spat as he roared nearer and nearer the swaying bag. "Think he can get away with sending information, to the Germans in broad daylight, right in sight of the whole Allied Front."

That was what flashed in his mind at first thought. The man was a German spy. Clever way of getting news to Germany. Then came doubt in Smoke Wade's puzzled mind. If this man in the basket was a spy conveying information to the Germans through his flag signals, he was a fool as well. He could see Smoke thundering down on him. Smoke was close enough now so there could be no doubt of that. He even saw the man in the basket glance at him—but the chap went on with his signaling.

A puzzled frown formed on Smoke's brow. He roared close and flashed past the balloon and its basket. He saw the balloonist grasp his two flags in one hand and wave him away with the other with a trace of irritation.

Around in a tight vertical and Smoke roared back. Again the man in the basket signaled him to keep away. Then at the end of that last sweeping gesture with his hand, the balloonist pointed higher and to the northeast.

Instantly, Smoke whirled in his seat and stared in that direction. The sight that met his eyes only increased his perplexity the more. For out of the northeast, hurling hell bent for the balloon, but still well off, a flight of five Fokkers romped down to the kill, straight for the swaying Allied bag.

SMOKE spun his head and stared back at the balloonist. He was waving his flags wildly. The balloon was still hanging high in the air, but now it was going down, with Yank wench crews working like mad far below.

The pinto Spad banked over and headed straight for that snarling mess of five Fokkers that stormed down. Smoke hunched over his stick. No sound came from his lips. His brain was in a fog. He couldn't seem to think straight. Couldn't begin to figure the thing out clearly. A man in a Yankee uniform signaling with flags, signaling into Germany.

Five Fokkers and that pinto Spad thundered at each other at their combined speeds of nearly three hundred miles an hour. Fokkers, at first mere specks, grew larger before Smoke with astonishing speed. There was the rattle of Spandau guns as Jerry pilots tramped down on their triggers and warmed their death-dealers.

Smoke answered with a staccato of his own deadly Vickers. Still befogged. Still uncertain—wondering—almost mad with curiosity. But Smoke Wade would never let those five Jerry planes down a balloon so long as it had the Yank insignia on it.

At first glance, he had hoped that the lead plane of that Fokker flight might be the crimson crate of von Stolz. If so it would solve one problem. It would tell him that von Stolz wasn't up to some deviltry away from the Front. Some hidden menace that would be, of certainty, a deadly one.

But no crimson plane led the flight. Every Fokker in the flight was painted the same color. Bright green, splashed with dashes of orange. A single flight from some routine *jadgstaffel.*

Every second that flashed by brought those two enemies more than a hundred yards nearer each other. Smoke shot a glance over his shoulder and down. That was where the balloon was now—down and going down much faster. And there in the basket, still waving wildly, the lone balloonist swayed.

"What in hell's he wavin' at?" Smoke growled. "Thet's what I'd like to know. And what I'm mighty soon goin' to find out directly, if my aim ain't so bad."

Almost within range now. Smoke tensed over his stick and waited. His hand poised over his trigger button, but his eyes were not across his sights. And his leathery, Arizona-bronzed face was wrinkled in ever so slight a grin.

His stick arm moved and his legs on the rudder bar. They were the only parts of his body that ceased to remain motionless. The effect on the pinto Spad was like magic. Still just out of range of those droning murder-makers, the pinto Spad leaped into the air. It screamed half over in a loop. The controls moved again with the same expert, accurate precision, and the Spad half rolled. All this in two seconds of time.

Fokkers, taken by surprise, saw their danger too late. Smoke had executed his trick so expertly and so quickly that they were wholly unwarned of their danger until it was too late.

They roared straight on in their dive for the rapidly lowering balloon. Straight through the place where Smoke Wade had been a moment before they tore, and now a pinto Spad, with the fierceness of a demon from hell, was screaming on their tails.

The leader shot a wild, frightened glance over his shoulder. The two Fokkers at the tip veered away in consternation before the downward lunge of Smoke's pinto Spad.

Now Smoke was glaring across his sights. His trigger button slammed home, and Vickers guns bucked and rattled as tracers fluffed out before the pinto's nose.

There was a slight movement of the rudder, two short bursts from Smoke's Vickers, and the two Fokkers directly behind their lead, the two that had held their formation, plunged for earth and eternal darkness.

Bam! The nose of Smoke's pinto dropped still lower. He sent a spray of flaming steel at one of the fleeing Fokkers, swung back for the leader and punched down.

Again came that frightened stare from the leader of the Fokker flight. A leader alone now. His teeth clenched. There was fright written on that German's round face, but there was brave determination as well as he saw death reaching out for him.

The bag was going lower and lower. Smoke caught a glimpse of the balloonist still working frantically with his flags, all the while facing Germany and toward Hill 167. Queer. But no time to figure that out now. The lone Fokker leader had turned forward in his seat and was punching down straight for the bag.

"Hate to blast a gutty guy like you out the sky, Heinie," Smoke drawled. "Hate to do it, but I got to do somethin', if you're set on murder yourself."

Before and below him the desperate Jerry leader was making a frantic effort, flying in a crazy zigzag course to reach the lowering balloon. Game fellow. Clever flyer. A good reason perhaps why he had been made leader of his *Kampflugg* in Germany.

Smoke shot a glance at the other two remaining Fokkers. They were dim specks to the north now, fleeing for home. Perhaps new men with orders to run if the going got hot.

Smoke was hurling down, taking careful aim. Hard aiming at that irregularly swerving target before him. And when he tramped down on his trigger button he did it with a half prayer that the shot wouldn't be vital.

A cloud of smoke belched from the side of the Mercedes cowling. Black smoke, but no flame. The propeller of the Fokker stopped straight across with an apparent grunt. The Fokker nosed down for a forced landing. It was well behind Yank lines. No hope of ever getting back to Germany. Smoke grinned.

"Ain't right to kill a gutty guy like you outright, Jerry," he mouthed. "Reckon yuh won't get treated bad. Ain't enough birds with guts in this world, say nothin' of in Germany."

The Fokker pilot made a fair landing south of the balloon wench, cracked a wing and nosed over. Smoke saw men running to his aid and capture. He swept the ground below for a possible chance of getting his own plane down safely. Everywhere was the mark of war. Shell holes and blasted earth. Not much chance of landing right there, if he didn't have to.

"I reckon," he mused, "best thing I can do is to go to general headquarters and see General Banks. Maybe he might like to know about this here signalin' to Germany. Right now I don't reckon this here balloonatic is a spy nor nothin' like thet, but I'm plumb curious."

IT WAS nearly a quarter of an hour later that Smoke Wade barged down on the little field near the general headquarters office where his friend, General Banks, commanded, and set the pinto Spad gently on the sod.

Smoke was calmly untangling his long legs from around the controls and getting to the ground when he stopped short and gaped down the field. The moving figure which had attracted his sudden attention was small. A man dressed in the garb of a Yank pilot.

"Well, I'll be a rip-snortin—"

A shake of his head cut off the words.

"Nope," he said, "must be I'm beginnin' to see things, but thet sure looks plenty like him. Yes, sir. Enough to be his twin brother, I reckon."

Once more he turned and stared at the figure climbing into the plane, another Spad that had been warming on the line when Smoke had landed. The man was entirely hidden by his flying togs. Only his mouth and chin were visible below the big goggles.

"It don't seem possible," Smoke mused with another shake of his head. "Don't seem possible thet two hombres could walk with thet same strut and swagger, like a cock-sure game rooster, but—"

On his arrival in General Banks' outer office, Smoke waited only a moment; he was admitted to the private office of the great general almost immediately.

Gray, old, shaggy-browed General Banks seemed very worn and tired as he tried to smile at Smoke. The big cowboy ace grinned across the desk.

"General," he drawled, "this here is sort of queer, what I come to see you about, and I reckon somethin' almost as queer just happened out on the field. So I'm here sort of askin' questions about two things what I'm plumb curious about."

General Banks nodded wearily.

"Go ahead, Smoke. Ask all you like," he said.

At once Smoke explained the strange sight he had seen over the Front, not half an hour before, the balloon observer signaling into Germany.

"Reckon thet's the funniest thing ever I did see," he finished. "Cain't figure no reason fer a balloonist signalin' Heinies from his basket. Ain't there no other way to send them a message? Already, from what I hear, they do plenty of interceptin' of our codes without our permission, say nothin' of messages they maybe might have a good right to hear that was fer them."

The great general nodded slightly, and his face took on an even more worried look.

"That is one of the main troubles right now, Smoke," he said. "I can explain that signaling, but we were trying to keep it a secret." He smiled. "Blast you, Smoke. You're the kind that makes it hard to keep secrets.

Thank the Lord the enemy haven't anyone just like you or we'd have a tougher time than we already have. But first, before I explain, tell me the second queer thing you have in mind."

Smoke nodded, opened his mouth to speak, but two things interrupted his next words. The one was someone coming into the office of General Banks. The other was the blast of a Hisso motor outside on the little field that adjoined G.H.Q.

Smoke spun and faced the officer that had so suddenly come in. He was a major. He stopped short when he saw Smoke, shifted his eyes apologetically to General Banks.

"Pardon me, general. I didn't know you were in conference. You told me to advise you at once when the half of the code had gone." He jerked his head toward the disappearing thunder of the Hisso motor outside. "Special agent 5-B is just leaving by plane for Paris with Section A of the emergency code. You can hear him taking the air."

General Banks nodded.

"Thank you, major," he said. "Thanks very much for informing me." He took a long breath. "Let's hope things will be better from now on. That's all for now, major."

The major left and closed the door behind him. General Banks seemed relieved when he nodded to Smoke to proceed.

At first Smoke laughed a little sheepishly.

"Maybe you'll think I'm crazy, general," he admitted. "I do myself, but then you can't tell, and the more I been turnin' this here over in my mind, since what I seen, the funnier it makes me feel."

Banks sat forward a little more tensely.

"It come just as I was climbin' out of my pinto Spad," Smoke went on. "Course I've seen lots of pilots walkin' to their crates and that, but this hombre struck me sort of queer. Maybe I should have gone up and investigated right there, but it seemed so impossible thet—"

General Banks nodded with a trace of irritation.

"Never mind the apologies. Smoke," he frowned. "Go on and tell me what you saw or think you saw."

"Cain't be sure," Smoke drawled, "but if thet hombre what was walkin' to thet Spad wasn't von Stolz in Yank flyin' togs, then von Stolz has got a twin what don't vary a hair from the baron in his walk and swagger—" he sighed deeply—"but I reckon it's just a pipe dream. Maybe it's because I've missed him over the Front fer close to two weeks now, and it's got me seein' things."

General Banks smiled.

"I guess that must be the explanation, Smoke," he ventured. "Certainly that man wouldn't be von Stolz, not here at general headquarters."

"Reckon not," Smoke agreed, "but you don't know thet hombre like I do, general. He's one clever rat. Maybe I better ferget about this here, though, and put it down fer a pipe dream. You was goin' to tell me how come a balloonist was signalin' with flags into Germany."

"Yes," said General Banks. "I will, since you've blundered into something that was supposed to be kept secret. Of course we don't mind your knowing, Smoke, but we've been trying to keep it under cover. You'll understand better when you know the details."

GENERAL BANKS settled back in his chair, jerked his head to another chair which Smoke took, and began.

"You know, Smoke," he said, "we've been trying to figure some strategic movement that would take the enemy by surprise and go a long way toward ending the war quickly. I believe we have hit upon that plan, except for one thing. The wheels are already in motion, but I don't mind telling you we're in a considerable jam.

"Perhaps you thought the taking of Hill 167 by the enemy was too easy to look like the real thing."

Smoke nodded.

"Let's hope the enemy didn't look at it like that," Banks continued. "At any rate our crack Regiment, the 64th, is still in what is now Germany."

Smoke stared, "Huh?" he said.

"That's right." Banks affirmed. "Here's what happened. While we held Hill 167, we built, unknown to the enemy, huge quarters in the mountain there to house the whole regiment. They were left there in hiding with supplies for a week or more. They have all the necessary guns and ammunition to retake that hill and blast the Germans much farther back than they were before; that is, if—"

He leaned forward across the desk tensely.

"If the order can get through to them to attack at the same time we are ready to strike from our present position, well south of Hill 167. You see, Germany has moved two of her crack regiments to hold the position given up by our forces. If those two crack regiments of the enemy are taken, the effect on the enemy will be demoralizing. The time set for that drive is tomorrow morning at dawn, but we don't dare send the order. That was what the balloonist you chanced to see was trying to put over to the men of the 64th. He was trying to inform them that they were not to send any more messages to us."

Smoke stared blankly. He shook his head.

"Reckon, maybe, I'm pretty dumb, general," he admitted. "I just cain't follow yuh no how."

"You will. Listen. You know the German Intelligence is very efficient."

"Too damned efficient and clever," Smoke snorted.

"Right," Banks came back, "But we've got to meet them and here's the truth. From test messages we've sent out we know that the enemy have practically every one of our codes and can read them."

"Huh?" gasped Smoke. "Yuh mean to say there ain't no way to send orders fer the attack to the 64th regiment without the Germans bein' able to decode 'em and learn just as much about what's goin' on as we know?"

General Banks nodded.

"Exactly, Smoke. That's the horrible part of this mess. But we have one hope left. Of course, we can't go ahead with our plans. For success the attack must come from our forces behind our present front line trenches and those boys in their dugout quarters under the top of Hill 167 where they're hiding. If we fail to get the message through without the enemy knowing it, the 64th may run out of food. Then, no telling what they may do. Of course we're in communication with them or can be, but the condition is just about as bad or perhaps worse than if all wireless intercourse were cut off entirely. We have one hope left."

Smoke's eyes narrowed.

"And I reckon thet last course is the emergency code I heard about just now on its way to Paris," he guessed.

"Correct," General Banks admitted. "In order to avoid all possible chance of this code being intercepted we held half of the code, section A, here at G.H.Q. The other half is at Staff headquarters in Paris. Section A is on its way to Paris now, should be there any minute; then orders will be sent in this new code for the attack to start at dawn tomorrow morning by both our forces on this side of the lines and the 64th regiment in Hill 167. If the enemy should get hold of this code, well, I'm afraid we're sunk and we'll lose the finest regiment that ever fought."

The worry was back on Smoke Wade's leathery face. He jumped as though shot when the door to General Banks' office opened and the same major who had come in before, bolted through.

He was wild-eyed, staring, panting.

"General," he cried. "General. The code. It's gone. Special Agent 5-B didn't take the papers. Someone else about his size has got them and left in that plane. We just found Special Agent 5-B knocked out and stowed in a closet off his office. His papers are gone. I passed the wrong man. He looked like 5-B with his flying togs on. I looked over his papers and passed him. He left for Paris in that Spad. He—"

General Banks was clutching his phone in trembling hands. Frantically he slammed the hook to get a clear wire. A blank, ghastly expression crossed his wrinkled face. He slammed the phone to the desk again and leaped to his feet.

"Phone's gone dead. Somebody cut the wires, perhaps. Can't get Paris. Can't get anything."

Smoke Wade was on his feet too. Half way to the door, he hitched his big six-gun a little higher on his right leg.

"Von Stolz," he barked. "I knowed I should have looked into thet hombre with his swagger."

"Smoke!" General Banks voice cracked out like a whip lash. "If that was von Stolz you're the only man who can save us in this. Hurry. Fly to Paris. Get to staff headquarters and stop von Stolz before he gets away. He'll have the whole code with him. Our last hope. We'll be cut off from the 64th as though they weren't on earth at all. Hurry, for the love of heaven."

Those last words were very dim as Smoke left. He was almost out of earshot of the general's voice. Headlong, he raced out of G.H.Q., dove through the main doors past astonished guards and headed for his waiting pinto Spad.

In every step he cursed himself for not investigating the owner of that familiar, boastful swagger of von Stolz. Everything was lost now, unless—unless he could get von Stolz before he left Paris with the code.

A wild leap carried Smoke over the edge of his pinto Spad cockpit into the seat. Already he had yelled to a mechanic. The propeller of the Hisso whirled and the engine barked. Smoke tensed at the gun, fed it forward slowly, angry that he must wait a little for the engine to grow slightly warmer. It had cooled off during his visit with the general.

That was a fortunate pause. Down the tarmac, General Banks puffed his way toward Smoke. He held out a slip of paper with words and his signature written upon it.

"Take this," he panted. "It'll get you through quicker. God's best luck, son. Thousands of lives are depending upon you."

Smoke gave a short nod, stuffed the paper inside his jacket and battered the gun wide open. With a wild roar the Hisso leaped into full being, and the pinto Spad shot across the field into the wind.

IT SEEMED that the Spad was only crawling on its way to Paris. It was only a few minutes' flight from the little field outside General Headquarters to the great Le Bourget field on the outskirts of Paris, but those few minutes that passed seemed like years to Smoke Wade.

Smoke never waited to circle the great field where ships filled the air above almost constantly. He dove straight down, took his wind direction from the landing T as he came down, found he was coming in cross wind, cocked on one ear to make up for the drift and touched wheels and skid smoothly.

He was out of his cockpit before the pinto Spad finished her roll. Desperately he shot a glance about the place for a Yank uniform—found one on a first lieutenant and ran toward him.

"See anything of a Spad landing here in the last ten minutes?" Smoke bellowed, still far away. "See a guy land with a funny cocky swagger to his walk? A little guy what wouldn't look out of place with a monocle in one pig eye?"

The lieutenant scrutinized Smoke for an instant, then shook his head. Smoke whirled and shot a glance down the line of ships along the field.

"A black ship with a red nose," Smoke pursued hopefully.

Again the lieutenant shook his head.

"It happens I'm in charge in incoming ships here," he said. "No ship of that description has landed here. Was it expected in Le Bourget? There's several other fields around here."

Smoke hesitated for an instant. His head was spinning.

"Get on the phone and call every field near enough to Paris to matter. Have them hold a black Spad with a red nose and hold the pilot that comes to claim it. Get that straight?"

The lieutenant paused. "Who's giving these orders?" he asked.

"Name's Wade. Captain Smoke Wade, and if that isn't enough," Smoke snapped, "here." He stuck the note from General Banks in front of the astonished eyes of the lieutenant. There was a quick salute and the lieutenant was off. Once more Smoke showed the brief order to clear the roads for Captain Smoke Wade. This time he got a motorcycle and sidecar and plopped into the seat.

"Staff headquarters, pronto, and tear off the tires, cowboy," he barked in the rider's ear.

Down in a cloud of dust, then zigzag through lanes of yipping taxies they tore. Once Smoke glanced at the rider in the saddle above him. The swarthy face was calm, slightly grinning as the expert hands guided the motorcycle through spots that seemed inches too small.

There came a sudden swerve of the machine and a squeal of brakes. The rider grinned at Smoke, shaking himself in the seat.

"Staff headquarters, sir," the driver said.

"An' how!" Smoke amended.

He was out like a shot and barging up to the massive door that stood closed behind four guards. The guards came to "present arms." Smoke stuck the note from General Banks before one. An instant for reading and he passed.

Inside, other guards stopped him. Again the note of authority and Smoke's voice cracked his demands.

"Reckon I'll see the head of the Intelligence right pronto. It's damned important."

The guard jerked his head for Smoke to follow. They passed down the long corridor and turned left. At an office door, the guard knocked. There was a brief pause and then the door opened. A small, frowning man blinked. Before he could say a word, Smoke thrust forward his note from Banks. The Intelligence officer nodded and motioned him in. He closed the door and they were alone.

"Got to see the head of Intelligence right now," Smoke began.

The little man before him frowned still more.

"He's busy right now. You'll have to wait unless you can tell me your business."

Smoke tensed. His big fists closed and opened again. Then, with a sense of futility, he nodded.

"O.K. If you're lookin' fer a load of trouble to handle, get a load of this. Special Agent 5-B just flew down here from G.H.Q. and brought section A of the emergency code. Probably you know this much, maybe not."

The other nodded with a trace of irritation.

"Of course I know it. I handled the matter myself. What of it?"

"You handled it yourself?" Smoke barked. "Well, get a load of this. That guy who came down here to get Section B of the code and make it complete wasn't special agent 5-B."

The little man stared. "Wasn't 5-B?" he demanded. "Why, you're crazy. I examined his credentials. Everything was O.K. I gave him section B of the code to make the complete set, and he left fifteen minutes ago to take the complete code to our wireless station on the roof of this building. He said he had already delivered section A to the wireless officer. I checked up on that and found that he had. So I gave him section B, as was called for in orders. But I haven't the slightest idea what business this is of a captain of airplane pilots."

Smoke's face purpled.

"Never mind that for now," he snapped. "Listen. I reckon you called the wireless officer at the station and made sure that the section B reached him O.K. after it left your office. In the pig's ear you did."

The little man stiffened.

"See here," he said indignantly, "Perhaps you don't know who you're addressing. I'm Morton, second in command here at the staff headquarters Intelligence Department. You'll address me hereafter in the manner befitting my position, and I've a good mind to—to have you thrown out."

"Throw and be damned," Smoke barked. "I don't care if you're the

King of England himself and the President of the U.S.A. to boot. You've had a fast one pulled on you, and I'm here to straighten it out. Now, get this. That wasn't 5-B what come here with section A. I don't give a damn what papers he had. Thet was the Baron von Stolz, one of the cleverest Heinie's in these parts, and I don't mean perhaps. Ever hear of von Stolz, Morton?"

Morton's face went white.

"You—you don't mean von Stolz, the famous ace?" he stammered. "That's absurd. How could he? How—"

"Don't matter how. Reckon he's on his way to Germany right now with the code, thinkin' we never caught on."

"RIDICULOUS," stormed Morton in self-defense. "That's impossible. I called the wireless officer about section B after 5-B had left my office. He said he had just received both sections, A and B, of the emergency code. The 64th have that code and orders will begin to go out tonight. Full orders for the attack tomorrow morning. Now get out before I lose my temper."

A thin smile crossed Smoke's face at that.

"Reckon maybe I had better go, seein' as how I cain't get nothin' out of you, Morton," he drawled. "But first, I want to mention this, in case you ain't thought of it. Von Stolz is clever, like a lot more of our Intelligence ought to be. Reckon he copied them two sections of the code, the last one on the way to the wireless station. Catch on?"

Morton shook his head and moved as though to push Smoke toward the door.

"That's impossible," he said. "He didn't have time."

Smoke chuckled then for the first time.

"Oh, hell, Morton, I don't mean he took a pencil and paper and copied it," he said. "Von Stolz wouldn't take that much trouble. What he'd do is photograph both of 'em with a little camera. Thet wouldn't take much time, Morton."

Morton sputtered.

"Yeah," cut in Smoke, "the only trouble with some of you birds is thet you got your jobs through some kind of pull, some of yuh, and you're so damned scart of losin' 'em you'd send hundreds of Yanks to hell rather than admit you're wrong. Tell yuh what I'll do. I'll lay yuh a little bet, and if you ain't a yellow-backed coyote, like I think yuh are, you'll take me up."

Morton's eyes blazed. He stood rigid.

"I'll bet yuh ten thousand francs, Morton, thet right now this here emergency code is on the way to Germany. I'll add to that, that this emergency code will never be sent to the 54th regiment, and just to make it look hard I'll lay my money thet a code goes over the air to the stranded 64th thet never was put in dots and dashes before, and if I'm wrong in any one of the three, you win the money. What yuh got to say, Morton? You game or just a yellow mug?"

Morton was shaking with rage. His fists clenched. He was nodding his head angrily.

"I'll take it," he said tightly. "I never heard crazier talk in my life."

Smoke brushed past him and reached for the phone with the faintest trace of a smile on his lips.

After much trouble he got the lieutenant at Le Bourget on the other end of the line and asked what luck he had had in tracing and holding the black Spad with the red nose.

"Got a report from the home defense field at LeCour. They had a ship land there. It took off just before I called—headed north."

Smoke cursed and hung up. He tried General Banks at headquarters. Wires must have been hurriedly put back in condition, for he got an answer almost immediately. He explained what had happened, and General Banks promised to come to Paris at once.

Smoke's third call had been inspired just before he made the bet with Morton. He called a signal detachment at the Front and asked to speak to two members of the company there. His face clouded as he got the answer.

"On leave?" he gasped. "Why, hell, what do they need leave for? Them two hombres don't need no rest."

The answer that came back was wholly unsatisfactory. They were simply on leave. The speaker at the other end didn't know or give a damn why.

Smoke's face clouded. His hands shook a little from the start the information had given him.

"Yuh—yuh wouldn't know where Joe and Tom Buck did go, would yuh?" he stammered desperately.

"They've gone to Paris, I think," came the reply.

Paris. Two men in Paris who could hold the key to success or failure of the desperate plan that Smoke had laid.

Morton watched him go toward the door like a man in a daze. Smoke never spoke to Morton on his way out or to anyone else. His face was vacant. He must find two friends from the West back in the States. Two friends, Joe and Tom Buck, who alone could save the 64th Regiment and turn what seemed now certain defeat into victory.

He walked for a block, as though surrounded by fog. He started for a gendarme, cursed and gave it up. He wasn't much on French. He'd have a lot to explain before a gendarme would even begin to know what he was talking about or what these two signal corps men might look like.

TEN minutes of fruitless searching along the boulevards then suddenly he jerked upright and stared at an approaching vehicle. It was an old horse-drawn victoria with a team hitched in front. The horses were coming at a gallop, and astride each horse sat a bronze, coppery-colored Yank with high cheek bones, riding like a wild Indian. Again and again wild yells and whoops belched from their lips as they weaved in and out of the traffic.

Smoke stopped, stared, gulped, blinked and let out a wild whoop in answer as they swung down the boulevard toward him. Gendarmes raced out before the charging horses, only to dart back out of the way while they had time.

A roaring laugh escaped Smoke's lips. He leaped to the edge of the curbing, tensed and then swung and leaped with the expert movement of the trained horseman born to the saddle.

His lanky form shot up on the nigh horse directly behind the rider. There was a quick exchange of glances, grins from the yelling copper-skinned devils and they charged on.

"Staff headquarters," Smoke yelled in their ears.

They nodded, shot up floppy salutes and yelled on, with crowds scurrying from before their wild charge. Smoke whirled on the rump of his horse, leaped clear and landed with a thud in the lap of the fear-paralyzed driver in the seat of the victoria.

The victoria skidded as they whirled about a waving gendarme and shot down the street toward staff headquarters. Smoke clutched the side of the swaying carriage and half stood, peering ahead. He gasped as he saw a figure climbing out of a car before Staff with the flag of a general. It looked like General Banks. It was. The general was staring aghast at the oncoming spectacle.

A swerve in the course of the victoria with the two figures on their charging horses—the heads of the horses came up and they reared. The victoria stopped and Smoke was out like a flash. He reached up, grasped Tom Buck, the taller of the two brothers, by the arm and jerked him from his horse. He yelled at Joe Buck, the stockier brother, to get down. Then he turned to General Banks, grinning.

"General," he said, apologetically, "this here looks maybe like a wild West show, but we was in a hurry after I found these two friends of mine, so we come just as fast as we could."

General Banks blustered. He stared from one grinning face to another.

"Well! Well, I should say so. What in the devil's the meaning of this foolishness?"

The driver of the victoria was demanding his money. Smoke whirled, stuffed a handful of franc notes into his pocket and grinned again at General Banks.

"Reckon I can mighty soon tell yuh, if we get away from this here crowd what's gathered and get where we can talk."

The general led the way inside the staff headquarters building with some hesitancy. A guard found them an office. They went inside and closed the door. Banks surveyed Smoke and his two companions. A smile crossed his face then.

"In a hurry to get here, eh?" he demanded. "I should think so, but it looks to me as though these two friends of yours were seeing Paris, Western style."

"Maybe you're right," Smoke chuckled, "but thet part of it ain't important. Fact is, this, general. Von Stolz got away with thet code this afternoon, like I told yuh, but I got a plan thet maybe is goin' to save the day. You said there ain't no code left now that Heinie ain't got. This trick von Stolz pulled settled thet. But I got a code. Joe and Tom Buck here is old friends of mine from back in Arizona, and they got a code what I ain't goin' to mention right now. Had too many German spies around already. Cain't tell. They might even have a dictaphone in this room. So all I'm goin' to ask is thet you see thet things is carried out on schedule. You know, fer the drive at dawn. I'm goin' to take one of these Buck boys with me and we're goin' to be ready to receive the messages and full orders by midnight tonight."

General Banks frowned in puzzlement.

Tom Buck stepped forward, with his brother Joe beside him.

"Where Smoke Wade goes, we both go," said Tom.

Smoke grinned. "Them is nice words all right, but it can't be done tonight. Both you boys know your wireless. I know thet because I remembered you was doin' thet ticker stuff with the signal corps. I'm takin'—" he glanced from one to the other. Joe Buck was more solidly built than his brother—"you with me, Joe. Tom, you'll stay here and send out the orders for the 64th as I tell you to. Joe and me, we'll be at the other end of the line, never mind where. You just send when the brass hats give you what to send in. Reckon Joe and me'll be where we're goin' by midnight. Start any time after that."

"But-but," stammered General Banks, "I don't understand this at all. What the devil are you getting at, Smoke?"

"A code, general," Smoke answered. "A code that Heinie never will catch on to, and one that damn few other people would know. Thet's what you want, ain't it?"

General Banks nodded. "But—" he objected.

"Never you mind thet right now, general," Smoke cut in. "You know you can trust me. Our backs is to the wall right now, and we're about sunk. All right. I got a way out, and I ain't even explainin' it to you, fer fear somebody might be listenin'. All you got to do is two things. Put Tom Buck here up in the radio station to send and give him the full orders. The other is to tell me how I can get entrance to this here dugout joint on the other side."

"Good Lord!" exclaimed Banks, "you're not going to try to get to the 64th—over there?"

Smoke grinned slightly.

"Somebody's got to be there what understands the code what Tom is goin' to send, ain't they? I reckon Joe and me'll get along—somehow."

For a moment General Banks' eyes softened and blurred. He laid a gentle hand on Smoke's broad shoulder.

"God bless you, son," he said. "I'll—do it."

Once, before Smoke Wade and Joe Buck left staff headquarters, Smoke gave orders to Tom. The orders came in just one word whispered close to the big, bronze ear of the leaner Buck brother.

Tom grinned when he heard and nodded.

"After midnight I send," he said.

IT WAS dusk when Smoke and Joe Buck raced toward Le Bourget in a Paris taxi. In the dimming light, Smoke took out the map of the dug-out city on Hill 167 and studied it. He pointed to the position marked with an X.

"Joe, that's where we get in, I reckon. Take a good look and remember the location. A big rock that rolls pretty easily and leaves an opening to pass through."

"I'll remember all right," Joe assured.

"Good," said Smoke. "It'll be your last chance to look at this map." He struck a match, touched it to the paper and let it burn until only a blank corner was left. Then he dropped it out the window.

A D.H. was waiting for them at Le Bourget by Banks' orders. Wind whistled under the wings as they roared into the night. Smoke studied a map of the country around Hill 167 and tucked the map in the side of the fuselage and droned on.

Darkness smothered them as they roared over the Front. He climbed steadily. Searchlights shot up from Germany and tried to hunt them out, but the ship was too high.

Without hesitation, Smoke reached for the gun and pulled it back. The engine idled and died. He cut the switch and peered down into the blackness. Very dimly he could make out the field he had picked from the map. He gripped the stick a little tighter. Landing was going to be tough in this darkness. He could just make out the open space. Couldn't tell anything about the smoothness of the ground.

Wheels touched softly. The ship rolled. There came a groan of the undercarriage and the D.H. swerved. Struts cracked and gave way.

Smoke cursed. The tail came up and went over with a silly *kerwumph* that left them hanging by their belts.

Joe Buck was out before Smoke could get his long legs untangled.

"You all right, Smoke?" he hissed.

"O.K., Joe. Let's get out of here."

Smoke pitched out on his head, and together they ran, half crouched, for the cover of trees. They heard shouts from the far side of the field and the sound of running feet.

Together, they gained the shelter of the brush and trees and turned instantly toward a great dark blotch before them. Still they heard shouts from behind. A brilliant light flashed and picked them out of the inkiness about them. A shot cracked out as they dove for closer cover.

They tensed in the shadow. A truck rumbled up. Men were yelling behind.

"Quick!" Smoke hissed. "On the truck."

They leaped out, reached the tail of the truck and ducked under the camouflaged tarpaulin. Once the truck halted for a sentry, was identified and moved along toward the Front and Hill 167.

Smoke peered from under the canvas and clutched Joe Buck's arm.

"This is our stop, Joe," he whispered.

Silently they dropped to the road. Before them loomed the great hill. They were trapped now, unless everything was a success. Trapped with the 64th Regiment waiting for death or capture—or victory.

Cautiously, they climbed the slope. Here and there they heard guttural voices. They avoided them. Gun crews waiting to blast Yank lines, newly thrown up.

Joe Buck stopped short and clutched Smoke's arm. It was pitch dark, but somehow this early American could see.

"There is a rock—there," he hissed.

They reached the rock, hardly thirty feet from a German gun placement. For a long time they tensed there beside the big stone, then they put their shoulders against it and pushed. The stone moved as though on a hinge. An opening was disclosed through which they crawled, then turned the stone in its former position.

They found themselves in a large corridor that curved a few feet from the secret entrance. Groping their way they made the turn, went on until they struck something soft and yielding. Canvas. A curtain.

It moved to one side, and Smoke stared and blinked in the light. Before him men leaped to their feet—but silently. Men, men, men. Guns and ammunition. Artillery pieces, ready to be dragged out to service. It took only a few moments to explain to the colonel who confronted them who they were and why they were there. Men would have cheered, but for the order for that ghastly, maddening silence and suspense. Joe Buck took his seat at the wireless sets.

MIDNIGHT! Joe was tensing at his ear-phones and key. Smoke leaned anxiously over his shoulder.

"We haven't gotten a message from headquarters for nearly twenty-four hours," the colonel told them in a shaky voice.

Smoke clenched his teeth and didn't answer. Perhaps the set was dead. Perhaps—Joe Buck jerked up suddenly and nodded.

"Coming," he whispered. "Very faint. Everybody still. There!"

He tuned and tuned again. He nodded once, twice more; then suddenly he began to write rapidly. The colonel stared over his shoulder as before.

"What the devil is that stuff?" he demanded of Smoke.

"New code," Smoke grinned. "You'll know as soon as my friend decodes it. Wait."

On and on. Again and again Joe Buck took the message to make sure he had it right. Night wore on. He tore the phones from his head and began to make a copy of the last message taken. Once through, he handed the message to the colonel. The colonel read and nodded.

"At five. That's the zero hour." There was grateful relief in his voice. A chance to fight at last. He gave orders to his officers in hushed tones. Guns began to move toward various hidden exits. Smoke and Joe Buck, their work done, each snatched a machine gun and were among the first to burst from the openings when the signal was given. What followed is history.

Two crack regiments of the German forces, caught between the 64th on Hill 167, and the Yanks advancing from the south, surrendered in their astonishment when they found they were trapped. Yanks poured up Hill 167 and over it. Artillery of the 64th, set up on the Hill after machine guns had cleared the way, blasted Bocheland far to the north.

And in the wake of the advancing Yank horde came General Banks, Tom Buck and Morton. Banks was jubilant, but puzzled. Morton was angry and chagrined. Tom Buck just smiled.

Smoke Wade grinned at all three. He was covered with sweat and dirt, and a trickle of blood oozed down his face from a scalp wound, but he didn't seem to notice that.

"Well," he demanded of Morton, "do I win thet bet or don't I?"

Morton nodded.

"You win all right," he admitted. "The Germans got that first Special code, for we tried a test message. We radioed in that code for the troops two miles east of here to prepare for a drive, warning them first not to. The enemy got it all right, because they drew some of their forces away from this immediate sector to protect that. But what I want to know," he flared, "is what in the name of common sense that jumble of grunts and groans, was that Buck sent on the air."

"That's what I want to know too," General Banks cut in.

"Sounded like a lot of foolishness to me," Morton snorted.

Smoke chuckled.

"Maybe damn foolishness to you, Morton, but it put over the idea. You got to admit that. And while I think of it, these here boys, Joe and Tom Buck, friends of mine from the West, has earned plenty. This here war ain't goin' to last ferever, leastwise at this rate, and they'll want to be buyin' a ranch fer themselves. So Morton, you can just pay over my winnin's to them. And thet mess of grunts and groans they were sendin' and receivin', thet was just their native tongue. Yuh See, these boys is full-blooded Cherokee Indians. Thet was just plain Cherokee Indian talk!"

Next Month . . . . .

Smoke Wade mixes with von Stolz in another hell-bent-for leather sky round-up!

"The whole flight's wiped out," Quinn gasped. "They—they didn't want us to see . . ." Then the wounded flight leader collapsed. Smoke Wade knew he could tell no more for days—if at all. What was it the Boches did not want seen? There was only one way to find out—and the Arizona skipper took it, riding his pinto Spad down death's sky highway with vengeance guns!

The Death Circus

Frederick
Blakeslee

"The flight's gone! Fokkers—fifty of 'em—they didn't want us to see. . ." But that was all the wounded Yank could say. What was this secret for which he had paid with his life's blood? Grimly Smoke Wade, vowed to find out—to smash his way through von Stolz's latest murder trap with vengeance wings.

The Death Circus

THE Arizona sun-bronzed features of the cowboy skipper of the 66th pursuit were twisted in a peculiar, anxious expression. His gray eyes, narrowed against the morning sun, stared into the sky toward the northeast, toward a lone Spad that half flew, half fell over the boundary of the field.

Smoke Wade stood like a statue as he watched. Instinctively his gun hand clutched the butt of his big Western six-gun far down on his right leg. Then, as though he suddenly realized the futility of that natural movement in time of trouble, his grip on the gun butt relaxed and he broke into a run toward the point where the disabled Spad was about to land.

The Spad hurled down. Smoke could see the flapping fabric on the right wing where archie or Spandau fire had ripped it loose. The plane bobbed twice as though uncertain whether to land or remain in flight. The engine was dead, prop stopped straight across.

A limp figure, with head lolling against the padding on one side of the cockpit, was fighting the plane down. Wheels touched, rolled, then caved in.

Crumph! Everything seemed to fold up at one time. The landing gear disappeared in a cloud of dust. The Spad shot ahead on her belly, jerked over on one wing and shuddered as she settled back and lay still.

Smoke Wade raced on. He reached the Spad a moment after the crash. A black cloud rose from the hot engine. He dove through this, flipped the safety belt free, clutched the limp form and heaved.

Flames spurted about him. He had the pilot in his arms and was running for the open space beyond the inferno that was already breaking.

Behind him something boomed as he dove clear of the wreckage. Flames shot after him. The gasoline tank had let go. Just in time.

Smoke whirled as he heard the sound and breathed a prayer of thanks. He shot a fearful glance at the young pilot in his arms. Heard the rattle of an ambulance as it jolted across the field from the tarmac.

He shook the pilot a little.

"Quinn," he said softly, "Quinn. What in hell's goin' on? Where's the rest of your flight?"

Slowly, weakly, the leader of C Flight of the 66th opened his eyes. There was sorrow and a touch of shame in that look that young Quinn gave Smoke Wade, his commanding officer.

"G-gone," he said. "All—four—gone. I—I tried to—"

The ambulance skidded to a stop. Two medics yanked a stretcher from the rear and came running. Smoke settled his burden gently to the canvas and patted the bleeding shoulder.

"Course you did, son," he said. "Reckon I wouldn't a picked you months ago for a flight leader if I hadn't knowed you had plenty of guts. Maybe too much. But what happened? Must a been all the Heinie crates was in the sky at once and you run smack into 'em—which don't sound reasonable."

They slid the stretcher into the ambulance. Smoke followed, sat beside Quinn as the ambulance jolted back across the field toward the hospital.

Slowly, Quinn's head nodded.

"But that's what happened," he said weakly. "Must have been ten flights of Fokkers altogether. Too—busy to count. First one hopped us from a cloud, then another. We'd just crossed the lines. A thousand feet. They—didn't want us to see—"

The eyelids quivered for an instant. The lips twitched, the body stiffened, then went limp. And that was all.

Smoke stared for an instant. Quinn out, maybe dead. Gently, hopefully, Smoke shook the younger man.

"Didn't want yuh to see what, son?" he pleaded.

Except for the jolting of the ambulance which threw him about on the stretcher, Quinn didn't move. Smoke tensed. A low curse escaped his lips. He slipped his hand beneath the bloodstained shirt. The curse, half finished, ceased. He could feel Quinn's heart beating very slightly.

Smoke carried one end of the stretcher into the hospital and watched while the medical officer made his examination. His eyes met the officer's when he looked up.

"He'll pull through, I think," the medico said, "but he's lost a lot of blood. He'll have a fight. Nothing must excite him."

Smoke nodded slowly.

"I reckon not," he agreed.

SMOKE left the hospital. Quinn would live. He was glad of that, of course. But what was it that the enemy did not want them to see? Were they preparing for a drive? Did they have some new devilish scheme that Quinn had discovered?

Smoke's long legs carried him toward the office of Colonel McGill, the field commander.

His two other flight leaders trotted toward him, to shoot anxious questions as to what had happened. Smoke answered as well as he could.

"But I cain't figure out what it all means," he frowned. "Quinn passed out when he was tryin' to tell me what it was that all them Heinie coyotes didn't want him to see. Reckon thet settles any news fer Quinn fer a spell. The doc says he's got to he kept quiet so's he can get well."

Brant, the leader of A Flight, looked puzzled.

"I can't get this straight," he admitted. "Last evening Snell and I had our flights out on evening patrol. I didn't see a thing of an enemy ship, did you, Snell?"

Snell, the smaller of the two flight commanders, shook his head.

"Not a ship," he agreed. "Haven't seen an enemy ship since we got the report three days ago that von Stolz and his circus had moved out of the sector."

Smoke's voice came in a hiss.

"Von Stolz," he said with the harsh accent of a curse. "I'd be willin' to bet and give plenty of odds that that Von devil is behind this. Reckon he got mighty discouraged when we bombed his drome a week ago, but I was too fast on the draw when I figured we'd got rid of him at last."

Brant and Snell walked on either side of Smoke down the tarmac.

"You know," Brant said, "I can't figure just where these ships could be kept. There isn't a field within this sector that is large enough to house fifty odd Fokkers since we blew von Stolz's old field to hell."

Smoke stopped short in his long striding. He was almost in front of headquarters. He shot a lingering glance down the tarmac to where a pinto Spad—painted black and white after his pinto pony back in Arizona—stood glistening in the sun.

"Hmm," he said half to himself. "Reckon now thet's a bright idea, Brant. I was goin' to have a talk with McGill, but on second thought I reckon thet wouldn't do no good. Not just this minute. I reckon I'll go take a look fer myself and the colonel might have some objections if I told him." He stared at Brant through narrowed eyes. '"Maybe," he said, "von Stolz is back in the air with a new circus. Maybe he's figurin' to get even and bein' as he ain't dumb, I reckon he's got a new drome that we can't lay eggs on."

He broke into a swift stride down the tarmac, waving a long arm at his two flight leaders.

"Adios," he called. "Be seein' yuh."

Smoke bellowed to his mechanic before he reached the field. He ambled into the cockpit of his pinto Spad, pushed the gun open, heard the gas suck into the cylinders as the mechanic spun the prop, then clicked the switch and barked:

"Contact!"

Wam! The propeller spun. The Hisso caught and snorted. He sat with a dreamy expression as he watched the temperature gauge climb. His face looked mild, hid the torture in his brain. The torture of knowing that four young pilots had gone to their death under that same sun a few minutes before.

Calmly he pushed the gun ahead and spun the ship. But behind that mask of calm his teeth were clenched.

Once in the air, Smoke turned toward the Front. He climbed as he flew. The glasses came out of their case and he stared through them as his altitude gave him greater visibility.

"Maybe," he said, "Brant is right. Wouldn't be surprised. Likely what Jerry didn't want Quinn and his boys to see was the place where they keep their crates."

He climbed higher and higher. Now he was sweeping the German side of the lines with his glasses. Then he watched two suspicious looking clouds above, one to the right of him, the other to the left.

"Funniest clouds I ever did see," he mused. "Flat as pancakes, I reckon. Never did see one cloud thet shape, let alone two."

Again he swept the German side with his glasses. The morning was clear and bright. Except for those two clouds, flat as pancakes, the sky was clear as a mountain spring.

SMOKE sighted the old drome of von Stolz far to the north. That had been blown up several days ago. It appeared to be in the same condition. His eyes ranged over other parts of the terrain. He remembered the country as though he had a map before him at the moment. The terrain was very rough where the Arennes mountains came down into France. There was little space for flying fields.

One plot he remembered was beneath a rugged-faced mountain. The map he recalled, showed it large and level. He found it stared down at long range. The glasses brought it near. He shook his head. The whole area was dotted by tiny specks that glistened in the sunlight. Puddles of water. No, that couldn't be the field. Besides, there were no hangers there for ships.

He shot a glance at the two clouds above him and grinned. He caught sight of a ship at one end of the flat cloud to his right.

"They'll be down in a minute, Jake. We'll be ready to give 'em a surprise party."

Smoke sat motionless, seemed to be staring ahead, but out of the corner of his eye he saw tiny specks tumble over the edge of the cloud and scream down.

Even when they were close enough so that he could hear the whine of the Mercedes engines he did not turn. A slow grin spread over his face. He tensed at the controls. Grew rigid. Took another look out of the comer of his eye, cursed softly and waited.

Tac-tac-tac! The rattle of warming Spandau guns still just out of range came to his ears. Now! Now he would be expected to turn. Every second counted now. The Germans would expect him to turn in astonishment at the sound of their warming guns.

But Smoke Wade did not turn. Instead, he moved the controls with a surprising speed. The pinto Spad leaped and bucked and looped and rolled. His trigger fingers poised for an instant.

From an inverted position, Smoke saw one Fokker zoom to make a desperate effort to catch him in its fire. He felt the safety belt tighten about his middle as he hung head downward.

His eyes ranged along his sights in a flashing glance. Then—

Tac-tac-tac! Vickers guns bucked and spoke. The Fokker flipped crazily, half rolled and headed down.

For an instant, Smoke had pushed the stick ahead while he made the deadly shot. Now the stick slammed back in his stomach once more, and the pinto Spad groaned over in the completion of the loop.

Before him four Fokkers struggled to dive free of his surprise lunge. Smoke picked one on the left, banked sharply in a vertical turn. His feet pushed the rudder and his guns spoke again. The Fokker leaped into the air, burst into flame and tore for hell.

Once more the controls moved sharply under the expert hand and feet of Smoke Wade. The pinto whirled and lunged for another Fokker. But that Jerry pilot was already on the run. All of the three remaining Fokkers were on the run, it seemed.

Smoke cursed, pushed wildly on the gun, found that the Hisso was doing her best and cursed again. A puzzled look came into his narrowed eyes.

"Thet's funny, I reckon, Jake," he said to his pinto Spad. "Thought there was close to fifty planes in the air when Quinn's boys went down. And now—"

The last sentence was cut off by the snarl of Spandau guns from behind him and above. Smoke whirled in his seat and shot a glance upward.

Fokkers poured down. They were upon him. No time to pull the trick he had pulled before. The last second that counted was lost. He must fight it out, gun for gun.

All too late, he realized the trick. A small flight had plunged at him from one cloud. While his efforts were concentrated upon that enemy flight, a horde of enemy ships had cut loose from another cloud and were slamming down now with blazing guns.

Already yellow tracers were ripping their way through his right wing. He heard and felt the drum and vibration of Spandau steel as it slashed through the covering of his tail. And at point of that attacking mass of Fokkers, spread out to cut off any flight for his own lines that he might try to make, Smoke recognized the crimson ship of the Baron von Stolz.

Anger colored his face with a red flush that showed bronze against his dark skin. Controls moved, rudder and stick. Spandau slugs drummed closer to his cockpit.

Up went the pinto Spad. Up, up, and up it shot into the air in a twisting climb. Fokkers followed him, hung on their props. A few hundred feet and the pinto Spad rolled, to come out above most of the attacking Fokkers.

Smoke glared across his sights as he came down. The pinto Spad wavered almost in a stall. It picked up speed, began to plunge. Smoke's fingers pressed the triggers and sent flaming lead into the vitals of the nearest Fokker.

"You make three, if my count ain't off," he snarled as the Fokker blew apart in the air. "One more and we're closer to even for the day's trappin'."

HE kicked out, slithered to the right and zigzagged through a snarling pack of ships that hurled at him from all sides. That crimson crate of von Stolz had gotten out of range as he fled.

"Skulkin' von coyote," Smoke barked.

Glaring across his sights he could see nothing but that lead Fokker of his enemy. He'd get that crate or—

Bam! His instrument board flashed from before his eyes and left a gaping hole before him, a hole that squirted hot oil into his face.

Frantically, he brushed the searing oil out of his face and plunged on. Fokkers all about him. For the moment insane passion shook him.

He wanted von Stolz. To down von Stolz would end a lot of this trick murder that had been going on along the Front.

A checkered Fokker slashed before his sights, intercepting his lunge at the baron. Spandaus flamed from all sides. Smoke pressed his guns. Cursed. The left gun bucked in a short burst and died. The other never spoke at all.

Instantly, Smoke had his six-gun out and took aim. The six-gun boomed. The first Fokker had turned and was bearing in close. At that moment something seemed to happen to the head of the Jerry pilot of that crate. It jerked and bobbed once, then flopped against the cockpit padding while the Fokker fell spinning.

"Four," Smoke barked. "Now if I get you, you von devil, I'll figure we're gettin' closer to even for the—"

His heart suddenly seemed to stop beating. Or was it his Hisso? Yes, the Hisso. It missed. It caught and ran again. Black smoke belched from the side of his motor. Fokkers were boring in from every side. There seemed no escape.

The faintest glimmer of hope came with the momentary pick-up of his Hisso. Smoke knew it wouldn't be for long. He rolled, cut round in a tight vertical and headed for home with what seemed to be every enemy ship in the world on his tail.

Yellow tracers fluffed about him as he ran. The Hisso snorted and spat and groaned. It hung together somehow and ran at half speed.

He was going down in a steep power glide. His foot kicked the rudder back and forth at irregular intervals to throw the pursuing ships off their aim.

Enemy steel drummed on his fuselage covering, slashed through his wings. He felt the sting of a slug as it cut through his sleeve, felt the warm blood ooze down his arm from the skin wound. Hunched farther over the stick and hurled on down.

Fokkers swarmed about his tail like a pack of wolves—hungry wolves. The Hisso in the Spad was giving out, just managing to keep turning over. Smoke was diving for dear life toward his lines.

And as he skimmed two hundred feet above the front Yank line, all hell seemed to break loose below. Yank machine guns. Yank anti-aircraft, even at that close range, bellowed into action.

Fokkers wavered in their mad lunge to finish the famous Arizona ace before he could land safely. Wavered and snarled on with blazing guns.

Deliberately, Smoke's hand reached for the switch. The Hisso died completely, prop stopped. He was gliding down now. Gliding at the mercy of Fokkers that trailed him.

He turned in his seat and glared back. His six-gun came up out of the cockpit. He took aim. A crimson crate had slithered in behind him. Von Stolz was hurling to the kill of his enemy.

Blam! The Western six-gun boomed. Smoke cursed. The instant before his finger had pulled the trigger, von Stolz had seen that deadly gun come up over the cockpit cowling. The crimson Fokker leaped and bucked. An instant after Smoke's gun spat flame the Fokker shuddered and turned sharply.

As if by signal from their leader all Fokkers followed in a steep bank and roared back to their lines. The crimson crate was going down on the German side of the lines. Smoke caught a glimpse of that before he turned back to find a landing place for his pinto Spad.

But the baron wasn't injured. Smoke was certain of that. He had the uncanny sense of the expert marksman which tells him just where his bullet has gone before he can see the hole it has made. And so he knew that that jerky motion caused by von Stolz's quick hand on his control stick had thrown him off aim just enough. Probably the bullet had ticked the whirling prop of the Fokker just enough to cause trouble and force von Stolz to land.

Even in Smoke's own predicament, he smiled at the thought.

"Reckon I'd like mighty well to hear von Stolz explain how come he happened to get hit with one of my slugs," he drawled.

Then Smoke's entire attention was centered on bringing his pinto Spad to rest on the blasted earth below him.

EVERYWHERE the ground was torn by shells until it was a mass of holes and small hills. He swept the country in a desperate effort to find a place level enough to bring his pinto Spad down safely.

His keen eye caught sight of a small stretch of road where men were working. They were repairing it, so that a long line of trucks, waiting to the south, could continue their movement toward the Yank Front.

A movement of the stick and the pinto Spad was headed for the highway. A deep breath and Smoke's voice bellowed ahead of him.

"Out of the way. Comin' down." Then to the pinto Spad he said, "Hang on, Jake, old boy. We're goin' down, and if I ain't mistaken you're goin' to catch particular hell in this landin'. But I'll do the best I—"

Creak, crack! The Spad shuddered almost like a living thing as the wheels touched the uneven surface of the road. There came a lurch and a sickening settle as the landing gear gave way. The pinto Spad, pride of Smoke Wade and hated ship to the enemy, slid along on its belly and stopped.

Smoke climbed out. Men working to repair the road came running from the ditches at the side where they had taken cover. A little sadly, Smoke surveyed his pinto Spad and shook his head.

"Reckon," he said, "it's a good thing, Jake, that you're only a machine 'stead of my pinto pony back home I named yuh after. 'Cause if yuh was him I reckon wouldn't be nothin' to do but shoot yuh with your legs all broke thet a way. But likely you'll be back flyin' with me 'fore long when some of the boys get you back to the field and put in some new parts."

Smoke helped move the disabled pinto Spad out of the way and strode south past the lines of waiting trucks. He found a motorcycle rider with empty side car, rode back to his field in it and left orders at the main hangar to have the repair crew bring his ship in.

From there he went straight to Colonel McGill's office. The shaggy-browed old warrior shot an anxious glance at Smoke's blood-stained sleeve.

"What's happened, Smoke?" he demanded. "You're all right?"

Smoke grinned as he nodded.

"Reckon I'm a heap better physical than mental," he admitted. "I just went over the lines to have a look at the country. Nice mornin' fer it, colonel. Got jumped by the same mess of Fokkers, I reckon, what messed up Quinn and stole his flight and sent 'em to hell. Mighty near got me too. Guns jammed and the Hisso quit, and I just sent the boys up toward the Front to bring Jake in and put him back in flyin' shape."

Colonel McGill nodded gravely.

"I understood you'd gone out, Smoke," he said. "I don't suppose you'll ever stop taking matters in your own hands in time of a crisis."

Smoke grinned and shook his head.

"Reckon not, colonel," he said. "Been used to runnin' most every show I was ever hooked up with. Cain't get it out my blood. But I'm mighty near stumped this time. I know one thing. I'm mighty sure von Stolz and his circus, that's who it is, is makin' clouds to hide above. They put 'em just where they want 'em. Get smoke machines workin' and the whole *jagdstaffel* flies around in a circle droppin' smoke. Then they hang around above thet cloud. Them clouds I seen couldn't be anything else but man-made smoke screens. They're flat as pancakes.

"But thet ain't what's botherin' me, colonel. What I want to know is where them coyotes is hidin' their crates and what field they use to base at. It cain't be far away because them Fokkers stays up fer a long time, and if they come from way oft some place they wouldn't have much gas left to fly with when they got across from us. The Arennes Mountains don't leave much space for landing fields."

Smoke strode to a photographic map on the wall of McGill's office and pointed out two spots.

"This place, you know, colonel, is where we blew von Stolz's field off the map less than a week ago." He moved his finger to a blotched section, dotted by glistening pin points. "To the best of my recollection," he went on, "this place here right under that flat-faced mountain is the only field large enough for ships to take off and land. And thet couldn't be the drome 'cause there ain't no hangars anywhere around the field. These Heinie's is clever at camouflage, but they don't often fool old Smoke Wade with their crazy paint brush."

A peculiar expression crossed Colonel McGill's face.

"BESIDES," Smoke finished, "this space here under the mountain is covered with pools of water. See by the map. I reckon you couldn't take off a baby carriage without strikin' one of them puddles, let alone a flock of Fokkers."

Colonel McGill nodded.

"Yes," he said. "I know. That's what sticks me, too, Smoke."

Smoke eyed him.

"I don't get yuh, colonel," he said.

"It's what Quinn said," McGill confessed.

"Quinn?"

"Yes. Did he tell you where the ships were taking off?"

Smoke's eyes narrowed in surprise.

"Hell, no. He was just goin' to when he passed out."

"He's been delirious," the colonel went on. "He's been babbling something over at the hospital about ships taking off right through mud puddles and water."

"Huh?" Smoke cried. "What the—" He turned toward the door. "I'm goin' over and find out what goes on here. Just as quick as it gets dark and they get the pinto Spad in shape again."

"Wait!" McGill ordered sharply. "Not so fast. You've got a job cut out for you tonight. You're going over into Germany all right but not alone. You'll take the D.H. we have here at the field for the purpose and be ready to take off at eight. That will be an hour after dark. You'll take a passenger. A member of our Intelligence."

Smoke grinned slowly. "Reckon thet ain't so bad as I thought it was goin' to be, colonel," he admitted. "Me and this spy of ours'll go over and either find out what's goin' on or else—"

"Wrong again," Colonel McGill said. "You'll take this member of Intelligence over and leave him. You'll return then and get some sleep. At dawn every ship is ordered out on patrol. That's orders from headquarters. New replacements will be up from Issoudon to fill in the gaps left by the deaths of Quinn's flight. G.H.Q. orders you to be back to lead the patrol at dawn."

The smile fled from Smoke Wade's face. The bronze skin turned to a lighter shade. He cursed under his breath.

"Them brass hats is crazy," he said. "Send replacements up here and order 'em to go over into thet hell."

"There will be sixteen ships in the air from here," McGill tried to console.

"Yeah?" snarled Smoke. "Sixteen Spads. Five of 'em won't be as good as nothin' at all. That leaves eleven Spads.

Eleven Spads to protect five green kids from around fifty crates of von Stolz's new circus, barrin' four I knocked down a spell ago, gettin' blowed out the sky myself in doin' it. Swell break, that is." McGill gasped.

"Good Lord! Fifty of von Stolz's circus? I thought he'd given up this sector since we blew his whole field off the map, hangars, most of the ships and all."

"But he ain't," snapped Smoke. "He don't give up thet easy. If we could be sure of where he keeps them crates we might do the same to them, but we ain't. I'm certain of one thing. Quinn is talkin' crazy about his takin' off in that field under the mountain. I seen the pools of water standin' there myself. If there's water standin' as thick as I seen on thet field, I reckon the whole thing's covered pretty thick with mud. Besides, where could they keep their crates? Ain't a hangar in sight anywhere. Couldn't spot a man or a ship on the field. It don't make sense."

"Perhaps," McGill suggested, only half hopefully, "this spy you'll drop tonight will find something he can do about it when he gets over there."

"Yeah," Smoke said bitterly, "in maybe a week or a month. Meantime a lot of green kids is goin' to hell while a lot of good boys, my own boys—" his voice shook a little—"will be goin' to hell tryin' to keep 'em protected."

"Perhaps," McGill insisted desperately, "perhaps the spy will be able to find some way of destroying the ships or the field before dawn. In that event the patrol won't have any trouble."

Smoke Wade snapped a salute to his superior, turned on his heel and strode from the office. He went to the hospital, and found Quinn babbling in delirium. As Colonel McGill had said, his words, when they could be distinguished, were concerning many enemy ships taking off through mud, taking off in a field where no ships could or should take off.

Very gently, Smoke tried to ask a question now and then, but Quinn was beyond the point of understanding him. For some time Smoke sat and listened to the incoherent babbling, from which only an occasional sentence could be picked up. It was always the same. German ships taking off from that field. Smoke was wondering if perhaps the flyer had not been a trifle out of his head and only thought he saw Fokkers taking off from that impossible drome.

EVENING and darkness came. The D.H. was rolled to the tarmac.

Smoke climbed to the front seat and warmed the Liberty engine. Minutes passed. The hour of take-off arrived. A figure detached itself from the shadow of a hangar and strode toward the ship.

"Lieutenant Smoke Wade?" came the question.

The man was of medium height and well built. He carried a cap under his arm, a German officer's cap, and he wore a long coat that came to his ankles and covered whatever uniform he might be wearing.

Smoke grinned and nodded. "Reckon you got the right taxi driver, partner," he said. "Where to?"

The man unbuttoned his big coat. In the dim light Smoke caught a glimpse of the German uniform beneath as he reached into the inside coat pocket of the great overcoat. The man drew out a map and a flashlight.

"I'm known as C-2," he said. "I understand, Lieutenant, that you are particularly interested in this mission of mine. Colonel McGill has told me."

"Reckon you ain't far off," he said. "I'd give most anything to be able to blow von Stolz out of the air for good."

A strange light came into the eyes of C-2 at the mention of the baron's name.

"Von Stolz?" he said. "You suspect that this is his circus?"

"Suspect, hell!" Smoke flared. "I know it's his circus."

C-2 gave a short, stiff nod, flashed the light on and pointed to the map.

"Possible landing fields are not so numerous on the Arennes Mountain region," he said. "But I understand you are a skillful pilot. You can doubtless land me in this field?"

Smoke's eyes narrowed as he squinted at the spot on the map. He recalled seeing that field through glasses that morning. Had decided in fact that it was out of the question for use as a drome.

"If it was a daylight landing," Smoke drawled, "I reckon I'd bet ten to one I could make it without scratchin' a wing. But landin' in the dark from ten thousand feet and a dead engine ain't so easy. Climb astraddle of this crate and we'll see."

C-2 climbed. The Liberty roared and the D.H. swept out into the night and turned toward the Front.

Climbing, climbing, Smoke reached ten thousand feet above the Front, studied his map in the light of his dash lamp and counted the minutes against it.

One, two three minutes. They should be over the field now or easily within gliding distance of it.

Deliberately, Smoke's hand reached the switch and flipped the knobs. The Liberty died. Must go down upon the field silently. Give C-2 a chance to get well away from the field, then start the Liberty again and return, according to orders. Return to lead his squadron to their death. Smoke shuddered.

He brought the D.H. down in a gentle glide, turning in great circles as he lost altitude.

Down, down, with only the sound of the wind swishing through the rigging and over his wings. Wind that had a soft sound as it slipped by.

Below, guns boomed, and far to the south the sound of gunfire merged into a continuous roar like distant thunder.

Down to four, three, two thousand feet. Smoke was sure of his location. In the next minute, from fifteen hundred feet, he spotted the field to his right.

He could make it out very dimly. His teeth clenched. The field looked smaller, much smaller than he had remembered it from a higher altitude. Too late now to turn back. Engine dead, killed by his own hand. Must land.

Controls moved. The D.H. slid down in a slip toward a row of trees at the edge of the field. Branches tore through the lower wings and landing gear. The D.H. lurched perilously toward the dark blotch that was the field.

Wheels were touching, rolling. The plane rocked as it traveled over the uneven ground, then came to a stop.

Already C-2 was climbing out. He stripped off his great coat, hitched his belt and Luger pistol. Smoke climbed out to stretch his legs. He wouldn't be starting back for perhaps a half hour.

Smoke stepped beside C-2.

"Listen, C-2," he was almost pleading. "You got to find out where these crates of von Stolz's circus are kept. Got to blow hell out of 'em, see? If—"

Smoke's words ceased abruptly. A sound drifted to them from the side of the field. The sound of running feet. Smoke whirled. His gun hand went for the six-gun. He tensed. C-2 was just behind him.

SMOKE moved instantly, dropped to the ground, slithered under the D.H. and snatched a flare pistol from the front cockpit . . . *Blam!* Flames burst out and the D.H. began to burn. Smoke's big six-gun was in his hand now. Desperately he tried to see beyond the blinding searchlight that had just been turned on them.

He felt, then, a hard thing thrust in his back. A gun muzzle. Turning with a snarl, he stared into the frowning face of C-2. Germans were running toward them with drawn Luger pistols.

C-2's voice cracked out sharply.

"Drop that gun. You are my prisoner."

Smoke tensed. He glared back at C-2. Then, willingly, he handed him his six-gun, butt first. Clever trick, this. C-2 was acting as the German high *offizier* he played. Pulling a fake to make his part more convincing before the German soldiers who had caught them.

Then he wasn't so sure. C-2's voice cracked out again in a harsh laugh.

"I have tricked you, lieutenant. You thought you were bringing an American spy into Germany. You shall be dealt with accordingly." C-2 whirled to the *offizier* among the soldiers. "Take us at once to the Baron von Stolz. Tell him *Hauptmann* von Gruner is back."

At the mention of the name Smoke Wade's teeth clenched. He couldn't be sure. Was this C-2 an American spy or was it von Gruner himself? Von Gruner, he recalled, was a close friend of von Stolz, and had been shot down behind Yank lines three months before. His plane had burned and the famous ace had been taken from the burning wreckage and rushed to a hospital.

Smoke's head spun a little dizzily with conflicting thought. If he could be positive that this man was really von Gruner he might try to put up a fight. Perhaps it was a fake. Perhaps C-2 was really the spy after all. In that case he would never face von Stolz. Von Stolz would, of course, see that he was not von Gruner and could cause his arrest.

Smoke shot a glance about him in the dark. Not a chance of escape.

German soldiers had Lugers trained on him—on C-2 as well. They wouldn't be sure either until they met von Stolz. If C-2 was a real Yank spy they would both be stood up against a stone wall and shot as a spy and an accomplice. If C-2 was not a Yank spy, but von Gruner as he claimed, then Smoke would in all probability be shot for his act in bringing what he thought was a spy and landing him behind Yank lines.

They walked across the field and reached a road where a car stood. The soldiers herded Smoke and C-2 into the car. They allowed C-2 to carry both his Luger and Smoke's six-gun because they were obviously afraid to treat him as a suspect. After a short ride, the car turned in to a level space. Smoke stared in astonishment. There before him was the mountain that bordered the field dotted with mud puddles. Von Stolz here? But how? Where?

In almost immediate answer to Smoke's mental question the car drew up before the face of the mountain. There were words in German which Smoke could not catch. Then a small slab swung open.

SMOKE climbed out of the car. He stepped through the opening and found they were in a dark passage. The *offizier* commanding the German soldiers was with them. A moment later a door opened.

Von Stolz, with his close-cropped head and monocled eye, stood framed in the doorway. The *offizier* said something to him in German. Von Stolz' eyes opened wider, to focus upon the man Smoke knew as C-2.

Then he spoke one word that spelled the death sentence to any remaining hopes of Smoke Wade.

"Von Gruner. *Mein freund!* But you have changed since your accident."

C-2 laughed, prodded Smoke ahead of him through the door.

"*Jawohl,*" he said. "The American butchers did their work on my face very badly. I was burned after the crash. You are well, baron, and how is your brother Karl and rest of the boys?"

Von Stolz stared at C-2. Then he smiled, advanced in a quick step and threw his arms about C-2.

"*Gott im Himmel!*" he cried. "You are von Gruner! I recognize you now. But how did you escape?"

C-2 laughed.

"Escape is simple with the *dumkopf* Yankees and the help of our Intelligence," C-2 laughed. "Our Intelligence in Paris learned that a spy known as C-2 was to be sent here. They arranged for the disappearance of C-2 and I was sent in his place. And this American *Leutnant* brought me over tonight."

Then, for the first time, von Stolz's little eyes fell upon Smoke Wade.

"And to think, *freund* von Gruner," he chuckled, "that my old enemy, Smoke Wade, should be the one to bring you over. Ha-ha."

"That is funny, *Jawohl*," he went on. "For now at last, Smoke Wade, you are finished with your scheming against me. You will be shot as a transporter of spies. But first—" von Stolz winked at C-2—"you shall see what I think you have come to see."

Von Stolz's arrogance was getting the better of him.

"Come," he jerked his head.

The *offizier* followed with the Luger at Smoke's back. Von Stolz and C-2 led the way. Smoke was prodded through a small door.

The smell of dope, engine oil and gasoline came to his nostrils as they entered a darker room. Von Stolz reached a switch and the place became brilliantly lighted. Smoke stared.

They had entered a great, flat-floored cave in the side of the mountain. Rows and rows of ships stood there—the Fokkers of von Stolz's new circus.

"You have been gone several months," von Stolz smiled to his friend. "We have not been idle while you have been away, von Gruner. We have now an airdrome that is impregnable to air bombing."

Von Stolz pulled a switch near the front of the cavernous room. There was a grinding of machinery and the side of the mountain began to open.

A harsh laugh came from the throat of Smoke Wade.

"That would be a swell trick all right if you could fly when you got out of this hole in the mountain. You can't get off in that muddy field," Smoke taunted.

"No?" von Stolz said. "You are wrong again, Smoke Wade. We fixed the field so that your prying eyes would not see its smoothness. We placed large mirrors here and there, set in concrete to give the appearance of pools of water. But it is the finest field I have ever flown from."

C-2 SEEMED to tense. His right hand moved to the holster. He whirled—and his Luger spat. At the same time, he pushed Smoke to one side as the *offizier* behind him crumpled to the floor. Von Stolz barked a curse and moved for his own Luger. C-2 spun and covered him.

"Drop that gun," he snarled.

Smoke dove at C-2 then and snatched his own six-gun from the pocket of the Intelligence officer.

"Don't drop it," he countermanded. "You and me, von Stolz, is goin' to shoot it out man to man. We'll finish this thing right now."

Von Stolz was trembling. In spite of Smoke's orders the Luger slipped from his fingers and clattered to the floor. The baron's face turned ashen gray. He couldn't seem to speak for fear.

"Yellow, like I reckoned," Smoke snarled. "All right, if you won't fight it out on the ground, we'll fight it out in the air one of these day. I'd shoot you down where you stand, but I ain't that low. Come on, C-2. We're leavin' pronto."

At the open door the crimson ship of von Stolz stood ready to lead the flight. Smoke jerked his head toward the rest of the planes."

"Set fire to them crates, C-2. But first throw this Mercedes prop."

The prop whirled. The Mercedes caught, sputtered. C-2 leaped away, ran back into the cave hangar, touched matches to fabric. Ships burned and crackled.

Shouts went up from outside. Men came running. C-2 raced back before the belching smoke. He leaped to the wing of the crimson Fokker and Smoke pushed the gun ahead.

He turned for an instant to wave at von Stolz. Cursed. Von Stolz was running across the floor of the hangar toward the switch that would close the doors. He reached it, pulled. Machinery ground. The doors began to close—

Smoke clutched the stick. His hand flashed to his six-gun. There wasn't time to fire. Von Stolz had done his work. Done it well. There might be a chance to get out yet—a slim chance.

Straight for the opening that remained, Smoke hurled the Fokker.

The opening was growing smaller and smaller. The Fokker of von Stolz seemed eternally slow.

Wam! The plane shot out into the open. One wing caught for an instant, half swung the Fokker. Smoke kicked viciously, got it straight, sent it across the field and into the air as German slugs spat after them.

Once in the sky Smoke turned and glanced back at the slit left in the door. Smoke and flame belched through it in a whirling mass. C-2 grinned up at him from his position across the wing.

Back at the field C-2 explained to Smoke and Colonel McGill.

"I've been training for a month to impersonate the real von Gruner," he said. "I didn't know I was to meet von Stolz tonight until Wade told me he was across the lines. Von Stolz and Gruner were old friends, you know. Von Gruner and I looked something alike and there was the story about his made-over face to help. I pulled that crack about von Stolz's brother, Karl, knowing it would put the act over. But I don't know how long I would have been able to keep it up."

Smoke laughed.

"I reckon you sure put it over all right," he said. "Fooled me dizzy. I'd a bet ten to one that you was von Gruner after I seen the way von Stolz took you in his arms."

C-2 chuckled.

"And for the moment I wouldn't have taken that bet," he said.

Next month follow

SMOKE WADE

. . . as he fights a terrible new menace—the Black Death. Even the Boches are afraid of this horror weapon which they have chained to use against the Allies, but cannot control! Yet Smoke Wade sets out to defeat it—and part of his plan is a hell-bent expedition up the River Rhine by submarine!

Line up with the cowboy ace as he fights new dangers . . .
. . . Meet a pair of old friends—the Cherokee Indian brothers

September BATTLE BIRDS—For sale on August 10th

Steel
Coffin
Ace

Boche boats surrounded them—
Boche guns lined the river banks—
yet farther and farther up the Rhine
crept that lone Allied submarine.
A steel coffin carrying the six gun
ace and his two redskin buddies to
a strange air base hidden deep in
Bocheland!

Steel Coffin Ace

THE narrowed gray eyes of the Arizona-bronzed skipper of the 66th pursuit took on a hard glint—not without pleasure. A grin formed about his thin, straight lips. He stared far ahead at specks that were taking shape as he hurled his pinto Spad farther into Germany.

"Reckon there's always a heap of consolatin' in seein' even a sign of that red crate of von Stolz these days, eh, Jake?" He talked to his pinto Spad, named and painted for his pinto pony back on the Arizona range. He talked on as the specks took shape, became Fokkers flying in a vee.

"It means, Jake, thet when von Stolz is flyin' the sky and tearin' around like he's supposed to do, he ain't in no mess of mud and slime figurin' out tricks. Thet's him comin' at the point of his *jagdstaffel* of coyotes over yonder, I reckon. Looks to be in a mighty big hurry to get to me too, and I reckon it ain't 'cause he's got no good news fer me, nor nothin'. Boy, he sure is comin' like he means business this time."

The grin left his weather-beaten face. He frowned. His free hand dove to the case beside him in the cockpit and pulled out his powerful binoculars.

After a moment's survey of the German rear section he shook his head and placed the glasses back in their case.

"Cain't see a thing no way thet's out of the ordinary," he drawled.

"Ain't no German troop concentration. Cain't see no new line of trenches. Nothin' but what was here yesterday and day before pretty much."

He shot a glance at the Fokkers as they drew near. He rubbed his chin in the palm of his free hand.

"Nothin' to see or spy on, s'fer as I can see. Still, the cuss keeps right on comin' like he was madder'n a ring-tailed hop toad."

Still the planes were a mile away and more.

"Thet's him, though, Jake, ain't it? We'd know his style of flyin' left wing a mite low, any place, eh, boy? But we ain't goin' to waste time just a fightin' fer fun this mornin', much as I'd like to. From the hurry them Fokkers is in to stop me there's somethin' up. And thet's our job, Jake, to find out what 'tis, I reckon."

He turned east in a gradual bank and roared at five thousand feet above the rear of the German lines. Now and then archie grunted a lazy yellow mushroom up at him. Smoke's face grew puzzled once more as he watched the action of von Stolz and his Fokkers. They had slowed. They had actually turned. Didn't seem at all interested in following Smoke to the east.

"Hmm," Smoke grinned at the realization, "reckon they ain't interested in my flyin' east. Let's try it the other way, eh, Jake? Keep on this game of hide-and-go-find-me and we'll have von Stolz tellin' us just what 'tis he don't want us to see."

Stick and rudder moved instantly. The pinto Spad nipped on one wing, groaned in the tight vertical and slammed back toward the west at full throttle.

Smoke continued to watch von Stolz and the seven Fokkers in the entire flight. His grin grew still larger as he saw the effect his turn had had on the Jerry flight.

Crimson Fokker at point, the pack roared at him to cut him off. Smoke chuckled.

"Used to be a game we played when I was a kid," he said to himself and the pinto Spad. "Used to have a lot of fun playin' thet game. Called it hot and cold. Somebody'd hide and then the one what was it would go lookin' fer the fella. If the one what was 'it' was gettin' close they'd holler 'warm' or maybe if he was right there they'd holler 'hot.' And if they was a long ways away they'd say they was 'cold'. I reckon this here game is just as good as thet game for gettin' pointers. From the way you're actin', you von coyote, I reckon I'm gettin' a might hot to the thing you ain't aimin' fer me to see."

SMOKE measured the distance between the thundering Fokker flight and his pinto Spad. He calculated mentally the speed of each. Gave a short nod and pushed on the gun for all he was worth.

"Reckon we'll go through, Jake, and see the works," he drawled.

Spandau guns spat at long range when they saw they were beaten to the break.

Von Stolz and his Fokkers thundered after Smoke Wade and his racing Spad. The gap widened between them. Smoke took one last look over his shoulder, snatched the glasses from their case and peered through them toward the west.

His brow furrowed. Eyes narrowed. He was staring far to the west now, almost to the line of horizon. Something seemed queer. The earth appeared blackened in a wide stripe. Was it the earth that was black? It was so far away he couldn't be sure. Perhaps it was the air above the earth that looked black.

Smoke Wade spun and glared at the Fokkers racing toward him. He thumbed his nose at them.

"Reckon I give you more credit than was comin' to yuh, von Stolz," he drawled. "But you're too late. I'm goin' to take myself a look and see what the hell."

Smoke pointed the nose of the pinto Spad straight for the blackened smudge far to the west and let the Hisso hurl him nearer. From behind came the frantic jabber of Spandau guns. Two, three slugs thunked through his wing on the right, well out toward the tip.

He hardly noticed that now. He could see the blackness ahead more plainly. He raised his powerful glasses to his eyes and squinted.

"Hmm," he drawled. "Queerest thing I ever did see. Black smudge on the ground over there, just like somebody was burnin' crude oil or pine pitch wood. Only thing, there ain't no flame, so likely it ain't fire."

Nearer and nearer he roared. He could see the point from which the black smoke-like vapor was coming. It poured from several points along a front line of German trench. The wind was from the north. It carried the black cloud down across No-Man's-Land into Yank trenches.

Smoke couldn't see through the blackness at the point where it covered the ground. But beyond that point, to the south ahead of the advancing cloud, he made out men running for their lives before it. Men with gas masks and men without masks. Yanks running in mortal terror from something that they could not fight.

The horrible realization swept over Smoke instantly, Men with and without masks were running ahead of that advancing sooty cloud. Death was in that vapor. A new kind of gas, perhaps. Maybe a liquid—or even a fire without flame.

Smoke was baffled. He wasn't sure of anything except the fact that the cloud traveling before the wind was mowing down hundreds of Yanks that didn't have a chance to fight it.

Archie and ground machine guns belched forth their death as Smoke plunged down his pinto Spad in a twisting dive. Shells burst about him. Machine gun slugs ripped his wings, his fuselage covering.

Smoke never hesitated. He was headed for the men who managed those four nozzles from which the black mist poured. They were grotesque looking figures with strange masks covering their heads. They did not look up as Smoke roared down. Perhaps the headgear shut out even their hearing.

Vickers belched flame and steel from the nose of the racing Spad. Smoke wasn't smiling now. His teeth were clenched and he was cursing. Cursing as he slammed down and jabbed lead into the men who controlled the first nozzle.

THEY fell back, sprawled kicking. Others ran forward to take their place. The black substance continued to pour out with force. When the men holding it dropped, the nozzle lashed about like the tail of a snake.

Germans fell before it as the cloud poured into their own front line trenches. It was turned off almost instantly. Then Boches grasped it and swung it toward the Yank lines once more.

Smoke was thundering on to the next hose. Screaming hell came up to meet him from the hands of the ground crews. He sent his pinto Spad bucking like a wild cayuse—twisting, snorting. One after another the ground crews about each of the nozzles leaped, slumped, doubled with cries of mortal pain.

A sharp bank and he roared back. Von Stolz and his brood were there now to add to his trouble.

Smoke yanked his stick, kicked and glared across his sights from an upside-down position. He got one of the Fokkers in his sights. Pulled. Didn't wait to see what happened to that crate.

He rolled out, glared about. Found he was on the tail of another Fokker for the instant, sent that one down angrily. He searched the sky for that crimson crate of von Stolz. Found it. As usual von Stolz was out of range, hiding behind some of his flight. Smoke cursed.

He flipped down. Took aim at a fresh crew of the second nozzle that poured black smoke like vapor. Got them. He heard a rattle on his tail. Turned. Von Stolz was there, guns chattering a death chant.

Anger welled up in the leathery face of Smoke Wade. He purpled. Controls moved with lightning-like speed. Pinto Spad leaped and rolled. Rolled again as in surprise.

Von Stolz shot beneath. Smoke was after him instantly. But the baron had planned well. He who fights and runs away lives to fight another day. Apparently the Baron von Stolz liked living very much indeed. For at that very moment he was out behind what was left of his flight, running for home.

Left alone, Smoke plunged down at the nozzle crews again. There seemed no end to the supply of men who would come running to man the nozzles when the old crew had been killed. Rifles and Lugers and machine guns and archie batteries roared and crackled incessantly. Smoke tore on. Finally he grunted a curse in disgust.

"Hell and damnation," he rasped. "Them Germans keep sendin' up their young kids to be shot down as fast as I can press a trigger. This here ain't no game no more. It's plain slaughter."

He flipped the bullet-riddled pinto Spad on its ear, banked sharply and roared over the black mist that hung like blowing fog over the Yank trenches.

A shudder passed over him as he saw men stumble and fall from exhaustion before the advance of the death cloud. Saw them gasp and writhe as the fumes poured over them and shut them from his sight.

With a curse, he turned toward Ramou, the home field of the 66th pursuit.

DOWN slammed the pinto Spad on the tarmac. Smoke was out, running to the office of his superior, Colonel McGill. The old, gray-haired war dog looked up from under his shaggy brows as Smoke burst, unannounced, into his office.

"What in the name of common sense?" demanded McGill.

"Maybe I look crazy," Smoke began. "Reckon I do." He hitched his great six-gun a little higher on his right leg to a more comfortable position. "I just seen somethin' that ain't favorable to sanity. Gas thet the Germans is sendin' over against our poor devils in the trenches. To all appearances there ain't no gas mask among our boys that'll combat this black stuff. Don't know for sure whether it's gas or a fire without flame or what in hell it is. But I know one thing. It's got to be stopped. I blammed away until I couldn't hold a trigger button down no longer. I come back to get the whole squadron and bomb the damn place where Heinie is sendin' the stuff over. Alone I couldn't kill them off fast enough to make it worthwhile."

Smoke whirled toward the door.

"Just thought I'd drop in, colonel, and tell yuh what I was plannin' so's you'd know when you heard all the crates takin' off."

Colonel McGill leaped to his feet. He caught Smoke by the arm. The lanky cowboy skipper hesitated, turned.

"Wait, Smoke," McGill said kindly. "I have orders for you. You didn't give me a chance to tell you. General Banks wants to see you just as soon as you come in. He's over at G.H.Q."

"But I reckon I—"

McGill cut him off with a wave of his hand.

"Orders from G.H.Q. are orders, Smoke. You know that. Better get over there as soon as possible. This thing General Banks wants to see you on may be in connection with what you have just reported."

Smoke nodded slowly.

"Reckon you're right," he admitted. "Generals is to run things, after all. Sometimes maybe I take too much in my own hands, colonel."

McGill smiled with paternal kindness.

"What you undertake has always come out for the best, Smoke. I'll admit that."

"Thanks, colonel," Smoke said. "Be seein' yuh."

AGAIN the pinto Spad took the air. This time Smoke turned southwest toward general headquarters. Ten minutes later he landed in the little field he often used for the purpose, across the road from the great headquarters.

He was admitted at once to General Banks. The general was as straight, as dignified as ever. But his face was creased with many worry lines. He smiled with relief as he saw Smoke.

"I'm always delighted and grateful when you come, in, Smoke," the great general said, holding out his hand. "Perhaps it's because I only call upon you when I'm stuck and can't think of another way out. Then comes the fear that perhaps you may not be—er—able to come. I'd sure be up against it under those circumstances."

Smoke grinned.

"I reckon you wouldn't be the only one, general," he said. "But what's this I hear you got on your mind. Must be mighty important. Wait. Let me guess, will yuh?"

General Banks frowned.

"Guess?"

"Reckon so," grinned Smoke. "If you wasn't such a good friend of mine, general, I'd lay yuh a bet I could guess the nature of this here callin'. But bein' as how I ain't wantin' to make money out of yuh, I'll just guess that this here thing you're callin' me on has got somethin' to do with a black gas thet—"

General Banks' eyes opened wide with astonishment.

"Black gas!" he exclaimed. "Smoke. How in the devil did you know?" There was more than mere surprise in his voice. There was fear, horror.

The telephone jangled on the desk. General Banks seemed jumpy. He jerked and snatched the phone. Barked into the mouthpiece.

"Hello . . . Yes, yes . . . Oh, Good Lord! . . . Very well."

Bang! The receiver slammed to the hook. Banks whirled to face Smoke.

"I see now," he said. "I didn't know."

Smoke frowned.

"General, you sure are talkin' plumb ten thousand feet over my haid. Must be I'm pretty dumb, but I don't get none of this here."

General Banks took a long breath. He seemed to be fighting to control himself. He sank into his chair, spread out his hands in a half hopeless gesture.

"I couldn't imagine how you could guess about this black gas," he admitted.

"Then I suddenly realized that it could only mean one thing."

Smoke looked more puzzled than ever.

"You see," General Banks went on, "yesterday a member of our Intelligence returned from a month in Germany. He brought back considerable information of great value. Among other things he told us of a new horrible gas the Germans have developed. He has been unable to procure a mask that will guard against the gas. He isn't sure, in fact, that the Germans have a mask that will protect against The Black Death, as they call it. He has an idea that the Germans who work about it use masks with oxygen tanks attached."

Smoke nodded.

"Come to think of it, they did look sort of like they had oxygen tanks in 'em. They was too big for just head masks. I seen 'em less than an hour ago up in the Fesmes sector where they were turnin' some loose. Must be hell. Poor devils runnin' as far as they could and then droppin' from exhaustion. I was goin' back to bomb the outlets when Colonel McGill said you wanted to see me."

"I assumed you had seen the attack," General Banks said. "I didn't know it had come off until you practically told me; then this telephoned message told me the truth. The devil is to pay up there. The gas has been coming over for perhaps an hour. This is the first chance anyone has had to get the message through to me. That was a valiant idea to bomb the outlets, Smoke, but I have a much more direct way for you to stop this devilish work. I have a way by which you can get directly at the supply base."

Smoke's eyes opened wide.

"Huh?" he asked. "Supply base? You mean at the factory, general? Yuh know where the stuff is made?"

"Exactly," Banks nodded. "The Intelligence officer who just returned has the whole location and the plan for attack." Smoke moved to the edge of his chair. He lighted a cigarette, puffed and hung on the words of General Banks.

BANKS stepped to the side of his office. He pulled down a large map of Belgium, Holland and Germany. He traced with his finger, spoke in lower tones.

"There," he said, "is Dornsel. In that town this black gas is manufactured. It cannot be made anywhere else, apparently. From what the Intelligence officer says it is made from a peculiar oil that is taken from the ground at that point. This special crude oil must be used the instant it comes from the ground to produce the desired result. There is some gas in connection with it that must not be allowed to free itself entirely from the liquid. So there is the factory."

Smoke was on his feet, walking to the map, staring, perplexed.

"But, general," he objected. "Dornsel on the map there is plenty miles away from our nearest point of take-off. A guy wouldn't have the chance of a gopher in a wolf's mouth of gettin' back after he'd flown over and bombed the place there. Couldn't carry enough gas and bombs too."

"Of course," said General Banks. "That has been considered. The place will be bombed, of course, but the take-off will be from Germany, not Allied territory."

"Huh?" said Smoke. "I don't follow you on the jumps no how, general. Don't tell me yuh got gas stations reserved along the way."

Banks shook his head. He smiled a little. Relaxed.

"Watch my finger," he said. "You're pretty good at guessing, Smoke. See if you can figure how you'll get a plane into Germany."

Smoke watched. General Banks' finger was following a blue, irregular line on the map that was marked Rhine River.

A twisted grin spread over Smoke's face.

"Be pretty far to swim, I reckon," he drawled. "Only other way would be by submarine, maybe. Thet it?"

Banks nodded.

"Good guess. Here's the plan. There is a captured German submarine on the coast at St. Valery in the mouth of the Somme. It requires a crew of at least four to man it, including the officer in command. G-3, the Intelligence officer who brought back this information, will be in charge. You will choose two men to accompany you. G-3 is a former submarine officer. Already they are taking a special plane with folding wings to be stowed away in the room that has been especially built in the submarine. Your job, of course, will be to fly the plane with bombs, drop them on the factory and return to the submarine base where it will be in hiding here."

The general's finger had traveled through Belgium, up the Rhine River, moved up a branch past a town called Wesel and paused some distance up the Lippe River, a tributary of the Rhine.

"There," he said, "G-3 tells us, is an island, well hidden from view of either bank. The island is not inhabited. It has a level stretch of field that will be suitable for a take-off."

"Reckon thet sounds mighty easy—if we get thet far," Smoke ventured. "Can a sub go up the Rhine thet far?"

Banks nodded.

"The Rhine has plenty of depth far beyond the Lippe River. The Lippe River, however, might cause some trouble, but it would be a run of an hour or two up the Lippe River and that could be made with the electric motors of the submarine at night with the sub only partly submerged if necessary."

His finger moved from the island to Dornsel.

"From this island," he went on, "you see Dornsel is only about a hundred miles north. That can be easily made with this special ship and the few high explosive bombs. G-3 tried himself to blow up the factory for the black gas at Dornsel, but he says it is entirely too heavily guarded on the ground. However, there is no fortifying against aerial attack as they know we can't fly from France and return without refueling."

Smoke hitched his six-gun higher on his leg. Turned.

"When do we start, general?" he asked.

Banks smiled. His hand came down firmly on Smoke's shoulder.

"I knew you'd say that, Smoke," he said. "Start at once. The sooner that factory is blown to bits the fewer Yanks will die of the devilish stuff. Every minute counts. Do you want me to have any special two men sent as your assistants for the trip?"

Smoke paused for an instant. He nodded.

"Reckon so," he said. "Remember them two Cherokee Indians, Tom and Joe Buck? Connected with the signal corps. Cain't think of no one I could trust quite as much as them in a pinch. If you'll have them start for St. Valery right pronto, I reckon they'll find me and Jake, my pinto Spad, waitin' fer 'em."

THE pinto Spad took the air again, thundered over France to the west. Ahead he made out the coast line from ten thousand feet. There was something thrilling to Smoke about this new adventure.

"Don't know whether I'm goin' to like ridin' in one of these submarines," Smoke drawled to himself as he slammed his pinto Spad down to a field near the harbor at St. Valery in the mouth of the Somme.

Coming down he sighted a long, black thing. It looked like a floating pig, gigantic in size.

"Reckon thet's her," he grinned.

He landed. A bit reluctantly, he climbed from, the cockpit of his pinto Spad, turned it over to French soldiers to guard.

Smoke caught a ride to the docks of St. Valery. He asked a Yank sailor on the deck of the submarine a significant question.

"Ever hear of a hombre named Smoke Wade, partner?" he asked.

The sailor's eyes narrowed for an instant. An alert young man, quick of movement, keen-eyed, appeared behind Smoke suddenly.

"You're asking to see Smoke Wade," said the stranger.

Smoke turned. He grinned.

"Gee, no," he said. "I'm Smoke Wade."

The man who had appeared behind him nodded to the sailor on the deck. The gob disappeared below. The man smiled.

"G-3," he corrected. "You may want to call me G-D and a lot of other things before I get through for getting you in this mess, but I've been over. I've seen things."

Smoke nodded solemnly.

"I seen it, too, this morning, I reckon. We got to blast this gas off the face of the earth before more Yanks die. You likely seen it bein' experimented with in Germany. I seen it in action, killin' men. It's hell."

G-3 nodded.

"I don't doubt it. Let's go below," he offered. "Ever been on a submarine?"

Smoke shook his head.

"Not guilty; and I'll admit I never had much hankerin' to. Not for genuine pleasure. I got two men, Cherokee Indians, they are. They'll be here in another couple of hours. When do yuh figure to take off in this thing?"

G-3 laughed as they climbed down through a hatch.

"You don't take off in a submarine," he chuckled. "But I figure to leave port this afternoon, just before dark. We'll reach the mouth of the Rhine past midnight then, or should."

"How long you figure it'll take to make the trip?" Smoke inquired.

"Two days. That is, two days and three nights, including tonight. That should land us at the island in the River Lippe the third night from now. If we're lucky, that will be the night that the gas house is bombed at Dornsel."

"Brrrrrr," Smoke shivered as he dropped into the interior of the submarine. "For a hombre what is used to the great open spaces where yuh got room to move around, this place don't look like no paradise to spend a pleasant weekend," he groaned.

G-3 laughed.

"You'll get used to it," he chuckled. "Come in here. I'll show you your bombing job."

He pushed open a steel door at the end of the control room and stepped aside for Smoke to pass.

Smoke pushed through, straightened and said "Ouch!" His head had hit a steel beam beyond the door. Then he stared at the plane.

"Reckon I never did see nothin' like thet," he said. "Not quite."

"I'm quite sure you haven't," G-3 assured him. "They've just started building these planes. It's a rather compact model of a Bristol Fighter. Wings fold easily. You can see it doesn't take much space compared to the carrying capacity. This plane will carry full tanks of gas for four hours and three hundred pounds of bombs, besides the pilot. This plane, as you can see, is equipped with a land gear. Makes a much faster job."

Smoke walked round the ship with folded wings. His eyes shone with interest. He pointed to a second cockpit between the wings.

"Thought this was only a single-place bomber," he ventured.

G-3 nodded.

"It is. That isn't really a cockpit. That's where the bombs are kept." He pointed inside. "Six of them. Fifty pounds apiece. Couldn't put them in the wings because it would harder handling. In here they don't have to be touched until they're ready to be dropped."

AFTER an hour's inspection of the submarine they went on deck again. Smoke stepped to the wharf. He breathed deeply, lighted a cigarette and inhaled luxuriously. G-3 smiled.

"I ain't figurin' to get cooped up in thet thing no sooner than I have to," Smoke said as he sat down and let his booted feet hang off toward the water. Leaned back against a pile, he smoked on. The afternoon waned. G-3 busied himself with preparations for the cruise.

Two shambling figures, straight, bronze, black-haired, came down the wharf in late afternoon. Tom Buck, the taller, leaner of the two, said "Howdy, Smoke."

Joe Buck, the stouter, grinned as he nodded.

"The general says we go for a boat ride."

Smoke nodded.

"Yeah. But this time you don't even get a chance to see the world through a port hole." He pointed to the submarine. "If you figure you're goin' on a pleasure cruise in thet thing, you're crazy."

G-3 put in appearance. Met Tom and Joe Buck.

"We better be weighing anchor," he advised them.

Gobs who had been making last minute adjustments stepped ashore. Smoke, Tom Buck and his brother clambered down the ladder into the control room. G-3 followed them. The hatch above their heads was closed. G-3 turned to them to give instructions.

"Stand by and watch how I do things," he said. "You'll get the rudimentary idea of it before long. Motors are electric, of course. We could have brought many more men aboard, but—" and now a smile broke on his lips—"we might find it necessary to blow her up in the river after the mission is over. No need of leaving more men than necessary stranded in Germany."

"Huh?" said Smoke. His eyes narrowed. G-3 laughed.

Already the submarine vibrated. A whirring sound came from the rear end of the craft. They seemed to be moving. G-3 pointed to the dials, levers, explained what they meant, how they affected the movements of the submarine.

He ground a handle by the tower in the center of the control room.

"We're going down just below the surface," he explained. "I'm putting up the periscope. Look in here. This mirror before you. We can see where we're going by this."

Smoke nodded.

"I've heard of them, 'course," he said. "But I never could figure how one of these subs could go up a river without bein' seen by the shore. Anybody could sure spot thet thing stickin' up through the water and movin' along."

"I've thought of that, too," admitted G-3. "So I'm trying a new stunt of mine on this trip, since we plan to go by river. We could travel by night, but there isn't time to waste whole days. You probably didn't notice this periscope. The top looks like a duck. I hope no German peasant notices a duck traveling pretty fast up the river in a perfectly straight line tomorrow or the next day."

Smoke laughed. The two Indians grinned. But in Smoke's voice genuine mirth was lacking when he said.

"I sure hope no hungry duck hunter comes along what can shoot. I always wondered just how ducks felt. Reckon I'll know, maybe."

Toward midnight the rolling motion of the sea quieted. G-3 was busy every second. He was cruising in the dark, taking note of his speed, of his position. Then he turned the craft.

"We're in the mouth of the Rhine now," he said. "Better turn in and try to get some sleep. You'll have to relieve me some time tomorrow."

Hours later Smoke leaped from his bunk. He couldn't recall when he had fallen asleep. Must have been a long time ago.

"How's she coming, partner?" Smoke asked in deep concern.

G-3 smiled wearily.

"O.K. We've got a good start. River is good and wide and deep here. See?" he pointed into the glass.

Smoke stared, and shivered.

"Gives me a funny feeling to know I'm under a mess of water like that glass shows us ahead. This is no place for a desert ranger like me, partner. Damn glad I ain't flyin' these rat traps fer a livin'."

G-3 chuckled as he stepped away from the wheel.

"You take her for a while," he encouraged. "I'll keep an eye on you while I get some cans open; then if you're doing all right I'll turn in after I get a bite to eat and you can take charge for a few hours. We're going pretty slow for two reasons. We can't take a chance of running aground in daylight, let alone the dark, and then I don't want that duck to look too much as though she's going places in a hurry."

Smoke took the controls gingerly.

"I hope," he said, "I don't do very poorly. I'd a heap rather ride a whole string of buckin' horses and fight von Stolz and his gang to boot than try to fly one of these blind pigs."

BUT Smoke did sufficiently well so that he kept the submarine plowing the waters noiselessly for hours that day. Tom and Joe Buck took their turns but confined themselves more to oiling and keeping the great machine in running order.

Night came and the second day. The river became narrowed, and deeper too. Through the periscope they could see the ancient castles on the high cliffs above the river. Several times they slowed, came to a stop as a river boat passed. They moved with extreme care past towns and cities.

They neared Wesel at the junction of the River Lippe and the Rhine at the close of the daylight hours of the second day. Here would be the turning.

G-3 had been catching a couple of hours sleep. But he was at the controls when they got their first warning of real danger. Through the periscope they made out a motor boat leaving the docks at Wesel. It headed for them in the river.

G-3 tensed by the controls.

"Trouble coming at us," he hissed.

For a half minute he stood motionless, steering on a straight course. Smoke leaned over his shoulder, stared into the glass.

"Look," he said. "That varmint. He's gettin' ready to shoot at our duck."

Instantly, G-3 moved the controls. The sub dived deeper. They could only see water bubbling above the glass. The submarine was moving faster, faster.

"Got to run for it," G-3 said through tight lips. "Don't know whether they think they're shooting ducks or submarines. Suppose we couldn't hope to keen them fooled forever."

Minutes raced by. Minutes that spelled horrible death at the bottom of the river. G-3 moved the controls again.

"Got to come up and take a look. Can't run aground now."

The glass cleared. G-3 swung the periscope. The Boche boat was in hot pursuit. Another boat, a larger one, was joining in the hunt. G-3 cursed.

"Not hunting ducks," he said with certainty now. "Good thing it's nearly dark. We may beat them out. Got to move fast. They'll be—"

Blam! The sub shuddered. Smoke fell to the floor. G-3 was clutching a brace rod in one hand and staring into the glass. His face whitened.

"Torpedo!" he explained. "Just missed. Time torpedo."

He grew rigid. Stared fixedly at the instruments. Into the glass once more.

"Going to dive. Hope we don't hit bottom. Headed straight up the River Lippe now. Long stretch. Go by compass."

Controls moved again. The sub went deeper. Water bubbled in the glass once more. Then suspense. The air seemed choking inside the control room. Maybe that was imagination. Maybe not. Smoke couldn't tell. He only knew that he'd never felt so shut in, so utterly helpless in his life. He coughed. Tom Buck came and leaned over him. He gulped.

"Air not good in here," he said thickly.

Smoke shook his head.

"Lousy," he agreed.

"Don't move any more than you have to," G-3 cracked from beside his controls. "Something's happened to the oxygen machinery. Torpedoed probably. Have to come up before long. Engine's holding out. Pray we don't hit anything, if you can't think of anything else to do."

MINUTES seemed like days. Hours like eternity. Then when the air became so dead that Smoke saw black specks before his eyes, the submarine began to rise.

"Got to come up," G-3 choked. "Let's hope they've given up the chase."

Smoke staggered to the controls and peered into the glass. Only darkness there. It was dark. They'd have a tough time spotting them. He opened his mouth to speak. Gasped instead.

A beam of light slashed and blinded into the glass.

"They're still on the trail," G-3 said bitterly. "We're going up. Got to open the hatch to breathe anyway. A one-pounder is below decks." He pulled a lever. "It's up now. Ammunition in the store room. You three go up and do your stuff."

That was all. Enough. Smoke dove into the store room, past the plane with folded wings. Found the one-pounder shells. Tom and Joe were beside him. With arms full of shells they tore for the hatch that was already open. The air was most welcome. They still staggered as they ran back along the dripping deck to the gun aft of the submarine.

Smoke aimed the gun. The two Cherokee Indians shot home the shells. The gun blammed and barked again.

Four times the gun boomed, and then the searchlight went out with a violent flash.

"Get 'em?" G-3 called through the hatch.

"Not sure. Got the searchlight, I reckon."

"Good. The island's just ahead. Stand by for a crash. Goin' to beach the sub right on this end of the island. Have to blow her up after we get the plane off. Can't let Jerry get her so easy."

Smoke grasped a rail. Minutes passed. There was no sign from behind. The Boche boat might be sinking. It might still be pursuing them without a searchlight.

Bam! Crash! A terrific clanking, grating noise came from the forward part of the sub. Smoke felt himself jerked forward.

"Quick. Out the way." That was G-3 through the hatch. In the darkness a great arm rose from the after-deck of the sub. The whole top opened, split apart in two great doors.

Smoke peered down the hatchway into the control room.

"Here comes the ship," G-3 called. "Heads up—or down."

A whirring sound and the arm came up, up, higher and higher. A black bulk rose beneath it at the end of short cables. It swung clear. The derrick arm swung toward the shore. The plane lowered to the bank of the island.

G-3 was clambering out of the hatch. With the aid of Tom and Joe the plane was hurriedly assembled. Wings fixed. The plane stood complete, ready to go. Joe Buck was before the propeller. A blinding light flashed on them from down the river.

Smoke leaped for the cockpit. G-3 was pointing straight ahead.

"Get off at once. Engine ought not to be too cold out of hot store room. Find maps of Dornsel and the gas factory in the cockpit case. Plenty of flares."

"Contact!" Smoke yelled. Joe Buck whirled the prop.

"If you get a chance come back and pick up the two boys. Good Indians. Don't worry about me. I've got a German uniform in the sub. I'll get it on before I blow her up. Got more business over here."

Brrrram! The great engine roared on the fifth turn of the prop.

"Good luck!" called G-3. "Take off straight ahead. All clear."

Smoke's hand smacked the gun open. One spit and the engine ran smoothly. The searchlight caught him in the glare

Ping! Something whined overhead. The plane gathered speed, grew light. Rose. Smoke sat back and took a long breath.

He climbed higher and higher. No need of warning the whole German countryside that he was coming. He reached for the map case, drew out the maps.

Blam! A brilliant flash and a dull boom came from behind. He turned and stared back and down. The whole island was lighted by the blast. Pieces of metal flew high in the air. The sub was split wide open. Then darkness closed in again below.

SMOKE found the points marked on his map. He checked his time. Be about a one-hour run to Dornsel. He roared on. Nothing happened to vary the monotony. He sat back, rested and was thankful for a seat in the sky and not below the water.

Fifty minutes. He picked up a flare, swung lower. It didn't matter so much about Heinie seeing or hearing him clearly now. He was here. He dropped the flare.

The earth became lighted like day. He saw the town ahead, saw figures in the streets suddenly take life and run about like frightened ants.

According to the map the factory should be at the north end of town. He flung out another flare, found the building. Figures streamed from the doors in confusion. Several guards turned their rifles up at him. The flares blinded them so they could not take accurate aim.

Another and another flare went over the side; then Smoke Wade pushed the plane down, down in a terrific dive. Steel slammed against his wings. He pulled level just over the roof of the factory. His hand yanked the toggle lever.

Blam! Blam! Blam! The building heaved as he roared over. A sharp turn and he thundered back. Three more bombs hissed down. In the light of the settling flares he could see black, soot like vapor coming in clouds from the demolished building.

He paused a moment. Shuddered.

"Maybe you'll like a taste of your own stuff," he said, not angrily.

He turned then, flew by compass and the clock back the way he had come. He checked his gas. Tank three quarters full.

Fifty minutes' flying. His eyes were becoming accustomed to the darkness. He made out the River Lippe far below.

His hand reached for the switch. The motor died. He dropped the nose and began to glide down. He could make out the island by the river's dull gleam on either side of it.

Silently, with only the gentle swish of wind passing his wings, Smoke brought his plane down for a landing. All seemed still about him. He tensed in the cockpit.

"Whooo! Whooo!"

Very gently the sound of a sleepy hoot owl came from the trees at the side.

Smoke paused. He pursed his lips and answered. A figure emerged from the shadow, then another. They came running toward the plane with a soft, swift padding of feet.

"Quick. We go? Germans in boat."

Joe Buck leaped for the propeller. Tom poised on the step.

"We almost get caught," he said. "Plane land here after you take off. Think it you. Run out. Find out wrong. Ship go again after find out submarine is blown up. We make sure this time."

A light flashed through the trees on the other side of the field. Smoke's big six-gun was out in a flash.

Blam! The light leaped and went out.

A guttural voice cursed and groaned. More lights popped out.

The prop spun. The engine caught. Tom, shooting as he went, climbed into the front bomb cockpit. Joe leaped in beside him. Smoke pushed on the gun and took a last shot.

Sluggishly, reluctantly, the plane rose. Landing gear dragged through the tree tops. Staggered—regained speed—plugged on. Without a moment's hesitation, Smoke turned toward the south.

His eyes switched from the compass to the clock to the gas gauge. He held his altitude at a thousand feet. No time to waste in climbing. Minutes dragged. The gas seemed to pour into the engine.

Then, when the gas gauge said empty, Smoke made out pin points of flame ahead. Guns belched under him. German guns.

No-Man's-Land skimmed beneath him in the light of the flare. The first-line Yank trenches swept beneath. The second line. Out ahead he could see a field. He made for it.

Only a wheel and a wing were broken in the landing.

It was while Smoke and Tom and Joe were riding back of the lines in a truck that Smoke asked:

"How about G-3? He get away?"

"G-3 had a boat hid in bushes," Joe said. "He went ashore in that."

"Huh?" said Smoke. "Yuh don't tell me. Reckon thet bird sure planned out this trip all right. But from now on he can have his submarines. I'll take my cruises in a ferry boat, I reckon."

Joe grinned. "Tom says he'll take his in canoe," he offered.

NEXT MONTH—

Smoke Wade hurls his pinto Spad against the wings of a ghost buzzard!

"F-17 was gasping for breath. Smoke started to lift him, but the man shook his head. 'It's—all over. Let me talk. Listen. They're bombing—your field—tonight. Von Stolz and—his cousin. A—trick. Watch—for—' But before he could finish, death had marked him with its black, bony finger."

What was the warning he had failed to give? What grim danger was awaiting Smoke Wade? Be sure to read this gripping story in BATTLE BIRDS for October.

The
Gotha
Ghost
FREDERICK
BLAKESLEE

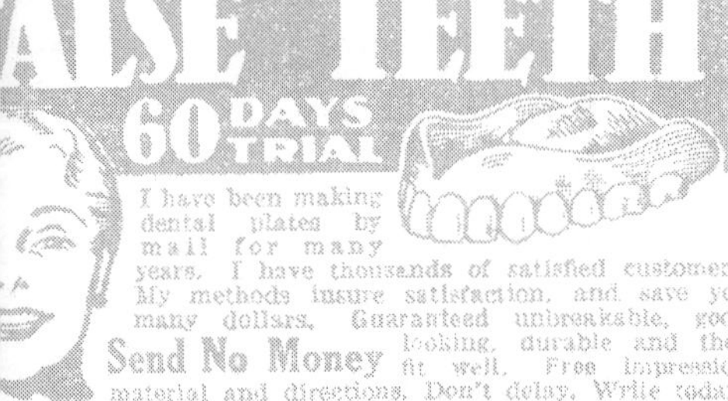

"I am the ghost of von Muhl. Tomorrow you will all die!" Ghastly, weird, the voice echoed through the mess room of the 66th. But there are more ways than one of slaying a specter—and Smoke Wade and his new buddy knew 'em all!

The Gotha Ghost

WHEN Smoke Wade caught sight for the first time of that intermittent white flash far below, he was squinting through his powerful glasses from an altitude of ten thousand feet above Germany.

His lanky form straightened in the seat abruptly with interest. The leather of his face wrinkled in a puzzled expression.

"What the hell, Jake?" he asked his pinto Spad. "Sure looks like some poor hombre is tryin' to send us a signal from Heinie land. Yep, sure does."

Instantly he lowered his glasses from his eyes and stared about the blue of the sky for other ships.

"Nope," he concluded. "Thought maybe somebody was signalin' to somebody else up here, but there ain't a soul in the sky but me. Wonder where von Stolz and his brood is this evenin'. Don't reckon they'd be turnin' in fer the night this early. Why, the sun ain't hardly down far enough to call it evenin', hardly."

While he talked to himself, he moved the controls. The pinto Spad moved instantly. Dove with power full on for an open field two miles down, well back of the lines.

As he came nearer he saw the flashes of white more clearly. They had only been tiny white specks when they had first attracted his attention.

Now the lanky Arizona cowboy skipper of the 66th saw that they were signals in code.

S.O.S. S.O.S. NEWS! NEWS!

"Holy tail-waggin' rattle snakes," Smoke said. "Reckon thet's some spy of ourn—or else I'm a ring-horned toad."

The pinto Spad screamed. The Hisso was going crazy in the dive. Down, down. Down to five thousand, four thousand. The dots and dashes continued to come. Smoke could see now that a man dressed in a German uniform was flattening and placing on edge again, intermittently, a square panel of white. Perhaps a frame with cloth over. Perhaps a white piece of card-board.

The man was staring up, waving frantically. Pointing to the south. Smoke turned. Gasped. Swore. A cloud of dust marked the flight of a racing car, headed for the field where the lone man stood.

Smoke jerked the controls. He sent the pinto Spad thundering toward the car just as it lurched to a stop near the field. Two men leaped from the car. Then Vickers guns chanted death. Smoke was staring across his sights, holding down the trigger. Three men about to leap from the auto sprawled over the side and lay still.

Smoke banked, sighted and pressed again. One of the two Boches who had jumped was still in the open. He crumpled in a strange, limp somersault. The other had gained the shelter of a hedge alongside the road.

Smoke sent a hail of steel into that hedge from above. He saw the man leap out, clutch his throat and fall. But when he shifted his eyes to the man who had been signaling with the panels, he knew he had gotten that last German a split second too late.

The signaler was down on his knees. He was holding one hand toward Smoke. Struggling to get up. He staggered there, slumped again.

Smoke kicked over, stuck the pinto Spad into a wild slip and romped down. Wheels touched. The ship rolled. Smoke was out instantly. He raced headlong to the still figure. Knelt down.

Blood oozed from a wound in the chest. The man was gasping for breath. Smoke lifted his head a little.

"Good Lord," he said. "You—you ain't F-17?"

A light of recognition came into the dulling eyes of the spy. The head nodded slightly.

"Yes—Smoke. Listen. Saw your pinto Spad."

Smoke half lifted F-17 from the ground. The man shook his head.

"It's—all over. Let me talk. Listen."

Smoke relaxed. Bent down closer.

"They're—bombing—your field—tonight. Von Muhl and—bombers. Von Stolz's cousin."

A convulsion shook F-17 as he lay there in Smoke's arms. Blood gushed from his chest, from his lips now. The eyes glazed, cleared again. The lips moved.

"A—trick. Watch—for—"

F-17 made a valiant effort to continue at the last. To finish his word of warning. But death marked him with its black, bony finger before he was through.

SMOKE seized F-17 in his arms and ran to the pinto Spad. Once this famous spy and Smoke had turned a trick against the Germans together. F-17 was dead. He'd be returned to his own side of the lines.

While Smoke ran he pleaded with the dead man. Perhaps he wasn't dead. Half crazily Smoke tried to make himself realize it wasn't true. F-17 had been such a swell guy. What was it he was going to say and couldn't finish?

Another car was racing toward the field as Smoke crammed into the cockpit with the body of F-17 on his lap. The Hisso barked. Guns cracked along the edge of the road. Smoke ducked, yanked the pinto Spad into the air and turned south.

The body of F-17 was growing cold when the pinto Spad settled to a gentle landing at the field of the 66th near Ramou.

Tenderly, as a father would carry a child, Smoke bore the limp form to the hospital. It took a medical officer but a few minutes to pronounce the final verdict.

"Dead!" he said.

Smoke nodded solemnly.

"Reckoned so," he said. "Wanted to be sure."

He turned and walked toward Colonel McGill's office as one in a daze. The grayed old war dog looked up—frowned as Smoke appeared before him.

"Good Lord, Smoke, you look as if you'd seen a ghost."

"Reckon I do," he said. "Remember that spy they called F-17? I worked with him on a little deal across the lines. We worked together. Swell fella, he was. Just picked him up over in Heinie land—dead. Said von Muhl, von Stolz's cousin, is comin' over with his bombers tonight to blow hell out of us here at the field. He said somethin' else I couldn't get rightly clear and he died before he could finish tellin' me. Somethin' about a trick to watch out fer. Reckon he knowed what it was—if he only could a lived a half minute longer."

Colonel McGill's face whitened slightly.

"Good Lord, Smoke. Bombing this field tonight! You're sure he said it was von Muhl's bombers? He's the cleverest bomb *Jadgstaffel* commander on the German side of the lines."

"Certain of it, I reckon," Smoke nodded. "What you propose to do about it, colonel?"

McGill tapped his desk for a moment.

"To tell the truth, I was just about to ask you the same question. What would you do?"

Smoke shrugged.

"Ain't really only one thing to do I reckon. Order every ship into the air and every man off the field. Thet's the usual thing, I reckon, when a field knows there's bombers comin' over to give 'em hell."

McGill nodded.

"I suppose you're right." He cursed and rapped his fist hard on the table. "It galls the very devil out of me to have these Jerries come over and scare us stiff so that we have to leave our field without even a guard."

"Reckon it does me too," Smoke admitted. "But with bombers comin' over to blow us off the face of the map, it don't matter much whether there's anything to guard or not. Not after they get through, if they do any kind of a job." Smoke grinned for the first time.

"Course maybe they won't, but yuh never can tell. It won't be like every pilot on the field was goin' to crawl off in a corner and die. Reckon when we get the word from the listenin' post at the Front that the bombers is comin', we'll be takin' the air. I'll lay anybody a hundred franc note against a plug nickel thet although this von Muhl and his egg layers place some of their nest decorators, they won't all go home and tell the folks it was a swell picnic. Me and the boys'll be up there when they come, and there'll be plenty of hell poppin'."

McGill looked relieved.

"That's the way I like to hear you talk, Smoke," he said. "You looked pretty well licked when you came in here a few minutes ago. I'll issue the order at once. Every enlisted man will leave the field an hour after dark. Only a few mechanics will remain, as many as necessary. They will leave as soon as you and your ships take off. Is every man in condition to fly, Smoke?"

"Reckon so," came the answer. "Heard Brant say he had a toothache this noon, but I don't guess thet'll keep him from doin' his stuff as usual. Likely he's either got it pulled or plugged by this time."

A HUSH fell over the evening mess as Smoke entered. Already the news had spread. McGill had ordered everyone to leave the field one hour after dark, with the exception of a few mechanics. Rumor had it that all ships would be ready to take off at a moment's notice. What did it mean?

Smoke told them.

"And remember this," he advised. "F-17 said there was a trick of some kind comin'. But he didn't say what it was. Every one of you hombres be ready to take off. Ships'll be kept warm until we get word from the listenin' post at the Front that the bombers are comin' over. Then we go up and do our stuff, *sabbe?*"

Heads nodded. Pilots shifted uneasily. Smoke swept them with his keen eyes. He sensed the atmosphere of tenseness about the place. Men didn't eat as well as they had before he had spoken. When he had entered there had been mystery in the air; now, at mention of a Boche trick, there was something akin to fear.

Smoke's brain throbbed for sudden inspiration. He caught Brant's eye, made a sign for him to come over.

"How's the toothache?" he asked.

Brant grinned for answer. Showed a hole in the lower jaw at the right with a mass of clotted blood.

"O. K., Smoke," he said.

"The boys look kind of jittery," Smoke went on in a lowered voice.

"You and Quinn and Snell are O.K. and the older men; but what's struck the replacements? They've been up here long enough to keep their feelings to themselves, it seems."

Brant nodded.

"Sure," he agreed. "I guess Carter has got them steamed up again. He's a strange sort of a bird. Good enough guy and all that. Older than most of the rest."

Smoke's eyes narrowed. He jerked his head to Brant and moved toward a table at the end of the room.

"Come on over and eat with me," he said.

Brant followed. When they were out of hearing of the others Smoke spoke again.

"What do you know about this hombre, Carter? Used to be on the vaudeville stage or something, didn't he?"

Brant nodded.

"Sleight of hand artist. Magician. Damn clever, too. He's got a lot of stories about black magic and spirits and that stuff. I don't think he means any harm. Sort of heavy on the practical joking side."

"Sure," said Smoke. He rose half out of his seat and stared about the mess. He sat down again and turned to Brant.

"Carter's over in the other end of the room next to Quinn," he said. "Go over and tell him I want to see him, will yuh?"

Brant left. A moment later he came back with Carter.

Carter was perhaps twenty-five or thirty; older than the usual run of replacements that came up from Issoudon. He had dark, penetrating eyes, a mouth, that curled up slightly at the corners as though he were about to smile any moment, and quick, alert hands with long, tapering fingers.

"Hello, Carter," Smoke nodded. "“‘Sit down."

Carter sat down. He looked puzzled.

"Hear you're a magician," Smoke ventured. "What's this practical joking I hear you been playin' on the boys, gettin' 'em all worked up sort of about black magic and this and that?"

Carter's upturned lips broke into a smile.

"Oh, that," he said. "I've just been kidding. Truthfully, I don't know any more about this black magic stuff than you do. But some of these kids seem so damned innocent I couldn't resist the temptation of giving them a thrill. I didn't mean to do any harm."

"No, but yuh are, Carter," Smoke ventured. "Some of these boys are only kids, as you say. That's all the more reason why they shouldn't be kidded. Their imaginations are too alive, I reckon. They cain't control their feelin' like you and me. I noticed things tightened up tonight when I mentioned a trick that probably was coming.

"Here's what I want you to do right now, Carter. The boys are close to the jitters. You're goin' to put on a show. Make it funny. Forget the mysterious and weird stuff. Make them forget it. Put on a magic act that'll make 'em laugh. Make' me the goat if you want to. Reckon thet'll be funnier yet."

Carter eyed Smoke suspiciously for an instant.

"Sure you wouldn't get sore, captain?" he asked.

Smoke laughed.

"Reckon you don't know me very well yet, Carter. Try it and see."

"O.K." Carter hissed. "Here goes."

AS Carter spoke, he burst into a roar of rippling laughter.

Pilots, old and new jerked their heads around. Carter was getting to his feet. He stepped to the seat of his chair, grasped Smoke by the shoulder and helped him stand up.

"Listen, you birds," Carter sang out with another ripple of laughter, "I just found out something about our commanding officer while I was sitting here talking to him. Boy, has he had you guys fooled plenty!"

A hush came over the mess. Every eye was on Smoke and Carter. Smoke's face had a puzzled expression—part of it was genuine.

"I just found out some things about Smoke Wade, gang, that you never dreamed of," Carter laughed on. "Listen. Shhhh. Any of you birds ever think Smoke was a lady's man? No, neither did I. And from what he says, the only time he leaves the field is to go hunting Heinies. Right?"

Here and there a grin spread over a still white face.

"Then watch closely," said Carter. "Because I'm going to show you how I know that Smoke Wade doesn't go hunting Heinies—not the male kind anyway—when he leaves here."

He turned to blank-faced Smoke.

"Hate to show you up like this, captain," he chuckled, "but this is too good to keep. That bulge in your right coat pocket. Look, everybody."

Carter's hand moved toward it. Smoke made a motion as if to stop him, but purposely too slow. Carter's hand beat his. And before the staring eyes of the pilots of the 66th pursuit squadron, Carter drew out something long and thin and black.

A pair of small, black silk stockings.

Smoke pretended to snatch them away, but Carter succeeded in holding them up triumphantly for everyone to see.

Quinn threw back his head and laughed. Snell chuckled. Laughter went the rounds. The spell of tension was broken.

"Listen," pleaded Carter, "I'm not half through. Wait. Hold everything. Don't laugh. This is serious. Look. Smoke's got something in his inside pocket. Boy, does he think a lot of this dame of his? And she must think a lot of him because she's given him a swell muffler to keep his neck warm. Look."

Like lightning Carter's deft fingers darted into the inside pocket. Flashed out again. He held up something pink and made of silk. Smoke ducked but not in time. Carter managed to hold up a pair of tiny silk panties for a glimpse to every eye. Then quickly he slipped them around Smoke's long, leathery neck. He jerked them away again. The pilots roared.

"Wait a minute," he shouted, "I made a grave mistake. This isn't a muffler, not for the neck anyway." He turned on Smoke in well-affected disgust. "Captain," he said, "I'm surprised. Astonished, in fact."

He had to shout to make himself heard. A replacement laughed so hard he fell out of his chair. Smoke's face was beginning to turn a color that more nearly matched the pink panties.

"Look at these silk pants," he yelled. "Not big enough to cover the tail end of a jack rabbit. Why, Captain. Wait, let me look again. I'm liable to find some hair ribbons before I get through. A big he-guy like you robbing the cradle. What's her name, Smoke?"

Carter's voice stopped. Every eye was on Smoke Wade. The color was rising higher in his thin cheeks. Then from the direction of the front door of the mess came a female voice, high, shrill.

"Oh, there you are, Smoke, you great big gorgeous man, you!"

Eyes turned swiftly toward the door. It was closed. No one was there. Carter was shaking with laughter he could hardly speak as he turned to Smoke.

"Let's see if we can find some hair ribbons," he yelled.

This time Smoke beat him to it. His face was crimson. He ducked under the extended arms and dove through the back door of the mess. He could still hear the pilots' laughter coming through the open doorway.

He stopped and wiped his forehead.

"Phew!" he whistled. "I told thet guy Carter he could make me the goat. Reckon he made me a whole herd of goats in a swell razzberry patch." He broke off in a chuckle as he heard the roars still coming from the mess. "Reckon, too, thet turned the trick. Bet there ain't a single replacement in there that ain't forgot about any trick bein' played tonight."

Later Carter came to him with a worried expression.

"I hope, captain," he said, "you aren't sore about tonight."

Smoke chuckled.

""Sore?" he said. "What do yuh take me fer? I told yuh to do it, didn't I? But I don't mind tellin' yuh I never got so fussed in my life. If there'd been a knot hole an inch bigger'n the biggest one in the floor, I'd a crawled through it, and don't yuh think I wouldn't. What I want to know is where in hell you got them silk things in such a hurry? I know damn well they wasn't on me."

Carter colored slightly.

"Just luck," he smiled. "I got them for a little French girl down in Ramou. Was going to take 'em to her tonight if this bombing business hadn't come up. Just happened to have them in my pocket."

Smoke grinned.

"And I suppose thet was her that yelled through the door at the right time?"

Carter shook his head.

"Don't make me blush," he said. "You've heard of ventriloquism, of course."

Smoke nodded.

"Of course. Mighty clever. Well, it done the trick. I ain't heard anybody mention this bombin' raid since."

Brant and Quinn and Snell, the three flight leaders, came into Smoke's office at that moment. Brant grinned at Carter, shot a sidelong glance at Smoke.

"Get those hair ribbons yet, Carter?" he asked.

"How would you birds all like to go to hell?" boomed Smoke. "I don't suppose I'll ever hear the last of this."

Carter left with a grin frozen on his face.

"You shouldn't," Snell laughed. "That was a damn clever trick. The gang is still laughing their heads off about it. Of course they realize it's a put-up job, but they've forgotten any fear that they might have had. They're new men."

"I reckon," said Smoke, "thet's about the swellest thing I could hear. Now, here's the dope for tonight. Every plane loaded with flares and all the ammunition they'll hold. Have the boys ready to take off at a minute's notice. We'll take off in a wide formation so's we can see each other by exhaust stack flame. I'm waitin' now for the first call from the Front listening posts. I'll let yuh know when anything turns up. We got to be high above the field when they come over. That'll be all fer now."

They left. For a long time Smoke sat alone in his darkened office. Any minute that telephone bell might jangle.

HOURS—one, two, three—moved on. Getting toward midnight. He was tense, listening more alertly now. The bombers should be coming over. He tried to figure what trick might be working against them. What could take place in a bombing raid that would be a clever trick? Nothing! Anything!

Brrrring! Smoke leaped for the phone.

"Smoke Wade talkin' . . . Yeah . . . Comin', eh . . . Thanks."

That was all. Smoke pulled on his flying suit, ran for the door and down the tarmac. Pilots waited by their warmed ships in the darkness. Smoke bellowed ahead of him.

"Start the engines, you buzzards. Pink underwear and all."

If tension had developed since mess it broke again then.

"Contact!"

As the word left pilots' lips, barked to the waiting mechanics at the props, there was a laugh in them. Motors roared. Ships thundered down the field for a formation take-off in the dark. Dangerous, yes, but less dangerous than to have everyone flying about, free lance.

Smoke took his position at point. Flame spat from his exhaust stacks. The Hisso screamed. Other Hissos joined in the bedlam of sound. The whole squadron, in formation, wobbled across the field and took the air.

Higher and higher they climbed. The night was clear. At ten thousand feet altitude Smoke leveled his pinto Spad and circled in a great arc.

He checked his watch. About five more minutes and the bombers should be over. He'd wait until the first bomb was dropped. That would tell for sure they were here. The 66th must be high above them to pounce down.

Blam! The first bomb, a trial shot, split the night with tongues of flame. In the light, Smoke could make out the bombers clearly. Five great Gothas in all. Cumbersome vehicles of war. Cumbersome, but capable of carrying hundreds of pounds of compressed death beneath their wings.

Instantly, Smoke's hand dove into the cockpit and came out, with a flare. It burst and drifted down. Other flares broke the darkness as pilots behind followed their leader's example. Then Smoke tipped the nose of the pinto Spad over and hurled down on full power.

Down, down. Vickers guns rattled in warming bursts. Spandau guns chattered defiantly in return from the front and back gunner's cockpits of the giant bombers. They were obviously taken by surprise, these five bombers. But they were going to fight it out.

Spads leaped and plunged and zoomed under blind spots. Smoke sent one Gotha down in a mass of flames. It was a horrible, impressive sight, the great machine turning and flopping like a mortally wounded beast out of the prehistoric age.

More flares burst above as the last flight, hanging overhead, now came snarling down to the battle.

Blam! Blam! Blam!

Bombs burst in and around the field. One hangar leaped high in the air and caved down, a heap of wreckage. The Gotha at point swerved and plunged east suddenly. Smoke banked and roared after it. But another Gotha banked in front of him; the gunner of the rear cockpit sent

Spandau steel into the right wing of the pinto Spad.

Smoke changed his course. He hunched over, glared through his sights, pressed the trigger. Vickers bucked and ranted. Thin white lines of tracer smoke slashed through into the pilot's cockpit.

The Boche crumpled. The reserve pilot took control, righted the Gotha. The nose gunner was firing at him now.

Another burst of flaming lead left the muzzles of the Vickers guns on the stocky nose of the pinto Spad. The front Boche gunner slumped from sight. The reserve pilot dropped over the wheel. The Gotha started down in a power dive.

Another Gotha was going down to the east. The flares were growing dimmer. Smoke searched the sky for the Gotha which had been at point. He found it. It was running for home.

Instantly, he pounced upon it, chased it out of the rim of the lighted flares. His guns bucked again and again in short bursts. The Gotha turned over like a lazy buzzard, slow and deliberate, then plunged and crashed two minutes later.

Smoke whirled his pinto Spad and searched the dimming sky. In a minute it would be dark once more. He saw the other Gotha, a mere shadow, far to the north. He turned toward it, pushed on the gun—but another Spad was already on it's tail.

The Spad dove, tried to come up under the Gotha's blind spot. Suddenly a tongue of flame shot out from the side of the Yank ship. Smoke held his breath. Who was it?

He couldn't tell at that distance. The plane was falling, falling. The Gotha was running for home. It was out in the dark, alone now. Not much chance of getting it. Anyway, Smoke wasn't so much interested in bagging it as he was in watching one of his boys in trouble.

"Slip her!" he shouted. "Slip her!"

But already the pilot was doing his best. Flames spurted from the engine. The Spad was sliding, blowing the flames away from the fuselage. Smoke romped down beside the disabled Spad.

Then it was that he saw the pilot. Carter was at the stick. Silk stockings and pink panties flashed before Smoke's face in vision. Carter, the boy, the man who had put over the stunt to make them laugh. Carter going down in flames.

Instantly, Smoke jerked the controls. His pinto Spad shot down to land. Wheels touched and rolled. Carter was coming down in a terrific sideslip. Flames continued to blast from the side of the motor.

SMOKE leaped from his cockpit. Stood ready, waiting, tense. It seemed Carter would crash in that slip. Then in the last split second, he kicked straight. Flames seemed to cover his cockpit. No, it was only one side of the cockpit. Carter was sticking his head out of the other side so that he could see. Wheels touched. The tail bounced.

A form catapulted from the cockpit as the plane touched the field. The ship made a half ground loop, stopped and crackled as it burned.

Smoke was running for the crumpled form. It didn't move. He reached Carter's side, turned him over. A gasp came from the injured man's lips. The gasp increased to a cough that seemed to come from the bottom of Carter's shoes. He sat up. Coughed more. Smoke helped him to his feet.

"O.K.?" Smoke asked in concern. "Reckon thet was the swellest show I ever seen."

Carter gasped for breath. He staggered a little, but he could stand alone.

"Phew!" he said. "Thought for a minute Renee wasn't going to get her pants and socks after all. I didn't dare breathe when the flames came at me out of the slip—done a couple of fire tricks on the stage. Know how to handle it. But I lit wrong when I jumped. Knocked what breath I had left out of me."

Carter turned and stared into the north blackness. About them other planes were landing in the light of more flares.

"Damn! Gotha got away," he said. "Got my engine or tank or something."

Suddenly, Smoke came up with a start. He had glanced past Carter to see a figure running to the middle of the field, toward a still form lying on the ground.

"Hey, what the hell?" he barked.

Instantly, he was running toward that bundle of something in the center of the field. By the light of the burning Gotha at the far side, and Carter's burning Spad, he could see quite plainly. And likewise the man who was running from the row of hangars could see him.

The man turned abruptly. Smoke eyed him. He yelled.

"Hey, what goes on?"

His six-gun was out in a flash and blammed across the tarmac. But he took particular pains not to hit the running figure. Perhaps it was one of his own pilots who had just landed. They were coming in all over the field now, taxiing to the deadline. But the man looked more like a mechanic. What was a mechanic doing at the field? They had been ordered to leave as soon as the squadron was in the air. They should have been gone more than a half hour now.

Before Smoke was sure enough to take accurate aim with his six-gun, the man had rounded a hangar corner and was out of sight. Smoke cursed. Kept on going toward the heap in the center of the field.

He reached it, gasped. Something queer here. A bloody face looked up at him. Eyes stared. Dead eyes that could not see. The corpse was dressed in, the uniform of a high-ranking *Offizier* of the Imperial Air Force, Bombers branch.

Smoke shuddered as he felt over the body. Probably wasn't an unbroken bone in the whole mass of bloody flesh. From a breast pocket he drew a slip of paper. Written upon it in both French and English were the words:

"Kindly notify my country that the Baron von Muhl is dead."

Smoke searched the uniform, but there were no other signs of identification. He stared up into the sky. The man had either fallen out of one of those bombers or jumped. And this was von Muhl? Smoke frowned. Something queer about it all. Why should a man jump or fall out of one of those bombers? He couldn't figure out an excuse.

At first when he had sighted the body he had jumped at the conclusion that the Boche had been thrown from one of the bombers when it crashed. But that was impossible. There wasn't a wrecked bomber nearer than a hundred yards.

Quinn came running up now from between the hangars.

"Smoke," he panted. "Guess who you shot down in that lead Gotha?"

"Huh?" said Smoke. "Don't tell me it's von Muhl, von Stolz's cousin!"

Quinn nodded.

"But how did you know?"

"I didn't. Read this." He handed him the note.

Other pilots gathered about them quickly. Quinn looked dazed.

"That's funny," he said. "I just came from the crashed lead Gotha. One of the pilots in the cockpit wore the identification tag of von Muhl."

Carter had come up silently. He laughed.

"Two von Muhls in the same night," he chirped. "That's hot."

Smoke nodded.

"Hot, but not so funny," he said. Then his lips closed and he stalked toward his office, which had been spared from destruction.

As he arrived at the door a motorcycle dispatch rider sputtered up, saluted and handed him a long envelope.

He took it, nodded a good-night to the rider and entered his office. There he lit the light and tore open the letter.

> *Special orders from GENERAL HEADQUARTERS—*
>
> *The 66th pursuit squadron is ordered to take off at dawn and fly above the Camai sector. Keep all enemy air craft from crossing our lines. Our ground movements must not be seen by the enemy.*

SMOKE got up. He reached deep in his foot locker, brought out two bottles of cognac and walked out on the tarmac. His voice rose and floated across the field, which was dotted in three places with holes made by bursting bombs.

"Attention, you buzzards. Report at mess pronto."

Men of the 66th followed Smoke into the mess building. The bombs had done little damage to the field. The aim of the enemy had been thrown off by the surprise attack. Two hangars were down and several acres beyond the tarmac were blown up, but aside from that there was little to hinder regular operations.

Smoke placed the two bottles on the table. Glasses were filled, clinked. He grinned, held up his orders and read from them. Quickly, when he had finished, he glanced about the faces to see how the news had been taken.

"After we leave here," Smoke said, "we'll turn in for a wink, I reckon."

Snell laughed.

"And somebody better stay with you, Smoke, to see that you get yours."

Pilots laughed easily. Smoke laughed with them. Good sign. Tough assignment tomorrow. Von Stolz would be out to avenge the death of his cousin without doubt. There would be plenty of action.

Men drank and talked and ate crackers. Carter came in after Smoke had given the orders. He sat beside Smoke who repeated the orders for the dawn patrol. Carter nodded solemnly. It seemed he had suddenly forgotten how to laugh. He leaned close to Smoke.

"Maybe I'm crazy," he said, "but I've just got a hunch. I think it would be best to send these birds to bed right now. Break them up."

The words had hardly left his lips before a dim, moaning sound resounded through the mess. It seemed to come at once from nowhere and everywhere. It grew in volume. Men ceased their talking, grew tense.

The sound began to waver, took shape, spoke words. Words in a stilted German dialect.

"I—I—I—I ammm the Gho—o—st of von Muhl. My death will be—e—e avenged. Tomorrow you will—all—die!"

Smoke turned in astonishment, he stared blankly at Carter next to him. Carter was motionless. Again the weird voice repeated the warning; Smoke watched his companion without moving an eyelash.

When the voice came the third time, he rose in half-crazed fury. Snatching Carter by the shoulders, he shook him.

The ghostly voice never wavered, never changed from that dull monotone.

"For God's sake, captain," Carter pleaded. "I haven't anything to do with it. That's straight. What do you take me for?"

Baffled, Smoke let him go. Nodded slowly. Stared at the table in front of him. The voice died away.

Smoke looked up quickly, searched the faces of his pilots. White faces before him. The thing they had just heard seemed so ghastly, so unreal and yet so real. Everyone had heard that strange voice. The voice that came from nowhere, but that filled the room, seemed to echo against the floor and the ceiling and the four walls.

In desperation, Smoke glanced at his watch. It was a few minutes past one. He got to his feet, forced a laugh.

"Carter here is carryin' his jokes a mite too far," he snapped. "Him and me'll have a little session after you go turn in. Dismissed. Report at four tomorrow morning for breakfast before patrol. That's all."

Carter got up, white-faced, tried to speak. Smoke pushed him down roughly, clapped a great hand over his mouth.

MEN filed out. They glanced suspiciously at Carter and Smoke knew that he hadn't convinced them of the older man's responsibility for the weird voice.

The last pilot left. Smoke called after him.

"Close the door, Brant!"

The door bumped shut. Smoke turned to Carter, but the other spoke first.

"For heaven's sake, Smoke, I didn't—"

"Sure. Reckon I know thet." Smoke cut in. "But I was the goat a while back, and now I thought you wouldn't mind."

"You mean you kept me here on purpose?"

"Sure did. I know you didn't do it, Carter. Certain of it. But what I want to know is, where it comes from and who did it. Besides, I had to have somebody to blame it on. Now my boys ain't sure whether you did or not. The uncertainty'll help 'em to sleep a heap better. What do you know?"

"Not much," Carter admitted. "Only this. Remember the bird who was running out into the field when we first landed and then beat it when he saw you making for that hunk of flesh that is supposed to be the body of von Muhl?"

Smoke nodded.

"I followed him after you quit shooting. As near as I could tell he went into the repair hangar. I just hung around then, not wanting to let him know I was on his trail."

"And you reckon he's got somethin' to do with it?"

"I'm sure of it, but I want to let it work out. I think I know where he's located. I can get him anytime I want him now. You see, I know now what he's up to."

"Sure, I do too, now," Smoke said. "This first guy we found with the note on him isn't von Muhl at all. He's likely some German what was killed in the last few hours, dressed in von Muhl's uniform and dumped on our field. They figured to pull a real scare by whatever this voice thing is. But they didn't figure on the real von Muhl bein' brought down, I reckon."

Smoke's gun hand reached down for his six-gun.

"Yuh say yuh know where to get this hombre, Carter," he said. "All right. Let's go."

Carter shook his head.

"Not yet," he said. "Listen. In my business I know something about showmanship and human nature. If this thing stands, it won't be so good, even if we prove to the guys it isn't a ghost. But if we can shift it into a joke and make it a laugh before we go up tomorrow morning, we'll win. Will you leave that up to me?"

Smoke paused for a long time in thought. His hand relaxed on the six-gun butt. He nodded.

"Reckon you're right, Carter," he said. "You sure pulled me out of one tough hole. I'll give yuh another chance."

TWO hours of tossing on his bunk. Smoke got up and hurried to the tarmac and across it to the mess. Pilots came in after him. Hollow-eyed pilots with dark rings beneath that told of sleepless torture. Smoke forced a laugh.

"You birds didn't dream about any of them ghosts Carter was kiddin' yuh with, did yuh?"

He laughed again, tried to get the spirit over. It fell as flat as a rotten tomato in a mud hole. Carter gave him the wink—smiled.

"I think our turn is coming," he said.

Cold, damp mist drifted in through the open door. Someone shivered audibly. Another and another. Smoke slammed the door. Men hardly touched their food; they sucked nervously at cigarettes.

Suddenly the room was filled with that moaning sound. It grew and grew; then above it, sounded the voice—hollow and monotonous in tone.

"I—I—I am—m—m the gho—ost of von Muhl. My—y death will be—e—avenged. This morning you will—all—die."

Faces turned white. Eyes stared at Carter. He was bending down, holding his head in his hands. The place grew deathly still. And in the stillness another voice, still deeper than the first, floated into the room.

"You—u—u are not von Muhl! You—u—u are an imposter. I—I—I—I am—m von Muhl's ghooost. I am going to kill these men, not you. *Heraus mit!*"

Someone snickered. Smoke gasped, got the cue and broke out into a roaring laugh. The first voice came again. Men stopped to listen, broke off in laughter again. Then came the second voice, denying the genuine von Muhl had just spoken.

Men of the 66th left the mess laughing. They hurried to their planes as dawn broke. Smoke called them together at the deadline.

"We got von Stolz's cousin last night," he said. "Now we go after von Stolz."

Spads roared into the air. Carter alone circled the field before falling into formation. Over the repair hangar, he turned and deliberately thundered down.

His Vickers guns spat flame directly into the loft of the building. Back and forth he swung, raking the entire side. Then he pulled out just before his Spad crashed into the hangar and joined the formation.

Smoke stared at Carter as he came up. Carter grinned, held his fist out with thumb down. They droned on in the graying dawn.

Mists hung heavily over the Front for a solid hour. Above was clear sky and the rising sun lighting the top of the cloud. Gradually the mist cleared. A flight of fifteen Fokkers stormed up from the north, a crimson ship at point. That would be von Stolz.

Smoke signaled at once for the attack. His squadron had the advantage of higher altitude. They romped down, guns chattering in a warming burst. The cowboy leader turned in his seat and surveyed his men. Grins of confidence came back to him. He returned that show of feeling with the same token, pushed on.

Spads and Fokkers came nearer and nearer to grips. The Fokker flight wavered. Von Stolz at point seemed undecided. Smoke pressed his triggers for another short burst to warm his guns.

Almost within range now. Von Stolz wavered again. He turned east. His Fokkers followed him. Vickers steel flashed out at long range from the guns of the charging Spads. Two, three Fokkers dropped from the tail of the big fleeing flight and hurled down.

Later, when the patrol was finished and they were returning to the field of the 66th, Carter slammed down in a hurry and ran to the repair hangar.

Smoke circled, came down and climbed out just as Carter was returning.

"I—killed him," Carter said. "Must have been a German in the guise of a mechanic. That bombing raid last night with no guards gave him a chance to set up his apparatus. A sort of high-powered telephone outfit with a wire underground from the repair hangar to a speaker on the floor of the mess. All the apparatus is in place yet." Carter looked worried. "It doesn't seem just right to shoot guys in your own hangar somehow. Hope I don't get in a jam for it."

Smoke chuckled.

"Jam, hell," he said. "Not unless it's strawberry," his grin broadened—"or maybe raspberry. But more likely it'll be medals for you, Carter. That was the slickest piece of ventriloquism I ever did hear this mornin' at mess. How in the devil did yuh figure out thet spiel?"

Carter grinned a little then.

"That was fairly simple," he said. "I studied on it all the rest of the night. And finally I figured that there wouldn't be anything much funnier than a couple of competing ghosts fighting to see who was going to do the scaring."

The Secret Squadron

He was an outlaw—his flight had condemned him, branded him traitor. Yet grimly Smoke Wade was flinging alone into enemy skies—a one-man squadron determined to stop a Boche slaughter trap with his own Spad wings as bait.

The Secret Squadron

CHAPTER ONE
Hell Mission

WHEN Captain Smoke Wade, the lanky Arizona cowboy skipper of the 66th pursuit squadron, stopped a terrific blow with his jaw and went down like a sledged steer, it seemed for the moment that the famous ace had met a better man. And it came just before the start of the great Moselle Drive.

But there was more to that incident. Much more. Both before that blow was struck and afterward.

It began shortly after Smoke had stalked into the office of Colonel McGill, C.O. of the pursuit field near Ramou where Smoke's "boys" were located.

The shaggy, gray eyebrows of the colonel were lower than usual that morning. A look which Smoke noted instantly upon entering.

A chuckle broke from Smoke's thin lips. A sound of mirth that was meant more to cheer his well-liked commander than to express any humor that Smoke might be feeling at the moment.

"Well, I'll be damned, colonel," Smoke drawled. "You look like you had a cross between the jitters and the hoof and mouth disease. What in hell ails yuh, anyhow? Somebody put a burr under your saddle?"

The bare trace of a smile played about McGill's lips—a slight smile of gratitude for the effort Smoke had made to cheer. But the anxious look lingered and the smile faded as he spoke.

"It's something, Smoke, that can't be laughed off," he said.

His fingers shook slightly, Smoke thought, as he picked a slip of paper from his desk and held it out for Smoke's lean, strong fingers to catch.

"Read that," McGill went on. "You may be interested, particularly when I tell you the rest of it."

There was an ominous ring to that last. Smoke's eyes widened as he read. He scanned the sheet the second time to make sure. Scanned it through narrow eyes that time.

Our agents in Germany inform that enemy-planes are concentrating. Uncertain as to point of meeting but many planes are known to have left their own airdromes in the past two days. Have no knowledge of their present location but suspect the enemy has knowledge of some of our plans and are concentrating all possible planes somewhere across from our planned point of activity.

"Phew!" he whistled. And the smile fled from his face as well. Then a low curse. "Somehow I had a hunch thet skulkin' coyote, von Stolz, was up to somethin'."

Smoke laid the note gently, almost reverently, back on the desk. Colonel McGill and Smoke exchanged significant glances.

"That," McGill nodded to the message, "was just phoned to me from Intelligence headquarters in Paris. Our agents in Germany have done good work. But they've gotten us tangled in a mess that isn't going to be easy to unsnarl."

Smoke was staring at the old colonel and through him. His steel gray eyes were shifted and fixed on a point out of the window behind the colonel seated at his desk. The lids were half closed. His lips moved slightly.

"Concentratin' across from the point of planned activity," he mumbled thoughtfully.

McGill cut into his thoughts.

"That's what I want to tell you next, Smoke," he said. "I've received quite a bit of information this morning and all of it damnably important. For two days now, headquarters has been planning a drive north of here. The Front at the moment is bounded by the Moselle River.

We plan to throw up bridges from a hidden area when the time comes for this drive, and then rush these bridges and take the other side of the river, after which, of course, we move as far into enemy territory as possible."

Smoke's eyes flashed as they turned on his C.O.

"Two days?" he repeated. "You mean you been preparin' fer this secret drive fer two days? Thet right, colonel?"

McGill nodded.

"Hum," Smoke hummed to himself. "Two days. And them brass hats 'thinks' maybe this movement of planes to some secret point of concentration might have somethin' to do with the preparations fer this drive, eh? Why, holy jumped-up rattlesnakes. A kid able to creep could figure that out."

McGill laughed and nodded.

"Of course," he admitted. "It's hard for those commanding from the rear to realize things as clearly as we up Front. But here is what worries the command most." His shaggy brows lowered and he scrutinized Smoke closely. "You haven't seen much of von Stolz and his crowd lately, have you?"

"RECKON thet's what worries me some," Smoke admitted. "Ain't seen none of the von Stolz outfit fer two days. Seen other Heinie planes, a few here and there, but nothin' to speak of."

"Then," nodded McGill, "I think we have plenty of cause to worry. You see, our attack will by necessity be a hazardous one due to having to cross the river in the beginning of the drive. The enemy have much the advantage there. A few plane loads of bombs dropped on those bridges at the proper moment and the drive will be over. And it looks from here as though the enemy are preparing for this."

"I reckon so, colonel," Smoke agreed. "Gettin' every plane along the Front thet they can spare to concentrate somewhere back of the lines and then be ready. And when the bridges is thrown across the river they come bombin'. Come in such plenty of numbers thet it ain't goin' to be easy fer us or no one else to stop 'em from layin' their eggs."

Colonel McGill shook his head gravely.

"You said us or anyone else, Smoke," he repeated. "That's wrong. There won't be anyone else."

"Huh?" Smoke mumbled.

"Read this," the colonel said pushing another paper across toward him.

Smoke did read it. With mouth agape and a slow grin spreading over his leathery features, his eyes scanned the lines.

General headquarters is not certain of the reason for this mysterious move on the part of enemy planes. They may have definite information; they may have seen something of our activity and may be making a wild guess. Therefore, we do not wish to make them any more certain by concentrating our planes at the 66th pursuit field at Ramou. If we do not show concern over their movement, they may decide they have been wrong or that we have changed our plans—which it is too late to do now. We, therefore, are placing our faith in air protection in the capable hands of your squadron commander of the 66th, Captain Wade. It will be up to him to protect our bridges from attack by the concentrated forces of the enemy.

At first when Smoke Wade had finished reading, a roar of laughter belched from his lips. Then suddenly the laughter ceased and his face clouded.

"The damned fools," he snorted. "A thing as important as this and they hang the whole thing on me and the boys. Not, of course, thet I don't appreciate the honor. But how in hell are we goin' to hold back half the enemy planes in the sky?"

Colonel McGill shrugged. A twisted grin crossed his face but for only a brief space of time.

"You see, Smoke," he said, "sometimes even a great ace can get himself in a jam by being too good. They seem to figure you for a superman. They think you can handle the job or they wouldn't give you the assignment."

Smoke didn't answer. He sat staring past the special order he held in his hand. Staring fixedly at the toe of his well-worn boot.

"It ain't nothin' to do with myself," he said. "But the boys. We're goin' to catch plenty of hell and—"

His voice stopped and his fists clenched. He couldn't see why this had to be heaped on his squadron and none other.

"We've got to do our best," McGill cut in. "Two replacements are coming up to fill in the gaps and make a full squadron. They'll be here any—"

A knock sounded on his office door. Then an orderly entering in answer to his booming, "Come in."

"Lieutenants Jones and Raynor, sir," the orderly announced. "Replacements reporting for active duty with the 66th, sir."

"Show them in," the colonel answered.

Two pilots were ushered into the office. A small, likable little fellow with a boyish face and an easy grin. That was Jones.

Raynor was different. He was tall and broad-shouldered and lanky. He was of about the same build as Smoke Wade. But where Smoke walked with the stiff-legged, pigeon-toed clump of one born to the saddle and high-heeled Western boots, Raynor had a swaggering gait that showed not the slightest signs of an inferiority complex.

Smoke liked young Jones instantly. But there was something about Raynor that antagonized him, that made his right hand creep down his leg instinctively and clutch the old six-gun.

Introductions. Handshakes. Salutes. Somehow, Smoke felt like a specimen in a museum for that moment. Eyes were upon him. The eyes of Lieutenant Raynor. They were looking him up and down, and on the broad, weak mouth of Raynor there was a trace of sneering. His words held a similar meaning.

"SO YOU'RE the famous Smoke Wade we've been hearing about back at the training fields," Raynor said.

And his hand, fully as large as the brown paw of Smoke, pressed viciously down on the bones of the cowboy skipper.

Pain shot up Smoke's arm. There seemed no excuse for this act. Perhaps it was jealousy on the part of Raynor. As though the replacement were saying to himself, "I'll show this hook-nosed bird at the start that I'm as good a man as he is." That feeling of jealousy that rarely comes between two men, but when it does seems to consume even good judgment and common sense.

Smoke's face flushed with pain. At first he was tempted to clamp down on the hand of the other. His own handclasp was always firm. But there was no need of making a fool of oneself just because you had strong hands.

The grip of Raynor relaxed. There was that sneering smile yet, as though he were saying—"Well, I licked the air wonder at the first encounter."

Foolish, childish stuff. But that seemed like Raynor. And Smoke let it go for the time being and tried not to notice.

Later when they prepared for a patrol before noon mess, Raynor and Smoke tangled eyes once more.

It was while Smoke was standing near his pinto Spad—the flashing pursuit ship that he had painted in blotched pattern and named Jake for his favorite pinto pony back on the Arizona ranges.

Two Indians, friends from the West whom he had worked with before and who were now permanently connected with the 66th at his request as signal men and mechanics, stood near the pinto Spad and worked on final checks of the engine and guns.

Joe Buck, the shorter of the two Cherokee Indians, climbed to the cockpit. Tom Buck, the taller, more angular of the two brothers, dug in his toes before the prop and called for contact.

Then the Hisso roared and began to warm for the patrol. At that moment, for no reason at all, Raynor came swaggering up with that same grin on his weak face.

"I suppose I'm going to get some extra special demonstrations of how to knock Heinies over," he said.

Smoke just looked at him for a moment. Raynor shifted his gaze once and came back with his eyes.

"Look here, Raynor," Smoke drawled evenly. "I don't know just what you got in your head about me. Maybe you think I'm a four-flusher or somethin'. I don't know."

Pilots were gathering at that moment for special, last-minute instructions for the flight, but Smoke didn't seem to notice them. His eyes were narrowed and only on that weak face before him, that now seemed to want to turn away.

"But you'll find out, I reckon," Smoke finished, "that you'll get along a heap easier with the 66th if yuh quit actin' like a kid and more like a man."

A flush of red flashed into the face of Raynor. His eyes snapped. His lips opened and stayed apart as though words would come—but he just couldn't force them out. And before he could make it, Smoke cut him off with orders.

"We'll fly in three formations," he announced. "Brant, you lead the point flight. Snell and Quinn, you can take care of the tip flights, I reckon. Raynor, you and Jones tuck yourselves in tip positions in Brant's flight so you'll be where you can get broke in easy and safe. And me, I'll fly a hundred or two above and keep watch to see how everybody does.

We got strict orders to keep every Heinie behind the lines and make 'em like it. The special thing we got to do—if possible—is to find a new drome the Jerries is supposed to have set up somewhere over on the other side. If we get tanglin' prop wash with an E. A., give 'em plenty of hell. That goes for everyone but you two, Raynor and Jones. You two, get in a burst if you can at a Heinie and then run like hell. Thet'll do fer the first lesson."

Pilots moved toward their ships. Smoke jerked his head to the two new replacements.

"Remember," he said. "One burst if yuh see a Heinie and can get close enough. One burst—and then run like hell, no matter what happens."

"Yes, sir," Jones said with a snappy salute.

Raynor simply glared, then he deliberately turned his back and strode toward a new Spad which had been assigned to him.

Smoke's eyes were glued to the replacement's back for a long moment until it disappeared beneath the cockpit cowling. The lanky cowpoke shook his head sadly.

"Sometimes," he mused, "humans is like cattle. Now and then comes a ornery cuss what wasn't never worth raisin'. Looks like Raynor's one of them kind. I'd give a heap to know what's eatin' him."

Then Smoke was climbing into his own cockpit. Tom and Joe Buck were pulling the chucks from under his wheels.

"Clear!" they called above the whine of the Hisso.

And ship by ship, the whole 66th pursuit squadron thundered into the air.

CHAPTER TWO
The Checkered Pfalz

TWICE on the way over, Smoke saw those hateful eyes of Raynor turned up to him. He gave him stare for stare, shook his head in perplexity and droned on.

Smoke checked for the tenth time the flight of his three formations below. Then the powerful glasses came from their case at the side of his cockpit and he squinted through them across the sky ahead.

For almost two minutes, he sat hunched forward and gazed across the horizon. Then suddenly he came up in his seat, with a jerk. He had spotted something high above.

"Phew!" he whistled. "Is thet cuss up in the air! Must be right up scrapin' twenty thousand, maybe more."

Slowly a grin spread over his face. Slowly, he nodded to himself.

"Reckon thet tells the story. He's a watch."

He shifted his glasses so that they trained on the earth below, on the twisting Moselle River across which bridges would slither before long—pontoon bridges for Yank soldiers to cross.

"Yes, sir. He's watchin' up there. First sign of the bridges and he runs back and tells his gang at the field—wherever it is—thet they better get goin' and blow the bridges to hell."

The grin broadened. He pushed on the throttle. Stuck the glasses back in their case and brought the nose of his pinto Spad high above the horizon in a steep climb.

At the same time he caught Brant's eye and motioned his signal. Smoke was going up to have a look at this enemy plane he had spotted. Brant would be in command of the whole squadron in his absence. Brant was to continue into Germany with the three flights.

"We'll see," Smoke grinned, "if we cain't draw some of these Heinie air devils out of their hidin' place."

He watched the lone plane again through the glasses as he climbed toward it. It was above and Smoke was taking a terrific chance in zooming up to have a look.

Up, up and up. Smoke was growing colder. Altimeter said fifteen—sixteen thousand feet. Going higher. Smoke squinted and frowned.

"How in hell high up is thet devil," he gasped. "It's gettin' so I'm thinkin' maybe I ain't goin' to make it thet high."

Eighteen, nineteen thousand.

Movements were hard for Smoke. The rare air played tricks with his senses. The cold air numbed him. The Hisso was groaning and pleading for more oxygen. It wasn't within three hundred revs, of full throttle. Still the gun was all the way ahead.

And the Fokker—he could see it plainly now—hung a good three or four thousand feet above him. Smoke could see the pilot with a strange head-gear over his face, staring down through glasses at him and the ground below.

"Don't look—like—I'm goin'—to make it," Smoke gasped.

He circled for a moment, then snorted in disgust.

"Reckon thet's too much fer me. Jerry's got maybe a super-charger on his engine and oxygen tanks to breathe with. Soon as he gets ready to come down, another'll come up."

He glanced to the northwest. From far off he saw them coming. A double flight of Jerry crates. Pfalz! Pfalz with their wasp-shaped thin fuselages at the tails. They seemed headed straight for the place where the Fokker hung safely out of reach.

Smoke saw Brant's flight turn at sight of the enemy squadrons. But they hadn't sighted the hidden enemy drome yet. Smoke was sure of that. For he had been watching the whole country as well as that enemy plane above. Those Pfalz had come from farther to the northwest than the human eye could see against the ground haze and mist.

At the same instant, those Pfalz pilots seemed to see the Spad flights. They turned. Smoke dropped the nose of his pinto Spad too. No use hanging around up there with that Fokker out of reach.

The Hisso went crazy in that long dive. Wings shuddered and the fuselage groaned. His breath came easier. His body began to thaw out. He was heading straight for the Pfalz flight that had turned now and was heading for the northwest again.

But Smoke had altitude. Plenty of altitude. And his speed was telling. He dove ahead of them and slammed down with flaming guns to head them off. He knew they wouldn't land at their secret drome if they knew he was watching for them to do so.

Tac-tac-tac! His Vickers guns blasted a hole right in the middle of the Pfalz flight as they tore at him. The lead plane went down in a mass of flames. The other four Boches broke up and split four ways. The three Spad flights were snarling down from the south—Brant at point. Tense Spad pilots coming in to the fight.

Smoke whirled and tramped on his triggers as he saw one of the Pfalz turn, cornered, and lash into the first Spad flight at long range.

That Pfalz went down.

SUDDENLY, out of that mass of Spads, a lone plane shot down and out. A new Spad. A Spad with a pilot whose head and shoulders stuck from the cockpit like Smoke Wade's.

His Vickers guns were rattling in a long burst.

"Raynor!"

Smoke's voice cracked suddenly at recognition. The pilot of the lone Spad that had left the formation was the tall replacement with the sneering smile and the build like that of Smoke Wade.

Smoke kicked round and hurled down the long run to help. But even before it came he knew it wouldn't be long. The headstrong Raynor hadn't tasted fear of the enemy as yet.

The Pfalz he was attacking—a checkered ship—had ducked and turned. Raynor had delivered half a dozen bursts without doing more than punching holes, through the Boche's wing.

Tac-tac-tac!

"Get the hell out and run for home before it's too late," Smoke yelled at the top of his voice.

But his voice was cut off by the blast of the Hisso engine.

Smoke saw that next maneuver coming even before it happened. It was the simplest move in the world. The Pfalz pilot had seen his chance.

Bull-headed Raynor was snarling down, putting everything he had into the final kill. And with none too good marksmanship at that. He was tearing in recklessly—the move of one who has had luck and had seldom known accident or mishap.

Wam! That Pfalz shot over and rolled. The maneuver came with perfectly timed skill. Fine pilot, that German.

And a wise one. For at the same instant that he made his flip and was staring across his sights at the unlucky Raynor, he saw, out of the corner of his eye, that famous pinto Spad of Smoke Wade.

Tac-tac-tac! A quick, hurried burst slashed from the Spandau guns of the checkered Pfalz. The sight of Smoke Wade snarling in had changed his aim, had taken his mind off the job of killing Raynor.

Yellow tracers slashed out close to Raynor's cockpit. Too close for comfort. Raynor turned and stared back. His face was ghostly white but his jaw was set.

Then a strange thing happened. Just as Smoke was poised with thumb over his trigger button, the Pfalz pilot shot an arm into the air and waved a salute. His next move was so quick that it took Smoke off guard and when he realized what had happened the Pfalz had rolled again, jerked to the right in a quick vertical and was thundering for the northwest, well out of range.

Raynor kicked round. His nose dropped and he started pushing wildly on the throttle for more speed—going on over Germany after that checkered Pfalz! His face was no longer white with fear but had the purple of insane rage upon it.

Smoke darted toward him. Another Pfalz had screamed down to hell and the third had turned and was running for home like that checkered one.

Tac-tac-tac!

"Stop, yuh damn fool!" Smoke bellowed.

At the same time he sent a burst of Vickers lead across the nose of Raynor's crate. Raynor turned deliberately for an instant, glared up at Smoke—and droned on in pursuit of the checkered Pfalz.

Smoke had the higher position—the advantage. He used it then. Used it to save Raynor in spite of himself. He stuck the nose of the old, battle-scarred pinto Spad down and let the powerful Hisso go crazy.

Again Raynor looked back over his shoulder. This time his face went white again. That whirling prop of Smoke's plane was very near. Dangerously so. Threatening to chew him to bits at any moment.

Wam! The stick shot back in the Spad. The nose leaped in the air as the ship raced just over Raynor. The blast from the whirling prop struck the new Spad and sent it floundering in a terrific eddy of air. Flop, flop. Raynor began to fall hardly knowing what was forcing him down. And before he could regain his level flight, Smoke had kicked over and was snarling back.

Bam! Raynor got another dose of that prop wash that made his plane uncontrollable for a moment. He had turned. Been forced round. Didn't know just where he was going. He heard again the roar of that Hisso of Smoke Wade and he turned them in the direction that Smoke was pointing. Turned for home.

SMOKE WADE did three things shortly after his pinto Spad hit the tarmac of the home field once more. He called the pilots about him, faced them seriously.

"Did any of you birds see anything that looked like this secret drome where the planes are concentrated on the Heinie side?" he asked.

Brant shook his head.

"Not me, Smoke."

Others agreed. No one had seen anything that even suggested an enemy airdrome.

"Okay," Smoke nodded wearily. "Dismissed."

They broke up. Smoke stalked across to where Raynor was turning to go to his quarters, helmet and goggles in hand.

"Just a minute," Smoke said in a low voice so that others could not hear. Raynor whirled, his face flushed.

"Listen," he snarled. "You're a captain and you outrank me so go ahead and give me hell for doing what I damn pleased upstairs just now. See if I care."

Smoke hesitated. His mouth closed with a snap. He stared with those cold, level steel gray eyes of his for a long time without speaking. Stared until Raynor's eyes dropped, only to look up again nervously. Then Smoke did a strange thing. He reached out and placed a hand on

Raynor's shoulder. A last vain attempt at making a friend.

"Look here, stranger," Smoke said. "You ain't gettin' no place makin' a damn fool out yourself. What you got against me? If you're half a man you'll spit it out to my face."

"Yeah?" Raynor snapped. "Okay. Then here it comes. I don't like your type, see? You're the kind that gets all the glory you can at the expense of others. That's why you didn't want me to take a crack at any of those Heinies out there. Scared I might take one or two away from your guns."

He turned to face Smoke more. Raynor's finger poked his superior in the chest as he spoke and Smoke, boiling inside, but curious, let him do it for the moment.

"Well, get this, glory hound," Raynor almost yelled, "I'm out to get my share of Jerries too, see? I've heard about how some of you big aces make us little fellas drive in the Jerries so you can pick 'em off and run up your own scores. Well, I'm here to get mine, see?"

And with that, Lieutenant Raynor, new replacement from Issoudon, spun round and stomped down the tarmac, leaving Smoke staring after him with an expression that was crossed between disgust and puzzlement.

And a few minutes later when Smoke was in Colonel McGill's office, he expressed his thoughts in words.

"I cain't make out Raynor unless he's one thing—and thet's too crazy," Smoke announced.

McGill raised his eyebrows in question.

"Only way I can figure him out is as jealous over a record he ain't got," Smoke guessed. "Ain't never seen one of them hombres, but I've heard there is such a thing. Fellas that get sore at somebody else thet can do somethin' better than they can."

McGill seemed impatient. It seemed strange to him that any one man could take Smoke's mind off other things of war to this extent. But to Smoke Wade, "his boys" were plenty important. A replacement whose confidence he couldn't gain always worried him even more than some dangerous mission.

"Too bad," the colonel cut off, "but what about this place where these enemy planes are concentrated?"

Smoke shook his head.

"Ain't seen hide nor hair of nothin' thet looks like a enemy airdrome in thet sector. Certainly not big enough to house half the planes on the other side of the lines. But now this here replacement Raynor, I reckon I'll have to give him what he wants. He's been askin' for a good lickin' of some kind ever since he landed here a few hours ago. I guess I'll have to—"

"For heaven sake, Smoke," Colonel McGill barked suddenly. "Stop talking about this replacement Raynor and tell me more about this damnable enemy concentration."

Smoke blinked.

"Oh, yeah. Reckon thet's right. Well, I seen some things out there and I got an idea. Maybe it'll work to help us locate the field where those enemy planes is supposed to be hidin' until they get their chance to sneak out and blow up the bridges."

Colonel McGill leaned forward, tense, eager.

"Yes. Go on."

Then Smoke's face broke in one of those maddening grins.

"Well," he drawled, "Rightly I got to ask General Banks in command of the troops in this sector if he'll work this stunt with me."

Colonel McGill groaned, then nodded.

"All right. But hurry. That drive is supposed to start before long. About another day or day and a half I believe. We've got to work fast if we're going to clear the sky of enemy planes. What's this plan?"

"Just a little trick," grinned Smoke. "Yuh see, I figured it out while I was over there when I seen a cuss in a supercharged Fokker higher'n we could go. He's watchin' fer the first sign of the bridges to be shoved across and then he's goin' back and land and give the word and out'll come all the E.A. loaded with bombs to start blowin' up the bridges. Thet's when I want to be there—to see where they come from, so we can blow up their drome and their crates."

"Huh?" Colonel McGill was staring in open-mouthed astonishment. "Why confound it, man, you're talking like a lunatic. After the bridges we put across the Moselle are blown up, what good will it do then to find out where the new drome is and blow it up? By that time the enemy planes will have done their work and likely they'll be headed back where they came from."

"Oh," chuckled Smoke, "it ain't goin' to be exactly as bad as that. They won't really blow up the bridges! But I got to get to General Banks now and get his permission and cooperation."

Smoke grinned, saluted and turned toward the door.

"Tell yuh all about it if it'll work," he called back to his puzzled C.O. as he stepped through the entrance and struck the tarmac.

Going back to his quarters, he passed the quarters of A Flight. From inside came hushed voices—something suspicious in those voices.

"Come on, six. Six my point Come on six."

A smile curled the corners of Smoke's lips—a smile that faded as he opened the door softly.

CHAPTER THREE
Crooked Dice

HUDDLED around a cot in A hangar were grouped several pilots:. Jones was rolling the dice. Brant was looking on from a distance. Raynor seemed to be taking all bets—and from the looks of the bills tucked between his fingers, winning them.

Softly, Smoke stepped nearer. He licked his lips. He hadn't been in a good crap game for a long time. That was a lot of money Raynor had in his hand.

"Crap!" Jones rolled and lost.

Instantly Raynor swooped up the bones. Jones got up reluctantly with a sheepish grin.

"That cleans me for now."

Raynor glanced about hopefully for some other sucker. His smile of invitation faded quickly as his eyes fell on Smoke Wade. Smoke was stepping up to the cot. One hand had been thrust into his pocket; it came out now with plenty of franc notes.

"Maybe I could sit in Jones' place," Smoke volunteered. "Just fer a few minutes."

Raynor nodded without smiling.

"If you're not afraid of losing," he said coldly.

"I ain't," Smoke said.

Raynor blew on his hands, shuffled the dice and rolled.

Seven! A natural. Smoke put down more money. Again Raynor rolled. And again—seven!

Smoke's hawk eyes were on those dice now. Funny that seven should be rolled twice with a four and a three.

Bam! Smoke put down his dough and the roll went out.

Seven! Four and a three. Third time in succession.

But Smoke was ready then. Ready and waiting. He'd looked at those dice once too often. There were threes on all sides of the one dice and four on each side of the other.

The sight of those crooked dice sent the hot blood racing to his head in rage. Raynor was not only a jealous fool but he'd cheat to win. Cheat boldly and openly. Smoke wanted to plant a fast right to that weak mouth and smear it with blood. But there was another way. For Smoke Wade had a way of making dice talk—an honest way that was skill and not thieving.

So, instead of smacking Raynor where he sat, Smoke lurched. It was as though he had been leaning on the cot too hard and his hand had slipped, throwing his body toward the dice. Already his fingers clutched another pair of dice. An honest pair. These he dropped on the cot as he fell and his hand snatched the crooked dice before Raynor could complete a frantic effort to get them first.

Raynor got the dice . They looked exactly like his own—except that they had a different number on each side. His face went crimson. Smoke did not speak, but his eyes said plenty as they burned into the eyes of the crook at the other end of the cot.

"Roll!" said Smoke. That was all.

He tossed a hundred franc note in the center. Raynor hesitated. A rifle lay on the cot beside him. A rifle that someone had just brought back from target practice. Raynor glanced at that rifle with the look of a caged animal.

"Roll!" Smoke repeated.

Raynor rolled. A five popped up and on the next roll a seven.

"Not so lucky now," Smoke said with meaning.

He let his money lay. Two hundred francs. He picked the dice. Raynor grew tense, looked as though he wanted to back out, but then covered the bet.

Smoke rolled. A seven turned up—a five and a two. He left his winnings on the cot, and rolled again.

He rolled an eight that time. Made three passes and then made a three and a five. Raynor swore bitterly under his breath.

And while he rolled, Smoke slipped the crooked dice into his pocket to get them out of the way.

Smoke lost a point and the dice. He had cut down on his betting. Now he pocketed his winnings and bet a hundred francs. Raynor took the dice.

"Two hundred francs," he mumbled.

"Five hundred," Smoke taunted—"if you got guts."

Raynor rolled—snake eyes. He lost and kept the dice. He had one hundred-franc note, left. Desperately he slammed it to the cot and shot the dice—shot for all he had. Shot honestly, because he no longer had his crooked cubes.

Seven! He let it lay. Smoke covered instantly.

Five! Again and again Raynor tried to make that five. His nerves were giving way. He was a bum loser.

Seven! Raynor lost. Smoke leisurely reached for his winnings. As he did so, the other whirled. His shaking hands clutched the rifle beside him and he lunged, butt first. *Wam!* Smoke saw it coming but too late to dodge.

THE blow struck Smoke Wade flush on the jaw and hurled him backward with terrific force. There was no denying that Raynor was strong. Doubly so when he was in an insane, jealous rage as now.

Back—back the lanky cowboy skipper hurled across the floor. And all of the time he was fighting to get straight—to come out of the fog that the blow had caused. Everything was spinning. His legs wouldn't work. His eyes wouldn't focus. He felt weak. Too weak to get up when finally he stopped that motion of falling and ended in a corner of the billet.

But some other force overpowered him then, took command. It was part rage and a sudden awakening to his position. He had played with Raynor too long. He should have given him a licking before now. But he had waited, as always, until the last minute. As always, he wanted to give the other fellow the benefit of the doubt. Now he had done his share. He had done even more than turn the other cheek.

Raynor had lunged again, with the butt of the rifle thrust forward as he came. His face was crimson and grimacing like that of a maniac.

But Smoke wasn't worrying about his face. He saw but one thing—a spoiled, childish man before him. He even went beyond seeing one who had wronged him and in place of that he saw just a human being who needed a licking for his own good.

Slowly, uncertainly, Smoke Wade staggered to his feet. Rage had flooded over him uncontrollably for a split second. But now he was growing dangerously cold and calm.

His eyes stopped their dazed wandering and focused narrowly on that livid face of Raynor. There seemed something in them that was impelling. Something that worked a spell on Raynor and slowed his mad advance.

"Put up thet gun!"

The words lashed out with the authoritative crack of a mule skinner's whip.

Raynor hesitated. Hesitated for a split second.

Smoke stood feet wide apart. His hand stole significantly toward the six-gun at his side. It was only a threat. He was still a little dazed.

But Raynor saw the move and his grip on the rifle relaxed; then he let the gun drop from his hands.

"You damn yellow-bellied four-flusher," he snarled. "Have to grab for that Jesse James gun of yours, eh? And you're supposed to be the boy air wonder of the Yanks."

Smoke boiled inside, but he didn't answer just then. His hand did touch his six-gun, but only as he unbuckled the cartridge belt that held the holster.

He stripped it from him with ominous leisure. His eyes during that time never moved from the face that was slowly turning from crimson to white.

Others about the room were coming in. Brant stepped beside Raynor warningly.

"You better lay off," he advised, "unless you're looking for a chance to commit suicide."

Raynor's face was steadily growing more ashen, but he stood his ground.

"Think I'm scared of that glory hound," he snarled. "I started this and I can finish it. Get out the way."

PERHAPS it was the fact that there were others of his flight and squadron about that prompted Raynor to push on instead of wisely backing out. Or perhaps he underrated Smoke Wade as a fighting man.

He lunged forward. A hard right shot out, followed closely by a smashing left from Raynor as he tore in. Smoke was ready now. His jaw ached but he didn't notice it. His head was clear and his legs would hold him. That was all that was necessary.

As Raynor lunged and struck out, Smoke stepped to the left. That move came just in time. Raynor had charged with rage driving him on. He saw his mistake after his start—too late to change.

Wam! The big right fist of Smoke Wade leaped out from somewhere as Raynor's fists slashed just past him. Smoke caught Raynor in the stomach.

There was a quick exhaling of breath and then a thud that echoed through the quarters.

That thud came as Smoke whirled and crossed with his left to the point behind the ear of Raynor.

The whole thing happened so quickly that hardly anyone in the room realized what had taken place. But there was Raynor going down against the cot and—Smoke saw that next move just in time. He leaped forward. Brant jumped just behind him.

Bam! The big six-gun had flashed from its holster, where Smoke had tossed it on the cot, and had spat flame and steel. But Smoke had seized the wrist just in time to throw off Raynor's aim.

The gun flew from Raynor's hand and plunked on the floor. Someone picked it up and held it.

It was then that Smoke lost himself for the moment. Rage smothered him. Rage at a cheater who didn't have a fair thought in his system.

Raynor was struggling to get away. His face was turning green with fright. He was cornered. He knew that Smoke Wade could lick him now. Knew that Smoke was the better man in anything he wanted to name—crap, flying, fighting—anything. But it was too late now. Smoke's right came hard and struck. It struck and struck again. Smashed that sneering face until blood spurted over him and the floor.

Raynor was weak; he was out on his feet. But Smoke who was, if anything, smaller and lighter than his opponent, was holding him there and letting him have everything in both fists by turns.

"Yuh dirty low-lived rat," he bellowed. "Yuh yella-bellied skunk. Yuh low-lived son of a jack-ass. I'll teach yuh to cheat in crap when you're in the 66th!"

Wam-Bam-Biff!

Raynor was limp. His face was a mass of pulp and blood; his eyes were glazed.

Suddenly Smoke seemed to get hold of himself. He stopped short, gasping for breath. He held Raynor at arm's length and stared at him like a man suddenly awakened from a nightmare.

"Fer the love of Heaven," he said, "did I do thet?"

And when no answer came back except the obvious stillness of the man who looked on, thrilling to see Raynor get at least part of what he had earned, Smoke shook his head sadly and blinked a couple of times. Then without a word, he tossed the limp form over his shoulder and stalked out the door and down the tarmac toward the hospital.

He entered the receiving room, placed the unconscious pilot on a stretcher and turned to a gaping attendant.

"Reckon I messed him up plenty. Right sorry about it. See if you can make anything out of him. Don't reckon I done much good."

And with that he stalked out of the hospital and walked with serious face cast down toward his pinto Spad, which was standing on the line.

"It looks," he mumbled to himself, "like I failed. Yes sir, I reckon I ain't goin' to be able to make much of Raynor after all."

He climbed into the cockpit of the ship. Tom Buck came running.

"You look worried," he ventured. "Something wrong?"

Smoke turned quickly.

"Huh? Oh, you Tom. Not much. Tried to lick some sense into a replacement." He rubbed his chin tenderly. "Kind of hurts when I strike one what ain't got it in him, thet's all. Wind her up. I'm goin' over to general headquarters."

The third turn started the Hisso. Then with the motor still warm, Smoke roared into the air and a few minutes later came down on the little field outside G.H.Q.

GENERAL BANKS sent for him instantly when he heard that Smoke Wade was waiting. The eyes of the old war-dog general were deep-set and haggard. He hadn't had much sleep apparently. He leaned anxiously across the desk.

"How are things?"

There was a note of desperate hope in his voice.

Smoke forced a grin and then looked sober once more, because his jaw hurt when he tried to smile.

"I think I got things about figured out, general," he said. "Jerry has got their planes concentrated somewhere back of the Front right near that point where we plan to cross the Moselle river with pontoon bridges. But they ain't showin" themselves and we cain't find hide nor hair of any place that looks like it even might be their hidin' place. Not a sign of a buildin' big enough to house two or three planes—say nothin' of anythin' that would hold fifty ships."

General Banks nodded. His eyes shifted to his desk top. He looked baffled—cornered.

"But I got a trick maybe'll work. I found a Fokker scout flyin' higher'n we can go. Must be some Fokker with a super-charger and a oxygen tank. I figure this way. He's there watchin' to see when we throw up the bridges. Then he'll dive down to this hidden drome and give the alarm. All their crates will come tearin' out of hidin' loaded with bombs and blow the bridges to tell when they're full of swell Yank doughboys."

General Banks nodded with a trace of irritation.

"Of course," he ventured. "We figured that. What has that—"

"Wait now," Smoke said "Just you hold your mustangs a minute longer and I'll tell yuh. Now suppose this here scout only thought he seen the real bridges goin' across the Moselle River. Suppose they was just sort of board rafts that would show up to look like pontoons but wouldn't make a damn bit of difference if they was blowed up."

General Banks eyes widened. A smile broke across his face and his fist thumped the desk top.

"By George, I believe you've got it, Smoke," he cried. "This scout then will come down and land at the hidden field and—"

"About the way I figure it," Smoke ventured. And I'll be up there with some of my outfit—or all of 'em—to make 'em think we're over to start the real drive. I'll see where he lands; thinking that the drive is on, they won't care if we see their hiding place, because it will be too late for us to spread the alarm. But they will only bomb the fake bridges. Just blow a few boards out the water that'll look good from the air. We will have discovered their hideout and we can come and blow 'em off the face of the earth with the help of other bombers before they realize that they been tricked!"

General Banks had risen to his feet excitedly as Smoke finished. He held out his hand to the cowboy ace.

"Smoke," he said fervently, "you're a wonder. That stunt will work. I know it. I'll rush orders through at once. They should be running these fake bridges across the Moselle in an hour. Just a mess of boards fastened together like rafts. You'll be there with your squadron to watch."

"I reckon we will, general," Smoke grinned. "I can count on thet then? We'll turn the trick on von Stolz and his concentration."

"By all means," Banks beamed. "And I think I can safely say that you've saved the day again. Smoke."

But General Banks was taking a lot for granted—as he was to learn within a few hours.

CHAPTER FOUR
Tarmac of Death

THE SUN was getting lower in the west as Smoke flew back from G.H.Q. He hummed a favorite tune and his voice rose and fell, smothered by the roar of the Hisso.

Way down on the Injun reservation,
Forty miles from civilization,
Lives a tribe, called I'll be Damned—

His thoughts went back to Raynor and his face clouded. Landing, he gave orders to prepare for a patrol at five o'clock. Then he reported to Colonel McGill's office. The eyes of the C.O. shone proudly when he heard of the scheme.

Smoke went to the hospital then—but he didn't ask to see Raynor, just inquired how he was getting on. He was told that the replacement would come round all right. He wasn't as badly marked as Smoke had at first feared; blood had done much to make him seem terribly mutilated.

Smoke felt better after that. Ships were blasting along the line now—Spads of the 66th pursuit. Spads that were warming for the afternoon patrol that was to be an important factor in his trick. Pilots were appearing on the tarmac.

Every plane of the 66th was there. Every plane, that is, but the new Spad of Raynor. Smoke called the pilots in a circle about him for last minute orders.

"We're goin' after somethin' thet's all-fired important," he said. "We're pullin' a fake bridge party and we want to see where this Heinie watch-dog lights when he goes down to spread the alarm. After thet there'll be some fightin'. But they'll have a lot more planes than we will and don't take too many chances. We got nothin' much to gain fightin' against odds. The main thing is to spot their hidden drome and then we can go over and blow 'em off the face of the earth tonight."

Pilots of the famous pursuit squadron climbed into their ships. They spun as chokes came out from before the wheels. Spads hurled into the air in the lowering sun.

Nearer the lines they droned. Smoke's gray eyes were slitted to see into the rays of the sun to the west. The River Moselle lay ahead—the river that should be spanned shortly by fake bridges.

As Smoke drew closer, his eyes widened. Something was happening down there now. He could see bursts of gun fire. Shells were breaking on the German side of the Moselle. General Banks was more than keeping his promise. He was actually making the whole thing look like a real drive starting—barrage and all.

Instantly, smoke's powerful glasses came from their case and up to his eyes, as he scanned the heavens above. His face darkened. A frown appeared in the slit between his helmet and the glasses. The sky seemed empty. His heart seemed about to plunge for a moment. He cursed softly.

Suddenly, his heart leaped. He had spotted that lone watching plane up there. It was coming down!

Down, down! Smoke was following him with his eyes. He had a long way to go before he reached their level. Smoke slapped his gun open and tore past Brant at point. At the same time Brant saw the diving Fokker and pointed. Smoke nodded as he passed. Shot his open palm into the air and waved it side-wise—His signal to leave that plunging plane alone. They were not to attack.

Then he dropped down before Brant and led the squadron in a gentle circle toward their own lines. A temporary trick. But he climbed as he flew.

Turning, he watched the diving Fokker over his shoulder. He hoped the Boche would guess that he hadn't been seen—and still, that really made no difference now. What he wanted, was to spot the enemy's hidden tarmac and then fly away, without showing any hint of his discovery. Then as soon as darkness came, the 66th would return loaded with bombs and blow up the drome.

BUT Smoke didn't get his wish this time. His flight had completed their gradual turn. The lookout Fokker had streamed down to their altitude, headed straight for what seemed to be a dense forest.

Smoke stared, picked up the glasses and glanced through them. He took the glasses away from his eyes and stared without them; then they came up again—and he muttered something.

"Looks funny down there. Afternoon sun ought to be makin' shadows if them is trees. But there ain't no shadows. Nothin' but blotches thet looks like trees—"

Then in the next breath: "He's landed. Looks like he's planted his ship down right on top of those trees. But thet couldn't be cause he's rollin'."

Curiosity led Smoke to his next move. He didn't cut off his circle and head for home as he had planned. Rather he dropped his altitude. The whole squadron of the 66th followed.

The very ground seemed to open in small holes in a row. Smokes' eyes were popping. He pushed the stick and hurled closer. Down, down! He could hear the screaming Hissos of the rest of his outfit hot on his tail.

Before his astonished eyes a dozen enemy crates shot into the air from as many of those slitted holes in the ground. Twelve enemy ships, all Pfalz, catapulted out of somewhere below the surface of the earth.

Smoke cursed. A baffled, angry expression came into his eyes.

"Well I'll be damned," he snorted. "This ain't doin' so much good as I hoped. Not when these devils is livin' under the ground. How in hell will bombs do us any good?"

The twelve Pfalz were climbing swiftly. Smoke was making a turn for the south again. He hesitated before he started to run for home. There was no use getting his boys into this jam and yet—this was war. The more of those Jerry devils that were picked off—

He shook his head at the thought. No, that would endanger his boys. And to no good end, since the bridges that were being thrown across the Moselle River were fake.

Bam! Before he could make a definite decision, another volley of planes belched from a dozen slitted holes. This time those catapulted planes were Fokkers. And at the head of that flight flew a crimson plane—von Stolz!

The Yank's fist shot up in signal for attack. The nose of his pinto Spad dropped and brace wires screamed with the racing wind.

Von Stolz seemed to recognize that pinto Spad almost the instant that he and his crimson Fokker had been shot from its slit in the ground.

Smoke was tearing for him, hell-bent, the entire 66th strung out behind him. Von Stolz shot a worried glance over his shoulder and banked sharply to the south.

Smoke cursed. He whirled in his seat and caught sight of the crimson Fokker making its escape behind the rest of the *jagdstaffel.* Out of range now. Too many enemy crates to barge through before he could reach von Stolz for another try.

"Reckon though," Smoke drawled, "the varmint's learnt a little more about this here pinto Spad and what we can do, hey Jake? I notice he didn't stick around for any fightin'."

Tac-tac-tac! Yellow tracers slashed past him from behind. He heard them scurry into the left lower wing with a pinging noise, and he moved his controls without looking around.

The pinto Spad groaned with the strain of that split-second maneuver; when it was finished, Smoke was staring down the sights and tramping on his trigger.

That Fokker turned on one wing and dived for hell.

About him was a bedlam of sound. Out of the corner of his eye, as he banked to duck out of another line of yellow tracers, he caught sight of two dozen more plane flights being hurled into the air.

The air was screaming with ships. He saw a Spad turn over and burst into flame. Smoke leaped round in his seat and tore in after the Jerry who had caused that murder. At the same time he recognized the Spad. One of Quinn's newer replacements. Game kid. He was standing in the cockpit looking back at Smoke.

Smoke cursed and prayed at the same time. For the gutty kid did something to his insides in that moment. He was about to die. A horrible death. And he was standing there for that brief moment before death, holding a rigid salute— salute to Smoke Wade, his commander.

Then he jumped into space.

SMOKE twisted his head away. His eyes were moisted and narrowed.

They were taking deadly aim on the head of the Fokker pilot who had committed that killing.

Tac-tac-tac!

Flame and steel belched from his guns. The Boche's head flopped. Another death of a gutty Yank had been avenged.

The fighting now was terrific. More than half of the enemy planes had rushed to the Moselle River. Even above the rattle of machine guns and the screaming of engines, Smoke could hear the full boom-boom of the aerial bombs being hurled to those trick bridges.

A great feeling of despair welled over him. He was cornered, baffled. His trick had worked and failed at the same time. Spads hurled out of the fight at his signal and turned south, with enemy planes trying to get in their bursts from behind for the kill. Spads that were flying a desperate, zigzag course.

Then for the first time, Smoke noticed the flight of Pfalz that had catapulted first from the slots in the earth. The whole patrol was droning south. They were across the lines and making a turn to come back over the Moselle River. "What the hell you doin' down there?" Smoke barked.

Swinging his flight away from the other enemy crates, he headed toward that mass of Pfalz.

As he neared he saw the checkered Pfalz at point—the same ship that had nearly gotten Raynor.

At the same moment, the Boches seemed to swerve in their course, as though purposely to avoid him.

Smoke's teeth clenched as he pushed on the gun.

Nearer and nearer the two flights hurled. And it seemed that Smoke was right. The Pfalz turned behind the lines again rather than face the 66th. They tried to make a wide circle and come back on the other side, farther to the east. But Smoke and his boys speared them with the first burst three thousand feet and slightly to the north of the 66th's tarmac.

Smoke hurtled toward the checkered Pfalz with blazing guns. The Yank's muzzles belched flame and tracer smoke. He was sure of his kill—until the Pfalz leaped and swerved out of the white ribbons just at the right time.

Tracers had scurried into the engine cowling instead of the cockpit as Smoke had hoped. Black smoke belched from the side of the ship. The prop stopped. Nose went down. But the pilot wasn't hurt. Instead he was quite close to Smoke now. And he grinned and waved as he began gliding toward the field of the 66th.

The balance of the Pfalz flight had tried to break through the Spads. Several had succeeded. Two had gone down with death riding the wings. Now, seeing their leader crippled, all hurled out and made for home.

Smoke was riding the tail of that checkered Pfalz for the field. He couldn't figure this pilot out. It might be a trick. The fellow was such a skilled fighter—and yet he wouldn't fight!

The Pfalz landed. Men with automatics came running for the capture. As Smoke taxied in beside the enemy plane, the Boche was climbing out of his cockpit. Slowly he pushed up his goggles, took off his helmet—and then the cowboy skipper gasped.

CHAPTER FIVE
Traitor's Drome

HAL," he shouted. "Von Halbauer!" And while mechanics and officers of the 66th stood with mouths open and automatics in their hands—not knowing what to do with either—Smoke and the German pilot of the checkered Pfalz were embracing each other like long-lost brothers.

Others of the 66th were landing. Colonel McGill came hurrying up to demand :

"What in the devil goes on here, Smoke? You two friends?"

"I'll say we are," Smoke barked. "Yes, sir. Hal and me used to pal around together out in the Rockies."

Colonel McGill's face clouded with perplexity.

"This Hal as you call him," he asked puzzled. "Is he a German, or an Allied soldier in the uniform of a German?"

Smoke's face clouded for an instant. Then he grinned.

"I reckon we'll have to consider that my friend here is a prisoner of war, Colonel. Thet right, Hal?"

The German nodded, with a rather sheepish smile.

Colonel McGill's perplexity deepened. He stared from one face to the other.

"I'm afraid you'll have to explain a little more fully," he admitted. "I don't get it at all. A German in the Rockies?"

"Reckon thet guess ought to take a prize at a guessin' party, colonel," Smoke admitted. "Yes, sir. Colonel, meet my friend Count von Halbauer. Before the War, his family owned one of the biggest ranches in Arizona. Used to come out huntin' summers. I worked fer 'em when I was a kid and the count here—well we used to pal around together when he was there and I wasn't too busy work-in'. We was kids together."

The coolness of the colonel melted then before the explanation of Smoke and the warm smile of the young German. There was a firm hand clasp.

"We used to have wonderful times together, Smoke and I," von Halbauer explained. "Smoke was three years older than I was. He taught me to ride and shoot and rope cattle. I heard of him when this war took in the United States. I've heard much about him and his pinto Spad. I've known Smoke so well that I helped him break in Jake, the pinto pony he named his Spad for. But I've always tried to avoid his sector—have succeeded, in fact, until today."

Smoke chuckled and winked at the colonel.

"You should have heard me cuss him for a yellow-bellied coward up there when he wouldn't fight, colonel," he told him. "But now I know and I'll take it all back. Cause they don't come finer than Hal here."

The count seemed delighted with the compliment. He beamed. They started walking toward the tarmac together, a curious mob of pilots and mechanics following behind. Out of the tail of his eye, Smoke caught sight of the swollen face of Raynor.

His jubilation at finding a long lost friend over-rode his common sense and good judgment. He called out to Raynor, saw him try to duck and then change his mind. A minute later, Smoke was clasping him by the arm.

"This, Hal is the bird you almost got this morning, but missed when I scared you off, remember? Lieutenant Raynor, Count von Halbauer."

A cold nod. That was all Raynor extended in greeting to the captured German ace.

COLONEL MCGILL cleared his throat. "I suppose it's going to be tough breaking you two up. But as a prisoner of war, your friend, Smoke, will have to be under guard and held prisoner."

Von Halbauer bowed.

"To be sure," he said. "That is to be expected. But it would be nice if Smoke and I could talk over old times together."

Smoke nodded.

"I'll go to prison with yuh," he offered. "So we can chew the fat about stuff that's done. This is hell, having this war going on now."

It was, strangely enough, Raynor who cut in at that moment. And he made a suggestion that didn't sound like Raynor.

"Why," he ventured," wouldn't it be proper to have your friend, the count our guest at mess tonight. You could come for him, captain, and bring him over. I think we'd trust you not to let him escape."

Smoke turned slowly and stared at Raynor. The face was bruised and swollen still from its beating. But the sneer seemed to be gone. Smoke's mind was spinning rapidly. He couldn't figure this bird, Raynor. Maybe he had actually knocked some sense into his head after all.

"Thet's a right potent idea, Raynor. Mighty nice of yuh to suggest thet." It was getting dark now. "Mess ought to be ready—" he glanced at the watch on his oil-smeared wrist—"in about an hour or so. Sure. I'll come for yuh, Hal."

Smoke walked as far as the colonel's office with his friend. He left then for his own quarters to change into a better looking uniform and to wash for mess.

His joy at meeting Hal faded when he was alone in his room. Other thoughts crowded in. A swell guy like von Halbauer fighting against him—hooked up with von Stolz!

He washed and changed his clothes for the special mess. He smoked one cigarette and then another, and suddenly realized that he was nervous about something. Something that didn't sound just right. What about Raynor? What had prompted that suggestion on his part? He was not that sort. At least he hadn't seemed to be. Well, maybe the licking had done some good.

Smoke glanced at his watch and lighted a third cigarette. It was time for mess. He started for the door. And once outside, he strode toward the guard house.

A sound came to him and then his feet were traveling faster. An engine had blasted. He hadn't given orders for a plane to take off after dark. It was hurried. Someone wasn't waiting for the plane to warm up.

Smoke dashed across the field as the Hisso, choking now and then, dragged a Spad across the field and climbed slowly into the air.

Men were running toward him. He heard his name shouted.

"Smoke Wade let him out," sang out the voice. "I saw him."

Smoke ran faster in the direction of the voice. He came to a number of pilots, who had assembled from different directions.

"Hey, who in hell said that?" Smoke bellowed. "Who's out?"

Then there was a voice at his elbow that was familiar. A firm hand out of the darkness on his arm.

"I'm afraid you know all about it, Smoke." There was almost a choke in that voice. It was Colonel McGill.

Smoke flared angrily.

"Say, what in hell is this?"

"Your friend, Count von Halbauer," McGill was saying, "just escaped in that plane. And you let him out. Helped him saw the bars. I saw you helping him start the Spad he escaped in."

SMOKE seemed stunned. His friend, Colonel McGill, charging him with this crime of a traitor! He stared at the serious face of the old colonel in open-mouthed astonishment. Then when he could speak he said:

"You—you seen me—start a Spad fer him?"

Smoke glanced about in the darkness, like a caged animal looking for a hole of escape.

"But—but," he stammered, "how could yuh see me, colonel? Bein' dark like it is."

"I saw you plainly enough," Colonel McGill nodded. "No one could mistake your lanky form and that walk of yours, even in the darkness. You might as well come clear. There's no doubt in my mind about it."

The voice ended shakily. Men were gathering about the two on the edge of the tarmac. McGill lowered his voice and spoke again.

"I'd about as soon be hung as have to find this out, Smoke," he admitted. "I wouldn't have believed it except for seeing you myself."

"But look here, colonel," Smoke was getting his normal tone of voice back. He actually laughed. "This here thing must be a joke or somethin'. Why I ain't been near Hal since I left him in front of your office. Word of honor." McGill shook his head stubbornly. "But I saw you, Smoke. There's no use denying it. I can't say that I blame you in one way, if this fellow, Count von Halbauer, is as close a friend as you say. But this is war. Come along."

Colonel McGill reached to the side of Smokes' right leg and lifted the old Western six-gun from its holster. Smoke made no effort to resist.

The sting of distrust, the ache of hopelessness, gnawed at his very vitals. He felt like giving up without a fight. His own men were against him. He heard the voices of those he knew in the crowd. Asking questions. Here and there he heard a word from some lips that made all his past efforts seem futile.

"You'll be given a fair court martial," Colonel McGill was saying as he led Smoke toward the guard house.

Smoke stopped short near the door of the guard house. He turned slowly, thoughtfully and stared into the darkness beyond the deadline. He pointed out across the field.

"Just where do yuh reckon it was, colonel, thet yuh seen me helpin' Hal start a Spad engine?" he asked.

CHAPTER SIX
"Stop Yank!"

COLONEL MCGILL turned too. He hesitated for a moment, then he pointed down the field a little to the north. Away from the administration buildings of the field. "It was up there," he said. "But what's the use of asking as though you didn't know, Smoke? I saw you, I tell you."

"Thet's quite a ways up the field for you to be walkin' just about mess time, ain't it?" Smoke persisted.

"I had a reason for going there at that time," McGill said.

"A reason?" Smoke repeated. "Maybe a private reason—yuh couldn't tell me?"

"No," the colonel said. "I'll tell you. I received a note of warning. A note warning me that you were planning to help von Halbauer escape."

"Huh?" Smoke exploded, "a note warnin' you thet—well I'll be damned! Who in hell sent thet note?"

"Oh, it was straight enough, I'm afraid," Colonel McGill said. "It simply mentioned that you had been seen taking some hacksaw blades from the repair hangar. I presume one of the mechanics there sent it although there was no name signed to the note."

Smoke nodded slowly in the darkness. He turned toward the door of the guardhouse with a hopeless gesture.

"All right, colonel," he said. "I guess you're set about this thing."

Without another word, Smoke Wade passed through and walked down the lighted narrow hall toward a grated cell, the door of which stood open. The door clanged shut behind him and a key turned in the lock. Then he was alone.

FOR a long time, Smoke sat on the cot with his head in his hands—the picture of dejection. Not once was his mind on his own plight, but rather on the job that had been placed in his hands. The job of ridding the air of the enemy concentrated planes. Of the poor devils, the Yanks, that would go to hell when the real bridges were thrown across the Moselle River and the horde of enemy planes came bombing them—too many to be stopped by Smoke Wade and the 66th. All so futile now. He, Smoke was held by his own men. Held for committing a crime which he didn't do.

He got up and paced the floor.

"Anyone would know that lanky form of yours and your walk, even in the darkness."

Again and again these words of his C.O. came back to him. Still he couldn't seem to work anything tangible out of them. Someone had framed him. That was certain. There must be a German spy in the 66th. He went over his pilots, one by one in his mind. Only one fellow that he would suspect of anything out of the way.

"There's Raynor," he said to himself. "Raynor 'd do most anything if he thought of it and it was ornery. But Raynor ain't no German spy. He's too dumb and he ain't got the guts. Nope. Couldn't be thet Raynor's the spy what let von Halbauer go."

One hour passed. Smoke sat down again. His brain was spinning as he tried to make something out of nothing. He had definite information. He had found the secret enemy drome. But the drome couldn't be bombed successfully. There was no use in dropping bombs on those slits in the ground; they were long but very narrow—just wide enough to permit an enemy plane to be shot through and into the air.

Plans wouldn't formulate themselves somehow. He seemed standing against a great stone wall. He was a prisoner. He could clear himself—perhaps. If he could find out the guilty one who had tricked him..

Clump-clump-clump! Came the sound of boot steps in the narrow hall before the grated door.

Brant looked in through the grating. He grinned.

"Thought I'd come in and see how you're getting on," he said. "Rotten deal, shoving you in prison like this, but I can't say that I blame you for letting a friend out, even if he is a Heinie. Von Halbauer seemed like a swell guy."

Smoke nodded.

"Hal is a swell guy," he said, "but I didn't let him out. In fact I didn't have anything to do with him. He wouldn't expect me to help him get free any more than I'd expect him to help me if I was caught in Germany."

Brant smiled.

"Stick to your story, anyway, Smoke," he counseled. "It may get you out of it."

Smoke flared.

"Damn it, Brant," he said, "I'm not stickin' to anythin' but the truth. I didn't have anything to do with the escape of von Halbauer. Not a damn thing."

Brant stared hard at Smoke.

"Say," he said suddenly, "I'm beginning to believe that you didn't. What the—"

"Sure. That's what I say," Smoke cut in. "Somebody, a German spy here at the 66th likely, must have helped von Halbauer get away. I can't say I'm a mite sorry. I'm glad to see a grand guy like Hal get back. Must be hell rottin' in a prison camp, even one of ours."

"Any idea who might have done it?" Brant inquired.

Smoke shook his head.

"Raynor's the only one I can think of among the pilots who might try somethin' like thet and I cain't figure what he'd get out of it. He ain't clever enough nor gutty enough to be a German spy."

"No," agreed Brant, "but Raynor hates you worse than poison. He'd do almost anything like this to get you into a jam."

Smoke grinned and shook his head.

"Hell, man, what you talkin' about? No man would turn traitor to his own country to make it tough goin' for anyone he didn't like—even Raynor. Nope. You're barkin' up the wrong tree. What's the news, anyhow? Hear any more about the comin' drive."

Brant nodded.

"Word just came over from G.H.Q. Be ready to take off at dawn and fight like hell. They're throwing the real pontoons across the Moselle just before dawn."

A low curse hissed from Smoke's thin lips. He stood staring past

Brant into space. He was trying to work out something. Then half to himself, half to Brant in a low whisper he said:

"Got to get out of here. Somethin's got to be done."

Again a pause for an instant. He whirled.

"Listen," he cracked. "I got to get out of here. And I'm goin' into Germany and try and find out what's goin' on. I got to find some way of stoppin' them planes from comin' over."

"Huh?" Brant gasped. "How in the—"

"Don't know," Smoke hurried on. "But it's got to be done. You got your orders to go out and stop them devils from comin' out of their holes in the ground and blowin' up the bridges. Well, I got to stop 'em from startin'."

Brant's mouth dropped open.

"And look here," Smoke raced on in his hushed voice that the guards at the end of the hall could not hear. "You're in command of the outfit now, Brant. You're the skipper in my place. How much confidence you got in old Smoke Wade?"

Brant's eyes narrowed.

"Confidence?" he asked. "All the confidence in the world, Smoke. You're still the skipper as far as I'm concerned."

"Thanks, boy," he said. "Thanks for thet sentiment, Brant. I reckon then, Smoke'll be givin' another order. Maybe my last one. You give orders at dawn to load every plane with bombs. Come hell-bent and drop them bombs as close as yuh can on the slots in the ground the E.A.'s is catapulted from."

Brant nodded.

"Then," Smoke raced on, "next order is to go get my two Indians, Tom and Joe Buck."

"Right!" Brant's hand shot through the bars for a moment.

There was a hard hand-clasp between the skipper of the 66th and his next in command, then Brant was gone.

SMOKE glanced at his watch and paced the floor. It was getting along toward nine o'clock. Got dark quite early this time of the year. He was tense now. Strung to a high pitch waiting for his two Cherokees.

Then he heard their footsteps—a soft padding sound—as they

were passed by the guard and strode down the hallway to his cell. They stopped before his door. Smoke winked at them. In a hushed voice that was barely audible, he said:

"Start an argument with me. Then we'll fight through the bars. Get plenty of noise going. Sock me plenty and knock me down. Then beat it when the guards come, and get the old pinto Spad ready to leave in a hurry. I got it all planned out now. The drive is comin' off at dawn. Got to get out and get goin'."

Smoke started that argument himself. He cursed at both of them. Cursed them loud and long as though they had sided with others, as though they thought him guilty of being a traitor.

And faithfully, Joe and Tom Buck shouted back threats about what they would do if they could get their hands on the lanky cow-poke.

Fists were flying through the bars. There came the sound of running as guards hurried near. The fighting became furious. Grunts and groans—then Smoke fell back with a cry of pain.

He had seen the guards coming, and at once forced his face tight against the out-thrust fist of big Tom Buck, as it slashed through the iron bars. The blow knocked him backward with well-feigned force. Smoke sprawled on the floor of the cell. He groaned and stiffened—then relaxed. Out of the corner of his eye he saw that the Indians were running back the way they had come.

Smoke half-closed his eyes, trying to give the appearance of being unconscious and still see what was going on about him.

He heard rather than saw the key slip in the lock of the door. Then the iron door was swinging open. Two guards came in. One stood his rifle against the side of the door jam, and hurried to Smoke's side. The other brought his rifle with him, dragging it where it could not be brought into action too quickly.

The guards were about to bend over him. Now was the time to act.

Like a wildcat, he sprang. His list shot out, first to the jaw of the guard who was armed.

Smack! Smoke spun and crossed with his left to the jaw of the other astonished guard.

Thud! Hardly had that first guard slumped, when the other fell beside him. Seizing the rifle near the door, Smoke plunged into the hall.

He broke to a fast walk that slowed as he came to the end. One guard was standing outside; he looked at him as he passed—looked rather closely. But it was dark. Smoke strode boldly past and around the corner.

Circling the guard-house, he hurried away in the darkness. Ahead he heard the blast of a Hisso starting, heard an inquiring shout.

Smoke broke into a run, dropping the rifle for faster speed. Above the roar of the warming Hisso, came the pounding of feet. Someone was running across the tarmac from the other direction.

"All set, Smoke," he heard a shout. Then came a curse.

Smoke could see only dimly in the darkness. He made out the form of Tom Buck and near him one that was shorter and stockier. One who was swinging a wicked fist way from the knees. Joe Buck in action.

At the same time, Smoke saw another figure. A figure much like himself. Lanky and broad-shouldered and thin waisted. Raynor!

Smack! The blow connected and Raynor fell backward. Other running feet came from farther away. Joe Buck whirled and darted to Smoke's side as he climbed into the cockpit.

"Thought at first, Raynor was you. Looks just like you in the dark," he said. "Had to stop him."

"Right. Thanks. I'll tend to him later. Tell Brant what you just told me. Got to hurry. Duck before anybody catches you."

WHAM! The throttle of the pinto Spad slammed ahead. The Hisso was cold but there wasn't time to wait for a warming. Out through the darkness, the pinto Spad thundered its way. Smoke looked back. Lights were blinking now at the field—lights of those who had come running to learn of the escape of Smoke Wade. And the lanky cowboy skipper turned in his seat, grinned and thumbed his nose at them.

Then he switched on the light over his instrument board and dropped the map holder. He hunched over, studying for some time, while the great Hisso hurled him toward the Front at a high angle of climb.

His finger traced a line on the map to the location of the secret drome. Near it was a field well surrounded by a woods. That would have to do.

He couldn't make out anything clearly below except lighter and darker blotches of shadow. Gun fire pricking through the inkiness showed him the front lines. He glanced at his watch, calculated the minutes.

He climbed higher and higher, keeping track of the seconds. Archie blasted up at him and flashed with shuddering detonations. But those were chance shots.

He turned, then, in a lazy circle at ten thousand feet. Turned toward his own lines—and his hand eased back on the gun.

The Hisso of the pinto Spad ran slower and slower until it was merely idling. When the sound could no longer be heard two miles down, Smoke deliberately reached up and cut the switch, without knowing by sight where he was or just what lay beneath him.

Down, down he circled. He was flying cautiously; wind was purring through the wings and brace wires—making a soothing sound that could almost put one to sleep.

But Smoke's very life hung in that next move. The landing would tell the story—a landing in a small field behind the Boche lines.

He grew tense as he glided down. Germans might suspect and be waiting. The field might have been blasted by shells since he had last seen it. It was too dark to see any holes that might pockmark the level space of meadow.

Down, down. Tense, hunched forward and staring out one side of the wind-shield, Smoke slipped on toward earth. The field appeared before him in a grayish blotch. It grew larger. Then trees were looming in front of him.

The pinto Spad swished into a fishtail and slid in. It straightened. He held her off when close to the ground. It was hard to gauge his distance in that darkness.

Crumph! The groan of the landing gear—and then the low rumble of fast-spinning wheels. He was down. The roll was carrying him across the field to the other end. Trees were there too. Trees overhanging the field.

Smoke stepped from the cockpit and picked up the tail. He turned it around so that it pointed to the open meadow once more, and dropped the tail under the trees.

HE HAD reached the other side of the field and was climbing through the hedge when a light flashed upon him. For the moment he stopped motionless—but only for a split second.

He whirled and his right hand flashed to where the old six-gun should be. But it wasn't there. He remembered that Colonel McGill had taken it from him. The light went out. But he knew now that someone was in that undergrowth—and he was caught without a gun!

He was running like mad now. The light flashed again behind him. A voice called out softly. Smoke couldn't distinguish the words. His heart and feet were pounding so hard, he couldn't hear anything else.

Farther behind came shouts and voices. More lights gleamed and cut their knifelike rays across the fields. His legs were getting sore. They weren't used to running so fast and so far.

Crack! Crack! There was gunfire from behind.

Crack! Ping! Shots increased. Bullets whined past his ear. He turned sharply to the right and plunged into a wood. The light flash was still following—the light that had first picked him out of the darkness.

Smoke cursed in exhausted gasps. That fellow was a persistent devil. Why didn't he shoot? The Boches behind him were shooting!

He glanced over his shoulder as he raced on. The light had gained. The fellow was coming like a racing car. Smoke wasn't such a bad runner but this fellow had him beat.

The mob of shouting shooting Jerries were about a quarter of a mile behind. Smoke could see them spreading out as they came. They were going to trap him in some way. No doubt he was running into a snare. Some blind alley from which he couldn't escape.

Guns spat flame. Bullets whistled about him and thudded into the trees ahead. The light behind him went out.

Smoke slowed his pace suddenly. He heard a muffled cry—saw the light wavering. Something seemed to hold him. And as he slowed he could hear that voice behind. Hear it clearly.

"For God's sake, Yank. Stop!"

At the same moment, Smoke's legs seemed to give out and his toe caught on a root. He plunged headlong to the ground. Tried to get up. Was doing so when the thud of feet—unsteady feet—came closer through the darkness and the light flashed in his face. Then he was knocked down again by another form that fell upon him.

CHAPTER SEVEN
Prisoner

THE voice came again. Smoke was pushing the form from him; he felt a warm fluid flowing over him as he struggled to get up—and knew, even before the man spoke, that it was his life's blood.

"Listen," said the man. "I—am a spy. American. Tried to get you when landed. Send a message. Couldn't shout too loud for fear Germans hear. I'm dying now. Got a message to send back. Maybe you can—get it over."

Smoke was holding the other's head now. He could feel the body getting weaker all of the time. How that spy had run those last few feet bleeding like this was a mystery.

"Reckon I'll get it back if it's possible," Smoke said. "What is it, partner?"

"I've—found the field where—enemy concentrated," the spy said. "About a kilo to the east from here—toward where you were headed. Underground hangars. Enter in the west end. Dress as mechanic. Maybe you can do something. Want to get message back. Germans know all about drive coming and bridges—across the Moselle. Going to blow them up. Maybe get in hangars—and do something—to stop—ships. Pass word is—"

The voice broke and the spy was gasping frantically for breath.

"Yeah," Smoke encouraged, "the pass word, partner. What is it?"

"Pass word—is—*schnell*."

That last word was written indelibly in Smoke's memory. Then the American spy went entirely limp in Smoke's arms. He was dead, Smoke could do nothing else for him.

He repeated that pass word over and over again as he leaped to his feet and ran on.

His pursuers had gained ground; they were almost at the point where he had left the dead spy. But Smoke had taken a moment to rest back there and he was fresher now.

Suddenly, Smoke wasn't so sure of getting through. More lights slashed the night ink with their brilliance; one caught him and silhouetted him where he ran.

Frantically he ducked to the right where there were no lights, only to hear men yelling on that side, also. Men who came racing in like a pack of hungry wolves. Smoke's teeth clenched. He cursed. "If I only had my old smoke-pole," he groaned. "But then, maybe I wouldn't stand so much chance. I ain't got a light. I wouldn't lay no wild bets thet I'd get out of this—mess."

Ping! He ducked away from a whining slug as it smashed branches and sang in his ear. Another bullet plucked at his sleeve. But those shots only put wings on his feet and kept him running.

His brain was spinning with fatigue. He wondered how much longer this could go on. The Germans had circled him on three sides and were steadily closing in. He managed to duck and get clear of the lights for a moment—

Then suddenly everything changed. One minute he was alone, with yelling, shooting men behind and on both sides. Now bright lights flared before him. Three guttural voices demanded: "*Wer ist da?*"

Smoke stopped as though he had run smack into a stone wall. He turned to the right. Men were pushing from that direction. As he hesitated one of the gutteral voices spoke again. "One move and you die!" That was enough. No gun to defend himself. He was worn out from running; his legs were wobbling. And blinding lights were shining in his face now from every direction. He couldn't see a single one of those many Germans that must be behind them.

"Hold up your hands!"

Smoke was already putting them up.

Germans stepped in front of the light. They held Lugers against his back. Pointed them at his middle. He was the center of a veritable arsenal of hand fire-arms.

An *offizier* confronted him.

"You! Who are you?" he demanded.

Smoke grinned back good naturedly.

"The Prince of Wales, *mein Herr*," he chuckled. "Who'd yuh think? General Pershing?"

"*Ach, du bist ein dummkopf*'," the *offizier* ranted. "This is no time for joking. You are a prisoner of war. What are you doing here?"

Smoke's grin broadened. They were searching him for weapons.

"To tell the truth," he said seriously then, "I come over with a Cook's tour. And I just got lost from my party."

"*Ach*." A Luger jabbed him in the back. "*Kommen*. We shall see if you will make jokes of things."

Smoke began to march. And for the first time, he realized that he was on the border of the secret airdrome.

THEY skirted the field and walked along the edge of a wood beside it. He could see here and there a building among the trees. Could hear laughing and singing from two of them. The *offizier* who had questioned him was walking beside him now. Smoke turned to him.

"Mind if I put my hands down?" he ventured.

"*Nein*," came the answer. "That will be all right. You have been searched."

"And maybe you'd take me to see a friend of mine who's here on this drome. A *Leutnant* von Halbauer. Ever heard of him?"

"*Ach, Himmel*, you do not mean the Count von Halbauer, *Mein Herr*?" in astonishment.

"Right," chirped Smoke. "The count to you. Friend of mine. I'd like to be taken to him, if it's all the same."

"*Jawohl*."

They turned and approached a building among the trees. Smoke could see now that the quarters for the men were among the trees. Only the ships were in the underground hangars.

The *offizier* stopped before the door and knocked. The door opened presently, and a pilot with wings and medals stood framed there in the shaft of light.

"We have a prisoner out here who says he knows *Leutnant* von Halbauer. Is the count in?"

"*Nein*," came the answer. "He has gone for special answering of questions. He himself just returned a short time ago from being a prisoner of the enemy. He should be back any time."

The flying *offizier* squinted at Smoke.

"Bring him back in a little while—or better still, I will tell von Halbauer about it and he can send for him if he wishes to see him tonight. *Das ist alles.*"

Salutes, and the door closed. Flashlights again, and Smoke was marched away. They tramped back the way they had come to an old stone farmhouse on the edge of the wood. Smoke had seen three similar buildings along the forest line.

The *offizier* motioned him inside. Smoke obeyed. Mechanics in overalls lounged about the interior; it was evidently a mechanics' billet. Their eyes popped at sight of the Yankee uniform. Smoke grinned at them. He might as well keep up a cheerful front.

Then a stairs going into the cellar. And down there darkness and windows too small for him or any other human to crawl out of. Damp smells filled the heavy air. He heard a key turn in the oak door that barred the cellar stairs. For the second time that night he was a prisoner.

At first it seemed easy to get out of that place. He could loosen stones, he thought, around the small windows. He could make the openings larger in time. But how much more time was there before von Halbauer would be sending for him?

Smoke was making his third turn of the cellar wall, feeling his way and testing the flint-hard, stone sides, when he stopped short beside a window opening. Voices had come from somewhere. Likely the mechanics talking upstairs. The floor was very thick and he couldn't hear them except in this one place.

Here the floor did not cover completely. A cupboard had been built out over a hole in the floor, and the barrier to sound was thinner. But even at that it came very indistinctly.

Smoke pushed against the cellar wall to hear more plainly. He had caught something that sounded interesting. Something about Mercedes engines.

Closer and closer to that opening he pressed, pushing hard against the stone wall at his shoulder and listening with tingling ears. The words became more distinct. Began to make sense.

"This *Verdammt Amerikaner,* Fritz," said the voice. "I wonder why he came over." A laugh. "I have thought sometimes how easy it would be for an enemy, if he came properly dressed as us mechanics and knew the pass word, to block a whole drive like the one that is to take place at dawn tomorrow."

Smoke stiffened. He pushed harder. Something moved at his shoulder. Something yielded.

The one addressed as Fritz laughed too.

"But there are many things, August," he said, "that could be fixed to stop a flight of our planes—or of the American or French or the English planes for that matter."

"*Jawohl,*" said August. "Many things. But everyone would need a tool for changing. With this that I am thinking of, one needs only his fingers to ruin a whole motor in less time than it takes to tell it."

"*Ach, was ist?*" demanded Fritz.

"Can you not guess?"

Smoke Wade in the basement was trying his best to guess. He feared that before the word was out the speaker might move. He even feared that his hearing would go bad from the strain—or that he could not translate enough of the German to fully understand the secret.

Smoke pushed harder against the heavy stone at his shoulder. It moved again. But he was so intent on catching the words above that he paid no attention to the loose stone. August was going on.

"Remember the oil pressure relief valve on the base of the engine, Fritz?"

"*Ach, ja.* You are a clever one to think of that. What the enemy would do if they knew that and could get to our motors for, say, a second or two apiece, *nicht wahr?* Unscrew it altogether and we get no oil pressure at all. The oil would not lubricate the bearings of the motor and in a few seconds they would burn and melt apart."

They laughed together.

"*Ach,* you are a clever one, August, to think of that," Fritz commented.

"*Ja,* but it does me no good. The enemy would give me much to think of that, *nicht wahr,* Fritz, but we are true to the *Vaterland,* of course. We would not sell knowledge like that for millions, *ja?* Ha-ha-ha."

Scuffling of feet above. Smoke tensed. Was someone coming down or—A yawn explained it. A yawn and Fritz's voice saying he thought he'd turn in.

SMOKE'S heart was pounding like a trip hammer gone crazy. Back to his mind flashed that rock that had moved. He pushed on it once more. It moved again. A stone that weighed perhaps three hundred pounds was loose in the side of the wall. Loose and, if pushed aside, might help to make the window hole large enough for a full-sized man to crawl through.

Suddenly, he tensed. His ears tingled. Someone else was coming across that floor above. Several soldiers had just entered. He could tell by the heavy boots clumping overhead.

His brain spun dizzily for an instant's indecision. Should he hurriedly haul that rock away and take a chance of being caught as he escaped or—

Voices upstairs now that he couldn't catch. He leaned far in under the wall of the house where he had listened before.

"You should feel honored with your guest in the cellar," the *offizier's* voice sang out. "The *Amerikaner* in the cellar, according to our description of him to Count von Halbauer, is none other than Smoke Wade, the famous Yankee ace who flies the pinto Spad."

Excited conversation. Clumping of feet. But Smoke frowned. So von Halbauer was back! They were coming to get him. His chances of escape were slipping. And still he must get out and put into action the idea that the two mechanics had given him. The trick of unscrewing the oil pressure relief valves from each engine, so that they would have no oil pressure when they prepared for the drive at dawn.

Smoke turned frantically once more to the rock. He must make another try. All odds depended on this. Thousands of lives at stake and resting on his shoulders. Perhaps the whole war in the balance if this drive was lost.

With all his might, he yanked on the loose stone. It came a little more, and then lodged fast on some point that he couldn't discover in the darkness.

He jerked and yanked again in desperation. The stone held where it had lodged. The cellar door was opening. The *offizier* was calling down for Smoke to come up.

With a groan, Smoke Wade turned from the rock that might have set him free and stepped to the bottom of the cellar stairs.

CHAPTER EIGHT
Satan's Bet

A BEAM of light pierced the darkness of the cellar from the top of the stairs. The *offizier's* voice came down to Smoke.

"His *Excellenz*, Count von Halbauer, awaits with his *offiziers* to entertain you at a special mess in your honor, *Herr* Captain Wade," he called down.

"*Jawohl. Danke.*" Smoke answered as he climbed the stairs.

He noticed that this time Lugers were not thrust quite so viciously into his back. There was more respect shown now. Mechanics who hadn't turned in on their cots for the night and weren't asleep stared wide-eyed at Smoke as he stalked toward the front door.

"*Ach, Himmel.* The cowboy ace," he heard one whisper to another.

Smoke turned and bent a grin on the speaker, who flushed with sudden embarrassment.

Then out into the night and through the trees that skirted the cleverly camouflaged field. They came again to the larger stone house, and the *offizier* stepped to the door and knocked, while other guards stood about Smoke.

The door opened and von Halbauer himself stood there smiling. He bowed as Smoke came to meet him. But there was something distant and cold about his manner.

"And now I may return the honor that you were going to bestow upon me," he smiled. "But perhaps not as gallantly as you did for me."

Smoke shot him a puzzled glance. What in the devil was he talking about?

Smoke held out his hand. Von Halbauer took it for a moment and let it drop again. Then Smoke's eyes flashed about the room and saw the other *offiziers;* out of that crowd of pilots of the Kaiser's Imperial Air Force, he spotted one he knew. The Baron von Stolz was there, monocle and all.

The baron fitted his monocle more tightly into its socket and grinned.

"*Ach,*" he said, "This is a pleasure indeed. I have had you as a guest before, Captain Wade. *Jawohl.* But this is exceptional tonight. And I warn you, you shall not escape this time."

The baron's eyes fell on the Yankee uniform that Smoke wore.

"*Ach, du lieber,* what a pity," he groaned. "You, what you have proved yourself to be in the last few hours, and yet you are not in a German uniform so that we could shoot you as a spy."

Smoke's eyes burned into the scarred face of the little baron. Von Halbauer tried to break the tension that was increasing with the passing of every second.

"Let us sit down and begin," he announced.

He shot a significant glance at von Stolz. A look that told Smoke plenty of the count's dislike for the baron.

"Since this is my party, given in honor for my friend, Captain Smoke Wade, I shall arrange the seating positions.

He turned to Smoke.

"You will sit at the head of the table, on my right here," he said.

"And you, Baron von Stolz," the count announced. "You will sit at the other end, if you please."

For a moment it seemed that von Stolz was about to turn apoplectic. His face clouded and turned purple.

"Very well," he snapped. But his eyes said: "I'll get you later for this. Both of you."

It was obvious that the cocky little baron von Stolz wished to sit near Smoke Wade for some reason. And it was as plainly obvious that the Count von Halbauer wished the baron as far away from him as could be.

The baron stomped to the seat he had been given. Even the back of his neck was crimson from rage. Smoke grinned at von Halbauer.

"Thet little squirt, von Stolz, looks like he's about to bust out in flames," he ventured.

"And it wouldn't worry me much if he did," von Halbauer smiled back. "Of all the birds I've met, he—"

The count stopped as conversation died and eyes turned to him. Still Smoke could feel that puzzling frigidness in the air about him. There was a tenseness about von Halbauer, as though the whole thing were distasteful to him. The count was acting the perfect host, but without warmth.

SMOKE felt other eyes glued upon him. Curious eyes. Unsmiling eyes of the pilots of von Halbauer's jagdstaffel.

He suddenly felt the strange sensation of an unwelcome guest. He was a Yankee, yes. But what had he done to deserve this treatment from his old friend, von Halbauer? The count had certainly been delighted enough to see him on the other side of the lines when he had been taken a prisoner.

Everyone was seated. Smoke caught the glint of a sneering grin spreading across the face of the little baron at the far end of the table, as he rose. Eyes were shifting to him. He stood up to his full height and held a stein of beer before him. He bowed.

"A toast," he shouted. "For long I have waited for this moment. *Ja.* And now it has come. To toast *mein* enemy, Smoke Wade. Before I could have only toasted him as a famous enemy airman.

Now, after what has happened in the last few hours, I can toast Captain Smoke Wade, not only as an enemy pilot of note, but as a traitor to his country as well. *Jawohl. Hoch!*"

Smoke Wade leaped to his feet. A wild rage took hold of him.

Before his glaring eyes, Germans were drinking. Draining their steins in toast to him—not as a war ace but as a traitor to his country. They grinned and winked at each other.

Von Halbauer had risen too. He was holding up his hand for silence.

Smoke's voice cracked out above other noise.

"What in hell goes on here?" he shouted.

Without waiting for an answer, he strode toward the Baron von Stolz. The little fellow saw him coming, and his hand jerked toward his Luger.

"*Kommen*, traitor," he shouted. "It would be a pleasure to shoot you where you stand, swine."

Smoke seemed not to hear him. Didn't hear anything. Von Halbauer was calling to him, moving after him hurriedly. The great fists of Smoke Wade were doubled as he clumped forward.

"Traitor, eh?" he snarled. "Traitor! That's it. We'll see, yuh loud-mouthed little squirt!"

Von Halbauer leaped for Smoke. The baron had drawn his Luger and was raising it to shoot. And Smoke, in a mad rage, taunted him.

"Go on. Shoot, yuh yella-bellied little rat. I got nothin' but mah bare hands. But I'm comin' just the same. 'Cause I know you're yella and yuh don't dare shoot me—like this."

Then von Halbauer grabbed Smoke, and other German *offiziers* rushed in. There was a fierce struggle. One Boche went sailing backward from the Yank's fist.

Smoke lashed and hurled about, with German *offiziers* flying in every direction, only to come lunging back for more. And the little Baron von Stolz, with drawn Luger, was struggling to get through the crowd, trying to bring his gun into play. "Make way," he called. "Let me finish the swine. The *verdammt dummkopf.* He called me names. Let me at him."

His words were cut off by a blow that didn't come from Smoke Wade. Von Halbauer had suddenly leaped aside and ducked through the others. His right and then his left flashed with a thud to the baron's jaw.

As the little baron sagged and the monocle flew from his face, von Halbauer clutched his Luger hand. Just in time he pointed it at the ceiling. The bullet crashed through the timbers.

With a terrific wrench, then he yanked the gun from von Stolz's fingers and flung it far to the other end of the room. Smoke was suddenly beside him. Von Stolz rolled over and groaned. Von Halbauer turned, a little breathless, to Smoke.

"I'm sorry," he said. "Please accept my apologies, Captain Wade." Smoke stared at him, deep in mental fog.

"Captain Wade," he repeated. "Hell's bells, Hal, thet's the first time you've called me anything but Smoke, to my knowledge, since we was kids together. What is all this business of traitor and thet stuff?"

"You mean," von Halbauer exclaimed, "you don't know anything about it? Surely, you're joking. About letting me out of prison? Whatever the rest of us might think of that move, we've been gentlemen about it. And it was no excuse for von Stolz's insults just now." Smoke nodded slowly. "I was arrested by my own outfit and locked up as a traitor. I'll admit thet. But how in hell did you find it out, Hal?"

"Find it out?" exclaimed von Halbauer. "*Ach,* what do you mean? I recognized your figure. And you spoke in your regular drawl. You called me Hal. No one else has ever called me that name except you."

"Huh?" Smoke exclaimed. Then he cursed. "Well, I'll be damned. So thet hombre what let yuh out looked like me, eh? Did yuh see mah face?" Von Halbauer shook his head. "Of course not. It was dark, and it was not necessary, anyway. Your form and the way you talked told me it was you, although I will admit you didn't talk much."

A slow, twisted grin suddenly crossed Smoke's face.

"Why, the low-down, skulkin', yella-bellied coyote. Raynor!"

He turned and grinned at von Halbauer.

"Listen, Hal," he drawled. "I reckon you do think pretty little of me at thet. You figured I'd let you out and turned traitor to my country by doin' it. Kind of disappointed in old Smoke, eh? Well, I cain't say thet I blame yuh. After all, this is war and we're doin' our best to win for our own side. But what would yuh say was I to tell yuh thet I wasn't near or even in hearin' of a big shout from you at the time you escaped?"

Von Halbauer's face lighted with hope. But there was still fear and doubt there. "If you said it was so, I'd believe you, Smoke," he said. "And nothing would please me more. Ever since I was a kid, you've been my idol. Smoke. You've even been my idol as a flying man, fighting against me. I've always wanted to be like you. But when you or your double let me out this evening and helped me escape—well, it sort of did something to me—inside. Like a shell going off there. I'd give almost anything to know that it wasn't you."

"Yuh better start figurin' where you're goin' to give this anything," he chuckled, "because it wasn't me. Maybe you recollect a crazy hombre named Raynor I introduced yuh to on the other side?" He told Hal of Raynor's hatred; of his vengeful trick.

Von Halbauer nodded slowly, and for the moment the smile of pleasure left his face. Von Stolz was moving on the floor. Coming back. Regaining consciousness.

He sat up unsteadily. No one helped him to his feet. Apparently few, if any, cared much for the cocky little baron. When he stood up he glared at Smoke Wade. He felt for his gun, turned whiter when he found it wasn't there.

"My only regret," he snapped to Smoke, "is that you will never fly again so that I could even things with you in the skies."

SMOKE grinned down at him and laughed. That made the baron plenty mad.

"Tell yuh what I'll do," Smoke said. He drew a handful of franc notes from his pocket—the money he had won from Raynor in the hectic crap game. "Course, these is franc notes, but I guess we could figure some way out of makin' a exchange, von Stolz. I got better than a thousand francs here. I'll lay you one to ten of the equivalent in marks equal to ten thousand francs, that this drive of yourn ain't goin' to take place at dawn as you plan. And just to make it look hard, I'll add to thet, thet I fly again. *Leutnant* von Halbauer will hold the money."

Smoke turned to the count.

"Thet all right with you, Hal?"

Von Halbauer nodded. "*Jawohl,*" he said.

And Smoke turned back to von Stolz, who was standing with face crimson, shaking a little with rage.

"Or," Smoke flung at him, "is thet bet askin' too much? Maybe you ain't got the guts to put up thet much money. Or maybe you're too scairt I'm goin' to get away and win thet bet."

Von Stolz eyes snapped.

"*Ach,* swine,'" he ranted. "Of course I take an easy bet. *Leutnant* von Halbauer, I shall give you my bet presently. And I shall also take steps against you for your conduct to me a few moments ago."

Von Halbauer bowed stiffly.

"And remember when you do, baron, that I shall bring as witnesses every *offizier* in this mess to testify as to your conduct unbecoming a gentleman before my guest."

With a snort, von Stolz whirled and stomped from the mess. Von

Halbauer smiled now, with genuine pleasure.

"Let us return to our seats. I believe we can all get along nicely without the baron. He was not invited to this mess, anyway. This is my *Jagdstaffel.* And now that the baron von Stolz has gone, let us hope we will have a happy time."

They took seats. Von Halbauer rose from his chair at the end. He raised his stein and smiled down at Smoke and began to speak.

"I trust this cursed war has not blinded us to the admirable qualities of many of those in the opposing forces. Gentlemen, I propose a toast to one of the finest humans I have ever known. To Smoke Wade, *Mein Heiren. Hoch!*"

CHAPTER NINE
Death's Hangar

WHEN the mess that had been held in his honor was over, Smoke and von Halbauer, with guards trailing, walked together through the woods back to the place where Smoke had been held prisoner.

For some time he had been fearful that they would change his place of confinement. Of course, he wasn't sure whether it would do him any good to go to the old place. That loose rock had lodged again just before the guards had come for him. Could he loosen it? An idea came to him. Von Halbauer was talking.

"I'm sorry, Smoke, that we can't offer you more comfortable quarters tonight," he ventured. "But tomorrow you will be taken into the interior after questioning in the morning. I've had a cot taken to the basement for you to sleep on. It's the closest thing we have to a prison here. Everything has been put up in such a hurry."

Smoke laughed.

"Reckon I've slept in lots worse places than that, Hal," he said. "Don't you be worryin' about me."

But Smoke Wade was getting worried. In the east the first gray streaks of dawn were showing. A sign that he would have at most a bare half hour to escape and perform his work of halting the entire flights of the enemy planes.

They shook hands at the door of the house. Guards accompanied Smoke to the cellar steps and he went down alone. The key turned in the door above. He could hear the heavy snoring of one of the German mechanics on the first floor. The sound made him sleepy. He blinked and slapped his face to stay awake.

A cot with blankets had been placed in the cellar. Smoke grinned at it in the darkness.

"Reckon yuh done thet even before yuh knew I wasn't a traitor, Hal," he ventured.

As soon as he heard the heavy footsteps die away above, Smoke hurried to the large, loose stone in the wall.

He had pulled at it to get it out. Now, instead, he pushed with all his might. It moved. His heart leaped.

He felt around it to discover what had wedged it and found another smaller stone, which he quickly dislodged. Grasping the large rock again, he pulled.

It came. Came slowly, because it was heavy and fitted into the wall very snugly. Suddenly, it tipped toward him. He tried to catch it. Tried to ease it down to the floor of the cellar, so it wouldn't make noise when it fell.

But his hands slipped on the moist surface.

Crumph!

The whole house seemed to tremble as the stone landed. He tensed for a split second and listened. There were sounds upstairs. Someone was unlocking the cellar door.

Smoke felt the opening in the wall. It was almost large enough for him to squeeze through. Frantically, he tore at it and pulled more rocks out. There was no need of caution now.

"*Was ist?*" the voice called down the stairway.

Smoke didn't answer. He was tearing wildly to make the hole larger. His fingers were bleeding and sore. But he couldn't let up now.

A flash light slanted down the stairs.

The hole was big enough now. But before he could get through, Smoke realized that the Boche would be in the cellar and German slugs would be sizzling through his carcass.

He whirled to the cellar stairs, crouched beside them. Footsteps sounded on the boards. The big fellow was coming down, squinting in the light. Smoke's eyes were used to the darkness now.

Bam! Smoke shot out from his hiding place and put all his strength into that right hand uppercut to the chin. The Boche went down with a grunt.

Smoke regarded him thoughtfully for a second. He was a large man dressed in mechanic's overalls. Those overalls! No man was ever stripped as fast as that German. The monkey suit flashed from his still body as though by magic. And Smoke darted for the opening in the cellar wall, with the outfit under his arm and the Luger in his belt.

The hole was a closer fit than he had suspected. He heard excited voices on the stairs as he wriggled into freedom. There were loud exclamations from the cellar window. But he wasn't waiting to hear those now. He was running for dear life under cover of the trees.

FAR enough away to be safe for a moment, he stopped, panting, and struggled into the mechanic's monkey suit. It was plenty large for him.

Then, with the suit on and the Luger shifted where he could draw it when needed, he walked rapidly toward the drome.

The words of the dying spy came back to him.

"Can get in with mechanic's suit. Pass word—*Schnell*."

That would be it. The entrance would be at this end. He was looking for it when a sentry challenged him. "*Wer ist da?*"

Smoke's German would have given him away. But he had his one ace in the hole. The pass word. He tensed for an instant. Got his mouth in the right place and sort of gargled the word. "*Schnell!*"

The guard hesitated. He talked rapidly. Smoke couldn't get it all. His hand crept toward the Luger. But he got something about first mechanic and nodded. "*Jawohl,*" he said.

The guard stepped aside. A mound behind him opened, and a light gleamed through from inside.

Smoke's stock soared again and he stepped through. As the door closed behind him, he made out a lighted corridor underground. And ahead was a great, vaulted room with plane after plane standing on the line.

No one was about. The guard had spoken the truth. He was the first mechanic, if indeed that was the guard's meaning.

There was row upon row of Fokkers and Pfalz. He went to work. The oil pressure relief valve on the side of the Mercedes base under the cowling was easily accessible. He turned it with his fingers. A dull click sounded—Then it came off in his hand.

Two seconds of time and it was out. He worked faster. Sped from one to another. Now footsteps were coming from the corridor through which he had just entered—mechanics.

He finished in the first hangar and darted through the passage that linked the two end underground hangars. Plane after plane lost its oil pressure relief valve. Lost it to be stowed away in the over-all pockets of Smoke Wade.

Mechanics were coming nearer. He passed on ahead of them to the next hangar and the next. He worked like mad now. He had almost half the planes fixed so they would burn up in a minute of running.

On and on he raced, always ahead of the other mechanics. The relief valves he had taken out of the many planes were weighing down his pockets. But he must carry them until he was well away from there, so that there would be no chance they could be found.

He had searched the tenth of the twelve hangars when the first of the mechanics walked in and sighted him working at an engine.

He snapped a question at Smoke.

Smoke turned and smiled. But he didn't dare answer because his German was too poor. The other came closer. He was a sergeant, and possibly in charge of the hangar.

"*Was tun sie?*"

They were alone for the moment.

The sergeant was getting mad. He came closer, demanded to know who Smoke was and reached significantly for his holster.

But Smoke beat him to the draw. The Luger flashed from his coverall into his hand. It smacked as it struck the sergeant's skull.

Smoke slid the gun back into his belt. Bending, he dragged the limp form under the tail of a Fokker then went on with his work as the other mechanics entered.

There was evidently no one among them with authority. They were merely grease monkeys. They paid little attention to him. He worked on—passed to the eleventh hangar. Cleaning it, he went on to the last hangar.

Success, complete, was waiting for him there—until another sergeant entered. And that one held a Luger in his hand.

Smoke had cleaned the relief valves from about half of the Pfalz pursuits and had just sighted the checkered Pfalz of von Halbauer. He smiled to himself as he moved toward it. Hal would get a surprise. A good joke on Hal. Nothing that would do him any harm.

"Put up your hands!" came the order in German.

SMOKE whirled and found himself facing a businesslike Luger. But he was too fast for the Boche sergeant. Smoke did two things with lightning-speed—flopped flat on the floor, and drew his Luger, spitting flame and steel.

Bullets screamed over his head as the other Luger blasted. It was all up now.

The sergeant crumpled with a groan and pitched over on his face. Men came running through the connecting corridor.

Smoke darted aside and raced through the mass of Pfalz planes. No time to take any more souvenirs now. He must get out. Before him on the wall were switches beside a long ramp. He pulled everything he could see in desperation.

A loud explosion—a whizzing sound—and a Pfalz shot up the ramp. The great doors in the face of the ground opened before it. The Pfalz hurled into the outside air and crashed—just as Smoke plunged out after into the growing day.

Shots rang out behind him. He was being followed hard. He leaped for the cover of the wood behind the row of underground hangars. On and on until it seemed his feet would carry him no farther. He would get to his ship somehow unless it had already been discovered.

Dodging this way and that through the woods, he lost his pursuers. They became only a yelling mass of men who couldn't see him through the trees.

Then out into the open—across a field—and diving into the cover of a hedge along the side of the field. On and on. At last he broke through a hedge across another field and stopped short. Two Germans had turned, with guns pointed. They had heard him crashing through the thick growth and were now ordering him to halt. But Smoke still had action in his fatigued body.

The Luger was in his hand. And it spoke a string of shots that came almost as close together as machine-gun fire. *Blam! Blam! Blam!* The two guards tried to fire. But Smoke's slugs beat them to the trigger. Behind them stood Smoke's pinto Spad, which they had been stationed to guard. They whirled and staggered back, to fall the one across the other.

Smoke dived from the edge of the field and flipped the switch. He leaped for the prop and spun it.

CHAPTER TEN
Dead Man's Debt

B*LAM*! The Hisso blasted wide and thundered, moving the pinto Spad ahead over the ground. Smoke ducked under the lower wing and leaped from a flat position, just in time to catch the edge of the cockpit as it jolted past. *Crack! Crack! Ping!* Sound of shots and the ping of bullets tangled with the roar of the racing Hisso. His engine was cold, but he couldn't wait for it to warm.

The pinto Spad lifted and wavered. Trees were coming at him at sixty miles an hour. Smoke held down straight for them to build up speed.

Sput-sput! At the top of that zoom, with tree branches tearing through the landing gear, the Hisso cut out cold.

Blam. As though he had just turned the switch back on, she cut in again and roared. He climbed from then on. Climbed and stared into the southwestern sky of morning.

Ahead were tiny specks—A full dozen and more. Spads—Spads of the 66th pursuit. Smoke could tell them from their formation peculiarity. They were flying sluggishly—loaded with bombs.

He turned then and stared to the right where the Moselle River glistened in the morning light. And through the mist that drifted up from it he could see pontoon bridges spanning its width, and men racing over. Guns were flashing. A few seconds later the shells burst in Germany.

He dropped the nose of his Spad and roared down to the German side of the river. The Yanks had just crossed at several points. Germans were trying desperately to hold them back with machine-gun nests, which were placed plentifully along the bank.

The pinto Spad romped down. Vickers guns belched tracer smoke. Machine gunners squirmed and sprawled in their nests. The rattle died for a moment, and then began again as Yanks gained those positions and turned the Germans' machine guns on the Heinies themselves.

On and on Yanks raced into German territory, taking ground along a three-mile front. It was a giant move. And Smoke romped ahead of them until his Vickers guns were glowing cherry red from shooting and threatened to jam.

When the Yanks had moved far to the north, he turned to join his own squadron. They had reached the hidden drome now. Brant leading. Not an enemy plane was in the sky. Smoke grinned. His trick had worked—or rather, the trick of the German mechanic, August.

"Someday I'd like to meet that young Heinie and thank him for givin' me the idea," Smoke chuckled.

He swung low over the secret drome. His boys were roaring over the row of openings that were hangar doors at the ends of their ramps.

Blam! Blam! Boom! Bombs were bursting in profusion near and about those doors. He saw then at close range for the first time why that field hadn't been suspected. Small, different colored blotches of grass had been planted, to supply the light and dark shading of a forest roof when seen from the air.

Bombs gone, Smoke signaled to lay off. Enough damage had been done. The drive was a huge success. And besides their gas was about gone. Archie and machine-gun fire was getting too hot.

With Smoke at point, they turned back for their own drome across the lines at Ramou.

SMOKE saw Colonel McGill on the tarmac when he came in to land, and the smile of pleasure fled from his face at sight of this old friend who had distrusted him.

But before he could climb from his cockpit McGill was holding out his hand.

"Smoke," he said, "what can I say? To say I'm sorry doesn't begin to fill the requirements. I should have known you. Should have trusted you. But the fact that I thought I saw you was almost too convincing to deny."

"Reckon so," Smoke nodded. Cain't say I blame yuh, colonel. But what in hell's happened since I sneaked out on yuh?"

Colonel McGill jerked his head toward three figures coming down the tarmac.

"That's Raynor there," he said. "Brant tipped me off to the suspicion. They're just bringing him back to the guard house from my office. I've been giving him a pretty thorough examination. Got a confession out of him. I can't understand him, but I suspect that it's insane jealousy. A sort of spoiled boy and a rotten loser."

Smoke said nothing. He was watching Raynor walk down the tarmac toward the guard house. Other planes had landed or were landing. One stopped near the prisoner. The pilot, one of Snell's flight, dropped to the ground without turning off the switch.

Smoke shook his head as he watched.

"Poor devil," he said. "They'll shoot him for that, colonel. That's what I'd a figured I had comin' if I'd been guilty."

"Either shoot him or send him to Leavenworth for life, which would be worse," Colonel McGill said.

"Too bad," Smoke repeated. "This war is sure—"

He broke off in a cry of alarm. Something was happening to that idling plane. Raynor had broken from his guards and reached the cockpit. The motor roared, the Spad whirled and headed across the field. Smoke started to leap after it; then he turned and headed for his own pinto Spad.

He reached it. Tom Buck had appeared from somewhere and was before the prop. Smoke leaped and shouted at the same time.

"Contact!"

The prop spun and spun again. Nothing happened. Then the Hisso barked and coughed. Smoke cursed. A shout from the colonel's lips.

"Look, look!"

Smoke whirled and stared. Far to the north another plane droned toward them—a Pfalz with checkered covering.

Smoke forgot about starting his pinto Spad. Slowly, like a man in a dream, never taking his eyes from that checkered plane, he climbed from his cockpit. Tom Buck stared and no longer pulled at the prop.

Raynor was climbing desperately. Climbing and roaring toward that oncoming checkered Pfalz. The two planes thundered closer and closer together.

"I reckon," Smoke said slowly, "the army won't have to worry about wastin' bullets on—Raynor."

Silence again. Everyone was watching aghast. Then something strange happened. The checkered Pfalz swerved to avoid the stolen Spad. But Raynor kicked toward him viciously. Again and again, for the second and third time, that checkered Pfalz, under the hand of Baron von Halbauer, swerved and tried to avoid fighting. But childish, bull-headed Raynor had other ideas.

The Pfalz screamed into the heavens suddenly as bullets came closer. There was nothing else to do. Like lightning, its direction changed. Spandau guns chattered their demon chorus—and the Spad hurled down, Raynor clutching the stick in a grip of death.

Still no one spoke. The checkered Pfalz swerved and came on. It dropped over the boundary of the field at full throttle. The pilot's hand went up in salute, then dived beneath the cowling to reappear instantly with a small sack.

The sack lashed out in the slip stream and dropped a few feet in front of Smoke. The pilot waved again. Smoke bent to pick up the object.

The very slightest grin broke on his face as he opened it. There were many German marks in that sack. Many marks, together with a thousand francs.

To the puzzled glance from Colonel McGill, he explained:

"Made a bet with von Stolz a few hours ago. Von Halbauer held the money. I won. Thet's all."

Colonel McGill shook his head gravely. He shot an admiring glance at von Halbauer, who had turned and was tearing back over them, saluting as he went.

"Count von Halbauer must be a wonderful fellow," he said.

And as he spoke, the colonel's hand came up in gallant, admiring salute to this enemy *offizier.*

Smoke was already saluting beside him. He nodded slowly in perfect agreement with McGill's words.

The two held that salute until von Halbauer and his checkered Pfalz was out of sight. But long before it went below the trees, Smoke's eyes were misty and the hand that saluted shook a little with emotion.

His voice choked as, just at the moment when the checkered plane passed from view, he said, half in curse, half in prayer:

"Damn—war!"

Sixgun
Circus
FREDERICK
BLAKESLEE

With Smoke Wade in disgrace and a couple of stuffed dummy officers in charge, it looked as if the great Allied drive would be a flop. But it takes more than iron bars and Boche tricks to keep the cowboy peelot from trumping a black-crossed ace!

Six-gun Circus

GRAVE conference was taking place in the general headquarters office in Ramou sector. There was the alert grizzled old war horse, General Banks himself. There was another general—a Brigadier.

General Banks was speaking gravely to a lanky captain of the Yank air force. He nodded to the other general.

"Smoke," he said, "this is General Frane. General Frane, Captain Smoke Wade. You've heard of him, of course."

The two nodded and shook hands. Strange picture that. A little bantam rooster sort of a general—Frane. He looked up to acknowledge the greeting of the lanky Arizona sun-bronzed ace and skipper of the 66th pursuit squadron. "Reckon I'm pleased to meet yuh, general," Smoke bowed. "Special if you're a friend of General Banks here."

General Banks coughed and cleared his throat.

"Friend of course, but more than a friend," Banks said, Smoke thought with a trace of stiffness. "You see, General Frane has been sent up by Staff in Paris. We're preparing for a drive north of the Behre sector. You know that already. You've seen our activity and you know of the orders to keep back the enemy planes so that they can't sight on our preparations. You've done well, you and the 66th. But now comes the real test. The drive will start very soon. Plans are being rushed."

Smoke nodded.

"Reckon I seen things pickin' up," he ventured. "Just when is this drive comin', general?"

Smoke saw the brigadier general glance at him strangely, then he turned to Banks before that ranking officer could go on.

"Isn't it unusual," General Frane inquired, "for a captain to ask a question of such importance, general?"

Banks cleared his throat nervously.

"Not in the case of Smoke Wade," he answered with finality. He turned to Smoke, disregarding the little general beside him. "The drive Smoke, since you asked—and I was about to tell you anyway—is to begin forty-eight hours from this morning. At dawn. Two days away."

Smoke nodded.

"Thank yuh, general," he said.

He shot a glance at the little, squirming brigadier in the chair at the end of the desk and grinned back at Banks.

"This is what I called you over for, Smoke," Banks went on. "I am being called back to Paris for a short time on special duty. General Frane has been sent up here in my place to command the coming drive. I wanted you to meet him since you'll be taking orders from him—from now on. For the present your orders are to keep back the enemy planes—at all costs."

Smoke saluted.

"Yes, sir," he drawled. "I reckon thet won't be hard from what I've seen of enemy air lately. Von Stolz don't seem to be very hot about comin' over on our side of the lines. It's kind of worried me a little at that though. Not seein' him fer the last few days."

General Bank's face took on a more worried look.

"I wouldn't be too sure of things in the air, Smoke," he ventured. "We have a pretty strong hunch here that the enemy has recently gotten the idea that a drive is coming within the next week or so. If that is true, you'll see plenty of von Stolz and his devils before long."

Smoke' nodded again.

"Yes sir. I reckon so. Thet varmint don't stay out of sight fer long and it always worries me more when I don't see him than when I do. Cause I get a pretty strong hunch thet he's up to some new deviltry when he ain't around."

"Yes," said General Banks, "that's been proven in the past. Very well then. I think that's all for now." He rose. General Frane got up, as though reluctantly. Salutes—and Smoke turned for the door.

He had a peculiar feeling as he left the office. A vacant sensation. As though he felt something he could not describe. As though he were losing a good friend—permanently. Like a premonition that a buddy wouldn't come back from a flight.

He strode down the corridor toward the entrance to the building. A guard stepped in front of him and presented arms, then to port so as to block his way.

Smoke didn't understand. He stepped to the side to circle him. The guard moved that way. Smoke scowled.

"Hey, what is this, a old time holdup?" he demanded.

The guard spoke.

"Order from General Banks to hold everyone inside the building. Just issued the order by the special signal bell he has on his desk. Orders, captain, that's all I know, sir."

Smoke's eyes narrowed.

"Well I'll be a ring-tailed thingamajig-jig," he burst out. "What in hell is—"

He stopped short in his drawled exclamation as swift footsteps sounded in the corridor from the direction that he had just come. He turned. Gray-haired, weathered old General Banks was striding down to meet him.

"Sorry to hold you up, Smoke," he said, "but I wanted to see you alone."

He nodded and answered the presenting of arms as the two passed out of the door. And to the guard he said: "Thanks. Order rescinded now."

They walked out of hearing of the entrance and then stopped.

"I wanted to explain, Smoke," Banks said. "I don't know so much about it myself. But there seems to be some politics working through Staff at Paris. At any rate, Frane is the prize boy of this sector now and I—well I guess they figured the old war horse was getting too ancient to command another drive. So they've sent Frane up to take my place and he'll be in command—from now on."

"Him?" snorted Smoke. "Why that damned little shriveled-up hunk of shrimp. What in hell does he know about directin' a drive? Where did he go to college?"

General Banks smiled slowly—sadly.

"I guess that's a pretty good guess at where he learned his stuff, Smoke," he ventured, "but I shouldn't say that. Give him a break. After all, we old boys have to pass on. Maybe I'm reaching that point now and—"

"General," Smoke flared, "if you don't stop that crazy talk I'm liable to lose my temper and bust you one and thet ain't meant fer a insult neither. But we got pretty close together and don't think thet I'm a-goin' to stand by and see this squirt come gallopin' up with his movie clothes and his book learnin' and take you for no ride. No, sir. Smoke Wade ain't goin' to stand fer thet no-how."

"Just be careful, Smoke," advised the old general. "Don't get into any trouble for me and remember, while Frane seems pretty cocky now, still he's got a right to his chance. Give it to him, Smoke. A fair chance to make good on this drive. I know you will. And now—"

General Bank's eyes became misty. He held out his hand.

"I didn't want to leave, perhaps for good, Smoke, without saying good-bye and shaking the hand of the finest soldier of the air or ground I've ever known—"

Hands met.

"Shucks," choked Smoke.

Then he filled up. He turned quickly for his pinto Spad in the little field outside general headquarters office; and as he strode swiftly in that long, clumping, swinging gate of his, he heard General Banks call:

"Good Luck and God bless you, son."

SMOKE slapped the gun wide open on his pinto Spad and hurled it into the air. He dug savagely at his eyes and mumbled something about a "damn fool cryin' like a kid."

He raced down angrily over the little town of Ramou that bordered his field of the 66th pursuit. He cut the gun.

"Hell," he snapped, "if they don't shoot your friends in this man's war, they transfer 'em so's yuh cain't see 'em no more. And thet guy Frane. Well—" he grinned slowly—"maybe Banks'll be back again soon. Frane don't look like he's the kind that a guy would put much money up on was he a hoss."

Wheels touched and rolled. The pinto Spad stopped at the deadline and Smoke untangled himself and stood.

An orderly stepped up and saluted. Obviously the orderly had been waiting for Smoke's return.

"Major Turner wants to see you as soon as you land, sir."

Smoke turned. He hitched the big Western six-gun slightly higher on his right leg where it would be more comfortable. He licked his thin lips. His leathery face wrinkled in a frown.

"Who'd you say wants to see me?" he demanded.

"Major Turner, sir," the orderly repeated.

"Well who in hell is he and where'd he hail from?" Smoke drawled. "I heard of a lot of turners. Pancake turners and such but I ain't never heard of a Major Turner—leastwise around this grazin' country."

"He's the new C.O. of the field, I believe, sir," the orderly offered. "Just arrived, I think for the duration of the drive or something. Colonel McGill left hurriedly for Paris. Special orders.

"Well I'll be damned," Smoke sang out.

He stomped off toward field headquarters which had been commanded ever since he had come there by Colonel McGill. McGill had been like a father to Smoke.

"What is this, a conspiracy to take away all my friends?"

He stomped into the little office. Without waiting to be announced, he barged into the private office. For the door was open and he could see a big surly-faced, square-jawed youngish man behind the desk. There was an oak leaf on each shoulder. A major. Smoke saluted, but without interest.

"Reckon you're Major Turner," he said. "I'm Smoke Wade. Heard you was wantin' to see me, major."

The other looked up, startled. His face clouded.

"What's the idea of rushing in here without waiting until I'm ready to see you?" he demanded.

Smoke hesitated.

"Well, I figured you was in a hurry so I came gallopin' in the same way. Hope I ain't startled yuh too much."

"Nonsense," blustered the larger officer. "Listen. Orders. I'm in charge here for the drive. Get your squadron out on patrol at once. Keep in the air all day. Don't let the enemy cross their lines. Never mind why. That's all you need to know."

Smoke nodded slowly. His eyes were burning into the eyes of Major Turner. They glared across at each other. Instant enemies from the start.

"Reckon I don't have to ask why," Smoke drawled. "I already know. So them is orders, eh. O.K."

Smoke strode to his own office. He picked the phone up with an air of disgust and called the main hangar. A voice answered. An unfamiliar voice.

"This might be who speakin'?" Smoke demanded.

"Sergeant Peters," came the answer.

"Sergeant Peters," repeated Smoke. "For the love of a pack of wolves, who are you?"

"Chief hangar sergeant, sir. Just arrived on duty to take the place of the regular sergeant who left on a week's leave."

Smoke blinked as though stunned. He hesitated.

"O.K." he groaned. "Get out all the ships and warm them."

Bam! The receiver clicked on the hook. He picked it up again and paused once more. Then he slammed the receiver up once more and strode out. He walked toward the mess where he found his three flight leaders—Brant of A and Snell of B and Quinn, leader of C Flights. Other pilots were there also. He looked about. Peered at faces first and then sighed.

"Well, at least," he ventured, "you're all here. I'm beginnin' to see things and plenty of 'em. Mostly they're new faces. In case you birds don't know it, we got a new C.O. One of these correspondence-school majors from what I've seen of him so far. Feels his hardware a heap. Well, anyhow, we go on patrol pronto. Ships goin' out on the line right now. Orders to keep Fritz back of their lines—at all costs. And let's hope we don't see no more of von Stolz and his pack of coyotes 'n we've seen for the last few days."

BUT the hope of Smoke Wade was not realized. The entire 66th hurried into the air within twenty minutes and turned toward the Front. Hardly had they come in sight of their own lines when the air became thick ahead with tiny specks. Specks with balanced ailerons and winged-axle landing gear and snub snouts on the fronts of the fuselages.

Fokkers!

Smoke's eyes narrowed. At that distance he began to count. He had fifteen Spads including his pinto crate. The whole fighting personnel of the 66th. But in that mass of enemy planes they were easily outnumbered, two to one.

He counted until they were dangerously close. Counted thirty-five planes and wasn't finished. Then he stopped to signal orders for the dogfight and the warming of guns.

Tac-tac-tac!

Smoke's grin was gone. He sat his bucket seat, hunched over, and glared ahead. His teeth were clenched. It would be a matter of seconds. Keep the enemy back—at all costs.

Then he turned in his seat and a, sickly feeling came to the pit of his stomach. He was staring into those faces behind him. Veterans and green replacements. Some with white faces. Others with their faces merely flushed and dark with the thrill and excitement and worry that they felt.

Instinctively, Smoke loosened the old smoke pole in its holster by his side. He turned around and faced the Fokkers again. They must not pass.

At point of that giant flight he could see a checkered plane hurling along. Where was von Stolz? The thought worried him more. Not there.

Smoke's head was working rapidly. Trying to figure out the best method of attack. How could fifteen ships attack a swarm of almost forty Fokkers and expect to live—to say nothing of keeping those forty Fokkers back from crossing the line?

They were already above the lines. The first tangle of wings would take place directly above No-Man's-Land.

For the instant, Smoke glanced back to the south. Back on the Yank side of the lines. There was preparation there. It was plain to see from the air. Even now the German squadrons could see the added life and numbers of men and activity below.

He cursed the thought and rushed on. Nearer and nearer.

Then the plan came. He signaled his men. Raised his arm in a mystic sign that only his birds of the 66th knew.

Instantly every Spad nose dropped. Hissos whined and screamed. The pilots began slight turns. But that was part of the trick. They were trying to make Jerry think they were going to dive and run for it. But they were turning slowly. The first Fokkers were coming down after them.

Tac-tac-tac!

Spandau steel stabbed out with yellow lines of smoke like ribbons streaming out behind. But Smoke and his buzzards were taking their chances. Taking desperate chances for a gain.

Another signal from his hand—and the noses of those plunging Spads weaved upward. Hissos groaned. Fittings and wood and wire groaned with the terrific strain of the pull out. Then up and up against the bellies of those trailing Fokkers.

Tac-tac-tac! Vickers guns answered the staccato of the enemy guns. White tracers this time filled the air and slithered into Fokker fuselage bottoms. Tracers that went true with the aim of Smoke's men.

Fokkers wavered and fell. Taken by surprise, their pilots couldn't turn quickly enough when the noses of those Spads zoomed and the Vickers guns shattered.

Three Fokkers turned and fell, with Spads trying to flee from beneath them. Other Fokkers went down. Smoke tried to count the kills of that first attack. There had been fifteen Yank planes and nearly forty Fokkers. Now, he spotted again in his mind. Eleven had gone down from the savage Vickers guns of the 66th.

His masterful surprise attack had cut that enemy flight to slightly less than twice the number of Spads. But now the odds were much less than even. The chance for a concentrated surprise attack was gone. It was every man for himself. Smoke groaned and tried to find any of the green replacements who needed help.

He spotted one and raced down. Cursed because he was a split second too late. He wheeled and glared across his sights at the fleeing Fokker that had committed the murder.

Tac-tac-tac!

His guns spoke in another short burst and the enemy crate flopped over in a convulsion and burst into flames. He whirled and glared about.

Brant was having trouble. Two Jerries were on his tail and his guns weren't working. He was feverishly tugging at the clearing arms.

Smoke raced to him, leveled his sights and tramped down on the trigger button.

Tac-tac. . .

Then something happened. Something that stabbed a knife of fear and apprehension into his being. His guns jammed. The right one first—and then the left. Both stopped.

FOKKER devils were snarling down from behind. He tried to race for freedom while he fought with his useless guns. But Fokkers screamed in ahead and cut him off, turning him back toward Yank lines and the rear.

Tac-tac-tac!

He jerked at his arming levers and cursed as yellow tracers slashed past. He shot a glance at the others. Saw three Spads in that swift shift of his steel gray eyes, that were having trouble also with their Vickers guns. Something was queer.

He fought on to clear his guns. Fokkers dove and plunged to keep him from turning into Germany. They seemed possessed that he should keep going for home. Everything seemed wrong. Everything seemed crazy. They should be driving him and the others—helpless with jammed guns—back into Germany and force them to land. Take them prisoners.

With a frantic effort he got his guns cleared and fired a short burst. His hand and feet moved instantly. The pinto Spad leaped and rolled.

Tac-tac-tac! There was a chance now. Brant had his guns cleared too. A column of smoke lay from a plane that had gone down. Smoke stared far down it, saw a burning plane at the end of it. A Spad. He could make out the circles on the wing that hadn't caught fire yet.

Tac-tac-tac! Down went a Fokker to pay for that one. And another from before Brant's guns. They were gaining. Perhaps they'd be able to drive back the jerry devils in spite of their superior numbers. Perhaps—

Smoke gasped. For out of the north came another horde of enemy crates. Fokkers too. And this time he recognized the lead plane. It was crimson. It was the red Fokker of his arch-enemy of the skies, the Baron von Stolz.

Behind von Stolz came a giant flight of enemy planes. Reinforcements. So the Baron hadn't been decent for any good purpose. Smoke nodded and cursed softly under his breath.

"I had a hunch," he groaned. "Look at them crates come. 'Bout thirty in thet outfit, I reckon. And we're supposed to drive 'em back across their lines and keep 'em there!"

Savagely, he stabbed at another Fokker. Vickers guns chattered—but all too short.

Tac-tac. . . Jammed again. He tugged and sweated and cursed. Luck had forgotten him. Forsaken him for good.

He suddenly sensed the strangeness of the situation. They were all being driven back over their lines—back toward their own field at Ramou.

"If thet ain't the craziest thing I ever heard of," he drawled to himself—and fought on.

Back—back the Jerry pilots forced them. Smoke tore at his guns as they drove him south and headed him off from turning. Nothing he could do. Von Stolz and his devils had joined the other flight. The air screamed with diving, plunging crates.

Then, halfway between the field and the Front, Smoke yanked a swollen shell from each breach and cleared his guns.

Back into action once more. The pinto Spad leaped and turned over in a wild maneuver.

Bam! Smoke was glaring across his sights at the checkered Fokker of the leader of that first great flight. He had it in his sights. He could see the field ahead.

Tac-tac-tac! He tramped down on the trigger button once more in the instant that he came smack on the checkered plane. He saw his tracers flash out. Saw them scurry toward the checkered Fokker. They punched through a wing because the pilot had seen his move and had jerked his plane in a tight vertical out of the way.

Missed! Smoke cursed. Then he was sitting bolt upright as the Fokker turned over lazily and the prop slowed.

"Well I'll be a—" Smoke howled as he stared. "I'd a swore I missed the cuss. And look there. He's goin' down. Prop's stopped stone dead. Everythin' crazy this mornin'."

The pilot of the lead Fokker of that first flight was going down. His propeller had stopped and he was gliding swiftly straight for the field of the 66th at the edge of Ramou.

Smoke was after him' like a terrier, making sure he would, land. That it wasn't a trick. But it couldn't be a trick. The propeller had stopped. It couldn't be started again in the distance that was left.

Fokkers were turning back. Ground crews from the Front and about the field had been giving them plenty to think about. Another Spad was hurling for hell. Two Fokkers had just crashed. Altogether it was no decisive victory, in spite of their driving the Yank planes behind their own lines.

SMOKE slammed to the field, in his bullet-riddled Spad and landed beside the downed German leader. The big six-gun was loose: in its holster but not out. Smoke, could draw like lightning if, necessary.

He had seen the new chief hangar sergeant before, starting on the deadly patrol. Now he saw him again, coming at a run across the field with drawn automatic. He was headed straight for the Fokker.

But Smoke reached the ship first. He confronted the German. The sergeant came running up at that moment.

"I'll take care of this Kraut," he said, moving closer to take command of the prisoner.

Smoke hesitated. There was something about this new hangar sergeant that didn't strike him favorably. In spite of his better judgment, he nodded.

"O.K. sergeant. And heaven help you if he gets away. They'll, want to be questioning him before he goes back to the prison camp."

The sergeant grinned, and nodded. It seemed genuine enough.

"Don't you, worry, captain, I'll take care of him all right Got a special feeling for him. This Jerry killed a swell guy from Colombey Les Belles where I was before I come here; I got some squaring to do. I hope he does try to get away."

He moved his automatic suggestively of his thoughts.

Smoke was about to follow at some distance when he heard a voice behind him. He turned.

"Captain Wade, Major Turner wants to see you, sir," an orderly announced. "He's in a devil of a hurry and mad enough to—"

"Reckon he would be," Smoke nodded.

He glared, at the smoldering mass that had a few moments before been one of his Spads. One of his boys was in hell now—or wherever luckless aviators go. Smoke cursed and strode rapidly toward the office of the new C.O.

Turner looked up as Smoke slammed through the door.

"Well," he demanded, "what's the excuse for not holding back, those enemy planes?"

Smoke stared at him for a moment. Then he suddenly burst forth in a series of adjectives that went back five generations into the family of one, Major Turner. The major stared.

"So that's the kind of a guy you are." Smoke raved, in conclusion. "We go out and fight our heads off and do the best we can. We've knocked down three Fokkers to every loss we've suffered. And still you bawl me out. Well, maybe you can get some fun out of the German ace we captured alive. He's in the charge of Sergeant Peters. He took him to the guard-house. And that's all I know, you prime leather-lunged, fat-headed yellow jellyfish."

Smoke whirled on his heel. He couldn't trust himself longer. He heard quick steps behind him—a bellow of rage. Then a powerful arm caught him and turned him around.

Turner stood there, shaking with rage.

"I've a good mind to—" Turner began.

His fists were clenched. But something seemed to hold him back. Smoke's voice was chilled as dry ice as he came back:

"I'd sure be delighted to have yuh start it, major," he said through clenched teeth.

Smoke waited to give the major the chance to come through. But nothing happened. Big Major Turner flushed deeper, then whitened slightly and backed away a step. A snort of disgust from Smoke and the lanky cowboy ace turned and stomped out of the door.

He was surprised to see a mechanic working on the Fokker as he came back down the field. Walking closer, he was more surprised when he saw that it was the new chief hangar sergeant, Peters. Peters was alone. He was working on the motor, he had the magneto apart and was just putting it together again.

"What goes on here?" Smoke demanded.

Peters had seen him coming. He seemed set.

"Just putting this Fokker back in condition," he said. "Wasn't much wrong with it except a part of the mag had been hit by one of your slugs, sir."

Smoke's eyes narrowed.

"Who gave you orders to do this?" he demanded.

"Major Turner," came back the instant response.

"You and the major are pretty thick, aren't yuh, Peters?"

"Well I know him," Peters ventured. "I've worked for him before. I expect he had me transferred up here with him."

"Yeah?" drawled Smoke. "And I suppose they're goin' to take that Fokker behind the lines when they get it runnin'. Thet right?"

"Yes, sir."

He walked back thoughtfully toward his office. His head was dizzy from the strange things that had taken place. Nothing was right. And now this Fokker being fixed up at once.

He reached his office and paused. He heard the blast of a motor behind him. A Mercedes. Peters had started up the Fokker. Was taxiing it to the dead line. Bringing it over to—

Smoke gasped. The Fokker was heading straight for the two hangars behind which stood the guard-house. Smoke stared in that direction. He could see no guard about the local jail. Still—

Suddenly a figure leaped through the door of the guard-house. A guard came running around the corner and tried to fire as he ran. His aim was bad. He fired again. Peters had climbed out of the cockpit of the Fokker and was—or seemed to be—making some adjustment with the engine while it ran.

The old six-gun was out of its holster in a flash, but the distance was great. Too great. Smoke took aim and pulled anyway.

Dust leaped just ahead of the running German ace. Smoke ran at top speed, firing as he went. Peters seemed not to notice the running figure. He was engrossed in making his adjustment.

THE German ace reached the side of his cockpit and leaped. The Mercedes roared. Peters as though suddenly surprised, leaped away just in time to keep from being struck by the whirling tail.

Smoke took careful aim with his six-gun and fired again. That was a hit. But how good a hit he couldn't tell. He saw the Fokker swerve as it took off. It seemed for the moment about to crash, then it righted itself and roared on toward the north.

Smoke dove for his own pinto Spad. He clicked the switch and leaped for the prop. He pulled through and again. Nothing happened. Down and over. Hisso sucking gas. But no explosion.

The Fokker was vanishing into a small dot. Smoke gave up in disgust.

He stood watching the enemy plane grow smaller and shook his head.

"Somethin' damned funny about everythin'," he muttered in baffled rage. "I'd a swore I didn't hit thet Fokker in the engine. But if I did, it didn't take Peters long to fix it as good as ever."

He spun round and stared about for Peters. His hand strayed toward the butt of his six-gun back in its holster. But he didn't have to look far for Peters. A big headquarters car had turned into the drive. Little General Frane was getting out importantly. And Major Turner, with Sergeant Peters beside him, was greeting the general.

Smoke stopped as he saw a strange move. Both Peters and Frane had pointed toward Smoke. Pointed directly at him from a distance of perhaps two hundred feet.

Curiosity and rage prompted him to stride toward them. Major Turner shouted an order that he did not catch, an order to men with rifles and fixed bayonets who had come running at the shouted warning that the German ace had escaped.

General Frane glared at him and held but his hand.

"I'll take your revolver, Captain Wade," he said sternly.

Smoke's eyes narrowed. He didn't understand. But even from cocky General Frane an order was an order. He lifted the old six-gun tenderly from his holster and handed it to the general, butt first.

"I'll give this to you for safe-keeping, major," Frane told Turner. He turned to face Smoke again. "You're under arrest, captain," he announced.

"Under arrest?" Smoke cracked.

"That's what I said. You helped that German escape. I warned General Banks against telling you of the exact time for the drive to start and the date. But he thought he knew best. Sergeant Peters here saw everything and has guessed the rest very neatly. You made believe to down this German. Peters tells us there was nothing wrong with that Fokker. He just tried to repair it and it was O.K. He was taxiing it over to the hangar when he saw you assisting this German in his escape. Beyond a doubt you told him of the time and the place for the drive."

Smoke looked aghast from one face to another. Everything seemed crazy today. For the moment he was speechless.

"You have ruined this drive. It will be failure. Months of preparation—and for nothing." General Frane was working himself into a nice lather. "Some of you spies do your work well. You even spend months getting into the confidence of your superiors as you have done so that even you may turn one good trick against the Allies when the time comes."

Smoke glared at him. Then the corners of his mouth turned up in a derisive expression.

"So Peters told you all this, eh?" he said.

Peters seemed brave with the two officers to back him up.

"That's one of the main reasons why I had Peters transferred with me," Major Turner snapped. "You thought you were pretty clever, Wade, but it takes a good man to fool Sergeant Peters."

Smoke nodded slowly.

"Yep. I reckon it does. But it ain't goin' to be long before you're goin' to get the foolin' of your life, Peters." He turned to the general. "And I reckon you're right about there bein' nothin' wrong with that Fokker and him escapin' after he's been told the time and place for the drive. And I'll gamble right now thet he's hell-bent on his way back to thet field he took off from in Germany to tell 'em about the comin' drive."

"You admit your guilt then?" demanded General Frane.

Pilots of the field, saddened pilots, were gathering. Brant and Quinn and Snell and those of their flight who were still alive and not in the hospital were there.

Brant stepped up at that moment.

"Pardon, sir," he objected, "but I've known Captain Smoke Wade for a long time and I know that—"

"Silence," barked general Frane. "Who the devil are you?"

"Brant, sir," came the answer. "Senior flight commander."

"Good. Listen to orders. Only one way of saving this drive now. Observers of the 37th tell us they have spotted a supply dump for the force opposing our drive. They can tell you where it is. Get in touch with them. I've just heard from them. They say the only ones who can get through to bomb that dump will be a squadron of pursuit planes. You'll be in command here with the arrest of Wade. Get going. Bomb that dump. At all costs, mind you."

Smoke flared then.

"Damnation," he bellowed. "They ain't got a chance, general. They—"

Bayonets prodded Smoke in the back at a sign from the general. He tried to wriggle away from them. They were persistent.

"Silence," the bantam general shouted again. "Take him away, men. And see that he doesn't escape."

Smoke turned in desperation slowly toward the guard house. He paused. The guards stopped. Something had clicked in his mind. He faced General Frane.

"You think fer sure thet this drive is goin' to be a flop, don't yuh?" he demanded. "And you think I ain't got no way to turn a trick. Well, how's your sportin' blood, general?"

General Frane glared.

"What the devil are you talking about?" he demanded.

"Just wonderin' if you'd like to make a little bet. I'll give you odds of ten to one. I'll bet ten thousand francs against one thousand of yourn thet this drive is a success and thet it's all on account of somethin' I do about it. What yuh think of thet? Or maybe you're a welcher."

General Frane colored.

"I'll take that bet," he exclaimed. "Take it and collect."

"Maybe," grinned Smoke as they led him to the guard house.

ALL that day and into the night he worked out his plan.

About midnight, when the guards were the sleepiest and the new shift hadn't come on, he heard a voice at the grated window.

"Smoke!" It was Brant's voice.

"Thank the Lord for you," Smoke breathed back. "Got to get this mess untangled. How do I get out?"

"Here," said Brant, passing some hacksaw blades through the grating.

"Reckon thet'll do," Smoke grinned in the darkness. "What—what happened on the bombin' raid?"

"Can't you guess," Brant hissed back. "No use committing suicide. We went out with the bombs. Ran against tough fighting with four or five times as many enemy planes, so we turned around before it got too tough, dropped the bombs in the German trenches and came home."

"Good," nodded Smoke.

He was already sawing—sawing. Softly he worked the blades on the steel bars. They went through fairly easily.

One bar through. He went on to another one. That one through. Smoke pushed with all his might. Bent those bars out of his way and slipped between them, Brant helping him down on the outside.

"What now," Brant hissed as they gained a good distance from the guard house.

Smoke grinned. "Reckon we do a little kidnappin'," he ventured. "Got to git ma smoke pole first—and then comes Major Turner."

They moved toward the commandant's quarters. A window was open in the rear of the building. A guard passed close. They waited. Smoke slipped through the window. He could hear the steady breathing of the big flabby major in his bed.

But first he felt for his gun about the room. He found it in a desk drawer, slipped it back with a deep breath into his holster. He felt about the room. Someone else was coming through the window. Brant.

Smoke found a long robe cord and a shirt. He took these and turned the major over on his face. There was a startled snort and then the major was awake—but not soon enough.

"One peep out of you, Turner and I'll drill yuh, so help me," Smoke hissed.

Turner stiffened. Swiftly Smoke bound him and placed a gag in his mouth. Brant stepped to the window.

"All clear!"

Out of the window and into the darkness with their heavy burden before the guard returned. It had been easy so far. They carried Turner toward the hospital. A waiting ambulance stood a little way off. Smoke grinned and jerked his head toward it.

The motor started and they were moving down the road toward general headquarters. Smoke recalled where General Banks had slept in that building. Probably General Frane, who was taking his place, would sleep there now.

The ambulance stopped before the building. Guards presented arms. Smoke, in his officious captain's uniform, received instant recognition.

"General Frane just called the hospital," he said. "He's taken sick sudden. I come to help."

The guard stepped aside quickly. Smoke and Brant carried a stretcher boldly past the guard, leaving Turner in the car. They softened their footsteps as they came to Frane's room. Smoke tried the door. It wasn't locked. He stepped inside, Brant right behind him.

Then the room was flooded with light, as Smoke's hand pressed the button.

The little general leaped upright and blinked. Smoke was grinning at him across the barrel of his old six-gun.

"General," he said, "I come to save this drive fer the Yanks in spite of yuh. If you do as I tell yuh you'll be all right. If yuh don't, I'll let daylight through your over-important little carcass just as sure as little green apples grows on trees."

General Frane suddenly was seized by a fit of shakes.

"What—what do you want me to do. You'll get shot for this!"

"I'll get half-shot someday maybe," Smoke grinned. "And I want yuh to call up and issue some mighty important order. Orders that every squadron fer ten miles either side of the Front from us takes off at dawn and lands at field thirty-two."

General Frane's eyes widened.

"Field thirty-two," he gasped, "why that's fifty miles east of here. That can't possibly do any—"

He was beside himself with fear and rage and misgivings.

"I'm doin' the orderin' just now, general," Smoke reminded him. "Me and old smokey here. Get to that telephone and start spoutin'."

General Frane obeyed. He put in his call. To make sure there would be no mistake or trickery, Smoke held the muzzle of his six-gun against the base of the skull of the little general as he talked.

Frane gave the order. It was verified by those who recognized his voice. He hung up the receiver.

"Is that all you want?" he asked.

"Yep, except for a little confinement," Smoke told him. "Yuh see, we ain't aimin' to have this order countermanded. So we're takin' yuh fer a nice little trip."

He bound and gagged the general and together he and Brant, with a blanket thrown over Frane's face, carried him out on the stretcher and slid him into the waiting ambulance.

Halfway back to the field Smoke turned off on a road. In an abandoned house they left the two, still securely tied. It was growing light when they turned in at the drome. They didn't bother to take the ambulance to the hospital. An orderly was waiting for Brant. He stared at Smoke and blinked.

"But I thought, you were arrested, captain," he stammered.

"Oh, they forgave me last night after dark," Smoke grinned. "What's on your mind?"

"Orders from G.H.Q., sir. Report to field thirty-two at once. All ships. Special orders from General Frane. I've been looking all over to tell Major Turner but as you're second in command I'll deliver the order to you and Lieutenant Brant."

"Hum," grinned Smoke, "you don't tell me. Well, thanks."

Ships were barking on the line. Smoke walked in the protection of the hangars toward the warming planes. There was someone down there he wanted to see.

He saw him. Sergeant Peters. Peters, the liar. Peters the spy.

Peters saw Smoke at the same time that Smoke saw him. There was a sudden leap and then Peters was running wildly, guiltily for the cover of the hangars. Smoke brought up his six-gun and took careful aim. He pulled.

Peters' head jerked on his shoulders and he fell face down.

FIELD thirty-two was located over on the eastern Front, over where the Vosges Mountains came down into the flatlands to the west. By noon that day more than two hundred planes had landed there. Trucks with huge loads of ammunition and bombs had rumbled up. Smoke was in command.

And Smoke issued the orders too. Planes were constantly landing and taking off. Planes loaded with bombs—bombs that were blasted and wasted on the quiet Boche sector directly across.

Questions flew hot and heavy. Why were they bombing territory where there was nothing to blow up but woods and here and there an encampment of Germans taking life easy? Why waste all those bombs?

Planes circled and snarled down into thinly-held trenches until none but the dead held the line in territory that was little wanted by the Allies.

As night came, Smoke's face bore a worried look. Still he should have nothing to worry about. No casualties. No one injured. Two hundred bombers and pursuits were in the air almost continuously until dark and there had been no fights. But his face was much worried as the night wore on. He drew Brant aside about midnight and asked:

"You sure you know your stuff now. What you're to do?"

Brant nodded eagerly.

"O.K., then. Get goin'," Smoke nodded. "And good luck."

Men were sleeping about him. Sleeping anywhere as there weren't enough accommodations for all of them at field 32. Men grumbling and kicking. Then the first gray streak of dawn. Smoke was up and starting the engine of his pinto Spad. Until then he hadn't taken the air. He had remained on the ground to direct and order and command.

But now he would go. Planes slashed into the dull gray of morning. And still that worried look was on Smoke's face as he scanned the skies. In disgust he landed and issued more orders.

"If it works we'll win," he said. "If not, we're sunk. Anyway it's dawn. The drive should have just about started. The barrage anyway. I'm expecting enemy crates over now. Put on a swell fight and knock down as many as you can. Then beat it for the point of drive. And after helping there, return to your own dromes again."

Back in the air. Straining eyes into the west and north. Then Smoke was sitting up and the worried expression had fled and in its place was a grin of triumph. For far ahead in the west came a mass of Fokkers. Eighty or more. Von Stolz was at the head of them.

Smoke turned and glanced behind. Bombers and pursuits were leaving the field and rising. They hurled toward von Stolz and his buzzards. Now von Stolz was outnumbered more than two to one.

A wild tangle of ships. Tracers fluffed through the air in a dull haze. But it was only for a minute. Then a crimson Fokker darted out of the mess and high tailed for home. And the other Fokkers followed their leader who couldn't take it in a tight spot.

Spads and Nieuports and Camels trailed and sent many enemy ships to their death in that wild retreat. Then at Smoke's lead, the great victorious flight wheeled and headed for the point north of Behre—the point of the great drive.

Smoke stared through his glasses and cheered.

For Yanks were sweeping over behind the barrage—sweeping over the top amid fierce fighting. Yank planes dived down without interference and strafed those ground troops silly. Suddenly the resistance from the Germans diminished. There seemed to be trouble in the rear, as if their ammunition was giving out. Smoke stared north and saw a great hole in the ground. A hole where a great ammunition dump had been.

He turned the pinto Spad back toward his own field, where he found a staff car from Paris with the flag of a general flying on it.

General Banks, serious of face was waiting for him.

"I heard about this fuss and your arrest. Saw it come through on the dispatches," he explained, "and I took the matter in my own hands and came up to see what in thunder was going on. I've just gotten the reports on the drive. It's a gigantic success." A smile broke his seriousness. "And I've got a pretty strong hunch that you've had something to do with it, Smoke." Smoke grinned.

"Reckon I have had a little," he ventured. "And that reminds me. I got to get a couple of guys out of their confinement. I got a bet to collect." General Banks stopped him. "Wait a minute," he counseled, "I haven't finished yet. What's all this about anyway? The shooting of this sergeant named Peters and the disappearance of Major Turner and General Frane?"

Smoke told him briefly. The general's eyes opened wide when he heard of the way in which Turner had permitted the spy, Peters to put it over him.

"I'd hate to be in their shoes, either of them," Banks said, "when Staff gets hold of this. But what I can't understand yet is your reason for getting all the planes in these sectors around here over to field 32. There wasn't anything going on around there."

Smoke chuckled. "No?" he said. "You'd a thought there was somethin' goin' on if you'd been across the lines. We just raised particular hell for nothin' at all. I was tryin' to draw von Stolz away from the point of the drive. He'd naturally think with all that fuss we were gettin' ready to pull somethin' over in thet neck of the woods and he'd come with his whole flock of devils. Well he did—and that's when Brant got the chance to slip through to the ammunition dump with a load of bombs and blow up their reserve supply. Brant done more good to help the drive than anyone else, general."

Banks looked at Smoke peculiarly for a moment.

"Oh, yeah?" he said.

Injun Buzzards

FREDERICK
BLAKESLEE

"Wheeee-yip-yip!" High and sharp that cry rang through battle skies. The Indians were on the warpath—only two of 'em, but a pair of hellion redskins plus Smoke Wade, are equal to a squadron of Fokkers any day—as the Boches found out before that Wild West campaign was half begun!

Injun Buzzards

CHAPTER ONE

Vanished Staffel

"DOGGONE my hide!"

That exclamation sprayed from the thin lips of the sun-bronzed Arizona cowboy skipper of the 66th pursuit squadron for the third time in that early morning light. And it had burst forth in the same way for five dawns before that.

The lanky cowpoke ace was staring about the sky through slitted eyes. He had been staring that way ever since he had left the home field at Ramou and had swung Jake, his pinto Spad, across the lines into Boche air.

Then for the fourth time the exclamation came, in typical Smoke Wade fashion.

"Doggone my hide, cain't make it out. Von Stolz's old field is as lonesome as Death Valley on a Sunday afternoon."

He stared down at it mournfully and shook his head. A worried look was growing deeper in the steel-gray eyes. He stuck the controls forward and let Spad howl in a dive.

Down it shrieked, straight for the silent tarmac of the famous German ace and his *jagdstaffel.* A month before, everything in the line of anti-aircraft batteries would have suddenly gone crazy below him. But now it was like desecrating a ghost town with the noise of his motor.

Hangars—the canvas ones that had been erected after Smoke's last raid—were all down. There remained only the marks on the ground where the grass did not grow so thickly and black spots here and there where the oil had dripped from the bases of the Fokkers.

Nothing more. Smoke shook his head in bafflement. The Hisso was winding up in the long dive toward three thousand revs. He eased back on the stick as the earth slammed up at him. Shook his head again as the pinto Spad moaned upstairs.

"Been missin' him fer five days now. Ain't seen hide nor hair of the varmit nor any of his devils, so thought I better come over lookin'. But I reckon this here is as much of a fool's mission as I ever come for. The whole kit and works has went and they didn't leave a forwardin' address near as I can see."

Up shot the pinto Spad. Smoke shrugged. He didn't turn for home. Instead he glanced at the gas gauge to make sure of his supply.

"A hour and a half more flyin' time," he mumbled under the roar of the Hisso. "Thet'll be plenty of time to cover the front and have a little fun—" his face lighted in a grin—"just fer a special reason, I reckon."

He pushed the gun full on. Then, at two hundred feet above the ground, Smoke Wade proceeded to make a personally-conducted tour of the lines behind the Front.

He thundered over shouting Germans. Roared about them flying a crazy, zigzag course like a lunatic. His thumb tramped down on the trigger button often. Germans fell before him, or dodged into brush at the sides of their roads where they traveled.

And each time Smoke grinned to himself. He wasn't deliberately trying to take human life. Smoke was no waster. But he was laying a trap for his arch enemy, the Baron von Stolz. And he was using Germans to bait that trap.

On across the rear of the Front he droned. The pinto Spad leaped and bucked and bounded like the wild pinto pony had done years ago when Smoke Wade—a youngster then—had broken him in as his own horse.

Down and up and over that pinto Spad cavorted.

Tac-tac-tac!

Lead spattered from the Vickers guns mounted on the nose of the blotched Spad. Shots from archie guns and ground machine gun crews and rifles answered. But Smoke Wade was never there when the bullet arrived.

His eyes shifted from searching the sky to picking new masses of Germans to harass with his deadly steel. He knew it would take some time to carry out his plan. But eventually—

He spotted farther to the west a long line of trucks moving toward the Front. And above those two trucks were twin Fokkers hovering about.

Smoke's eyes lighted. He kicked over and stuck the nose of the pinto toward those two crates. A grin wrinkled his face. His slitted eyes were trying to make out the markings on those ships. Of course neither of those planes would be that of von Stolz. The baron had to have the whole outfit behind him before he stepped into the open. But it might be some of von Stolz's crew.

Nearer and nearer the pinto Spad hurled. At first those two Fokkers had been mere specks in the sky above the truck train. Now he could see them more clearly. His heart began to sink.

"Cain't be, I reckon," he drawled to himself mournfully. "Every Fokker in von Stolz's outfit has a red nose on it. And von Stolz's Fokker is plenty red all over. There ain't either one of them crates what's got a bit of red on 'em."

He thundered nearer. The Fokkers had already seen the pinto Spad. They seemed to waver for a moment and then turn.

MOTOR for motor, Smoke and the two Fokkers hurled at each other, Smoke held his fire. He caught the bursts of fire from the Spandaus of the two enemy planes. Grinned slightly at that.

"Plenty green at this here air fightin', I reckon," he ventured and hurled on. "Thet shootin' before they're within good range is always a sign of nervousness."

Tac-tac-tac!

Both ships were firing. Smoke was holding his, shielded behind the big Hisso. Just the top of his head showing slightly while he aimed his guns.

Then—

At the last split second, Smoke tramped down on his trigger button. But not until the ships plunging at him had swerved. The one turned to the right, the other ducked to the left.

The nose of the pinto Spad moved to the right just a hair and for the first time in that fight, flame tipped the guns of Smoke Wade. But for only a split second. A short burst of a few rounds.

Wam! The Fokker that had turned to the right suddenly seemed seized by a convulsion. It dropped its nose. The pilot had fallen dead upon the stick. A few seconds later it crashed beside the truck train.

When that nose had showed the first sign of going down—in fact when Smoke Wade's keen eyes had caught the jerk of the pilot's body forward with Death clutching at him—Smoke had kicked and pulled.

The second Fokker had turned to the left. Smoke was on his tail instantly. And his thumb tramped again when the gray eyes had taken careful aim.

Tac-tac-tac!

Flames, smoke and then the second Fokker had crashed right on one of the heavily loaded tracks. The whole thing suddenly became a mass of flame. The train was stopped.

Smoke kicked over and shook his head sadly.

"Sorry had to take it out on you green kids," he said. "But if this here stunt works, it's got to be somebody."

Then his guns were blazing in a steady stream as he thundered over the long line of trucks that stretched for two miles deeper into Germany.

He zoomed at the end. He couldn't go on like this forever. Glanced at his gas tanks. Only an hour's gas now. And he was at least ten minutes from his own side of the lines. Almost twenty minutes from his own field. That would leave forty minutes to—

He came up with a start. Far, far to the west, over where the rim of the world began and then seemed to drop into space, something strange caught his eye.

The nose of the pinto whirled and he roared toward that point. His hand crept to the case beside his seat and the powerful field-glasses came out.

He stared through them for a long time. Shook his head and stared again.

"Well, what the hell do yuh know," he exploded. "If thet don't look like a bunch of Injun signal fires then I never—"

He stared harder until his eyes seemed to bulge from their sockets.

The air had been fairly still when he had taken off. He remembered that. Hardly any wind. Now, there miles away to the west, deep in Germany were columns of smoke—three, columns that rose high in the air.

Smoke continued to stare as he drew nearer. Minutes passed. Twenty minutes. A half hour. He was looking down on a forest. The whole country in that sector seemed filled with trees.

He checked his map, sat at a good altitude and studied it. The map said that the woods composed the Vergon Forest. He'd heard of it. But he hadn't had much occasion to fly over it. Pretty well behind the lines on a Front he hadn't worked so much. Up toward Belgium.

The smoke continued to pour out of the trees. And the marvelous thing to him was the volume of it. It came from three distinct places—and it came steadily without a let-up. Now and then flames belched from the tree-tops along with the smoke.

He shook his head, puzzled.

"It ain't no forest fire," he decided. "Couldn't be no forest fire. It ain't spread a mite since I first seen it. But there's plenty of flame comin' now and then and—"

He shook his head again. The thing commanded his attention. He couldn't get away from it. That smoke and occasional flame coming from the woods. For the moment he forgot von Stolz.

But that was the exact time that he should have been watching for the little devil baron.

His first warning that he was in danger was the rattle of Spandaus slugs. They were from above and they weren't mere warming bursts either. Even before Smoke Wade had time to turn in his bucket seat and stare at the diving enemy crates, his hands and feet worked instinctively.

The pinto Spad leaped, half rolled and veered away out of the line of fire. And just in time. For when Smoke had gone into that maneuver,

Spandau tracers had been tucking themselves through his lower wing where it joins the fuselage.

From a sidewise position, Smoke stared about him.

His heart leaped. He grinned. A crimson Fokker led eight red-nosed Fokkers in an attack on the lone Spad.

"I reckoned they wouldn't let me get away with rainin' hell over the Front without callin' you, Von," Smoke chuckled. "But they did take plenty of time doin' hit at that."

Tac-tac-tac!

A blast of tracers, yellow and weird looking in the clear morning light, slithered from the nose of the crimson Fokker that led the flight. Smoke saw the beady little eyes of the cocky baron staring across his sights at him.

Again controls moved and the pinto Spad leaped out of the way. Smoke was still grinning. He turned in his seat while three other Fokkers had tailed him up and over. Turned for that split second of danger and thumbed his nose at the little baron.

The face of the baron went purple. Smoke saw the play.

Tac-tac-tac!

Yellow tracers fluffed about him. But on the one side. On his right. He was being herded into a position so that the baron could come in for the kill.

Tracers to the right of him. The baron hiding on the left, behind others of his staffel who could break at the right time and let him through with the killing shot.

Then the nose of the pinto Spad dropped. Dropped straight down. The Hisso screamed. But the dive had no more been begun than the nose shot up like a rocket and the whole Spad groaned with the strain.

Up, up, and up. Smoke rolled once as he climbed. Shot out above the astonished baron, and his devils.

Then for the first time in several minutes he thought of his gas. Shooting a-glance at the gauge, the grin fled from his face.

Empty!

CHAPTER TWO
Injun Talk

A FLOOD of realization suddenly swept over him. Gas tank said empty. He'd known he was pretty close to the margin. But the excitement of watching the strange smoke columns below, and later in the surprise by von Stolz and his devils he hadn't kept very good track of the time.

As he kicked over again and came down for the start of a dive, he shot a glance to the south. Far, far away he could see tiny bursts. Those would be somewhere along the line where shells were exploding. Couldn't be gunfire. There was little or no smoke from modern war guns.

Smoke's brain was spinning. He shot the next glance ahead. Just as he had planned. Two Fokkers before him out front. Pick one and—He glared across his sights and pressed the trigger button.

Tac-tac-tac!

White tracers fluffed out and buried themselves in the cockpit cowling of that one Fokker. Smoke held. The Jerry pilot hurled straight into the death-flying slugs and crumpled in the cockpit.

Smoke kicked to the left. He might as well get as many as he could before he went down. Not a Chance of getting back to the lines with an empty tank. Make as much of a showing as possible while he still flew.

Down on the other Fokker. But that red-nosed devil was wise—and cautious. He was gone up, over and out of range when the Arizona guntoter shifted his guns for him.

Tac-tac-tac!

Another Fokker bore in to ride Smoke's tail. Another cut across his nose with flaming guns. Getting plenty hot.

Smoke jerked the stick and kicked the rudder. Up, up shot the pinto

Spad. Up and then over in a roll. And when Smoke came out of that roll he was riding the tail of the crimson Fokker—von Stolz's ship.

He saw the whitish, green face of the baron turn and stare back at him. Fright was there in those little eyes. Fright of the man he feared in the air without the aid of his staffel.

Smoke's gun poised above the trigger button. Poised while he took sure aim.

"Ain't aimin' to miss this time, Von," Smoke mumbled. "But I'm goin' to make sure that the first one gets yuh and not—"

Bam! From out of somewhere higher above him a form came hurtling through the air like a bullet. For a second Smoke took his eye off the sights to glance up. That finished the deal and saved von Stolz.

Out of the blue high above, a Fokker with a red nose had meteored down to save his leader. That red-nosed devil was headed straight for the pinto Spad. A maniac coming to save his master. A pilot with more loyalty than brains, willing to commit suicide to get his leader out of a jam.

Smoke swerved instantly. That cowboy ace knew when to duck and when not to. This was one of those times he should get out of the way himself. There could be no denying the set, grim look on the face of that young Fokker pilot. Likely some kid up from school who had the patriotic hokum stuffed into him clear to the Adam's apple about saving his leader at all costs.

As Smoke turned he cursed. He shook his head, then grinned.

"What was it Shakespeare or somebody said once about discretion bein' the better part of bein' valorious, or some-thin'? Well, son, you got valor all right, but I got a hunch you're just a plain damn fool. You sure done it thet time, though."

Smoke's maneuver carried him a little out of the fighting for an instant. And he saw an opening for a kill. He kicked round. The pinto Spad groaned. Nose dropped and he was high-tailing the rear end of that Fokker that had just caused him to lose a death shot on von Stolz himself.

Down, down, he streaked. Three Fokkers ganged up on his own tail. The kid in the Fokker before him turned and suddenly went white. Smoke hesitated. Kicked free and his grin came back.

As the pinto Spad shot out at the side and up before the chasing Fokkers could follow, he mumbled in his slow drawl:

"I don't reckon I ought to let yuh go, youngster. But on the other hand it don't seem just right to shoot yuh down right after yuh made such a swell showin' of nerve—er damn foolishness. Yuh ought to get a party pitched fer yuh by the baron fer savin' his life when yuh get back. Well, enjoy yourself. I won't be stoppin' yuh—this time."

And then for no reason at all, except force of habit and curiosity to know why his gas was still holding out, he glanced at his gauge. He sat up with a jerk.

Tac-tac-tac!

Fokkers had found him again in their sights in that moment of pause. Dirty yellow tracers fluffed past. He moved the controls by force of habit. His surprise seemed for that moment, overpowering. "Well I'll be a—"

HE WAS staring at the gauge. It was moving. It didn't say "empty" although he could see the letters peering around the corner of the dial at him. But he still had gas. Just about gas enough perhaps to reach the lines. Couldn't waste any more with this fighting.

"Must have got stuck or somethin' when I went crazy that first time," Smoke mumbled as he roared in a zigzag course to throw the Jerries off his tail.

Von Stolz saw the move and read it correctly. He stormed in now bravely to cut Smoke off from his own lines.

Smoke came back now with a burst of Vickers steel. The baron ducked. Likely he had misjudged. Perhaps he had thought Smoke's guns had suddenly jammed and that had been the cause for his turning tail and trying to run for home.

Von Stolz plunged out of the way. Other Fokkers bore in on Smoke's tail.

Tac-tac-tac!

Smoke strained his eyes to see the rear of those crooked trenches as he hurled south. Just coming into sight. Yellow tracers fluffing past.

He kicked to the right and the left, back and forth, desperately trying to throw off von Stolz and his pack. He pushed desperately on the throttle for more speed. The old Hisso was doing her best. But that was only about a mile an hour faster than the Fokkers could do that followed.

Tac-tac-tac!

Spandau guns were concentrating on him now as he hurled nearer the lines and escape. There came a perfect haze of steel about him. Steel that whistled and left little yellow ribbons behind them.

Smoke cursed. The thing was getting his nerves. They were nearing the German Front. Things would begin popping then.

His big six-gun slithered out in his right hand. He turned in the cockpit, took careful aim and let go.

Blam! Blam!

Smoke knew the vital part of a Mercedes engine. He picked it in that nearest Fokker. One slightly faster than the crimson crate of von Stolz.

The engine sputtered and something flew from the side of it, out through the metal cowling. The prop stopped entirely with a jerk and a groan that even Smoke could hear above the thunder of his own motor.

Other Fokkers had to leap or veer around that one as it began to glide down. That slowed them a little. He hurled on in his wild course. Twisting, turning. The course took away from his speed, but he dared not fly straight.

He glanced at his gas again. The gauge was going down, down. He looked fearfully at the lines. Before, he had been sure he would have to land in Germany. There hadn't been any fun in hoping he wouldn't. The gauge had become stuck and lied to him. But now he was on edge. Keyed up. He might just make his own lines—or he might not. There was uncertainty now. And he sat hunched over the stick, staring ahead once more.

Suddenly, all hell seemed to break loose about him. He was over the German action sector, just behind the Front. Guns of every description opened on him. Archie and machine guns and a moment later men in trenches poured volley after volley through the struggling pinto Spad.

Holes appeared in the wings, where an instant before had been clear fabric. The pinto Spad was bucking and cavorting like the wild horse the original pinto had been.

A great gaping hole opened up through his right, wing. It was perilously close to the front spar. If that front spar went, Smoke would go with it.

Smoke was flying like a demon now. Up and down and over he plunged the pinto Spad. He stared about him. He didn't have time to keep track of the Fokkers behind, but he knew the archie fire was letting up around his tail and was heavier ahead, so that they wouldn't chance hitting their own pilots.

Out across the Front he stormed. Over No-Man's-Land. The barrage kept up from the German front-lines. Then suddenly it broke in volume until the fierce rattle of Spandau guns on his tail seemed but a mere, half-hearted, whispered warning of Death.

He turned now. His rudder and tail fabric was partly in ribbons. Still somehow, they managed to hold together and give him enough surface for control of the crate.

Smoke stared behind that tattered tail group. Von Stolz was in the lead. He had lost ground, but he and his staffel were making a frantic attempt to put the curse of death on Smoke before he reached his own lines.

Flame belched from every Spandau gun. Yellow tracers flicked out and bullets screamed past. There seemed no place left where Smoke could dodge that deadly steel. Then from in front of the thundering Hisso came another sound. A roar like that of an earthquake, punctuated here and there by the incessant rattle of Yank ground-machine guns.

Everything on the Yank side of the lines seemed to be just missing Smoke Wade and his pinto Spad by the barest margin. And then it was that the first slow grin in many minutes crossed his face.

"Damned if yuh ain't just like a bunch of Yanks," he muttered. "Take any kind of a chance with my neck, yuh crazy-fools, just so yuh get some of von Stolz's outfit. And I'd bet a thousand to one that yuh wouldn't hit me either."

Now he was within gliding distance of his own side of the lines.

"RECKON I could at least crack up sort of respectable," he muttered. "Got a good notion to go back with what gas I got and show thet von varmint where to head in, maybe."

Then for two reasons he decided not to. The Yankee ground fire was driving von Stolz and his Jerries back.

And the other reason was that a sudden noise from his motor warned him something was going to happen. It was a cough and then a gasp and a wheeze as though the Hisso had suddenly taken asthma.

The prop wavered and slowed. No need to look at the gas tank now. Better look for a place to come down.

Smoke was looking plenty. Everything below seemed blasted. And still he must land.

Along a road from the rear, a truck moved with a jolting, lumbering motion. Smoke tried to gauge the distance. He might land right in front of that truck. Might!

He bore down on the vehicle, saw the face of the driver grinning up at him. The driver thought he was diving for fun. He thumbed his nose.

Smoke yelled at the top of his lungs.

"Look out below. I'm comin' down pronto."

Again the driver thumbed his nose. But he did seem to move the truck ahead a little faster. Just fast enough to do the trick. That was all Smoke needed.

Down, down. He tried to stretch his glide as much as possible. Again the driver looked up and thumbed his nose again. A tarpaulin was slung over a frame in the back end of the truck. The front was open.

Smoke could have cleared that truck by two feet. But there was something about that truck driver that egged him on. He held a steeper dive, aimed right for the driver—then pulled back just at the right time to roll the wheels of the pinto Spad on the ribs that held the tarpaulin at the rear.

As he swished over, he saw a body dive from the side of the driver's seat. And out of the corner of his eye he caught the driver tumbling in plenty of hurry into the mud of the ditch beside the alleged road.

Then Smoke was touching the road with his wheels. He slowed his speed as much as, possible. Bumps and jolts and flops and then the Spad was rolling on the harder surface of the road.

As it stopped, Smoke got out. He stared back two hundred yards and grinned at the man who was picking himself up out of the muddy ditch.

Men were running across an open field. They were in the front-line area. A shell burst some five hundred yards to the right.

Smoke broke into a run.

"Hey, got any gas on thet truck?"

The driver was cursing and rubbing the mud out of his eyes. Smoke whistled and grinned broader.

"Phew!" he sang out, "Anybody'd think you'd been a Mule Skinner before yuh took to truck nursin' with thet vocabulary, I reckon."

The driver got his eyes cleared enough so he could see. But just before that he opened up again in profane derision of any so-and-so who would dive a guy and near crash him so he would have to take to the mud to save himself.

The driver then spotted Smoke. He broke into stammering.

"Oh, er excuse me, captain. Didn't know you was a—"

Smoke laughed "Don't blame you a mite I reckon. But maybe thet'll be a lesson to you too, son. Don't go to thumbin' your nose at no air pilot, special when he's low and can see yuh. Thet's liable to put all kinds of fool notions inter his Head. But have yuh got any gas? I got to get the bus filled up and hop off again."

Before he finished the driver was lifting the tarpaulin. He heaved out a five gallon can. Grinned.

"My emergency gas," he said. "I can get it filled up when—and if—I get back without Heinie spotting me. Got to get this load of ammo through."

A few moments to pour the five gallons into the tank. Smoke paused as he took hold of the prop, shook his head sadly as he stared at the pinto Spad.

"Good thing, I reckon, you ain't flesh and bone, Jake," he drawled, "cause you'd take a heap of time gettin' well after what you been through today, boy. Let's go."

He pulled through. Once, twice, three times. The Hisso started. Men coming across the field reached him. An officer asked if they could help.

Smoke thanked him and pushed on the throttle.

Blam! Blam! Two shells burst within two hundred feet of where the plane had stood. But Smoke was in the air and climbing.

"Reckon we foxed yuh thet time, Jerry," he grinned, "but yuh didn't leave me much time fer nappin'."

Ten minutes later he romped down over the boundary of the field at Ramou and roared to the deadline.

His two Indian friends, Tom Buck the taller, lankier and Joe Buck the smaller, stockier brother grinned when they first greeted Smoke. But their faces grew longer as they examined the pinto Spad with its holes and torn sections.

Tom Buck traced a line of holes along the fuselage covering just a foot behind the cockpit cowling. He shook his head gravely.

"That come plenty close, Smoke," he said. "Someday you go out on lone patrol and you not come back maybe."

Smoke turned as he stepped to the ground.

"Huh?" he demanded. "What you been doin' Tom? Goin' tuh fortune tellers again, or just overflowing in white mule and dreamin' crazy stuff?"

It was Joe Buck who spoke next.

"Smoke, you teach us to fly. We go everywhere you go. Take care of you, Smoke."

"Huh?" Smoke exploded. "Take care of me. Well, I'll be a ring tailed thingamajig if thet ain't a good one." He roared with laughter. "Take care of old Smoke Wade. Well, doggone my hide. Why damn you red devils, you'd be raisin' hell over the Front and you'd keep me busy gettin' you birds out of trouble."

Slowly then, a thought seemed to permeate the brain of the lanky Westerner. His eyes narrowed suddenly.

"Say," he ventured, "come to think of it, I could have used you two a while back. Seen somethin' thet looked like a signal fire over there. What's three heap big smoke columns mean out of a thick woods in flat country?"

CHAPTER THREE
Fledglings

THE two redskin brothers looked at each other, frowned in perplexity for a moment, then turned to Smoke.

"Three fires?" asked Tom.

"Reckon thet's right," Smoke nodded, "My mathmatics ain't never been too good but I always been able to count considerable past three. There was three fires all right. At least I seen three columns of smoke. Heap big ones too."

Joe Buck came in with an explanation. ""Three fires never mean much," he ventured. "You sure they were three separate fires, Smoke?"

"Sartain I'm sure. Thet's what I said, ain't it?"

"Yeah. But Cherokee make one fire and use blanket to make smoke rise and stop. Signal that way. Not know so much about other Indian nations' smoke."

"All right," countered the bronzed ace, "then what's three puffs of smoke from a single Cherokee fire? Not thet this here smoke I seen has anything to do with signals, maybe. But I just sort of got a hunch."

"In our tribe," Tom Buck was explaining, "three puffs of smoke mean the same as S.O.S. on the wireless code."

"Right," nodded Joe. "It means help. We need help. Send help if you can. Just like S.O.S."

Smoke pondered the idea for a moment staring absently at his well punctured pinto Spad fuselage and left wing. Then he shook his head with a baffled gesture,

"Don't make sense," he snorted in disgust. "Besides, them in the woods, whoever they are, they wouldn't build fires like thet size for signals. Not them. Why they was flames comin' out of the tops of the trees half the time."

Both Indians shook their heads instantly.

"That couldn't be hooked up with Indians in any way or their signals," Joe cut in hastily. "Indians as you know, Smoke, build a small fire that can be controlled easily. Then we put leaves and stuff that will make it smoke a lot when we want to signal. And after we're through we just kick it apart and throw a little dirt over it and get away before the enemy comes to find us."

Tom nodded.

"That's right, Smoke," he assured.

Smoke turned, puzzled and started down the tarmac. It was Tom who called after him.

"Don't forget we'd like to fly with you, if you'll teach us to fly, Smoke. We want to work with you."

Smoke nodded absently. He only half heard that request repeated. He was headed for the office of Colonel McGill.

He shook his head as he went on. The whole thing had him stumped. He stomped into the colonel's outer office and into the inner sanctum without even taking the time or the bother to knock on the door marked private. The orderly half rose from the desk outside the colonel's door, grinned, and sat down again as Smoke passed him without noticing him.

"Smoke's sure in a trance this time," the orderly said to himself.

Colonel McGill looked up with a frown from behind a pile of papers on his desk. His frown lessened as he saw Smoke and then noticed his face.

"You look as though you got plenty on your mind this morning, Smoke," he opened. "What's up? Heard you just got back from one of your personally conducted tours. Wish you'd take to commanding your outfit more, and do less about trying to win the war yourself, Smoke."

Smoke shot a quick glance at the shaggy, browned old colonel.

"Anything wrong with the way I command my boys?" Smoke asked instantly in a slightly hurt voice.

"No, of course not, Smoke," McGill hastened to correct. "But I've talked to you about this a million times. You do too much of this dangerous flying yourself. We'd be lost without you to command the 66th, Smoke. That's all. I'm afraid some time you—"

Smoke's face broke in a grin.

"Scairt I won't come back some time, eh? Listen here, colonel. I figure it this away. When my time comes I'm a goin' to move up or down whichever the big thief decides. And it ain't goin' to make much difference whether I'm takin' a nap in my cot or flyin' a crate with von Stolz and a dozen of his kind on my tail pourin' lead into me. When they turn over the page fer thet day and the big chief sees my name there, I reckon he'll just scratch my name off one page and write it in on the other. And thet's all they will be to it, colonel." McGill nodded. Then he too smiled. "I've heard you say about that same thing before, Smoke," he said. "But I've got a hunch you don't believe in that entirely yourself. If you did you wouldn't bother to fight so hard sometimes as you do. And you wouldn't fight me so hard to let you go instead of taking a bunch of the newer men over the lines. If your theory works, Smoke, those green kids won't be in any more danger fighting Heinies, than they would be on the ground—if it isn't their day to die."

SMOKE shuffled uneasily. Moved his weight to the other foot. Grinned sheepishly.

"Well, doggone, colonel," he admitted, "you ain't got no respect for a good theory no how, have yuh, colonel? I'll bet you been savin' up thet line of argument fer me fer some time now. Who the devil started this here mess of talk anyhow?"

Colonel McGill chuckled at his victory.

"Anyway, Smoke," he smiled, "I want you to realize how lost we'd be without you to run the 66th. I've given up giving you orders to stay on the ground. But let's forget that for now. Only for the sake of your boys, Smoke, be a little more careful, will you? Now what did you have on your mind?"

Smoke licked his lips and looked more sheepish than ever.

"Doggone," he exploded, "yuh almost made me ferget with your speech on dying, colonel. Oh, yeah. I was goin' to tell yuh what I seen. Yuh know, I been wonderin' where von Stolz went. Fer five days now we ain't seen hide nor hair of him."

McGill nodded. His face grew troubled.

"Well, this mornin' I made up my mind to go over and have a look at his drome. Which I did. And, colonel, thet drome is as deserted as a Sunday School. picnic after a family of skunks has taken command. Yes, sir. Just the marks where the canvas hangars used to be. Thet's bout all."

He told him then of his flight to the west, covering the sectors almost to the Belgian front. Of sighting the three columns of smoke rising out of the great expanse of woods.

"Damndest thing I ever did see," Smoke was saying. "These here three fires. And they must have been big ones too. Them trees that hides the fires must be a good eighty or hundred feet high I'd guess. And now and then the flames come spurtin' right out the top of them trees like nothin'. First when I seen the smoke from a long way off I figured maybe they was signal fires of some kind. But I reckon they're too big fer thet. I was tryin' to get a better look when thet von skulkin' coyote jumped me with a mess of his pack and I didn't have time to do much more'n get back to the lines."

"Did you see where von Stolz came from?" McGill asked.

Smoke shook his head.

"Reckon thet was a bad mistake," he admitted. "But from the first thing I seen of thet smoke I was pretty concentrated on it and didn't look around overly much."

"You say they jumped you from above?"

"Yes, sir, colonel."

"Then likely you wouldn't have seen them come from anywhere except out of the sun if you had been watching."

"Most likely, I reckon. But one thing I do know. There's some special reason why von Stolz has been moved, lock, stock and barrel to thet new sector. They don't want nobody messin' around there no how, and likely specially Smoke Wade and his pinto Spad. They sure done everything to keep me there but kiss me and I reckon they'd a done thet if they'd thought it'd do any good."

"Likely," McGill said dryly. "These three fires, now Smoke? You say they had considerable smoke coming out of them and then now and again flame came from the tree tops?"

"Reckon thet's right, Colonel. Only come to think of it, there wasn't so much smoke considerin' the size of the fire there looked to be."

Colonel McGill nodded. He tapped his desk top with his fingers for some time without speaking. Suddenly, he looked up at Smoke questioningly.

"Ever see—" he stopped short and changed the question.

"How were these fires or smoke columns arranged? In a triangle or a straight line, or just stuck sort of irregular?"

Smoke's eyes narrowed for a moment.

"Why, come to think of it, that's what made me think at first they was signal fires," he admitted. "They was in a straight line runnin' about north and south. Maybe fifty feet or more apart. Maybe a hundred."

McGill's fingers rapped the desk again nervously. He nodded.

"Smoke," he asked, "did you ever see a big steel mill?"

"A steel mill?" Smoke exploded, "you mean in them woods?"

"I'm just playing around with an idea," McGill said. "Did you ever see a steel mill, the usual kind, with the blast furnaces?"

"Why—why yes, fer a few minutes," Smoke admitted. "Seen them blast furnaces up to Pueblo in Colorado. The train I took out of Arizona, Santa Fe as I recollect, went near 'em when they shipped me to learn to fly."

McGill nodded.

"Was there anything about those fires or smoke columns you saw this morning that made you think of the blast furnaces in Pueblo? From your description they make me think of the ones in Youngstown, Ohio. I lived there once."

Slowly, Smoke Wade nodded his head.

"Why, yes, now thet yuh mention it, colonel," he admitted. "But—but these fires I seen in the woods this mornin' had a heap more smoke than them blast furnaces in Pueblo. It couldn't he anyhow cause what would they be doin' with blast furnaces in a woods thet's maybe eight or ten miles from any town or city?"

"I haven't the remotest idea, Smoke," McGill countered. "I'm simply grasping at straws as you might say."

"And straws in a blast furnace wouldn't last long, or do much good, Colonel," Smoke grinned. "Besides, like I say, they couldn't be blast furnaces cause there was a heap too much smoke."

McGill nodded tolerantly.

"Sure. But I've seen them start a blast furnace. And when they first start them there's plenty of smoke until they get things really going."

SMOKE'S eyes opened wider at that. He stared at the colonel for a long time without speaking. Colonel McGill stared back at Smoke. The brains of both were working rapidly. But to no obvious end.

"But listen colonel," Smoke burst out, "in thet woods and away from any town. Out there all alone. What in hell would they be puttin' up a set of blast furnaces there fer? Most likely it's somebody burnin' brush or—"

He shook his head in bafflement.

"Nope, thet couldn't be it. Can yuh imagine anybody spendin' time in Germany these times within fifteen miles or so of the Front cuttin' brush out of a woods and burnin' it."

Colonel McGill smiled slowly. But it was not a smile of humor.

"I haven't any more idea about it than you. I've just sort of been thinking out loud. There isn't the slightest reason why they should have blast furnaces in the woods there. But your description of the fire and smoke reminded me of blast furnaces starting up. It's at least something to think about."

Smoke nodded.

"I reckon so. Somethin' to go crazy thinkin' about if I get worse as fast as I have in the last twenty minutes talkin' about it," he admitted.

"Don't let it get you, Smoke," McGill counseled, "but don't forget it either. I'll gamble it's something mighty important and we've got to figure out what. Von Stolz is guarding that sector entirely too heavily for it not to mean anything. Now I've got a lot of work before me today, Smoke, so if that's all you want to report—"

Smoke nodded.

"I reckon thet's all," he said turning toward the door. He paused there. Seemed hesitant for a moment. Turned back to the colonel.

"Just one other thing," he ventured. "Somethin' funny."

Colonel McGill waited tolerantly.

"When I landed, both them Indian friends of mine I got moved here as mechanics seemed mighty worried about Jake gettin' shot up so, my pinto yuh know. And they both come bustin' out with the idea of teachin' 'em to fly so they could go along with me. I been sort of turnin' thet over in my mind since then, between thoughts of this other stuff, and it don't make such bad sense at that. Them boys can shoot like a couple of fools. And I got a hunch if they can fly a ship as well as they can ride horseback they'd be mighty valuable to the air service of old Uncle Samuel."

"You're asking my permission to teach them to fly, Smoke?" McGill asked. "Is that it?"

"Yes, sir. Thet was what I was aimin' at."

The colonel thought for a moment. Smiled.

"You'd likely put a saddle on the back of the pinto Spad with duel controls hooked to it and teach them that way I suppose," he ventured. He laughed then and shook his head. "No, Smoke. I'm afraid that wouldn't do. They're a couple of wild Indians in more than one sense of the word. We'd be getting into no end of trouble."

"No sir, I reckon maybe we wouldn't—get into so much trouble," Smoke argued. "I'm serious, colonel. Honest. We could take the old D.H. and put duels in hit and go to work on 'em. I'll take full responsibility of 'em."

Colonel McGill took a long breath. His eyes fell upon the pile of work on his desk.

"And after all, yuh owe them boys some things fer some of the stuff they've helped out in—beyond the call of duty, or somethin' like the medals read," Smoke persisted. "I'll be mighty careful and—"

McGill nodded then.

"All right," he said. "I haven't time to argue with you, Smoke. Not this morning, And after all, you're generally right by some twist of fate. Only remember this. You take full responsibility and they can't possibly get more than a sergeantcy at the best without going to ground school and taking special courses."

"Yes, sir," Smoke grinned. "They won't want nothin'. Reckon they'd be delighted to fly and stay just plain buck privates, colonel. I'll go tell 'em pronto. And thanks. I'll guarantee yah won't be sorry."

He was gone out the door leaving a very much relieved and busy colonel to tear into the paper work before him.

Smoke was trotting eagerly toward the place where Joe and Tom

Buck worked on the tattered remains of one badly riddled pinto Spad. Smoke's face was alight with the elation that he suddenly felt. For the moment, the strange circumstance of three fires in a row in the heavily wooded area near the Belgian Front was forgotten.

He shouted ahead of him as he came within ear-shot of the red-skin brothers. They turned and stared at the running figure of their commander, stared with puzzled expressions until they heard Smoke's voice.

"Get your flyin' togs and trot out the D.H. You birds are about to take your first lesson at sky ridin'."

And like the three smoke columns, those words to Colonel McGill were forgotten as well. Those words in which Smoke had guaranteed that his C.O. would not be sorry for his decision to let the two Indians learn to fly.

But the guarantee like the three smoke columns wouldn't be forgotten long. And Smoke would learn not far hence that he had given a guarantee that was going to make tough going ahead.

CHAPTER FOUR

Redskins Awing

AT FIRST in the training there was the usual skidding and slipping about the sky. Smoke yelled orders until he was hoarse. He turned and cursed the dumbness of the Indians—both Tom and Joe alike—as he gave them instructions by turns. And when he turned to glare at them after some fool maneuver, he only got a broad grin for his pains.

But they were learning. There could be no denying that. And having the time of their lives doing it

Things had suddenly quieted, on the sector near Ramou. And Smoke had purposely given orders for pilots of the 66th to remain in their own sector. He was saving that sector over near the Belgian Front for himself. Not that he wanted glory but he did want to run that show against von Stolz personally.

So while Smoke cursed and swore at the brothers as he gave them flight instruction, the boys—Smoke's boys of the 66th—stood by and grinned.

Landings and take-offs. Landings and take-offs. Both were able to get away with those within reason. A D.H. was nothing fancy for instructions. But it was the best at hand and must do. Smoke worked with them untiringly and the two Buck brothers seemed to have unbelievable stamina against fatigue.

Joe was getting so he could take the D.H. off, fly it around the field, do figure eights, cut his motor and land, without Smoke having to correct the stick from the front cockpit.

Tom had been a little slower. His eights were sloppy and his landings—those that Smoke didn't have to help him with, were plenty rough in spots, particularly on the last bound.

It was the fifth morning of instruction. Smoke confronted them grinning. Joe and Tom grinned back a greeting. He motioned to the Lewis gun Scaarf mounting in the rear cockpit where either of the brothers sat when they took instructions.

"Got any idea what that's there for this mornin'?" Smoke asked.

Both Indians stared at it, shook their heads. Tom brightened first.

"Maybe going hunting?" he suggested..

Before that the mounting had been removed while the D.H. was being used for instruction.

Smoke grinned.

"Yes and no," he countered with a wink. "That is, Joe and I are going hunting, Tom. Your turn comes some other day. Yuh see, Joe here is about ready to solo. I'm goin' to turn him loose if he does good on this trip. But we're aimin' over Germany together. Joe's goin' to fly us there if he can. Remember them three columns of smoke I seen a few days ago?"

Tom looked crestfallen. Joe nodded eagerly.

"Well," Smoke went on, "I reckon they been smolderin' about long enough without some attention. You and me is goin' over this morning and have a look. And we'll likely run into some shootin' before we get back. O.K. with you?"

A broad grin spread across Joe Buck's face. Tom had turned his back and was stalking slowly, sadly toward the hangar.

"Hey," Smoke called, "don't go way mad that a way, Tom. Your turn'll come in a couple of days."

Tom didn't answer. He disappeared into the hangar. He was gone a few minutes and came back with his bolt action army rifle slung over his shoulder.

Smoke stared at him.

"What's the idea of the artillery?" he demanded.

"You go hunting, I go too," Tom mumbled. He jerked his head toward the wood that skirted the field of the 66th.

Smoke nodded.

"Sure. Good. O.K."

Tom hesitated. Jerked his head toward the hangar this time.

"Telephone just rang. Someone want to speak to you, Smoke."

"Huh?" said Smoke, "Oh, telephone. O.K."

He trotted off. He found the receiver buzzing where it hung from the hook, but his shouts into the mouthpiece aroused no one except an orderly at a switch board demanding to know if somebody on the other end of the line had gone crazy. No. Nobody had called Smoke Wade, as far as he knew.

Smoke stomped out of the hangar. Joe Buck was, standing beside the warming D.H. alone. He grinned at the anger in Smoke's eyes.

"I think Tom fool you," Joe chuckled. "He tells you somebody wants to talk to you on the telephone and then he beats it out of sight before you come back."

"Yeah?" Smoke exploded. "Why the—"

He broke off in a chuckle then.

"I reckon before I get through with Tom he'll know better than to play tricks on his flying instructor. Wait till I get thet cuss alone in the air. Is that boy in for a ride! Ha-Ha."

Smoke put his booted foot in the stirrup beside his front cockpit. He turned to Joe Buck.

"All set?"

"O.K.!" There was something queer about the set of Joe's mouth. As though he wanted to laugh but didn't dare.

Belts fastened and the two settled in their seats.

"Take her off," yelled Smoke through the tube they had rigged up between the two cockpits.

"Right," came back from Joe.

THE Liberty roared. The D.H. slithered over the ground going faster and faster. The nose was too high for a take-off. Smoke barked through the tube. "Get that tail up. You're takin' off, not landing. How many times have I got to tell yuh to—"

The tail came up—too slowly. Smoke hit his stick in the forward cockpit a heavy crack. Surprise flooded his leathery face. The stick was already farther ahead than it should be to keep the tail up for the take-off.

He whirled in his seat and shot a glance at Joe, Joe wasn't looking at Smoke. He was staring past him looking ahead.

Smoke's perplexity grew. Something seemed wrong. But now Joe had the D.H. off the ground and they were climbing.

"Not so steep," Smoke bellowed back. "Want to stall?"

The D.H. leveled off again a little more. But slowly it worked into that climb. They were headed for the Front. Joe was holding his course well, but somehow that nose wouldn't stay down where it belonged for a slow climb, just slightly above the horizon.

Smoke placed a hand on the stick and wiggled it. Something felt very strange. The tail seemed weighed down. He could feel Joe Buck in spite of the fact that Smoke was supposed to be flying the ship now, holding the stick ahead a little for some reason.

"Hey," Smoke yelled back, "what the hell is in this tail?"

"I dropped my gold watch and couldn't get it before we started," Joe shouted back. "Must have slid back to the tail group."

"Oh, yeah?"

Smoke kicked viciously at the rudder and jerked the stick. The D.H. half rolled, turned upside down and then dove with the gun full on. He snapped it out with a jerk and grinned behind.

"Ought to have lost thet watch by now," he ventured.

Joe looked slightly white around the gills. But he managed to grin back. The tail seemed heavier now than ever. Then suddenly, it felt lighter on the stick.

Smoke shrugged.

"Hell I don't know what's the matter with this crate," he called back, "but if you want to take her, take her. Let's see what you'd do in this case. You'd go on likely like a damn fool I suppose."

He turned and Joe was nodding.

They went on. An hour passed. They had climbed high above the Front as they went over. Twice archie had grunted up at them but that was all. It was cold up there at fifteen thousand feet. Joe seemed to have the hang better of keeping the nose down and the tail up.

Far to the northwest, Smoke could make out the Belgian Front from the towns as their shape was shown on his map. He called into the tube.

"Getting tired?"

"Hell no."

"Let's have a little more right rudder, Joe. Swing a little more toward that forest down there ahead. There. That's better."

He stared then at the expanse of woods over which he had roared five days before. He came up in his seat. He was much closer to that woods than he had been five days before when he had first spotted it. The air was just as clear. Perfect weather for flying for two weeks. Not a drop of rain or a rift of fog.

"Well, I'll be damned," Smoke exploded.

"What's the matter?" That through the tube from Joe.

"Why, nothin', only there ain't no smoke columns comin' up like there was the other day. Thet's why I brought you along today, partly. Wanted yuh to have a look and see if you could figure anything out of it."

They roared nearer. Smoke pulled the powerful glasses out of the case. He'd had those glasses moved from his cockpit in Jake just for this trip. He stared through them—blinked and stared again.

"Well, I'll be a ring-tailed so and so or something" he bellowed. "There's spurts of flame comin' from three places in a line in thet woods. Right where I seen them three columns of smoke comin' the other day. But there ain't enough smoke to—"

He stopped short and leaned forward in his seat.

"Why damn me if them trees, some of 'em ain't burned around somethin' down there. Or else—"

His eyes were fairly bulging out of their sockets. He pushed on the stick instinctively. Pushed it harder until Joe dropped the nose and the Liberty began going crazy with the power dive.

"Let's go down and see what the hell's comin' off down there," Smoke cried. "I reckon I can see plenty now with them trees burned away like thet."

They were going down, too. The Liberty was screaming in the dive. Smoke shot a glance about them in the sky. Just one. Didn't see anything in the sky.

Fire belched here and there from three places in the woods. Three spots that were evenly placed in a line running north and south about fifty or a hundred feet apart.

Nearer and nearer.

"I'm lettin' you fly her while I look," Smoke called through the tube. "Don't let her crash, that's all. Pull her out when you get ready, but wait a while yet."

Down, down. Joe Buck was letting her go wild. Fifteen thousand feet of altitude shrunk in a surprisingly short time to ten and then to five and to two.

Smoke was staring through his glasses even at that altitude. Three giant cannon like muzzles stuck up at him out of the woods. At first he took them for huge guns. Like howitzers sticking their gaping snouts straight up.

But flame and not shells was coming: out of those three stacks. They were chimneys. Chimneys of great blast furnaces. Blast furnaces in the middle of a great woods. Absurd. But there they were, belching flame with little or no smoke as before.

"Pull her out," Smoke yelled.

Nothing happened.

"Pull her out!" he yelled at the top of his lungs in a very hoarse voice.

He whirled in his seat then. Stared at Joe Buck.

The Indian was also twisted round in his seat. He wasn't looking where he was going. Didn't seem to realize that they were traveling at better than two hundred miles an hour and had less than a quarter of a mile in which to come out of that dive and keep from ramming straight down the throat of that middle blast furnace stack to a horrible death.

Smoke almost froze as he turned too. For behind them, from high above, a crimson Fokker was streaking down with an odd dozen red-nosed Fokkers behind spread out in a snarling Vee so all could bring their guns to play at the same time.

SMOKE'S hand was on the stick. He jerked back even before he turned. The Liberty shrieked. The D.H. groaned with the strain. It seemed that the wings would sheer in that zoom. Smoke's teeth were clenched. His hand seemed frozen to that stick. It was only part way back. Didn't dare pull it out too quickly or something would have to go.

He stared down past the side of his cockpit. It seemed only a matter of inches, that space between the landing gear and the top edge of the middle blast furnace chimney.

A seering hot wave flooded over him, scorched his days' growth of whiskers. He felt the wing dope smolder. Smelled the choking fumes from that dope that was already to burst into flames.

It was too hot to cry out. Too stifling for that brief moment to even think beyond getting away from that flood of heat. Then it was passed and another menace, fully as great, swept down upon them with rattling Spandau guns.

Smoke didn't have to look behind to take in the situation. Von Stolz and his pack had caught them cold turkey. A lumbering D.H. that was supposed to be light of load, but which was tail-heavy. At feast fifteen minutes, perhaps more, from their own lines. A strained ship that might fall apart at any minute.

Tac-tac-tac!

Yellow tracers fluffed past. But Smoke could tell from the sound of those guns that they were still out of range. Von Stolz and his devils were simply warming their guns for the kill. They wouldn't know that Smoke Wade, flew in the front seat of this, D.H. How delighted von Stolz would be if he did know!

Tac-tac-tac!

Those last bursts weren't for fun. A half dozen Spandau slugs ripped past Smoke's elbow, crashed through the left wing and sent splinters flying in his eyes from the punctured longerons of the fuselage.

No more time to wait. Mustn't look up. The long chance.

Back came the stick in Smoke's lap. A scream, another roar, a shriek and motors tore all about him! Fokkers, taken by surprise, plunged every way to avoid that desperate loop that Smoke had hurled the D.H. into.

As he leveled out in that long dive at the end of the loop, Fokkers were still thundering past him on either side. Two sent a hail of Spandau slugs into the wings. They didn't dare aim any straighter than that at the cockpits for fear of crashing as they roared down.

Von Stolz had shot past very close. Smoke had seen his face clearly—and likely von Stolz had seen his. It didn't matter much now. They'd do their best to get them. Perhaps if von Stolz did recognize Smoke, it would help to make him more cautious.

Fokkers were snarling behind to come round again. Five made it and came hell-bent with blazing guns. Still nothing happened from those twin Lewis guns in the rear cockpit. Maybe Joe had been hit.

Fearfully, Smoke whirled in his seat. What he saw sent a thrill of mixed anger and admiration over him. He couldn't tell which was the stronger.

Joe Back was standing with his guns in his hands. He had obviously just taken hold of them and turned them on the turret. For he had been busy with something else.

There, behind the rear cockpit, was the secret of the heavy tail. Lanky Tom Buck had climbed out of the space just behind the rear cockpit He had moved up with his brother's help to a position a-straddle of the fuselage behind the gunner's cockpit. When Smoke saw him first he was just hooking the second toe under brace wires through holes he had cut or kicked in the side fabric of the fuselage.

He sat there for an instant like the bronze statue of a great Indian chief on his horse, except that Tom was riding backward, facing and guarding the rear of the plane. At that moment he raised the army rifle, took aim at a snarling Fokker.

CHAPTER FIVE
Shooting Fools

CRACK! The rifle of Tom Buck spoke. Just a split second after he had sighted a Fokker that was finishing a turn to open fire from behind.

Tac-tac-tac!

At that moment Joe Buck let go with both Lewis guns at a Fokker that slithered past the side of the D.H. Smoke stared.

The Fokker behind wavered and plunged. And from the engine of the second Boche ship smoke and flame sported.

Then Smoke had spun round and was glaring through his own sights. Almost had a Fokker there. Another movement to the right and he'd have him.

"Damn!"

He kicked. But he didn't dare throw the D.H. into the wild maneuver that was required for fear of hurling Tom Buck off his precarious position. He yelled through the tube to Joe.

Tac-tac-tac!

At first that was all that came back. Then:

"Wheeeee—yip—yip? What yuh want?"

"Tell thet crazy brother of yourn to get the hell down off thet turtle back before I throw him off," Smoke yelled.

Crack! Crack! Again and again the rifle in Tom's hands spoke. Another Fokker folded up for the day and plunged. Then Joe's voice in return.

Tom says to throw him off—if yuh can."

Tac-tac-tac! That was Joe going into action again.

Smoke let go with the works after that. Stick and rudder. His own guns began to smolder and bark and rave and buck. He stared about for von Stolz. For once in his life, Smoke was afraid the baron was about to die. Never before had he seen such rifle shooting from a moving thing as Tom was displaying. That lanky Indian up there riding backward, like the Indians of old being pursued in battle.

Tom was lying almost flat now across the turtle back, toes hooked under brace wires through the torn fabric at the sides. He seemed glued to the spot. And every time that Indian pulled a trigger, something happened out there in the air among the Jerries.

Smoke spotted the baron now in his crimson crate. He was out on the edge of the fight where he usually was. Smoke cursed and kicked the rudder.

Round came the D.H. and he headed for von Stolz. If he let these wild Indians go much longer they'd clean up even von Stolz. That was unthinkable. He was Smoke's meat when the time came.

He tore down through a maze of white and yellow tracer smoke. Fokkers scrambled out of his way, uncertain whether to prefer the front or the back of that deadly D.H.

Von Stolz remained just out of reach. Smoke maneuvered, jockeyed for position. Then by a chance turn to dodge another Fokker that seemed about to crash him, he found von Stolz within range, and almost in his sights.

A slight swerve to the left and that would be the end.

Bam! Something was snarling down out of the blue above. Smoke cursed took his eyes off the sights. A Fokker was coming in to save von Stolz.

Smoke's hand moved instantly. There was something familiar about that diving Fokker. He had seen it once before when he had von Stolz dead to rights in his sights.

And for the second time in less than a week, the brief space of time that Smoke had to dodge to keep from being crashed by the hurtling Fokker saved von Stolz.

The baron with his crimson Fokker leaped and rolled his ship. He was hurling away out of range. But Smoke wasn't watching him. He knew it would be useless. Instead his eyes were on the Fokker as it screamed past.

Smoke's head dove again before his sights. The nose of the pinto Spad moved round and down. He had turned to the right to avoid collision. Now he kicked to the left again and shot the nose down to follow the interfering Boche.

As the Fokker lunged past he recognized the pilot. The same, foolhardy youngster who had pulled the trick before.

Tac-tac-tac!

Smoke's thumb tramped down on the trigger button. Held it. His teeth were clenched and a curse sprayed through them.

"Cain't try them things too often," he mouthed. "You'll learn thet now, likely. Let yuh get away with the first one to give yuh a good time. Sort of went to your head, didn't it? Well, so will these—if the old aim ain't gone."

And Smoke was right. That Fokker never came out of its headlong dive for hell.

Tac-tac-tac!

Smoke whirled in his bucket seat. Tom was taking aim at another Fokker, at long-range now. Surprising what a lot of respect the tail end of that old D.H. commanded.

One Fokker was going down. Another was gliding far below with a dead engine. Joe Buck was whirling his guns like a madman. Smoke caught his breath. For an instant it looked as if Joe was swinging his guns straight on Tom's back. But he let up on the triggers just in time. Swept the guns past his lanky brother and opened again as a Fokker slithered around the tail at long range to come in around the front.

Tac-tac-tac!

Crack!

LIKELY it will never be known just who was responsible. But fire spurted from three guns at the same time. And simultaneously, the head of the Jerry pilot flopped over and his gasoline tank burst into flame.

Smoke spun back to the front of his seat. For the moment these two Indians were making the cowboy ace look a bit backward in his air fighting. That fact wasn't bothering Smoke in the least. In fact he was grinning broadly. He chuckled and shook his head. Then he glanced about the sky for that crimson plane once more.

The nose of the D.H. was free from Fokkers. Funny that. He stared farther to the north. The air seemed empty, until suddenly he spotted the remains of von Stolz's flight, their tails pointed toward Smoke and his redskins.

He swung once more toward those stacks in the woods. The fight had carried him a mile or two away. But von Stolz and his pack were on the run. The D.H. wouldn't stand a show in a chase. The Indians were too much for the Jerries.

The air was clear now. Smoke's grin was broadening. He tried to keep his shoulders from shaking but he was laughing his head off. Mumbling to himself as he laughed.

"Yes, sir. Damned if thet ain't bout the funniest thing I ever did see. Tom Buck sittin' up there like the wild redskin he is, shootin' his head off and callin' his shots regular. Man, how thet Injun can shoot!"

"And—" he broke out in a new fit of laughing as he eyed the tails of the red-nosed Fokkers running for home—"if thet ain't a sight fer sore eyes, seein' a mess of Fokkers runnin' from a old, decrepit D.H. with a crew of three instead of two. Man, oh, man, I wish the boys back at the 66th could see thet."

He plunged the stick forward. They were hurling down on those stacks again. The stacks were still belching smoke.

Something ripped out and whistled past the D.H. to explode higher in the air where they had been a moment before. Smoke ducked instinctively.

"Phew!" he whistled, "It don't pay to stay in one place long. No sir. We'll be goin' right pronto. But—"

Pluff!

Again another archie shell.

"I'll be back with some plain and fancy eggs that won't be for soft-boilin'. Must have got archie batteries set up in the last ten minutes, eh? Well, we'll take them too. Trees'll make it tough goin' fer yuh unless a guy is straight overhead."

He waved his arm down, thumbed his nose and ducked with a last look at the three spouting stacks.

Air was still clear. Only the tiny specks that were the ships of von Stolz running for home. Smoke watched them for a moment and frowned as he, too, turned toward his home field.

"Maybe," he ventured, "I ought to follow them and see where they go. Must be a long ways off, cause they been goin' plenty long now. Maybe later I'll find out. Be sort of funny to come over in a bunch and bomb the field and them funny lookin' smoke stacks and clean up the whole works in one raid. Reckon if we knowed just where—"

He turned back with a shrug.

"Hell, what's the use," he finished. "Von's taken plenty lickin' fer a spell and we got other things of more importance right now."

They were climbing higher and higher as they roared toward the lines. Archie batteries began grunting up at them from the back areas. The firing got hotter as they went farther south. Then it ceased as they stormed over No-Man's-Land and a few minutes later they romped down in a screaming zoom over the field at Ramou. Smoke shook the stick, and shouted his first command through the tube since he had told Tom Buck to come down off the turtle back.

"Land her," he snapped to Joe.

He felt the stick move. Felt it grow steady and let go. Even then he didn't turn to look at them. Smoke was afraid he wouldn't be able to keep a straight face.

Two bounds and they were down. Not bad for what Joe had been through. Smoke didn't move. Joe taxied to the dead line and the D.H. stopped and heeled over on the skid.

VERY leisurely, Smoke untangled his long legs from around the stick and dropped to the ground. He picked a cigarette out of a pack and lighted it and stuffed the pack into his pocket. Still he didn't turn. The corners of his lips were twitching. Then a voice from behind him. It was Tom's voice.

"I'm sorry if you're sore, captain," he said, "but I—I wanted to go along and I—"

Smoke turned very slowly. He eyed him through mere slits.

"Well, what you kickin' about? You went, didn't yuh?"

Tom moved nervously.

"Well, yeah, but—well hell, captain, I hoped yuh wouldn't be sore and—"

"Sore," Smoke suddenly managed to bellow. "Sore! I'll say I'm sore.

Who in hell do you think you are anyway? Sneakin' along with a holt-action rifle and pickin' off the cream of the Jerries in the fight. And me gettin' the jitters for fear you was goin' to pick off von Stolz himself before I got my crack at him.

"But you ain't satisfied with thet. You got to come back to the field and start to 'captain' me. Who in hell ever told you or anybody else to call Smoke Wade 'captain'. Ain't I know'd you long enough, so's when you get up in the world and start makin' a name fer yourself in the air you can go right on callin' your old, ordinary friends just like yuh used to without no handles to their names?

"And you ain't satisfied with makin' a monkey out of me by takin' half your life to learn to fly with all these air hombres about chucklin' behind my back. No. You got to go out and make a fool out of me pickin' off Jerries with a good single shot, bolt action rifle while all I got is a pair of machine guns to shoot with—and—oh, hell—"

Smoke whirled. Turned his back on Tom Buck. Turned his back simply because he couldn't stand and look at either of those blank faces longer without bursting out laughing in their faces. They were swallowing his line of anger hook, sinker and bait.

"Well, hell, captain, er Smoke," Tom blurted, "I—I didn't know you was goin' to—to take it thet way. Gee, I—"

That was the point that Smoke couldn't get past. There was almost a sob in the voice of the lanky Indian. He was sincerely sorry he'd hurt Smoke's feelings. Very sorry.

Smoke whirled back to face them and when he did his face was split from ear to ear with a broad grin. Then a roar of laughter bellowed from his mouth. He raised both arms and slapped each Redskin on the back. A resounding smack.

They looked perplexed for a moment. Then they began to smile too, a bit guardedly.

"Hell," Smoke thundered, "I was only kiddin'. Course I ought to put you red devils in the guard house fer the rest of your lives. Men got sent to Leavenworth fer less then thet, I reckon. But I never did see anythin' so funny as you sittin' up there astraddle of thet turtle back, Tom and scarin' the daylights out of them Jerry devils."

"You—you didn't mean nothin by bawlin' me out then?" Tom asked, still plenty suspicious. "I was all set to go to the guard house or get court martialed or somethin' fer that. But—" he grinned broader—"it would have been worth it."

"Mean it?" Smoke exploded, "Hell no. Course yuh oughtn't to a gone, but now that it happened I wouldn't have missed thet show fer a million dollars. No sir, not fer a million."

Then Smoke turned serious for a moment. He stuck an index finger into the chest of Tom Buck.

"But you listen here, long and lanky. If I catch you pullin' anything like this again, ever, I'll skin yuh and scalp yuh and hang yuh up to dry. Now mind what I tell yuh."

Then he turned abruptly on his heel while he could leave that feeling of gravity with the two, and strode toward the office of Colonel McGill.

MCGILL looked up from his desk. As usual he was busy. But not too busy to smile at Smoke Wade.

"Well," he asked, "how are the two Cherokees coming with their flight instructions?"

Smoke chuckled.

"You'd a think they was comin' swell if you'd been with us a hour ago. Boy, if von Stolz ever got sent for and couldn't come he did this afternoon. I was takin' Joe over to fly the plane on his first hop over the lines. We headed fer the forest where I seen the two columns of smoke and—"

Smoke stopped short suddenly and stared at the colonel.

"Say," he exploded, "I been so excited tellin' yuh 'bout these redskin devils thet I forgot to tell yuh the most important thing of all."

"Well, for heaven sake, start somewhere and finish that," Colonel McGill suggested.

"Sure," nodded Smoke. "Remember your talkin' bout blast furnaces and such?"

McGill nodded a little more interested now.

"Well, sir I reckon we got three blast furnaces stuck in thet woods over there. Yes, sir. Three blast furnaces now."

"Blast furnaces? How the devil do you know?"

Colonel McGill had suddenly clutched the edge of the desk. He was half sitting on the front of his chair.

"Seen 'em," Smoke drawled, "at least them chimneys looked just about like them stacks around Pueblo. And fire spurtin' from 'em, but—" he leaned forward and lowered his voice—"no smoke, not to speak of this time."

"Good Lord," exploded the colonel. He stared at Smoke for several seconds.

His brain seemed to be working rapidly. Then he dived through the pile of papers that, as usual, littered his desk top and came up triumphantly with a slip of paper.

He slid it across to Smoke.

"Read it," he ordered.

Smoke took the slip and glanced at it. He frowned as he read:

—*GGUNINVERGONF.*

His eyes ran over the meaningless letters again.

"Say, what the hell is this, colonel, a game or somethin'. Thet don't make no sense no how," he said.

"I know it," McGill said tensely. "Nobody else can make sense to it either. It came in a half hour ago—from Intelligence."

"Intelligence?" Smoke repeated.

"Right. Some wireless operator cut in on the message from German air. It was sent at terrific speed. What attracted his attention first was a weak signal calling for G-2. The sender was in a hurry. He only got part of his message sent so far as we know. Something must have happened—to stop him."

Smoke pointed to the message.

"And thet's all yuh got, colonel?"

"Yes." McGill reached for the message—"Look at the end. Those letters spell Vergon. Isn't that the Vergon Wood over near the Belgian front where you saw those blast furnaces?"

Smoke nodded slowly. He was standing now, staring at the slip on the desk. He didn't speak for a long time. Then he shook his head.

"Reckon maybe thet's got somethin' to do with what I seen," he drawled, half to himself. "Kind of looks like some poor spy devil sent the message and got caught at it."

Colonel McGill was thoughtfully looking at his desk and tapping it with his finger tips nervously.

"Three blast furnaces in the center of a wood. Three blast furnaces—" he repeated over and over again. Slammed his fist on the desk top.

"I'll be damned if I can think of anything they'd use a blast furnace for in a woods," he barked.

"Nor me, neither," Smoke agreed, "but I'm sure aimin' to find out more about it in the morning. Reckon Jake and me'll go droppin' a few eggs—even if it ain't Easter time yet."

CHAPTER SIX

Disappearing Fires

MESS at the 66th. Brant, sitting next to Smoke, seemed hesitant about asking something.

"What yuh got on your chest, Brant," Smoke asked around a mouthful of lamb stew. "I can see you're itchin' to say somethin'."

Brant smiled and nodded.

"I am Smoke," he said. "The boys haven't had much going on lately. We go out, take a joy ride and come back,

We haven't seen a Jerry crate in the air for about five days now."

Smoke forced a chuckle.

"Sure," he drawled. "Reckon thet's just like you birds. Give yuh plenty of action and yuh want a rest. Give yuh a rest and yuh want action."

Brant flared suddenly—something that Smoke hadn't seen him do for months, not since they had first met and had the showdown that made them friends.

"I don't like that crack," he snapped. "When did we ever duck a job? Of course, when some of the boys are too new and—"

Smoke's boney hand flipped through the air and slapped his senior flight commander on the back affectionately.

"Fer Pete's sake," he laughed, "ain't you knowd Smoke Wade long enough to tell when he's kiddin' and when he ain't? Course you're there when it comes to a tough spot. Show me the coyote what says you ain't and I'll bust him wide open. I was only jokin'. I know yuh ain't had no action lately, what with von Stolz moved out the sector."

Brant nodded.

"Maybe I shouldn't tell you this, Smoke," he began, "but some of the boys don't like your running this secret show of yours. We'd like to be in on it with you."

Smoke shook his head very slowly in return. He put a light hand on Brant's arm and looked the skipper of the senior flight straight in the eyes.

"Maybe they're right, too, son," he said. "I been sort of hoggin' things I guess, come to think of it. I reckon it's mostly because I didn't want to put you fellas in no danger spot. And maybe they think I been spendin' too much time with Tom and Joe Buck teachin' 'em to fly. And maybe I have. But I got a neat little job cut out fer myself tomorrow. And after that, I reckon you boys'll go along from then on. I don't blame 'em fer crabbin'. But there's some things what's done better with one crate than a dozen. You tell 'em fer Smoke that within thirty-six hours they'll get some action—thet is if what I got up my sleeve works out, and I reckon it's goin' to."

After mess, Smoke walked through the gathering twilight to his hangar. Tom and Joe had just returned from their mess. They were working on the holes in the D.H., checking the motor, examining guns.

"Reckon yuh won't need thet tomorrer, boys," Smoke ventured. "You won't be flyin' tomorrer. I got to do some lone stuff with Jake, so yuh better lay off your pet house-boat and get the pinto Spad in shape."

There was disappointment written on the coppery faces of the two. But nothing was said. They turned to the pinto Spad and began working with the holes and checking the motor. Smoke smiled.

"Thet's the way to take it," he said. "I know you boys is disappointed as hell but I got somethin' special to do and I cain't be givin' instructions tomorrer. Good night, boys."

He walked about the field. Couldn't get that strange mess of letters out of his mind. Couldn't stop thinking about a poor devil of a Yank spy who had been trying to send important information and had probably been caught in the act.

Again and again he turned that long meaningless word over in his mind. *GGUNINVERGONF.*

He turned in early. But although he slept soundly, he couldn't keep those letters from flashing in front of him. Flashing and going off again like a jiggly, electric sign. Vergon. That stood out. And something else was taking shape, too. Some other word—but Smoke just couldn't seem to make it.

Dawn and Smoke was dressed and gulping hot coffee and cakes. He strode then to his hangar. The pinto Spad was on the tarmac. Tom and Joe Buck looked exceptionally happy this morning' for some reason. The Hisso was already warm,

A check of the motor, revved up, inspection of the ship and his guns. He inspected the bombs under the wings. Six bombs there. He smiled and winked at the two redskins.

"What a lot of fun thet's goin' to be, droppin' them down them yawnin' stacks in Vergon woods," he chuckled. "Better bring about four hand bombs and pack 'em in the cockpit. Might need them, too."

He climbed into the cockpit himself and helped stow the twenty-five pound hand bombs into four spaces under his seat and beside him. Rather cramped room. The Hisso was idling now. Tom and Joe pulling the chocks.

"Clear?" Smoke barked.

"Clear!" came the answer.

The Hisso snarled and the pinto Spad took to the air, but slower this time with the heavy load of bombs.

Smoke turned away from the dawn, headed into the northwest, Again that jumble of letters blinked before him as he rode the pinto. No sense. He tried to shut it out of his mind. Couldn't. There was one word there that he couldn't get. A word that seemed to stand out and make some kind of sense and still—

He shook his head and roared on through the morning.

As he neared the Front he climbed. No need furnishing target practice for a bunch of Jerry archie crews.

A few batteries, scattered here and there behind the Front opened up under him. But he was too high.

HIS eyes strained into the northwest, and began to pick out that patch of woods far ahead. A patch that grew in size as he came nearer and became a great forest stretching out solidly except for a small clearing here and there.

His powerful glasses came out from their case beside him. The morning had been clear when he had started out. Now he was forced lower and lower by forming clouds.

The Vergon Forest was directly below him. He was searching everywhere for those blast furnaces, or the stacks that looked like them. But he couldn't find them.

There on the right—that clearing. It was long and narrow. Smoke stared at it.

"Well, doggone my hide," he exploded "I'd a swore thet them stacks was stickin' up with dead trees around 'em bout two or three miles west of thet field. Yes, sir. I'd a swore it. And now—" he scanned the tree tops with his glasses to make sure—"why there ain't a single sign of nothin' belchin' smoke nor flame. And there ain't even no trees burnt."

Again to make sure, he turned his perplexed face back toward the long, narrow clearing. His eyes had examined that before instinctively. A good airman always keeps watch for a necessary forced landing field.

Now he checked it for location again and swept to the west with his glasses. Nothing that looked, or even resembled the spot. Just a mass of tree tops for miles and miles.

Then as he stared through the glasses, sweeping the country and paying little attention to his surroundings for the moment, a strange white mist drifted in front of his vision and shut off the trees for the moment.

Smoke jerked upright, lowered the glasses, and glanced about him. Fog or low clouds were forming. He was forced down lower.

Angrily, he drove the pinto Spad for the tree tops. "Damned funny. Why the so and so fog. Never seen it come up so fast as this before in my life. No, sir. But then we been havin' queerest weather ever lately too. Imagine close to two weeks in sunny France without rain. Don't seem possible."

The fog smothered in closer suddenly. It was as though someone had dropped a whitish blanket of loose weave over the earth.

"Thet mess of blast furnaces or whatever the hell they are," Smoke snapped staring through narrowed eyes through the mist. "They was right here some place. Yesterday I could see the stacks all the way down to the ground. Now there ain't hide nor hair of the cussed things and—"

The fog suddenly became so thick that it shut out even the tree tops two hundred feet below. The stick shot forward. Smoke squinted, trying to penetrate the white death about him. Couldn't see a thing. Going down slowly, cautiously. Trees right down there. Mustn't smack into them.

The stick came back at the first shadowy form. The pinto Spad leveled and flew along with the landing gear just brushing the tops of branches.

Slowly, cautiously, Smoke made a turn. He was flying only with the aid of his compass now for direction. He was so low that he was in desperate danger of striking a higher tree at any moment. Still, he didn't dare lose sight of those trees. This fog had settled suddenly. It might be all over France and Germany, off the North Sea. And again it might be only a local freak of the early morning.

Turning like that, he headed back south the way he had come. Still he sought for that spot in the woods where he must drop his bombs. Couldn't find it. The whole thing seemed to have disappeared by magic.

Smoke cursed and shook his head. He was getting out of the area; he knew that five minutes later when the tree tops began to grow scarce. And he knew what lay beyond there. The Front was south—the German front.

The fog lifted slightly. Still. Smoke hugged the ground, making a hundred miles an hour. He throttled back for the fog. Any moment he might plunge into another band and he must not lose the earth.

Tac-tac-tac!

Guns belched from just ahead. German ground men had seen him coming, were waiting for him. Smoke dodged instantly. His hand came out of the cockpit with a bomb and he let it go over the side.

Braaam! Earth and stone and human parts screamed up toward him and the pinto Spad bucked from the concussion of that bomb.

"There, damn yuh," Smoke barked. "Reckon thet'll hold yuh fer a minute anyway."

He was skimming the bottom of the low cloud now. When he roared upon a large enough concentration of troops, bombs came out of the cockpit and hurled down. Then he was working his lever, dropping the bombs on field-gun placements and later on his way home, trenches of the enemy.

Then over No-Man's-Land and thundering over the heads of mud-smeared devils in the front-line Yank trenches. Beyond that the regular rear with supporting trenches and lines of trucks and men and guns coming up.

He swerved to the southeast.

"Don't look like this fog is ever goin' to let up," he muttered to himself. "Doggone if it ain't bout the thickest mess of soup I ever did see."

Things in France, that close to the earth didn't look as natural as they should. Still he must be coming out somewhere near Ramou if he held to that compass course.

Wam! Something gaunt and straight stuck up ahead. Controls moved instantly. The pinto Spad shot to the right and just in time. The wheels just missed rolling on the side of a church steeple.

A town slithered beneath like a sleeping thing half hidden in a shroud. Ramou. The field would be not far away.

He swerved left and blasted out over the field. No circling. The wind was from the right but he could come in cross-wind with a light load.

Wings cocked down into the wind, a short roll and then the roar of the Hisso as he taxied to the deadline.

CHAPTER SEVEN

Dead Man's Message

SMOKE climbed stiffly out of the cockpit and stretched. "I reckon," he mouthed, "this here soup is about—"

He suddenly glanced about. He thought he heard someone coming from the direction of the hangar—Tom and Joe of course.

But instead, it was the hangar sergeant from number seven; there was a peculiar expression on his face.

"Hey," Smoke ventured. "Where's Tom and Joe?"

The sergeant shifted nervously from one foot to the other.

"Well, yuh see sir—well—"

"What in hell's eatin' yuh," Smoke snapped. "Somebody got your tongue or somethin'? Hell's bells, fella, cain't yuh talk?"

"Yes, sir. Tom and Joe, they went."

"Went," exploded Smoke. "Went where?"

But already he was beginning to have misgivings as to what had happened.

"Well, sir, you see sir—"

"Yeah. Go on!"

That from between clenched teeth.

"It was shortly after you left, sir," the sergeant stammered. "I seen them gettin' the D.H. out and I knew you was gone and I heard you tell 'em before yuh went there wasn't goin' to be no flyin' today fer them. So I goes out and I says to 'em, 'hey, you ain't goin' to fly that crate today', and they says they was just testin' the engine after puttin' a new part in it and course they had to take it out on the line to test it since it's against orders to start the engines in the hangar unless emergency, sir. And so I says, 'all right' and I leaves 'em and goes back to my own hangar not wantin' to stick my nose in what ain't none of my business and they started up the engine and next thing I knew I seen 'em—Joe in the front cockpit flyin' her and Tom standin' in the back cockpit wavin' his rifle and yellin' like the wild Indian he is. And they was takin' off and climbin' fer the Front and—"

"And so you laughed at first and then you shook your head, I reckon," Smoke cut in, "and you says, 'Gosh all hell, ain't the skipper goin' to be maddern' hell when he gets back and hears about this!'"

"Well, yes, sir," the sergeant nodded sheepishly. "I did. But I thought maybe they'd be back before you—"

Smoke didn't get mad then. Instead he seemed to slump a little, like a man receiving word that he had lost a very close friend, maybe two. He turned without a word and stared to the north—stared into the pea soup that was down flat on the ground. He nodded very slowly several times. Then, for no other reason than to hide his emotions, he remarked as casually as he could:

"Well, at least we ought to get some rain out of this here fog. We need it bad enough, sure."

He turned then and strode off into the whitish mist that stuck like moist wool to the tarmac and the field.

He walked for some minutes mumbling to himself.

"They was good boys, them two. Crazy like a couple of loons, but they didn't mean nothin' bad. And how them red devils could shoot!"

He glanced almost constantly up at the gray fog above. Shook his head and cursed.

"Wouldn't do no good to go out lookin'. Not now. Hope if they got hit they got it over with quick. Poor devils."

He found himself in front of Colonel McGill's office. He turned and went in with a rather vacant stare. He hardly saw McGill look up at sound of his footstep on the threshold. His voice sounded far off when he asked:

"What on earth has happened, Smoke?"

"It's the Buck boys," Smoke said. "I shouldn't a done it. You ain't heard? No. Likely they saved the news fer me."

"The Buck boys? No, I haven't heard."

"They're gone," Smoke said.

"You mean dead?" demanded the colonel. "But how?"

"Likely they're dead," Smoke said. "They went off by themselves in the D.H. after I took off this morning in the pinto. This fog and they ain't back yet. Poor devils."

Colonel McGill eyed Smoke for a moment.

"They're probably all right," he ventured. "Maybe a little crash somewhere. That won't be anything to what they'll get when they come back after taking a plane without orders and—"

"Oh, the hell with orders," Smoke barked. He seemed to go to pieces suddenly. His face reddened with anger. "It's this fog. They'd been all right if they hadn't monkeyed so much. Any other mornin', maybe. Course I didn't give 'em permission to take the D.H. alone. But they're gone now. Cain't yuh think about anything but orders, damned orders? Hell, and this fog flat on its belly on the ground keepin' me here so's I cain't go out lookin' fer 'em and—"

"Silence!" bellowed the colonel. "Silence, Smoke, or by God I'll—I'll have you put—put somewhere for—"

He stopped short and stared at the lanky cowpoke. The wrath of both suddenly subsided. Colonel McGill shook his head.

"I'm sorry, Smoke. We both lost our heads."

Smoke nodded.

"Reckon so, colonel. I'm sorry too. But them two Injuns, they're mighty close to me. Sort of feel it's my fault, this happenin' to 'em."

"Of course you feel badly," the colonel nodded. "Too bad. They are good boys even if they are too wild at times. But tell me about your bombing raid this morning. I've been waiting to hear about that."

"Didn't turn out to be much"," Smoke admitted. "Caught in the fog and—"

"You mean," McGill exploded, "that you didn't spot the blast furnaces and drop the bombs there?"

"Yes, sir," Smoke explained. "Yuh know, thet was the funniest thing I've seen in a long time. Yesterday there was them blast furnaces spittin' flames right there in the woods with trees burned all around 'em. This mornin' I couldn't even find the spot."

"What?" McGill clutched the ends of his desk. "Couldn't find them?"

"Thet's what I said," Smoke nodded. "Not a sign of 'em. Not even a tree that looked brown or off color."

"Why that's impossible," McGill exploded.

"Sure. Reckon it is. But thet's the way it was."

"You're sure you had the right location in the woods?"

"Plumb sure, colonel. I been there three times now. I'd know thet woods if it was dug up and planted in the Gobi Desert I reckon. And thet spot just ain't there now. Thet's all. Course without the stacks and the flame and smoke or somethin', even burnt trees, I couldn't find the exact spot or I'd have unloaded the bombs right there anyways."

SMOKE WADE went from that headquarters office to his own. He snatched the telephone from his own desk and went to work. He called every post and headquarters and field and sector from one end of the Front to the other. Spent the entire morning calling. Glanced out of the window now and then, saw the fog still hanging over the field and cursed.

No news from Tom and Joe. An artillery outfit near Treamer said they had spotted a D.H. going over the lines at that point.

Smoke leaped to his big wall map, and found the little village called Treamer. Stared hard at it. Then he drew a line with his finger tip from Ramou to the approximate point of interest in the Vergon Forest.

"Well, I'll be damned," he exploded. "Treamer's just about on a line with thet spot in the woods."

He went out to a late noon mess after exhausting all the points of call he could find. He ate little, and talked less. Half through, he got up, lighted a cigarette and strode about the backs of the hangars.

He was still walking two hours later when an orderly found him. The orderly was excited.

"Smoke—captain," he blurted out. "Colonel wants to see you, pronto, right away."

Smoke suddenly galvanized into action. Fog was still down on the ground and growing thicker it seemed.

Smoke strode down toward headquarters office. The colonel was standing at the door when he entered.

"Listen," he began. "Just received devilish news from Paris. Paris is being shelled."

"Shelled," Smoke exploded.

"Shelled," repeated McGill. "It's horrible. Been going on since noon."

They were hurrying into the office. McGill handed Smoke the special orders he had just received. And the lanky skipper stared at them. Stared and cursed under his breath. The orders read:

> *ALL SQUADRONS TAKE OFF AT ONCE AND SEARCH ENEMY COUNTRY FOR BIG GUN. FIND BIG GUN AT ALL HAZARDS. IMMEDIATE.*

"Well, I'll be a ring-tailed thingamajig," Smoke roared. "The damned fools sendin' out thet order. Be suicide to take off in this soup and besides yuh cain't seen nothin' if yuh—"

He stopped suddenly and stared at Colonel McGill and through him. A new thought had come to his mind—something that seemed to sock him right between the eyes.

"Colonel," he said. "Colonel. Listen. Where's thet mess of letters what come from Intelligence yesterday. We couldn't make much sense out of it. But I reckon—"

"Good Lord," McGill exclaimed. "You've got it. You've got the idea."

He was hunting furiously in his desk. Found file paper and together they hovered over it on the desk.

—*GGUNINVERGONF.*

"Thet's what the poor devil on the other end of thet radio was tryin' to send us. The information where this big gun was," Smoke was raving.

McGill was nodding excitedly.

"Exactly. And the gun is right there where you spotted it. Right there where they had those giant blast furnaces in the woods."

Smoke was nodding slowly, studying the mess of letters. "Reckon so," he said. "Reckon so. See there." He took a pencil and added certain letters to the message.

biGGUNINVERGONForest.

"There," he said, standing back. "I reckon thet makes more sense. And I reckon we got thet question solved as to where the gun is. These here squadrons won't have to go out lookin' fer a big gun in pea soup. But what I cain't figure is why in hell they'd set up blast furnaces fer—"

"Listen," McGill cut him off. "These guns or this gun, whichever it is, must be plenty large to shoot to Paris. The report I got is that each giant shell that has landed in Paris blows up more than a full-sized city block. You can realize what that will mean if they keep it up and can call their shots. It means the wiping out of Paris, completely."

Smoke cursed under his breath as he nodded.

"Now this gun has to be enormous," McGill went on. "So big that it would be too large to move. So they build their blast furnaces for making the gun and they build the gun right there where it is to stay. Does that make sense?"

Smoke nodded. "I reckon there ain't no other explanation."

"Then if that is it," McGill exclaimed, leaping to his feet, "We have the whole thing as good as done. I'll notify G.H.Q. at once and tell them what we have worked out. There are two bombing squadrons near that point on this side. They'll bomb the entire Vergon Forest, Smoke."

Smoke nodded. Colonel McGill was putting through his call to G.H.Q. He waited a long time. Smoke paced the floor. Something was bothering him. He frowned.

Then McGill was talking to his superiors. Explaining what he and Smoke had discovered, both from the news and from the unfinished message that had come at first as a mere jumble of meaningless words.

"And if I might suggest, general," he was finishing, "There are two bombing squadrons located within easy reach of the center of the Vergon Forest. Yes, sir. I only thought perhaps they could go over loaded with bombs and finish off the big gun in short order sir. . . . Yes, sir. . . . Thank you general."

He hung up. Smiled with plenty of relief showing on his wrinkled old face.

"I think," he ventured, "that is that. After the fog lifts so that the bombers can get through I don't think we'll hear much more about that big gun shelling Paris."

"Well, maybe," Smoke said half to himself. "But listen here, colonel. You suggested thet this here big gun is so big thet they build it right there in the woods. Put up blast furnaces and thet and make the whole thing there in a hell of a hurry. Right?"

"Why, yes, of course," McGill nodded.

"Then I reckon thet gun would weigh maybe three, four times as much as a battleship, eh, colonel?"

McGill nodded again. His eyes were beginning to widen.

"Then," Smoke persisted, "if the big gun is so big what harm are a couple hundred air bombs goin' to do to it? Maybe kill off the gun crews. But they'll get more men to run her and keep right on goin'. Why hell, it'd take a whole damned arsenal blowin' up at once to do any harm to a gun as big as we're figurin' this one must be."

Colonel McGill stared at him for a moment. His smile of triumph fled, and his face turned a much whiter shade.

"Good Lord," he gasped, "I hadn't thought of that."

He sank weakly into his desk chair.

CHAPTER EIGHT
S.O.S.

FOR A long time the two commanders stared at each other. The one knowing the meaning of that last thought to the pilot. The other knowing the significance to the high command.

Then Colonel McGill reached for his phone without a word. Again he rang up G.H.Q.; and got the same general he had had before.

"I'm sorry sir," he explained, "but I'm afraid that suggestion won't work, general.... No, sir. You see we just talked it over at this end....Yes. You see our slant is that if this gun shelling Paris is so large as to blow up one or two entire blocks when the shell bursts, it must be enormous and no amount of explosive would harm it.

He paused to listen. Frowned at Smoke.

"Yes, sir, that's right, general.... Well, I'm glad you think my suggestion is worth something. Of course we may be wrong and.... oh, I see. Yes, I'm sorry I didn't think of it before."

The receiver clicked. McGill turned to Smoke.

"The general isn't sure whether the bombing squadrons have left. He made the decision and shot the order through at once when he got my message before."

The first smile of real humor since his entry crossed Smoke Wade's face.

"Reckon yuh don't need to worry none about them bombers havin' left," he ventured. "They wouldn't have time to warm up yet and it's likely thet this here general is about to learn thet they ain't goin' to even try it with a load of bombs in this here fog. It's murder, or suicide."

McGill nodded absently, stared at his desk top, tapped it with his finger tips.

"So what do we do now, Smoke?" he asked with a baffled, blank expression.

"Do? In this white hell that fills the sky? Hell, colonel, I reckon we'll accomplish about all we're goin' to by takin' big cheese knives and tryin' to cut thet fog. And I wouldn't bet thet yuh couldn't half and quarter it, neither."

He turned toward the door, paused.

"I'll be shovin' off just as soon as this damned fog gets a notion to climb out the way," he said. Then he stepped out on the tarmac and was enveloped in the white shroud.

He strolled down to the hangar where his pinto Spad was housed. Ordered it brought out and made ready for another flight.

"Bombs sir?" asked a mechanic who had taken the place of the Indians in caring for Smoke's crate.

Smoke hesitated, then nodded.

"Reckon so. Won't hurt nothin' and might come in handy."

He turned to go, then turned back.

"Never mind the bombs," he said at second thought. "Don't know what in hell I'd use 'em fer. Couldn't find the right place to put 'em this mornin'. And if I had, I reckon they wouldn't a done no good anyways."

He paced nervously, restlessly up and down the tarmac. He cursed the weather. Cursed his luck. Thick fog and still no sign of rain. The mist seemed soft and dry. Still it was genuine fog. He was sure of that.

He went to evening mess early, ate lightly and came out again. Another orderly from Colonel McGill's office. The colonel wanted to see him. He strode swiftly toward headquarters.

"Another order, Smoke," McGill said. "Here. Read it. Something new from G.H.Q. Looks as though they're taking our thoughts on the subject of the big gun."

Smoke took the message. Read:

> *"All squadrons stand by for taking the air at once. A large part of Paris is in ruins because of this big gun in the Vergon Forest. We cannot bomb it because of its size. We plan a hasty, desperate drive to take Vergon Forest and the big gun. Only the success of this drive will save Paris and later London and the war."*

"Damned fools," Smoke rasped. "Double damned crazy fools. Why thet gun is maybe twenty miles back of the German lines. Ain't a chance in the world of takin' thet much woods before the gun blows up the whole of London and Paris too. Take drivin' fer maybe two weeks to take it. There's wood clear from the front line Heinie trenches clear beyond the gun position. I know. I been over there. There'd be a Jerry behind every tree with a machine gun to pick off Yanks and Britishers and Frogs as they made their advance."

Colonel McGill shrugged, held out his hands in a gesture of hopelessness. Smoke whirled and stormed out of the office. It was darker. Still if the fog would lift, it was early enough in the evening to see plenty.

Toward the west a light streak appeared in the sky. Smoke squinted at it. Hoped and prayed that it was what he suspected. Then the truth came with the blowing of clouds. And the setting sun was peeping through that fog. The fog was lifting. Clearing.

A wild yell, a whoop of joy escaped Smoke's thin lips. He could still fly this day. Still look for Tom and Joe.

He broke into a run for his pinto Spad that stood on the line and yelled at the mechanic.

"Wind her up and get her hot."

He turned and stared about him as he heard the blast of the Hisso. Brant was coming toward him from the mess.

"Brant," Smoke hissed. "You'll be in command now until I get back. I'm goin' over around the Vergon Forest and see if I can spot anything of the redskins. The colonel'll be givin' yuh orders directly. Stand by for a big push. I reckon you'll get all the action you and the boys been lookin' fer now. Only fer the love of your old skipper, be careful, boy."

Brant had only time to nod before Smoke was running for his plane and the cockpit. Then he was kicking the rudder and the pinto Spad was spinning round and heading into the wind with a roar of defiance to the elements,

OUT through the lifting, thinning fog, Smoke thundered. Sun just tipping the rim of the world. There would be light for some time yet. He pushed on the gun. Sky clearing ahead. Good sign. He'd scour that forest for the two boys until it was dark—or something.

He wasn't bothering to fly high to escape archie and ground fire now. Didn't have time. Must get over there as quickly as possible. The sun was going down even as he blasted over the Front and Germany opened with her welcoming burst of fire.

Smoke was flying like a fool, dodging this way and that. Puffs about him, mostly behind. Then he was out of that rear line German sector and thundering deeper into the forest.

His eyes stared out ahead. Flying at a mere thousand feet he could see everything plainly and some distance ahead. He couldn't spot the place where the blast furnaces had been.

His gaze shifted to the long narrow field. That strip of clearing in the vast forest was just within vision. He could make out the dip in the trees where it was but he couldn't see the clearing.

Then he was sitting up straight, staring at something about a mile or two west of that field. Something that was rising slowly in a column. A smoke column.

Smoke aimed for it instantly. Something familiar about that column. Looked like those columns of smoke he had seen as a kid coming from the jagged hills in the West—Indian smoke.

And something else happened at that moment to clinch his attention to that spot. The column stopped its steady rising. Stopped and started again. It did this three times. Then it went on climbing for a moment.

Stick and rudder moved. He pushed again on the gun but the Hisso was doing her stuff at top speed.

Down, down she plunged. Smoke had swerved from his aim of the spot where the smoke was rising and was heading for long, narrow field a mile or so to the east of the smoke column.

Again and again came that puffy signal. Three puffs of smoke and then the column continued upward. Tom or Joe were making that by holding a coat or shirt over the smoldering fire and then raising it up.

He stared ahead hopefully, expectantly. Where was the D.H. He sat up higher and strained to see. The sun was going down. It was getting harder to see since Smoke was still almost in the glare of the setting sun and the rays blinded him while the earth below was growing dark.

But he managed to make out something odd there in the trees. Bits of color. Red and white and blue stripes. That would be the rudder of the D.H. half hidden by the foliage.

Coming nearer he made out more of the plane. The fuselage rear and one of the wings hanging in a tree.

He slipped on one ear to the narrow strip of clearing to the east. It was rougher than he expected.

Smoke cut the switch. He was down to stay. Germans or no Germans he was going to do his best to get to Tom and Joe.

The big six-gun came out of its holster far down on his right leg. He leaped from the pinto Spad and plunged into the forest straight toward that spot a mile away where he had seen the smoke column.

He was astonished at the tangled growth which made going hard—and slow. He pushed on, tearing his clothing. Cursing the hold-up. Any moment, he might run into a German who might be waiting for him behind any tree. But the Boche'd get a load of six-gun lead before he'd be taken.

It seemed an eternity before he reached that point from which the smoke had risen. The sun had gone down; it was almost too dark to see down here in the thick woods. But he could smell the smoke of that fire. Funny he didn't see anything of the two Indians.

He spotted something gleaming phosphorescently through the trees in the dimming light. That would be near the fire and them. The plane. The D.H. had crashed in the tree tops.

He hurried toward it. Reached it. Could still smell smoke but didn't see the fire or anyone about. A queer sensation flooded over Smoke Wade at that moment. Was this some sort of a trick? But how could it be? He had seen the signal fire and this time he was sure it was distinctly Indian. Why, Tom and Joe had told him themselves that the signal of three puffs meant—

Smoke whirled from the crash. No sign there. Not even a sign of blood about the place. No bodies. He breathed easier. At least they couldn't be badly hurt. Perhaps captured. Maybe this was a trick to trap Smoke himself.

He smelled smoke more plainly as he left the wreckage. Passed a clump of bushes that he pulled aside and there before him were the glowing embers of a small fire.

He stared about him in astonishment. No one was there. The place was vacated. It was almost pitch dark now. The embers shed a glowing light on the trees.

Smoke's brow furrowed in perplexity. His hand tightened on the butt of his six-gun. He knew he had been a long time getting there since landing, due to the thickness of the forest growth. But why should Tom and Joe leave? There was no doubt in his mind but that the fire had been built by the two Indians.

Smoke stood motionless, alone in a great, heavily-treed place. Alone and baffled. Only the crash of the plane and the remains of the fire. It was as though a ghost had built that fire.

He listened breathlessly. Not a sound came to him. The forest was still as death, except for once or twice the sleepy twitter of a roosting thrush.

CHAPTER NINE
Injun Round-Up

STRANGE sensation flooded over him. He couldn't describe it. It was as though someone had suddenly constricted the sides of the forest—shut him in behind walls that were suddenly moving together compressing the air about him.

He found it suddenly a little close. As though the air were packed tightly about him by some hidden force.

His next sensation was astonishing. The ground under his feet shuddered. All these things in hardly more than a second or two seconds of time.

His ears felt full and throbbed. He could feel his heart beat way up in his temples.

Then, like a grand finale came a rumbling sound from the west. A rumbling that grew in volume until it was deafening. It heightened into a thunderous roar unlike anything that Smoke Wade had ever heard before.

BRRRRAAAAMMMMM!

And when it had spent itself, it melted again to a distant rumbling echo. It left Smoke a little cold and clammy. He turned. Stared about him.

He didn't have to be told what that sound was. It was the baying of that giant gun, baying for the blood of innocent women and children in Paris or perhaps London. A projectile was already on its way to cause the murder—of who?

Smoke shuddered, cursed and stared about again, baffled. At a loss for once in his life to know what to do, where to go. Then, out of the darkness, something caught his eye on a tree next to the glowing embers of the fire.

There the side of a big spruce had been slashed with a knife. It had only been done but a short time. He could tell that for the pitch was just beginning to ooze into the cut.

His eyes narrowed. Someone had done that who knew woodcraft. A signal perhaps on the tree. He stepped past it. Stood beside the tree and squinted into the dimming light ahead.

There was another on another tree. Smoke leaped forward now. He knew the answer. Tom and Joe Buck had gone on. They had left a blazed trail through the forest for him to follow. And he did, with as much speed as the tangled growth and the darkness would permit.

Stumbling, half falling and catching himself to go on, Smoke tore through that forest But it was slow at best because of the obstacles and the nature of the blazed trail that he followed. So dark now and then that he often had to stop and make a circuit of the trees next before he could spot the next blazed tree.

Minutes passed. They seemed like hours. But it couldn't have been terribly long now. That big gun wouldn't remain idle any longer than necessary.

He began to get that stuffy, congested feeling again. Then came the shaking of the earth and the forest about him and at the end, the ear-splitting, spine-chilling bellow of the big gun sending out a projectile that was sentencing another group of humans to eternity.

After that was over he pushed on. It was so dark now that he had to feel his way as he went. Had to feel the trees before him to find which had the blazed slash on it before he could go on. It became obvious that Tom and Joe had made their way as soon as they had seen that Smoke caught their signal, straight for the giant gun.

He pushed on and on. Again and again came that rumble of the big gun. Coming nearer all of the time. Smoke caught the idea. When he felt the first hint of the sensation, he stuffed fingers in his ears. That eased the shock.

Pitch darkness. The next time the gun went off he saw the flash in the darkness through the trees. The enemy weren't even hiding the location of the gun. Must be sure they couldn't be harmed with Allied bombs.

Perhaps another half hour before that gun went off. Smoke was ready. He had spotted the intervals of time. Just about every half hour as nearly as he could guess.

When the big gun blasted that next time he was ready. He stood behind a big tree, stuffed fingers in his ears and waited.

BBBRRRRAAAAMMMM!

Smoke felt the tree rock behind him with the giant blast. He stood there tense, still holding his ears closed until the blast was completely done and the echoes had died away in the distance. He stepped out from the tree and crept on, more cautiously now. Germans would have a guard somewhere about.

Something moved ahead of him. Smoke raised his six-gun, but held his fire. He tensed. Stepped behind another tree.

That something was moving more and more. Coming nearer him. Then out of the darkness, a voice, hissing a name.

"SMOKE!" It came in the voice of Joe Buck. Smoke's heart leaped. He stepped into the open. Jumped ahead.

"Joe!" in muffled voice.

The stockier of the two brothers met him halfway. Even in the darkness, Smoke could see the grin on the coppery face.

"Ain't mad, Smoke?"

"Hell no, not if you and Tom are O.K."

"We got out without much. Tom's up ahead scoutin'. I stopped to wait for you and tell you. Listen. You saw where we crashed? Stayed up until the fog drove us down and we ran out of gas. Didn't come out so bad, but we wrecked the old D.H."

"The hell with that," Smoke chuckled, "just so you birds got out and could walk away, thet was a good landing aviator. But what in the devil is the idea of sneakin' off on me?"

"We wanted to get around the big gun before dark so we could take a look. We spotted her plain from the flash just before you got our signal. I climbed a tree and spotted her goin' off. Some heap big gun, this one."

"Yeah, but what's all this sneakin' around here? Yuh don't reckon to steal her, maybe, Joe?"

"No, but somethin' almost as good," Joe came back. "Listen. In order to work this gun they got to have men there to run her and get ammunition to her. Well, if we fix it so they can't do that, they can't shoot the gun, right?"

"Right," Smoke nodded in the darkness, "but how in hell—"

"Easy. Tom's gettin' the bearings. We build a fire all the way around her. This forest is as dry as tinder. No rain for weeks. We touch her off, get brush fixed in piles around in a circle and then set it off."

"Huh?" Smoke exploded. "Well, I'll be a—say, did yuh happen to think while you're doin' this they're goin' to pick yuh off easy from inside thet circle?"

Joe grinned.

"Not if we do it Indian fashion," he persisted. "Got horses here. A whole corral full of 'em and nobody much watching them. They been hauling in the big shells with horses because they hadn't got roads good enough for trucks, and we're going to do a little horse stealin' tonight along with everything else—that is if you're willing, Smoke."

"Willin'," Smoke snorted. "Just you tell me what to do and I'll come to doin' it as I can, Indian fashion."

They moved on together through the wood. A short, cautious crawl through the brush and Joe stopped Smoke. He was listening.

There came the sleepy call of a night thrush. Joe's tension let up. The call seemed to come from a little thicket just at their right and ahead.

Then from Joe's lips came the answering call. A moment later, Tom Buck, lanky and grinning, stepped noiselessly beside them.

"Everything all right," he said. "No guards around outside. Just guards close around gun. Not even much guard around horse corral. We make it easy."

"Hope yuh know what you're talkin' about," Smoke grinned back. "Lead on, long and lanky."

They stopped short. Again that tense feeling and then the deafening bellow of the big gun. Close by. They threw themselves to the ground. Held tight to their ears.

A blinding flash, the echo of the sound and then silence again except for a shouted order now and then that came faintly through the trees from about the big gun.

"First," Tom hissed, "we make a runway around like this."

In the darkness, Smoke could see him picking carefully at dead brush about the circle inside of which the gun was cooling.

"This," Joe whispered, "is burned tree tops and brush from blast furnaces. They take down and throw to all sides. Then they put false cover over top of opening in woods and cover with false leaves that always green. This old half-burned brush make good fire."

They worked on into the night tirelessly. It was a long job. Smoke guessed the circle they were forming around the giant gun stretched a good mile in circumference.

The big gun continued to roar at half hour intervals. They began to get used to expecting it at about a certain time. Were near enough so they could hear the order to fire coming through the trees from the commander of the crew.

BBRRRAAAMMM!

They'd fall flat, hold their ears, and get up to work on. It was past midnight before they finished. They ended near the corral. It was dark there too. Very little light showed about. Only a flashlight here and there, except at the fan mount where it was dimly illuminated.

From the cover of a clump of brush, Joe pointed to the corral and grinned.

"Think you can still, ride, Smoke?" he questioned.

"Hell yes, hut what the—"

"That way Indian spread fire. Ride around and throw burning brands into dry brush. It light all right."

Joe put his hands on Smoke's arm to hold him back. Smoke saw the lanky form of Tom slinking, snake-like, through the brush toward the corral. Joe pointed in the dim reflection of the light from the base of the big gun. Pointed at a sentry stalking slowly, sleepily across the gate of the corral.

"Get sentry, then we work in and let out horses."

"O.K.!"

Smoke crouched beside Joe and watched. Slowly, surely, Tom slipped behind that pacing sentry. No one seemed to notice him there. No other Germans seemed near.

Bam!

Tom leaped like a savage redskin of the Indian wars. Leaped upon the back of the guard from behind and a heavy wooden club crashed down on the skull of the German.

There was no time for the Boche to cry out. He slumped in his tracks, Tom leaped clear and slunk off in the brush.

JOE pressed Smoke's arm toward the corral. The horse smell seemed good in Smoke's nostrils. They stepped past the unconscious guard and opened the corral gate, then inside.

In the darkness, the horses moved restlessly. Joe and Smoke circled them and picked a horse apiece.

Halters on some. Nothing on others. Joe and Buck each took one with a halter. They tensed. A light flared outside the corral where Tom was hiding. That was the signal. Tom was lighting the fire brands at the end of the mile-long row of tinder dry brush.

Smoke and Joe leaped to their horse's backs at that. Heels kicked viciously into sides. A wild, Indian war-cry ripped from Joe Buck's lips as he kicked his horse into action.

Smoke raised his voice at the same time. The old cowboy yell of the ranges vibrated through the trees. Horses broke into a wild run. They were riding bare back—riding like fiends out of the corral.

Germans began to shout from every quarter. Germans were running. Running from the base of the big gun. But as fast as they came toward the galloping horsemen, they found that a roaring inferno had burst out between.

Tom passed the second handful of blazing brands to Joe, snatched up some for himself in one hand, caught the mane of a big black horse and leaped to his back.

Crack!

A rifle sang out in the night.

Round and round and round those three dare-devil riders galloped. The other horses raced ahead, dodging trees and leaping fallen logs.

One by one the fire brands were hurled by Smoke and Tom and Joe into the pile of brush that circled the great gun and the platform. Flames shot upward behind them.

The whole circle, a mile long, was on fire. Still they rode around it, raced their horses and yelled and screamed the war cry of the Cherokees and the high pitched yip-yip of the cowboy.

Germans tried to plunge through the flaming circle. Those who got through were mowed down by the guns of the three. The old smoke pole of the cowboy ace was getting almost too hot to hold. The flames were spreading; the horses getting tired.

The whole gun mount inside that circle was a roaring furnace that no man could stand. No more shots were coming from that giant gun.

But that would be only temporary. It couldn't last. When the fire burned out in the forest, new crews would come and Paris would be torn to bits in revenge.

Then suddenly the fire broke into a wild roar. A wind out of the north had risen in the early morning hours to fan the flames. Smoke turned and stared. The flames were spreading toward the south—toward German lines and the Front.

And flames were spreading in other directions as well. Smoke saw that with a sudden fearful misgiving. The flames were roaring out through the forest toward the field where the pinto Spad had been landed. Their only means of escape from the inferno they had started.

A wild shout belched from his lips. He pointed, turned, stared plainly baffled for a moment. The flames had gotten him twisted in direction.

"The field," he shouted to the Buck boys above the roar of the flames behind them. "Jake's in the little narrow field over east. Which way?"

Joe whirled on his horse. Pointed ahead of him a little more to the right than Smoke had guessed. They put heels to their horses and galloped for it through the tangle of woods.

Then as they left the roaring, gaining flames behind, the light of dawn was flooding above the tree tops. And above the thunderous roar of the flames that were sweeping over the tinder dry forest, another sound came to them. The throbbing drone of many motors of the air.

It was at that moment that they broke upon the long, narrow field where the pinto Spad stood, dimly outlined in the gray of dawn.

SMOKE leaped from his horse beside it. Tom and Joe were down. For a moment Smoke looked from one to the other. He listened to the roaring flames that were gaining on them now.

Smoke whirled and looked at the pinto Spad. Shook his head.

"Reckon, Jake," he said, "you ain't no truck horse. It just cain't be done."

Joe and Tom took in the situation instantly. They both seemed to speak at once.

"We'll stay. Isn't more than room for one to go up and out of this field."

Joe Buck said that, but his brother's voice insisting that he, Tom be allowed to do that, came almost as an echo. Smoke glanced over his shoulder at the flames coming nearer. He looked up at the sky full of planes far above them.

"Listen, you two," Smoke said. "I'm captain. I'm in command. I'm givin' orders now. The pinto Spad'd crash before she'd take all three of us out this little peanut of a field." He turned to Joe. "You ain't never drove a Spad, Joe but I reckon you can in a pinch. Get in thet cockpit. I'll throw the prop. Then Tom, you get on the wing and me, I'll dig in and get set for a stay underground , until this here fire devil gets gone."

Joe and Tom flared at the same time.

"Go to hell," Joe snapped, "with your orders. I'll stay."

"The hell you will, I'll stay," Tom barked. "Besides, a guy hasn't got a chance of getting out of this forest fire alive—unless he's a long lanky Indian."

The thunderous roar of the forest fire coming nearer was becoming almost deafening. They were shouting to make each other heard. Smoke glared. His hand moved more quickly than his eye. The big six-gun came out and he faced the two.

"Do I get my orders followed," he said grimly, "or do I have to enforce 'em?"

"I'll see you in hell first before I'll leave you," Joe flared.

"Shoot and be damned," Tom cried.

Then above the roar of the approaching fire came the scream of something from above. All three stared upward. Gasped. Then yelled.

A Spad was hurtling hell-bent out of the smoke-filled skies above. A Spad that had broken out of formations. Smoke was jumping up and down and yelling his head off.

"Brant—Brant. Nobody ain't never come at a more—"

He never finished that. They were running to stop the roll of that Spad.

"Go hop on, Joe," Smoke yelled and then the Indian obeyed.

Smoke leaped for his own cockpit and landed smack in it. Tom whirled the propeller. Three turns and the Hisso started. Two, three minutes for warming. Brant thundered out of the field with Joe on his wing to leave more room.

Smoke kicked round, pushed the gun full ahead and held on. Tom grinned up from the right wing. And he was still grinning as they headed for home.

But it was when they crossed the lines and Smoke looked back that he got the real thrill. The fire had suddenly turned. A north wind had driven the flames all the way to the German front lines. But now the wind had switched to the south. Heavy drops of rain spattered on Smoke's face and on the Spad windshield as signal of the coming storm.

The storm wasn't worrying Smoke. It was making him hop up and down in his bucket seat and yell like a school kid.

"Look," he yelled to Tom. "Look down thet a way and back. See. The drive is startin' and the Yanks is gettin' help from the Almighty himself. Yes, sir. Damned if the wind ain't shifted. The fire is burnin' over the whole forest. And now the south wind is blowin' the fire up north again and the rain is goin' to put it out.

"Look there! Down there! The Yanks and the Frogs and the British has crossed the front lines. They drove the Heinies out of their trenches and captured 'em. They couldn't go inter thet fire. And now all they got to do is march right into Germany as fast as the wind and rain puts out the forest fire from the south. They'll take thet big gun position sure nuff and just because you two Injuns thought of goin' back to old times and burnin' out a bunch of Heinies in the good old redskin method."

Then a frightened expression crossed Smoke's leathery face.

"Phew!" he whistled as they roared over the Allied lines for home. "Thet was a dose call. I'd a bet my shirt thet the Allies couldn't take thet gun placement in short of a couple of weeks. Phew!"

FEATURING THE WORLD'S GREATEST *SKY FIGHTER IN*

DOOM OVER PARIS

A FULL BOOK-LENGTH WAR-AIR NOVEL

COMPL
SCALE MO
PLANS
VICKERS F.

FLYING ACES OF THE PULPS

by Don Hutchison

ROBERT J. HOGAN'S lanky flying cowpoke, Smoke Wade, was but one of dozens, perhaps hundreds, of aviator heroes who flew the blazing skies of pulp fiction.

One of the great obsessions of the Depression years was with the romance of flying. To weary job seekers and downtrodden laborers, flying must have appeared a near miraculous escape from earthbound burdens, its practitioners akin to the gods as they rode the winds with white scarves fluttering in the slipstream. The trouble was that it cost a small fortune to actually own one of those crates. And you had to devote long hours achieving mechanical skill in order to fly them.

As usual, the pulps came up with a vicarious fix. Each month armchair aviators could take off from their corner newsstands with a choice of dozens of high-flying magazines, each promising delirious visions of winged glory. Although there were never as many air titles as detective, western, or even love, aviation fans remained a dedicated group of pulp consumers.

The magazine laying claim to being first off the ground was Fiction House's *Air Stories*, whose cover proclaimed itself "The First Air Story

Magazine." On the other hand, Dell Publications' War Birds called itself "The Oldest Air War Magazine." Both were published within a short time of each other in 1927. A third magazine, Wings, zoomed out soon after, ultimately achieving some kind of record by being the last aviation magazine to fold nearly thirty years later.

Most of the early stories were about air fighting in World War I, "the war to end all wars." The magazine logos reflected that fixation: Flying Aces, Battle Birds, Dare-Devil Aces, War Aces, Sky Fighters, and so on. Each was packed with romanticized epics featuring dashing Allied airmen and ruthless German foes locked in mortal combat above the clouds. Even the story titles soared: "Thundering Wings," "Sky Graves for the Gallant," "Brothers of Aces," "Sky Rider's Reckoning."

Since all pulps were essentially hero oriented, it was inevitable that the aviation titles would come up with some recurring fictional characters. Although never as plentiful as detective mystery men, aerial series characters did prove popular. The pulps produced dozens of daring young men in their flying machines. A few, like G-8 (and his Battles Aces), commanded their own magazine titles. Others were used to help boost the popularity of conventional aviation magazines.

And what names they had, those cavaliers in oval goggles! Speed Rossiter. Loop Murry. Coffin Kirk. Jinx Jones. Ace Dallas. Luke Lance. Buzz Travers. Ding Darley. There was even a flying jester named Phineas "Carbunkle" Pinkham, who didn't land planes—he crashed them.

Writer Arch Whitehouse, himself a Royal Flying Corps veteran with sixteen air victories, unleashed Larry Ledbeater and Todd Bancroft against the Japs. He wrote of Tug Hardwick and Beansie Baker in Flying Aces. Adventurous aircraft salesman Crash Carringer (reassuring name for a pilot!) appeared in the same magazine. Whitehouse also wrote a number of stories about the Coffin Crew, pilots Armitage, Townsend, Ryan and Tate. Erle Stanley Gardner dreamed up a hyperactive flying detective named Speed Dash. And Doc Savage's Lester Dent wrote of Hair Noon, a Coast Guard pilot.

MOST of the wind-bronzed high flyers were preposterously brave and handsome, with only their odd names to distinguish them. But a few stood out from the crowd.

A WWI series by Donald E. Keyhoe concerned the bizarre adventures of Philip Strange, "the phantom ace of G.2."

Strange's exploits appeared in *Flying Aces*, a tripartite pulp which routinely mixed tales of Spads and Spandaus with factual articles and detailed model building instructions.

Although Strange pre-dated G-8 and shared similar characteristics, he never achieved G-8's popularity. Known as the Brain Devil because of his ESP and other near-occult mental powers, Strange was an ex-child prodigy who had performed feats of magic, ventriloquism and hypnotism in showbiz. Like G-8, the Brain Devil was also an ace flier and Intelligence agent who used the art of disguise to confound the machinations of the Kaiser's evil scientists.

Philip Strange was the creation of Major Donald E. Keyhoe, who had flown in active service with the Marine Corps and had been an aide to Charles Lindbergh after his famous Paris flight. In later years he was to gain some fame and notoriety as the author who first brought UFOs to the attention of the public with five best-selling "fact" books including The Flying Saucer Conspiracy and The Flying Saucers Are Real. Critics of his UFO books often pointed out that he had once written masses of "far out" pulp fiction.

In the mid-thirties, Keyhoe sensed that youthful readers might be growing tired of beating the Boche. He developed a more contemporary barnstormer in Richard Knight, who was blind as a bat by day but eagle-eyed after dark. Not tied to the Western Front, Knight clocked considerably more miles than the WWI mental marvel, including flights to the Far East.

FLYING ACES boasted other heroes of the crimson skies. Arch Whitehouse was responsible for Buzz Benson, an aviation reporter and undercover man for the Secret Service. The Benson plots usually involved peril to the US Fleet in the Pacific, with Buzz zooming in to wreck havoc on bands of international crooks and not-too-disguised Oriental aggressors.

Another Whitehouse character, the Griffon, was Kerry Keen, young millionaire lay about by day and flying avenger by night. Whenever stratospheric evil threatened, Keen would don a scarlet silk-and-rubber mask and zoom out in his supercharged plane, the Black Bullet, from an underground hangar on his Long Island estate. (Years later, radio's Green Hornet would use the same shtick in an earthbound format).

Flying series heroes became so popular at one point that prolific author Harold F. Cruickshank managed to maintain the monthly exploits of three different characters—Sky Wolf, Sky Devil and Red Eagle in consecutive issues of three different Popular Publications titles.

One of the more unusual characters (by reason of sex) in the macho air pulps was Barbe Pivet, an aviatrix who appeared in a series written by Herman Petersen in *Air Stories* and later in *Wings*. A typical Pivet story, "Flaming Gas" (*Wings* Aug. 1928), has Barbe winging solo to the rescue and downing the villain's plane while her boyfriend watches helplessly on the ground.

And speaking of villains, Steve Fisher invented Mr. Death, a physically crippled Hun murder master who had "a face like powdered chalk." Death squared off with Yank flier Jed "Babyface" Garrett in a series of eight wild flights in *Dare-Devil Aces*. These ran from March to November 1936, and terminated with Mr. Death and his black Fokker still terrorizing the Western Front.

Arthur J. Burks, Marine pilot and prolific pulpster, wrote of Jim Swain, an aerial Robin Hood in war ravaged China. Robert Burtt picked up the aerial mercenaries theme with his stories of Battling Grogan and his Dragon Squadron of China. And Frederick F. Nebel turned out a series in *Air Stories* concerning tramp flyers Gales and Mike McGill, who roistered through the mysterious skies of the Orient in the early thirties. In a companion magazine, *Wings*, Joel Rogers pulled the chocks with that amazing gentleman Captain Death, top-kick of the sky sleuths.

THE INSTANT SUCCESS of Popular Publications' G-8 magazine led a number of publishers to attempt single character air hero titles. As might be expected, Street & Smith's entry in the air race downplayed the flamboyant excesses of their rival's zombie fighting Master Spy.

Bill Barnes, Air Adventurer began in early 1934 with a novel titled "Hawks of the Golden Crater." Compared to the likes of Coffin Kirk and Crash Carringer, Bill possessed the blandest of pulp hero monikers. The "Barnes" was meant to suggest "barnstormer"-in honor of those frolicsome gypsy fliers who found exhilarating freedom while courting aerial death. He even had a plane named the Stormer.

The initial Barnes novels were written by ex-cavalry officer Major Malcolm Wheeler-Nicholson, most of the others by Canadian-born writers Charles Spain Verral and Harold P. Montanye-all under the house name of George L. Eaton. The main plotline dealt with young flyer/designer Bill Barnes achieving fame and fortune as a daring air racer. With his prize money he assembles a gang of loyal aides and starts his own ultra-modern air field on Long Island.

Unfortunately, after some twenty full-length novels, Bill Barnes suffered the ignominy of seeing his pulp refashioned into *Bill Barnes Air Trails,* a large-size semi-slick. Bill's own adventures were reduced in scope to accommodate articles and model building departments. Poor Bill. Eventually he was squeezed out of his own magazine altogether, winding up as a back-of-the-book character in *Doc Savage* magazine.

ONE FLYING HERO who commanded his own book without fear of eviction was John Masters, the Lone Eagle. Named in honor of Charles Lindbergh, The Lone Eagle first spread his wings in September of 1933-a month before the debut of G-8 and his Battle Aces. Although doomed to fly forever in G-8's prop wash, he was the only air hero to last almost as long as the durable Master Spy-ten years and some seventy-six novel-length adventures.

Billed as "The World's Greatest Sky Fighter, the Lone Eagle was a legend of the Great War, a lone wolf ace of Yank Intelligence who appeared in the skies where the fighting was the toughest and under whose watchful eyes no Hun treachery could be perpetrated. But the man himself-John Masters-could not collect any of the glory which was his due.

The moment he stepped out of his mottled Spad he ceased to be the Lone Eagle. Like a cloak he flung off that romantic personality and became merely John Masters, a man whose drab uniform bore neither insignia nor rank, and whose papers showed him to be a newspaper correspondent from Chicago.

Perhaps it was the Eagle's austere life that made him less exciting than G-8. Perhaps it was just the nature of his magazine to be less flamboyant and thus less attractive to jaded pulp readers. The Lone Eagle covers were technically good, but they featured routine air war paintings at a time when routine air war magazines were glutting the market. By comparison, the G-8 covers glued your eyes to bizarre compositions juxtaposing snarling Spads and Fokkers with skeleton men and giant vampire bats.

What made the Eagle unique among pulp fliers was that he fought in two World Wars. In his February, 1940 issue, "The Nazi Menace," he aged twenty years in one month as he jumped from the heart of World War I into the new conflict. Once again John Masters had thrown in with the Allies, on condition that he carry no rank and wear no uniform except when necessary.

But something is missing in the new Lone Eagle-a sense of innocent adventure perhaps. War is never fun. It can only appear so when distanced by time and memory. In the early and mid thirties it was easy to romanticize WWI flying spies, their planes slicing boldly through the clear winds high above the verminous trenches. By 1940 the reality of a new horror in Europe produced a more sober, often times brooding fighting ace. Perhaps he was contemplating the fate of his magazine, which folded with the Spring 1943 issue.

MOST of the Lone Eagle novels were ghosted by F.E. Reichnitzer and Robert Sidney Bowen, using the house name Lieut. Scott Morgan. Reichnitzer wrote the early stories. He had been a Royal Air Force Camel pilot in the Great War, had been shot down in Belgium while on a bombing mission and imprisoned at Rasstatt. Once he had been placed before a firing squad and saved only when the commandant had a last minute change of heart.

Robert Sidney Bowen had left high school when the war began and had lied about his age in order to join the Royal Flying Corps. The youngest member of the RFC, Bowen went to France as a scout pilot and shot down a number of German planes and balloons. Later he became a newspaperman, test pilot, editor of Aviation Magazine and finally a prolific fiction writer.

Bowen also created the Captain Danger character in *Air War* magazine, although the series was soon taken over by pulp hero specialist Norman Daniels. Beginning in 1940 and running through 1944, there were over a dozen Captain Allen Danger novels in all, with titles like "Captain Danger's Nazi Hunt," "Captain Danger's Blitzkrieg," and "Captain Danger over London."

FEW of the World War II flying aces were as durable as their Great War counterparts. Two more captains-Captain Combat and Captain V-appeared briefly and then dropped from sight. Captain William Combat was the star of his own magazine, which lasted but three issues in 1940. A Yank-born RAF ace, Combat flew a Hawker Hurricane for the British 42nd Home Defense Squadron. Because of his mother's death at the hand of German flyers, the young American declared a personal war on the Nazi leader. A curiosity of the series is the publisher's reluctance to defame Adolf Hitler. In the novels the villainous Nazi leader is slightly disguised as Herr Gruber, a middle-aged man with a mustache and a small Van Dyke beard-and is so portrayed in the magazine's illustrations.

Captain V zoomed through seven short novels in Battle Birds from August 1942 to September 1943. He was the creation of Ralph Oppenheim, a writer with no flying experience who had produced one of the first air series-the Three Mosquitoes-and, with Captain V, one of the last. It is an ironic fact that few of the flying pulp heroes survived the war they fought in. They flashed and flourished for a brief time between the wars. By 1943 they were hit a one-two blow by crippling paper shortages and a growing disdain for the glorification of fanciful characters supposedly taking part in a very real-and increasingly painful-war.

ROBERT J. HOGAN PICTURED ON HORSEBACK FROM THE DUST JACKETS OF HIS WESTERNS PUBLISHED BY DODD, MEAD & COMPANY IN THE EARLY 1950'S (ALL RIGHTS RESERVED). The accompanying text reads in part: "Robert J. Hogan's first job after being graduated from St. Lawrence University was riding range for several ranches on the west slope of the Rockies. Since then he has been an amateur boxer, played piano for silent movies and hoedown dances, built houses, designed planes, manufactured leather goods and taught flying."

Smoke Wade: A Brief History

by Bill Mann

In the August 1931 issue of Street and Smith's "Air Trails", Robert J. Hogan introduced us to a rough and tumble Arizona cowpoke named Smoke Wade.

He had left the range and became the skipper of the 66th Pursuit Squadron in WWI France. Flying a Pinto colored Spad he called Jake, after his favorite Pinto ranch horse, Smoke always wore a six-shooter strapped to his leg and made frequent use of it during his aerial battles. He would often get in trouble with his superiors over his penchant for placing bets on just about anything, especially if it seemed like a long-shot. But Smoke would always win these bets, and everyone from generals to mechanics would be left owing him money.

In the air he would frequently end up dueling with his arch-enemy, the German ace Baron von Stolz. Like Doktor Krueger from Hogan's G-8 novels, von Stolz would come up with strange and deadly schemes to defeat the Allies. Smoke would always vanquish the Baron and foil his plans, but he could never quite finish him off, leaving von Stolz alive for the next month's story.

The Baron was not the only recurring character though. The Commanding Officer of the 66th was Colonel McGill, who Smoke looked up to like a father.

And at General Headquarters in Paris, General Banks was always looking to Smoke to solve whatever new crisis the Allied command faced.

Joe and Tom Buck were Cherokee Indians, and friends from Smoke's days on the Arizona range. After a stint in the Signal Corps, the Bucks now serve as mechanics in the 66th.

Also around in most every tale was Smoke's three Flight leaders – Quinn, Brant, and Snell.

After three appearances in "Air Trails" and one in another Street and Smith pulp, "Popular Complete Stories", Smoke Wade began his long run in Popular Publication's line of air pulps. The first story was in the August 1932 "Battle Aces", followed by forty-two more in "Battle Birds" and "Dare-Devil Aces". Beginning in April 1939, Smoke Wade began appearing as a back story in "G-8 and His Battle Aces". His final flight was in the very last issue of "G-8" in June 1944. But this would not be the end of Smoke Wade.

After the demise of the air pulps in the 1940's, Bob Hogan began writing many stories for the Western pulps, continuing into the late 40's and early 50's when the pulp magazine industry was all but dead. Like many of his contemporaries, Hogan turned to paperback novels to earn a living, and was very successful writing Western stories.

Three of his novels featured a familiar character, Smoke Wade, a cowboy who loved to gamble and always seemed to be in the middle of a scrap. And of course he had a Pinto pony named Jake.

From a historical standpoint, this second incarnation of Smoke Wade could not be the same cowpoke that flew the Pinto Spad in WWI. But Hogan obviously loved this character so much that he plunked him down in the "Old West" with pretty much everything but the plane.

Smoke's last adventures were in the novels "The Challenge of Smoke Wade" in 1950, "Stampede Canyon" in 1951, and "Savage Rebel" in 1952. "Savage Rebel" was later re-printed as "Wanted: Smoke Wade".

Ironically, many people remember Smoke Wade more from these three books than from all his sixty-four pulp adventures. One of those people actually got his name from the novels.

John Wade was born and raised on a Snake River cattle ranch in Hells Canyon, Oregon. He is a fourth generation cowboy and range land manager. As a boy he rode horseback six miles to the same one-room school house his mother had attended.

In 1959 young John was working a summer job at the Cache Creek Sheep & Cattle Ranch. The bunk house contained stacks of well thumbed paperbacks. One of them was "Wanted: Smoke Wade". He enjoyed the book so much he kept it, and carried it in his back pocket wherever he went. Upon returning to high school that fall, several friends began calling him "Smoke Wade" as the book was always with him. The name stuck through high school and four years in the U.S. Navy.

These days Smoke Wade is best known as a world renowned cowboy poet, storyteller, emcee, and freelance journalist.

I think Bob Hogan would have been pleased to know that Smoke is still out there, and that while he isn't flying a plane or shooting outlaws, he is still a cowboy at heart.

TITLE	MAGAZINE	DATE	VOL	NO
1931				
Wager Flight	**Air Trails**	Aug	6	5
Fly 'Em Cowboy	**Air Trails**	Sep	6	6
Aces In Dutch	**Air Trails**	Oct	7	1
Framed Wings	**Popular Complete Stories**	Oct 15	16	46
1932				
Sixgun Eagle	**Battle Aces**	Aug	6	3
Dead Man's Staffel	**Dare-Devil Aces**	Dec	3	2
Ghost Drome	**Battle Birds**	Dec	1	1

TITLE	MAGAZINE	DATE	VOL	NO
1933				
Buzzard's Trap	**Battle Birds**	Jan	1	2
The Death Fokker	**Battle Birds**	Feb	1	3
The Flaming Patrol	**Battle Birds**	Mar	1	4
The Sixgun Buzzard	**Battle Birds**	Apr	2	1
Hell's Buzzard	**Battle Birds**	May	2	2
The Bull's-Eye Patrol	**Battle Birds**	Jun	2	3
The Cowboy Flight	**Battle Birds**	Jul	2	4
The Death Circus	**Battle Birds**	Aug	3	1
Steel Coffin Ace	**Battle Birds**	Sep	3	2
The Gotha Ghost	**Battle Birds**	Oct	3	3
The Secret Squadron	**Battle Birds**	Nov	3	4
Sixgun Circus	**Battle Birds**	Dec	4	1
1934				
Injun Buzzards	**Battle Birds**	Jan	4	2
Cyclone Buster	**Battle Birds**	Feb	4	3
The Pirate Patrol	**Battle Birds**	Mar	4	4
Glory Hound	**Battle Birds**	Apr	5	1
The Black Ace	**Battle Birds**	May	5	2
Redskin Buzzards	**Battle Birds**	Jun	5	3
Knockout Ace	**Dare-Devil Aces**	Jul	7	4
The Cyclone Ace	**Dare-Devil Aces**	Oct	8	3
Maverick Buzzard	**Dare-Devil Aces**	Nov	8	4
1935				
Bull's-Eye Buzzard	**Dare-Devil Aces**	Feb	9	3
The Dynamite Trio	**Dare-Devil Aces**	Apr	10	1
Six Gun Dynamite	**Dare-Devil Aces**	Jun	10	3
The Rawhide Ace	**Dare-Devil Aces**	Sep	11	2
The Million Dollar Squadron	**Dare-Devil Aces**	Nov	11	4

TITLE	MAGAZINE	DATE	VOL	NO
1936				
The Scrap Iron Comet	**Dare-Devil Aces**	Feb	12	3
The Rodeo Buzzard	**Dare-Devil Aces**	Apr	13	1
The Fleabitten Ace	**Dare-Devil Aces**	May	13	2
Bomb Buzzard	**Dare-Devil Aces**	Jun	13	3
The Flying Horsemen	**Dare-Devil Aces**	Jul	13	4
Sixgun Tailtwister	**Dare-Devil Aces**	Aug	14	1
The Flare Patrol	**Dare-Devil Aces**	Oct	14	3
The Jail Buzzard	**Dare-Devil Aces**	Dec	15	1
1937				
The Hell Hound	**Dare-Devil Aces**	Feb	15	3
Vulture's Brand	**Dare-Devil Aces**	Apr	16	1
The Sky Puncher	**Dare-Devil Aces**	Sep	17	2
Ace In The Hole	**Dare-Devil Aces**	Nov	17	4
1938				
The Six-Gun Patrol	**Dare-Devil Aces**	Jan	18	4
Sky Bronco	**Dare-Devil Aces**	Sep	20	2
1939				
The Skyrider from Hell	**G-8 and his Battle Aces**	Apr	17	3
Sky Rodeo	**G-8 and his Battle Aces**	May	17	4
Where There's Smoke—There's Fire	**G-8 and his Battle Aces**	Sep	18	4
Leather and Lead	**G-8 and his Battle Aces**	Oct	19	1
1940				
Dead Pigeons	**G-8 and his Battle Aces**	May	20	4
Flight of the Cloud Buster	**G-8 and his Battle Aces**	Oct	22	1
The Devil Flys a Bronc	**G-8 and his Battle Aces**	Nov	22	2

TITLE	MAGAZINE	DATE	VOL	NO
1941				
The Sky Buster	**G-8 and his Battle Aces**	Mar	23	2
The Devil Sends an Ace	**G-8 and his Battle Aces**	Oct	24	2
Boomerang Patrol	**G-8 and his Battle Aces**	Dec	24	3
1942				
The Black Avenger	**G-8 and his Battle Aces**	Oct	17	4
1943				
Jitter Bomber	**G-8 and his Battle Aces**	Apr	26	3
Fly 'Em, Cowboy	**G-8 and his Battle Aces**	Aug	27	1
The Cowboy and the Baron	**G-8 and his Battle Aces**	Oct	27	2
1944				
Bullets for the Baron	**G-8 and his Battle Aces**	Feb	27	4
Six Gun Ace	**G-8 and his Battle Aces**	Jun	28	2

Made in the USA
Lexington, KY
16 September 2011